OF ASHES AND AFTER

FABINS

OHB

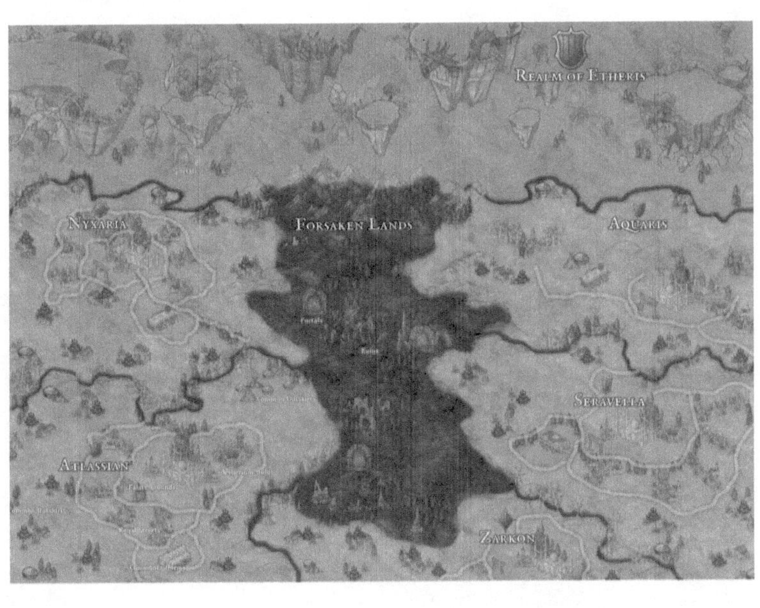

Realm of Etheris
Nyxaria
Forsaken Lands
Aquaris
Portals
Seravella
Atlassian
Zarkon

CHAPTER I
MIRABELLE

The arrow sliced through the air with a hiss, splitting the shaft of the one already lodged in the center of the target. It landed dead-on, fletching trembling from the force. Again.

I notched another. Released.

Again.

The *thwack* was duller this time, barely audible over the low rustle of leaves stirring in the still morning air. Northern grove was quieter than usual, no Tameables roaring in the distance, no guards passing with their heavy-footed patrols. Just me and arrows.

And silence.

I fired again. The string snapped forward with a satisfying hiss, another shaft split, followed by another moment of silence.

It was the same every morning. I would walk here while the others still dozed or brewed morning ale. Stood barefoot in the clearing, bow in hand, and fired until the burn in my fingers numbed everything else. I didn't know why I did it, because the pain didn't cleanse. The repetition didn't soothe. But it gave shape to the haze in my chest, and an order to the disorder.

A footstep crunched behind me. "I thought you'd finally

stopped trying to murder that poor target, Mira." Callen's voice cut through the hush like a breeze through still branches.

I didn't turn. "It's holding up better than I expected."

He stood behind me, his silhouette catching the light as he glanced at the splintered wood. "Split it down the middle again, didn't you? How many?"

"I wasn't counting."

He gave a low whistle, slow and impressed. "Ah, but I was. That's three arrows in a streak. Are you possessed?"

I turned toward him slowly, tucking a loose curl behind my ear. He leaned against a post near the edge of the clearing, arms crossed, his tunic sleeves rolled up like he always wore them.

He grinned when he caught my eye. "Well? Aren't you going to acknowledge the new definition of strength I've become?"

I gave him a flat look. He pushed off the post, stepping forward, holding out an arm. "Feel that tone. Pure, Telmorian-forged masculinity."

I pressed two fingers briefly to his forearm. "Slightly less like dough."

He gasped. "Just hold it for a moment and feel it."

"You want validation or a bruise?"

"I'll take whichever comes with prolonged contact."

Despite myself, a breath of laughter slipped out. He always managed to drag one out of me, even on the worst days. Especially on the worst days. And never pushed.

We gathered my things, the scent of oiled leather and pine clinging to the morning. As we turned toward the trail leading back to the central training range, Callen fell into step beside me. We walked for a while without speaking.

The path dipped into a grove of whiteleaf trees. The hush between us was soft, comfortable, even with the weight of the week pressing behind my ribs. Ahead, the trail opened into the training range, a wide, elevated platform surrounded by stone pillars and faintly glowing wards. Tameables roamed in the enclosure beyond, their bodies massive and strange against the early mist.

I looked up toward Celestia, trying, and failing, to block the flood of thoughts crashing back into my mind. Everyone was calling it the *Abyss* now. That was the name they'd settled on to explain away the fractures no one could stitch closed. The gaps. The missing hours, memories, and moments. The incidents without cause. The wrong men being remembered for the right things, Haldric's murder, the fragmented records of Etheris. The sudden shift in ranks and roles that no one questioned too deeply.

The Abyss, they said, had been born of the Untameable war, of Aether colliding with too much history and power in one place. As if war itself could sever memory, or grief could rewrite it. And I lived in the hollowed-out truth of it.

I was the Abyss. Every part of me that had once mattered—every moment *we* had lived, felt, chosen had been stripped clean. I was the secret they had buried. And they hadn't even remembered burying me.

We reached the outer edge of the training yard. The others were already there, Royals and Majors clustered near the sparring stones, Elders giving drills. I moved to slip in unnoticed, but Callen caught my wrist.

"Mira."

I looked down. A thin line of blood had trickled across my hand, reopened from gripping the bowstring. He shook his head in a gesture that was more weary resignation than disapproval and nodded toward the tent at the range's edge, where the healers sat waiting. I turned and crossed the field toward them.

It was almost a routine now, so the healer didn't look surprised to see me. Just held out a hand and motioned me toward the same bench where she patched me up every morning.

"Same hand?" she asked.

I nodded.

Her fingers moved in slow circles, pulling threads of her Aether through the air with healing fern and some blend. They wove over my palm, coaxing the skin to knit clean. The scent of dried lavender and fern bloomed faintly in the space between us. I stared straight ahead. The sting had dulled and now it was only sensation. Nothing that reached deeper than skin.

Across the range, the others had begun forming ranks. The Tameables stirred behind them, hulking silhouettes half-hidden by mist. Somewhere out there, Dreadclaw wheezed. He hadn't come to me in days. And I was too out of my mind to entertain his tantrums. And I didn't know if that meant he'd forgotten too, or if he simply let me grieve what I had lost—the life that made me believe in perfection; the feeling, so solid I could taste it, that I would be cherished for eternity; the whole life I had planned and built my heart around.

⸺⸙⸺

By the time I reached the main grounds, the others had already gathered beneath the stone arch. A breath of mist curled through the space, thick with morning chill and the distant scent of burned coal.

I slid onto the stone bench beside Lyria, who offered me a small nod of acknowledgment. "You missed Ophira's lecture on Dissonance yesterday," she whispered.

"I've heard about it before."

She snorted softly. "Not this version. This one comes with threats. Should be entertaining."

I gave her a faint smile. She'd become decent company of late. Our chambers were in the same wing, and she had the rare gift of talking without expecting anything in return when she was comfortable.

Elder Ophira stood at the front of the assembly, draped in her usual obsidian robes with that gold-banded staff she seemed to use more for intimidation than support. Beside her stood two others: a broad-shouldered man with pale hair and a patchy beard,

Elder Mavren, and a severe-looking woman in a green Sage robe whom I didn't recognize.

"The Celestial Dissonance begins in two fortnights," Mavren began, his voice a grind of gravel. "This is not a drill. It is a preview of their extinction, or ours."

Everything now was the Dissonance. Its history, our preparations, and the constant hum of terror. As a commoner, the outcome of these Celestial wars between Realms had been as relevant to me as the weather on a distant star. But now I was in the Legion. If Atlassian lost, I'd also lose it all. *It all.* What a grandiose way to say *my life.*

He scanned the assembly. "You know why you are here. For those still foolish enough to believe this is abstract, you are not training for a game. You are honing the only tools that will matter when the Clans break."

Cassian leaned toward Lyria, loudly whispering, "And here I thought this was the briefing for the seasonal ale-tasting tour—"

Ophira's head turned so fast I thought her spine might snap. "Cassian Alrith," she hissed. "If you'd prefer I toss you into the Abyss to experience it firsthand, do say so. Otherwise, remember we have only a limited number of nights before the Realms collide. To prepare for a war that will decide whether we live as conquerors or kneel as slaves. So unless you'd like your first taste of battle to be your last, I suggest you take this very seriously."

Cassian's smirk faded, though he recovered quickly, raising his hands in surrender. "Just ensuring everyone's awake and paying attention, Elder. No need for threats."

That was his way of goofing around and getting some attention. Cassian would befriend a rock if he thought he could leverage it for a promotion, or at least to influence our daily meal plan in his favor. He never shut up about how his years as a Major were just a prelude to schmoozing with the Royals.

"The only service you'll be providing if you interrupt again is as a cautionary tale," Mavren grunted.

Lyria shifted beside me, her knee brushing mine. "He's not

wrong," she muttered under her breath. "If the Dissonance is half as brutal as they say, we'll need more than luck to survive."

A murmur rippled through the gathered warriors. Delina, a Royal, arched her brow. "And what if the enemies have prepared harder?"

"Then we cheat," Callen said, grinning when Ophira shot him a glare. "What? You think they won't?"

She exhaled sharply. "Enough with the wits. It is a poor substitute for competence." She turned slightly and gave Mavren a nod to continue.

"Each Clan of Telmoria," Mavren continued, "will be matched with a rival, and those pairings will remain hidden until Alignment Day. When the Realms merge, everything changes. Terrains warp. And none of us will have time to recover if we stumble."

"What happens if we lose?" asked a Royal girl with a jeweled circlet tangled in her braid.

"We don't want to think about it," the Sage answered coolly, her hands folded like marble over her lap. "But since you asked: should we fail, Atlassian will forfeit its Sovereignty to the Dominion. Our Clan will be stripped of Aether and those who survive will be exiled to the commoners' territories—depending on what the winners decide."

I've heard it said enough times in the past few days to commit it to memory, yet it still strikes me as odd, how something this important isn't common knowledge to everyone. Then again, I was raised in a commoner's Dorms. We didn't spare much thought about which banner stood tallest. Victory meant little when it never changed our fate or the price of bread.

Sage's voice remained unshaken. "As we all know already, Atlassian has never lost a Dissonance in over two centuries. Our banners have flown highest through blood and wind, and we take pride in that."

"But pride," Ophira cut in, her tone now iron, "is no substitute for preparedness. And this will be the first Dissonance in living memory for which we have had less than five fortnights to prepare." Ophira's gaze swept over us. "The Abyss cost us more than bodies. It fractured time and left the Clan scrambling. We overestimated our stability, and now we must compensate for it."

Mavren added, "All our drills and formations have been tactically mapped over the past few nights with Sovereign. You will remain with the cohort you trained with before the Abyss. Your unit, your battle-family from now on. The familiarity of your formations is an advantage. The rest of the Legion will train under separate protocols and cohorts."

A pause. He turned slightly, eyes resting briefly on me. "Except our Tamer. As the only one with Tameables under her control, she could rotate between cohorts."

I inclined my head once, wordless. I had not asked for that title. But once Atlassian forgot who I was, Tamer was all they remembered me for. After the announcement of Damien's betrothal, I had stopped caring what they called me. Let them call me blessed or cursed. It no longer mattered. I just drifted through my duties with dull interest.

I hadn't even been present for Damien's coronation ceremony held just days after his betrothal announcement. I couldn't bear to see that stranger's face carved onto my man, my Etern. And yet, some part of me regretted missing it. But then, he had acted like a Sovereign long before they'd placed a crown upon his brow. I doubted the weight felt new to him at all.

A hush fell as Ophira spoke again. "And lastly," she said, "by request of our Sovereign himself, we welcome a new addition to your cohort, one whose insight will prove strategic, particularly regarding the ways of Nyxaria." We already knew the name before it passed her lips.

Lorenza stepped forward from the shadows behind us, her gown whispering against the stone. Nyxaria's Heiress.

Or Damien's woman.

CHAPTER 2

MIRABELLE

Amurmur rippled through our cohort—part admiration, part unease. My fingers twitched toward the half-healed cuts on my fingers.

"Thank you, Elder Ophira." Lorenza's voice was confident, yet melodious, like a blade wrapped in silk. "I look forward to learning Atlassian strategies." Her gaze swept the circle. "And contributing Nyxaria's...unique perspectives."

Cassian leaned toward me, loud enough for all to hear. "Is this just a fancy way of saying she'll stab us in the back with a jeweled dagger?"

Lorenza's laugh was light, effortless. "If I wanted to stab you, you'd already be admiring the craftsmanship of my blade from the inside." She tapped the ornate dagger at her hip. "Though I prefer steel to jewels for such delicate work."

She winked at him, then slipped into an empty space between two Royals. A few muffled chuckles escaped, and it lightened the scene.

I *should* stop comparing myself to her. I told myself that often enough to nearly believe it. Yet I couldn't help noticing how we were opposites in nearly every conceivable way.

She stood very tall, elegantly beautiful. The kind of willowy beauty that moved like water and spoke like silver. A well-raised Heiress through and through. One didn't need to see the sigil stamped on her breastplate to know it. She was composed without coldness, confident in her own skin, and knew how to win allies without trying.

Ophira's staff struck the stone beneath our feet with a sharp crack that sent sparks scattering across the pavilion floor. "We have no time for rivalry. You'll be training together. Fighting together. And yes, surviving together."

The Sage unfolded her hands, voice smooth as ever. "When the Realms align, you will have two—"

A sudden noise rose at the edge of the grounds. Low growls and a movement behind the mist. The murmurs died instantly. Through the shifting haze, a hulking shadow detached itself from the enclosure.

Dreadclaw.

I fought the urge to roll my eyes. The beast had been insufferable ever since Damien had kissed me during the Abyss battles. *Stars*, the creature had behaved like a jilted lover, as if there was anything left to be jealous of. Now he roamed the open, Aetherium-leashed grounds of his confinement, sulking.

Then he sneezed. A glob of acidic black phlegm splattered across Lorenza's gown, the fabric immediately smoking. Her startled gasp was still somehow graceful as she stumbled back into Callen.

"Oh dear," he drawled, steadying her with exaggerated care. "I do believe you've been...marked."

The tension shattered into laughter. Lorenza examined the ruin of her gown with composure, raised a brow at Dreadclaw. "Well. It's good to know I am memorable to you," she mused. "Charming...though next time I'd prefer something less rotten."

A fresh wave of chuckles rippled through the group. Even Mavren's lips twitched.

Her voice scraped against my raw nerves, and I instantly hated myself for the jealousy twisting in my gut. Lorenza hadn't asked for this any more than I had. She was merely another piece in the Elders' elaborate game. It wasn't her fault she'd been shaped so carefully, as if designed to fit Damien in all the ways I could not.

The noises returned, playful jabs, amused murmurs, the light hum of camaraderie that often followed shared embarrassment. I sat there in silence, letting the noise blur into meaningless chatter as I retreated inward.

Why was I the only one who remembered? I asked myself for the umpteenth time. Was it my Tether to the Tameables? Some flaw in the Crown's magic? Or just the Realm's idea of a cruel joke?

I didn't know. I hadn't known anything for weeks.

My first instinct after everything about us had been erased had been to run straight to Damien till Izmer had stopped me. I had plotted instead. I would rebuild his trust, piece by piece, until he would believe even the impossible.

So I did the only thing I could. I overthought every moment, picking them apart in vain. I even crafted a fragile plan: the ways to reach Damien, to earn his trust brick by painstaking brick. Perhaps one day, he would believe me, even if the truth sounded absurd or manipulative to every other living soul. But I was running out of time. And I'd only seen him once since his coronation, when he'd introduced Lorenza to our cohort. He hadn't even glanced my way. His indifference only sharpened my resolve, fueling an urge to make him see me.

The dreadful fact that Royal men could Bond with more than one partner, so long as they were of different bloodlines or wielded distinct Aethers, only deepened the snare of my miserable fate. If I were not fast enough, our fate was spoiled for good. The ritual with Lorenza would proceed, and she would be eternally tied to Damien. As an Heiress publicly Bonded, he would be honor-bound to see it through. Nyxaria would not accept the humiliation of a broken Bond after the deed was done.

A shift in the air pulled me back. As Lorenza had settled among us, most looked at her in surprise, some in approval. It was no small gesture on her part to sit among us, shoulder to shoulder, as one of the cohort rather than an Heiress above it.

Then, at last, the murmurs died. And we all turned our attention to the Elders as they began explaining what lay ahead, and how we must prepare to face the unknown—the rival Clan that would be assigned to us, whose name, Aether, and strengths were still a mystery we would have to unravel in the heat of the Dissonance.

Midway through, my gaze caught on Damien's figure across the range. He stood near the outer platform, speaking quietly with Nathan, brows drawn, arms folded in that way of his. Something hollow in my chest lurched. I hadn't seen his face or heard his voice in what felt like a lifetime. Pity I was reduced to this, aching for just a glimpse of a man who didn't care if I existed. Who had a Clan and another woman to occupy his heart. But I couldn't help myself, because he hadn't even been here for days, preparing for the Dissonance in whatever way Sovereigns prepared, and the silence he left behind was starting to feel deafening.

My hands curled in my lap, the urge to rise, to walk across the range, to say something—anything—battling with the helplessness pressing down on me. Every fiber of my being screamed to move, to act...but to do what?

To stride over and announce that the woman he'd promised eternity to stood barely twenty paces away?

He stood in polished leathers, the lines of his vambraces flexed as he shifted. His hair was slightly tousled by the wind, and the way the dark strands brushed against his brow was distractingly, infuriatingly perfect.

Then Lorenza's voice broke through the haze. "Forgive me," she said lightly, rising from beside us with a graceful sweep. "I have missed my betrothed more than I expected. It's been...days."

She didn't wait for dismissal, simply glided across the grounds, her damaged gown flaring behind her.

The sound of Elders faded in the background as I watched her cross the range. She reached Damien as he turned, and for a moment, they stood close. Her hand brushed his forearm lightly as she spoke, and he inclined his head as if listening.

I pressed my tongue to the roof of my mouth, forcing myself to breathe through it. *This was nothing. Look away.* Still, the way he leaned slightly toward her, just enough to hear without her raising her voice, made me watch them. It seemed I was indeed a masochist.

I dug my nails into my palms, letting the sharp pain anchor me. This weakness served no purpose. If I were to undo what had been done, I needed clarity, not this useless churning in my stomach for something trivial. And I shouldn't let emotions cloud my plans. After a few murmured words, they turned together, retreating toward the palace.

Something warm and wet dripped onto my thigh. I looked down to find my palm bleeding again, the carefully mended skin split open where my nails had bitten deep.

Dreadclaw's low growl rumbled through the ground, vibrating up through the stone benches. I didn't need to look to know he was watching me, those brooding eyes seeing too much.

———— ✦ ————

LYRIA CIRCLED ME, her stance light, her dark eyes sharp with focus. "You're holding back," she said, rolling her shoulders. "If you fight like this in the trials, you'll be gutted before the first bell rings."

I was not good at this and I had made peace with that. But I had improved enough to at least have a conversation mid-drill without losing a tooth, and Lyria had improved enough to mostly not narrate her own footwork aloud, which was progress for both of us.

We trained in the southern yard, surrounded by the clash of sparring and sharp calls across the field. The final phase of the Dissonance would allow neither Aether nor Tameables, so every afternoon was spent preparing for it, pushing ourselves until we were fit, or forced to become so. The rosters would be announced soon enough, but I trained regardless, bent on improving my most obvious weakness—namely, that I was not raised as a warrior and still had to negotiate with a sword about which end should threaten the enemy and which end should not threaten me.

I heard the others murmuring nearby, boots skidding against stone. Their sparring was methodical, muscles responding to commands. Their minds were focused on drills.

Mine was not. Still, I adjusted my grip on the practice sword.

"I don't plan on dying so easily," I murmured.

The leather-wrapped hilt bit into my palm, a reminder that none of this came naturally. Callen and Ophira had taught me the basics, how to swing, and how to stay alive. But I was still relying more on instinct and brute will than any real skill with a blade.

Lyria smirked, a flicker of fire in her eyes. "Prove it." And she lunged.

I parried, the force of her strike jolting up through my shoulder. Her blade came again, sharp and quick. I ducked under it, breath hissing through my teeth. For one staggering moment, I imagined throwing down the blade and walking off, back to the quiet rhythm of archery. But I stayed.

Through every swing and block, I stayed.

At the final exchange of the session, I feinted right to draw her guard, then dropped low and slammed my fist toward her ribs. She blocked it cleanly, shoving me backward with a grunt. "I have heard the Court is digging into your history."

A muscle in my jaw twitched. "Let them dig. They'll find nothing."

She spun, the edge of her blade singing through the air. I twisted just in time, her strike slicing past the fabric at my side.

"They don't like mysteries," she said. "Especially about commoners who command Tameables."

"What are they going to do, anyway? They need me alive." The words sounded bitter and I didn't like it. So I said nothing more.

I had wandered near the palace before noon, past the archway that led to the throne hall. I told myself I had only meant to pass through. But I had lingered. Hoping to see Damien, waiting for a chance to catch his eye.

Instead, the guards had dismissed me with cool indifference. "The Sovereign is occupied. Speak to Commander Nathan if it is urgent."

"I only need a moment—" I'd tried, my voice softer than I intended, almost pleading.

"I am afraid we cannot," the guard replied, his tone leaving no room for debate.

And then Lorenza had stepped out from his doors, with a shy smile gracing her features. She had smiled politely, almost absently, in my direction as she passed. I said nothing more to the guard. I just turned and left.

Now, Lyria lunged again, her strike aimed for my ribs—

All the thoughts, hurt, disdain, boiled over in me. I pivoted hard, dropped low, and slammed into her centerline. One arm caught her hip, the other her shoulder, and with a growl of force, I drove her backward.

She flew several feet before landing in a breathless heap on the stone. Gasps echoed. Callen clapped once. "Careful, Lyria. She's got a temper under all that brooding."

Lyria coughed, pushing herself up on her elbows. "Stars, Mira," she wheezed. "You trying to crack my spine?"

I blinked. "I—I am sorry." I offered her my hand, the words still catching in my throat as she rose.

We reset and sparred again. This time, when I twisted her arm too roughly, she countered. Sudden pain tore through my forearm. I recoiled, the stench of charred fabric and blistered skin thick in the air. She had accidentally wielded her Aether.

So much for not visiting the healers again. Lyria froze, her blade dropping slightly. Horror washed over her face. "Mirabelle—"

I waved her off, teeth clenched against the pain. "It's fine."

It wasn't. But I deserved it for hurting her, unintentionally or not. She'd only reacted on reflex, and her Aether had answered before she could stop it.

She stared at me, then exhaled sharply through her nose. "Healer."

"I can finish the—"

"That was not a suggestion." Before I could protest, she caught my wrist and started walking, pulling me along. "Let's get you healed."

I followed her silently, the sting in my arm paling beside the deeper ache inside me, a hollow pain I feared might never truly fade.

CHAPTER 3
MIRABELLE

I pushed the sleeve of my new tunic up my forearm. The fabric slid smoothly over the tender skin. The provisioning for the Dissonance preparation had been thorough. Sturdy boots, flexible leather corsets, tunics that breathed, and all treated to resist flame. I'd never understood how much my regular dresses hindered me until I got these clothes.

I flexed my fingers once, twice, then nocked the arrow. Drew the bowstring tight. Let the breath still in my lungs.

And released.

The arrow struck just shy of the center ring, a clean shot, but not a perfect one.

Behind me, boots crunched lightly on frost-dusted gravel.

"Well...I'm not in the mood to feel your arms," I called without turning and took another arrow. "My hand's too numb to appreciate the monumental gains you've made in a day, Callen."

"Your posture is compromising the release."

The bow slipped in my fingers.

I knew that voice, and it was not Callen's. It was a voice that lived in the marrow of my bones. Low, deep, and familiar in a way that made my heart flip in my chest.

I did not turn. Could not.

I made myself not turn, for one full breath, because I knew that the moment I did, my face would say everything I'd been rehearsing not to say for days.

"Your form is strong. But if you don't adjust your anchor point and shoulder alignment, you'll strain your draw arm," the voice continued, clinical and clear.

The bow slipped in my fingers. My heart lurched so violently I was certain he must have heard it. I turned.

And there he was.

Damien stood ten paces away, his arms folded across his chest. The pale dawn light carved him out of the morning mist, gilding the planes of his shoulders. His embroidered tunic was a deep black, fitted cleanly across the broad expanse of his frame, the collar carelessly open at the throat. He was still in his leathers, dust from the road faint on his boots. But he might as well have been wrought from starlight and memory, for how he burned my eyes.

Faint shadow of scruff lined his jaw, the kind he always kept. And still, he looked every inch the Sovereign. Regal and commanding.

Unreachable.

It had been weeks. Weeks since he'd kissed me like I was the only thing keeping him anchored to this Realm. Now, he looked at me with the detached, assessing focus of a strategist reviewing an asset.

"And you lean too far forward when you release," he continued, as if I weren't standing there on the verge of collapsing.

I could not speak. My heart still hammered so violently it hurt.

His hair was longer, the dark strands brushing his jaw. There were faint shadows under his eyes—*had he been sleeping?*—and a new faint scar along his temple. I wanted to ask what had happened.

Instead, I swallowed hard and managed to whisper, "I...will keep that in mind."

He studied me for a moment longer, then he gave a small, curt nod. "I heard about the burn," he said. "From training yesterday."

"It is manageable."

"I wasn't asking whether it was manageable. I was noting that we need you sound for the Dissonance trials. Don't overexert yourself. Conserve your strength for the Tameables. You know the Dissonance begins with trials that rely on them. We will need five of them—coordinated and disciplined."

I nodded. Too fast. Too stiff.

"With your Aether," he went on, "I believe that's more than possible. But Dreadclaw has not been cooperative, has he?"

I blinked and shook my head. "No. He's been insuffer—I mean...off."

"He is the most powerful of them all. Perhaps that's why he remains loyal to those who tamed him first. I anchored him alone all these years for that very reason." A faint frown creased his brow. "But with you, we will manage to forge strong Tethers. Eventually."

He stepped beside me now, facing the range. The scent of him —cold morning air, saddle leather, and the faint cedar of his bath —was a visceral ambush.

"I am aware we are not quite familiar with each other," Damien added, his tone carefully neutral. "That should not be an obstacle. Once Dreadclaw sees you working alongside me, his trust will follow. Then you can build further on your own bond with him."

The irony of that entire statement nearly choked me. Instead, I nodded awkwardly at him. "Of course."

That was all I could force out. After all the nights I had spent rehearsing. I had planned for days—nights—how I might begin again with engaging conversations. I had told myself I would build trust, earn his regard slowly, prove I was not mad, nor forgettable. But now, faced with his voice, his presence, the unbearable familiarity of a man who no longer knew what he meant to me, all I could force past my lips were a few useless words.

He turned, motioning for me to follow. "We will walk back to the Aetherium range."

I fell into step beside him, my pulse still erratic. The distance between us felt both too vast and too small.

"As I was saying," he continued, "we will be facing the opposing Realm's five most powerful Tameables. Our own five must be chosen carefully." He glanced at me. "I am entrusting this decision to you."

I stumbled on a loose stone. "To me?"

"Council's decision." His expression remained impassive. "I rarely place such trust lightly, but it seems you proved yourself during the Abyss."

Proved myself. So he remembers that part? My actions during the Abyss. He remembered the events, but not the context. Not the why. Not the *who for.* He remembered the warrior, but not the love that had armed her.

I wanted to say something useful and clever back to him. But my tongue was lead. "I...erm...appreciate the trust, Damien."

He went utterly still. Then, slowly, his head turned, and his eyes, which had been cool and distant, narrowed with a sudden, piercing focus.

I faltered, correcting myself hastily. "My—my Liege." The words felt foreign in my mouth. Like ash.

He turned to face me fully. His expression softened—not much, just enough for me to see it. "You may call me Damien," he said quietly. "If that is what you are comfortable with."

I could only nod. But inwardly, I screamed. Because the last time I had said his name, it had been a sigh against his lips in the dark. A plea. And now I said it like it belonged to someone else.

⟞⟡⟝

I WAITED IN THE GROUNDS, just beyond the arch-shaped gate that separated the physical world from the shimmering edges of the Aetherium Hold. This place was outside the barrier, but still in its reach. An invisible boundary enclosed the wide, uneven terrain, allowing Tameables to pass through under supervision. A controlled wildness like most things in Telmoria.

It was built for training with Untethered Royals and Majors, where escape paths had been etched into the perimeter stone and exits marked by glowing sigils in case something went wrong. It almost always did, with them.

I flexed my arm and glanced toward the barrier. My stomach coiled in quiet knots as I waited, but not over the training or Tameables. I couldn't get enough of the low timbre of Damien's voice, of the way he smelled. Of that painfully handsome face, and the rugged build that stole my breath every time I dared to glance his way. I was drowning in the warmth of his proximity, reveling in everything I'd been starved of for what felt like an eternity.

And then I heard them both. First, Damien's footfalls. Then the deeper, hollow thud that belonged to Dreadclaw.

They emerged through the Aetherium veil like a shadow torn from bone. Smoke curled faintly from Dreadclaw's shoulders, and his massive claws dragged along the ground with menace. Beside him walked Damien. Sleeves rolled to the forearms, and his dark hair swept back.

And Dreadclaw—*oh boy*—looked smug. Parading Damien around as if to say to the others, *Look who chose me, and not you.* I bit back a smile.

He hissed at me as they approached, a sound like steel dragged over stone, his forked tongue flicking out to taste the air between us. A performance I didn't really acknowledge.

"Easy," Damien murmured, resting a firm hand on Dreadclaw's smoked tendril. The Tameable rumbled low in its chest but obeyed, though its glowing gaze stayed fixed on me. The pull of his Tether brushing against my own.

You look terrible, his voice hissed in my mind. *Did you sleep in a ditch?*

I arched a brow. *Pleasant morning to you too. And you look like an overgrown lizard playing fetch.*

Dreadclaw's tendril gave a sharp twitch. A low growl began to build. I ignored it and approached them.

"He is temperamental," Damien admitted, frowning. "But he trusts you."

Oh yes, he trusts me to bring out the very worst in him. I schooled my expression into something neutral. "Yes."

Damien was already studying my posture again, always observing. And even with all that distance, standing this close to him again made me feel...real. *Alive.*

Dreadclaw stomped once, lowering his head until his snout hovered inches from my chest. Heat poured off him in thick, blistering waves. Then he lunged. Damien's hand already shot out, gripping my arm to pull me back.

I froze as Dreadclaw's massive body twisted past me, a burst of movement that shook the ground. His tendrils flared wide in a display meant to intimidate. The giant bully.

Damien's touch burned through my sleeve, and before I could stop myself, I leaned into his solid frame.

"Stay behind me." His voice was a low command at my ear.

I didn't move. For a stolen breath, I let myself rest against him, unwilling to let go of the steady warmth of his hold. "He won't hurt me," I murmured.

"You don't know that."

Oh, but I did. But I didn't voice it, if only to feel the protective weight of his hand a moment longer.

Dreadclaw hissed in my mind: *Tell him to release you.*

I shot the beast a warning look before turning back to Damien. "It's alright," I said gently, easing my arm free. "Let me try."

For a heartbeat, he hesitated. Then, reluctantly, he stepped back. And I missed the touch the moment it was gone. Maybe I should do something reckless, just enough to draw him close again. Or maybe pretend Dreadclaw was harder to manage than he was, so I'd earn a few more of these training sessions...preferably with Damien standing a little too close, his arm wrapping around me to *protect* me from this awful-mannered beast.

But before I could make good on anything, Lorenza's voice rang across the grounds.

"Hello!"

We turned in unison. She stood at the edge of the training grounds, one hand lifted in greeting. I returned the gesture automatically, while Damien offered only a curt nod of acknowledgment. Then I realized her eyes never left him. Her wave hadn't been for me.

Eww. And very much...ouch.

She strode toward us, her lithe frame draped in a fitted leather corset over a dark tunic, the ensemble accentuating the subtle curves. Her hair was pulled back and braided down. She was tall enough that Damien would never need to lift her when he kissed her— *Stop.*

A sharp tug on my sleeve startled me back to the present. Damien's fingers brushed my wrist, his brow furrowed. "You haven't heard a word I said, have you?"

I blinked. "What?"

His gaze dropped to my hand. "Stop pressing on your wound like that. You will tear it open."

I looked down. My fingers had been digging into the tender, half-healed burn without my realizing it, the skin beneath now an angry red.

"No, I didn't...mean to," I said defensively. "It wasn't intentional."

He didn't answer, only studied me a moment longer while I fidgeted. By then, Lorenza had reached us. She stepped into the enclosure with a soft laugh, brushing her hands on her thighs. "I hope I'm not interrupting."

You are.

Damien straightened beside me. "We are mid-training," he said evenly. "And it wouldn't be wise for you to step any closer to this Tameable." He nodded toward Dreadclaw, who still lingered in the shadowed end of the range, molten eyes trained on Lorenza with the fixed stillness of a storm watching a tree it might uproot.

I could almost feel his disapproval crackling in the space between us. Lorenza smiled, utterly unbothered. "I thought I might observe. Tameables are fascinating. And you would save me, wouldn't you?"

My jaw clenched at the way she said it, light and teasing, with a familiar ease that spoke of private conversations and shared moments I wasn't part of.

And yet I hadn't realized, until that moment, that Dreadclaw was also listening.

Get rid of her, his thought hissed through my mind like smoke beneath a closed door, *or I will do it for you.*

For me? He was choosing *my* side now?

Don't make a scene, I told him silently, even as a petty corner of my heart whispered otherwise.

As much as I wanted to throttle Lorenza for barging into our space, she wasn't the one at fault here. She had every right to stand where she pleased, to speak to him like that. She was his betrothed. The one with the title.

But I would get him back before that title turned into something irreversible. Not just with tantrums this time, I hoped.

"Should I stay?" Lorenza asked sweetly. "Perhaps I could assist with Mirabelle's training. Tameables are such strange creatures. Wouldn't it be good to have more than one voice to steady them?"

"No," Damien said without pause.

"Yes," I replied at the same time. We stared at each other for the span of a heartbeat. Even I didn't know why I'd said yes.

"If the Tamer needs help," he said at last.

Lorenza's lips curved. "Also, the council is waiting," she murmured. "They've finalized the envoy to Nyxaria. We need to confirm who we're sending. They're still insistent on Nathan."

Damien exhaled through his nose. The faintest flicker of annoyance crossed his face at the mention of Nathan. "I will join shortly."

Then he looked back to me, that unreadable calm returning. "I think you might be able to manage on your own," he said.

"But I'd rather not take the risk, not until Dreadclaw's fully aligned—"

Lorenza stepped between us, reaching up to adjust something at the clasp of Damien's tunic, a fold, a loose buckle, something that didn't matter. But it felt like a claim, even if she wouldn't have spared me a thought as a threat. Damien removed her hand without looking, jaw ticking.

A thunderous snarl ripped through the air, and before Lorenza could so much as gasp, Dreadclaw's massive tendril lashed out, sending her sprawling out of the Aetherium boundary. She landed hard, her perfect composure shattered, her face contorted in shock, pain and embarrassment.

"Back. Off," Damien commanded. The beast held his gaze, then gave a sulking huff and lumbered to a corner, the ground trembling with each step.

"I warned you," Damien said, his voice flat as he turned his attention back to Lorenza. But his other hand had already reached back, his fingers closing around my wrist. He tugged me to his side as his gaze flicked toward Dreadclaw, shielding me from a threat that didn't exist.

But I followed anyway, letting him pull me along like I was in need of saving. Because, *stars help me*, I was the sort of idiot who could still get butterflies from a single touch...and at the very wrong time.

We had only taken two steps toward where Lorenza had fallen before she was pushing herself up, brushing dust from her now-scuffed leathers. A thin trail of blood trickled from a scrape on her forearm. And she'd righted herself before we reached her.

"See a healer," Damien said, his gaze flicking to her injury. "Make sure it is nothing worse."

She glanced at the cut, then offered him a smile. "It will take more than a scratch to keep me down. But fine, if only to please you." She smiled and just walked off to the infirmary.

The moment she was gone, he started toward the palace, but I called after him. "Wait!"

He paused, glancing back, waiting.

I scrambled for an excuse. *I just want to be near you* wouldn't suffice here. "If—if I'm to be responsible for the Tameables in the Dissonance," I said, forcing steadiness into my voice, "then it's only logical I should be present for these discussions."

He held my gaze. "I was planning to arrange a separate briefing for you."

Oh.

"Well," I said quickly, "I can join this one too. If it's not... disruptive."

To my surprise, he nodded. "You can join."

I fell into step beside him, doing my best to mimic the composed stride of someone who wasn't internally celebrating like she'd just won a war. Dreadclaw's voice slithered into my mind, still Tethered to mine, dripping with amusement. *Pathetic.*

But I couldn't help the small, triumphant smile that tugged at my lips as I followed Damien toward the palace.

CHAPTER 4

DAMIEN

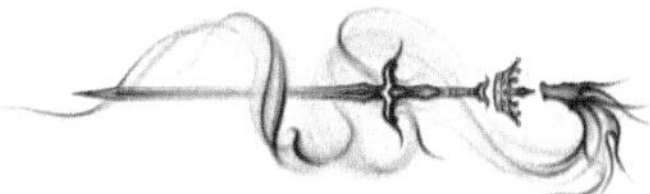

Around the long table, the Elders sat in quiet severity, flanked by Sages, and the occasional high-ranked Royals. Rowane lounged at my left, not seated so much as draped into his chair with the casualness of someone who knew he had already earned his place and had little desire to impress anyone further. Nathan sat to my right, arms folded, his expression impassive save for the way his jaw twitched whenever Nyxaria's name came up.

"We cannot afford to lose Nathan." Rowane's voice cut through the murmurs. "He is the backbone of our Legion. If Nyxaria insists on taking him as part of this alliance, then the price is too steep."

Sage Veyis exhaled through his nose. "The price was implied when we accepted their Heiress's hand in the Dissonance. Or have you forgotten that Lorenza's Aether alone could turn the tide in the Annihilation Trials?"

A murmur of agreement rippled through the council.

Three days. That was all the Dissonance offered. And the Annihilation Trial with no Tameables. Just Aether. We needed the alliances for that. Bringing in a warrior from another Clan—someone unknown to our opponents, unpredictable—could tip the balance. We won the last Dissonance by exploiting that very edge.

Lorenza, alongside Arthur from Zarkon, would serve as our primary weapons in this endeavor. But trading Nathan to secure this alliance had never been part of our strategy, nor would it be. He was not merely brute strength. He knew the Atlassian Legion in its entirety, understood its rhythms, its fractures, and its short-comings. He anchored the army, knew all warriors by name, by instinct, by history.

Nyxaria's request was nothing more than a calculated power play. They had no interest in Nathan as a leader. They wanted an efficient Aether-wielder on their battlefield: a weapon of rare capability, a warrior with the discipline to command and the raw force of Aether they cannot easily replicate.

And Lorenza could never come close to replacing Nathan. But if we were to refuse their demand, we could not do so empty-handed. We had to offer an alternative that carried real weight. Something they could not afford to dismiss.

"Their request is tactically clever." I said. "I will give them that."

"Admiring the craftsmanship of the blade pointed at your own throat, Damien?" Rowane murmured beside me, his dry tone laced with amusement.

"But he is our first sword. We can't afford to lose him for the second trial." I continued, brushing aside Rowane's quip, my eyes still on the board. "We have already agreed to send Rhylen to Zarkon. That is one pillar removed. But we can't weaken the very foundation of our Legion."

"We've offered a list of alternates," Mavren said.

"They don't want a substitute," Nathan said finally. "They want a bargain. They believe Lorenza's title is more valuable than whoever we might send."

My gaze flickered toward the Tamer, just briefly. Mirabelle hadn't spoken, but I noticed the subtle shift in her posture, the way her fingers curled slightly against the edge of the table. She was trying to look composed, but it was clear that she felt out of place, and her big green eyes lingered everywhere.

Every so often, her eyes darted to the speakers, curiosity flickering in moments she couldn't quite suppress. And every now and then, she glanced at me sideways.

This time, our eyes met. And she blushed.

Stars.

I clenched my jaw and forced myself back into the conversation.

"And if we refuse?" I asked, voice even. "Do we have an alternative option?"

"We risk souring the alliance," Sage Elara replied smoothly. "Nyxaria is the most stable of our neighboring Clans."

"We cannot let the alliance cost us our command," I said at last. "Find a second. One with enough prestige to satisfy their vanity, but not enough to cripple our defense."

"That won't be easy," Ophira said. "The next most prominent choice is..." She turned toward Mirabelle. "Mirabelle."

"She is not of Royal blood," Sage Elara said calmly. "The Nyxarian Elders would never accept it."

"She commands the most dangerous Tameable we've ever bound," Mavren said. "She's singlehandedly restructured our stables. That is worth more than lineage."

"It would offend Nyxaria," Elara murmured.

"Offended or not," I said, the words final, "she is not going anywhere."

A murmur rippled through the council.

"But her Aether—" someone began.

"Is Tethered to controlling Tameables," I interrupted. "Her shadows are defensive and for her own protection. Nyxaria will misuse her if we send her to them." My gaze swept the room, leaving no room for argument. "Besides, she is Atlassian's strength, and no one else's. We will find someone else."

Across the table, Mirabelle lowered her gaze, but her lips parted as if to speak. Then closed again.

"The matter is settled." My voice left no room for argument. "We will find another path with Nyxaria. I will reopen negotiations with Zarkon. They will accept another Commander for conditional trade. Rhylen will be reassigned in Nathan's stead."

I turned toward Mavren. "See to it." The council murmured their assent, though some looks of disapproval lingered. I didn't acknowledge it.

The door behind us creaked. And as if summoned by the very weight of her name, Lorenza entered. Ophira was the first to speak. "Nyxaria's request for Nathan is being...reevaluated."

Lorenza's gaze slid to me, softening with every step she took closer. "You disagree."

"I disagree with the price," I said flatly.

A beat of silence. Then she tilted her head and smiled. "Then let me speak to them. Perhaps they can be...persuaded."

"No," I said before she could say more. "You are already here. We won't complicate the terms any further. We will deal with it through proper channels."

She turned her head, slowly, and looked to Mirabelle.

"Unless," she said gently, "you would prefer to offer someone else in exchange."

"I am not for trade," Mirabelle said softly. Then her voice wavered. "I mean...the Sovereign has decided." She glanced at me, waiting for me to defend her. My knuckles turned pale where I held the chair.

Why had I never *seen* her before all this? She had been here all along. Not just surviving, but commanding. Our Tameables obeyed her where they snarled at the rest. And yet we had done nothing to prepare her. No proper strategy briefings. No sparring beyond necessity.

It was absurd. And worse, unjust.

"Mirabelle remains with our Tameables." I turned. "Lorenza, come with me."

I didn't wait for a response and walked out, toward the palace chambers.

"You're unusually protective of that Tamer," she mused, as the oak doors closed behind us, muting the scrape of chairs and the low clatter of voices swelling in our wake.

The grand central hall unfolded before us, its towering arches soaring high, crowned with intricate golden details that seemed to shimmer in the soft light. Staircases wound upwards, their marble steps gleaming under the glow of crystal chandeliers that reflected across the polished floors. A lone tree stood in the center of the hall, its green leaves a striking contrast to the ornate surroundings.

Lorenza's footsteps resonated softly on the marble as we walked, the silence around us filled only by the gentle echo of our presence in the vastness.

"She is Atlassian's best weapon against the other Clans' Tameables." I kept my gaze fixed ahead. "And she is not properly trained for other trials."

My footsteps slowed as we reached the staircase leading up to the Sovereign's wing. I had not taken my father's chamber. I remained in mine. Lorenza had been given one in our same wing, close enough to remind me of the arrangement with every passing day.

"I want you to stay out of this matter with Nathan," I said finally, ascending the stairs. "You might have already noticed. I prefer order in everything, and that it be handled properly, through the right channels."

"And alliances," Lorenza said, just behind me, "are not part of that structure?"

"They are," I replied, "but they are not the proper means to initiate negotiations between Clans. So, I would appreciate it if you could focus on what we have set out to do."

I pushed open the heavy doors to my chambers, stepping into the quiet sanctuary beyond. The Thralls had been there, the hearth burned low but steady, casting a warm glow over the chamber. Fresh linens draped the bed. For some reason, I had dismissed my Intimates during the Abyss. It hadn't mattered anyway. I was too consumed with keeping Atlassian alive through yet another trial we hadn't truly prepared for.

I crossed to the far wall, pulled open a drawer, and drew out a half-written letter sealed with red wax. I uncapped the ink vial.

"You're drafting the letter to Zarkon now?"

I hadn't realized Lorenza had followed me inside. "Yes."

She stepped closer, her fingers trailing along the edge of the desk. "Shall I help you with anything?"

"That won't be necessary." I looked back at the letter. "Take the time to yourself. Indulge in whatever you desire."

A pause. Then, "I could stay."

My quill stilled. I looked up. I had been mentoring her, helping her navigate Atlassian's intricate world of the Royals and Elders despite my own demanding schedule. Perhaps that was the very reason she was struggling to integrate with the rest.

"What do you think?" I asked, less for an answer and more to gauge her assessment of the situation. It was not customary to share one's own chamber with another black-blood—our own kind—prior to Bonding. Ritually or politically.

She met my gaze, her dark eyes trailed over me. "You've no Intimates now. Usually, that is how it is until the ceremony..." A slight, almost imperceptible shrug. "But you dismissed them all yourself, and I don't mind breaking a few impractical orders."

The offer hung between us. It was not crude, nor desperate. Simply stated, as if it were the logical progression of what my father had already implied to us both.

"I do mind," I said. "I prefer things uncomplicated, Lorenza. You—or anyone I Bond—will be here only after the rituals, should the alliance lead to it. Until then, you are here only for the Dissonance."

She did not avert her gaze, only inclined her head in acknowlededgment. "Very well," she said, though I could see her weighing the terms of our arrangement again. "You speak as if you haven't already been named Sovereign."

"I speak as one who intends to remain so. Which means I must see this through. And none of it includes redrawing personal boundaries to appease shifting expectations."

There was silence. Then, with grace sharpened by years of training and legacy, she inclined her head again. "Then I shall leave you to your tactics."

I paused, then added, more softly, "It is nothing personal. You should know that."

Her expression shifted into a shy smile. "I know you don't *not* want me. But I do think...everything is personal, to some extent."

She was wrong in almost everything she said. I would have treated anyone in her place with the same detached courtesy. This decision wasn't about her. And my mind had no room for thoughts that didn't serve my responsibilities. Correcting her, however, would be pointless. I remained silent. She turned and left without another word.

I waited until the doors clicked shut behind her, then turned back to my desk. But my thoughts did not return to the scroll. They kept drifting. Only two fortnights remained to refine three nights that would determine the fate of our Realm. To prepare strategies not only for the trials, but also for failure, for retreat, even for betrayal.

I scratched out the final line of the envoy letter, sanded the ink clean, and sealed it with the weight of my ring. Then I leaned back, eyes on the fire. Its quiet crackle was the only sound left to compete with the thoughts crowding my mind.

Green eyes. Burning with quiet things no one else seemed to notice. The Tamer who wasn't ready, who could cost us everything. But she should be trained and ready. Whether she wanted it or not.

CHAPTER 5
MIRABELLE

I began the slow ascent toward the Emberlock. The training ranges along the path were still crowded with Aether-wielders, mostly young Royals, moving through synchronized drills under Nathan and his two Commanders, their voices cutting through the air as they barked commands.

The first half of the day belonged to the Royals and Majors. I had seen enough glimpses between drills to recognize their method: break them down, then see who still fought.

In truth, I had not stayed long. I went to Amara's.

It was the second time I had visited since the Abyss swallowed my past. The first had left us both shaken. She'd pulled me in before I'd even finished the first sentence, hands around my back like she could hold the story inside me if she just held tight enough.

I told her what had happened. How the Crown had scraped us from Atlassian as cleanly as ink wiped from marble. Even she had forgotten every single conversation we had about Damien.

I had shared my well of sorrow—how I had buried grief beneath hope, found strength in routines, in taming beasts and in silence, and how I needed more time. But this visit was different. We'd already cried over it once; now she wanted proof I was doing something. Proof that I was fighting for myself. She sat across from me with the expression I recognized from childhood—the one that said *I am giving you thirty seconds before I start asking questions.*

"I needed time to heal before I could face it with sanity," I had admitted, pressing two small gems into her palm, trinkets I had saved for myself, now hers. "I'm still learning the rules of scheming inside Royal territory. Apparently, there's etiquette," I said, my smile a little wry.

She had laughed, though her eyes remained sad. "You? New to trouble? The Abyss must have stolen more than just memories."

I had left her with a pouch of nickels, new linens and a pair of soft socks she pretended not to like. And though I said little, I hoped it was enough to make her feel, if not rich, at least loved. I'd planned to ask Damien to assign her somewhere within the palace before the Abyss. And so much for that. Now even I don't belong anywhere near the palace.

Still, I was calmer today. Hopeful, perhaps. Not because of Amara, though she helped. But because I had glimpsed the barest sliver of an opening with Damien. And I hoped to be strong enough to crawl through it and get us back.

Because everything simply happened *to* me. Every loss, every silence, every cruel twist of fate, my whole life...had happened to me. And I was done. This time, I would make it happen *for* me.

And if nothing came of it, if the alliance held and Damien never looked at me as anything more than the Clan's useful Tamer, then at least I would not carry the ache of *what ifs*. I could say I tried, that I had not gone quietly. What I couldn't carry was the rot of having stood still and done nothing.

THE OUTER WALLS of Emberlock rose like a jagged crown above the field, spiked with iron and silver and old flame marks now. The Lock was forged in such a way that it could be transformed and reimagined to accommodate all kinds of games and trials. It was highly mercurial, and it amazed me how the whole look of it shifted from a gleaming citadel of sand and light to a dark, volcanic stronghold in a matter of days.

Now it was in an austere state: half from volcanic rock, half from fused obsidian. It housed preparation trials for the Dissonance, drills that mimicked the brutal, terrain-shifting trials we could face when the Realms aligned.

Almost everyone had arrived already. The yard pulsed with life: warriors stretching and chattering. Lyria waved at me from across the way, face flushed from a bout of sparring. Callen, of course, had a split lip and no shirt. Cassian lounged near the shade of the armory wall, rolling his shoulders and flirting with someone who was very clearly not flirting back. They were all preparing to face annihilation in less than four weeks. And they were laughing and chattering.

I stepped up beside Lyria. I was really warming up to her. She'd quickly become a frequent visitor, and more often than not, my mealtime companion.

Ophira's voice cut through the murmurs. "You will not know what the trials will be until Dissonance dawns. Today, you learn to survive with nothing but wit and will. Don't even think about wielding Aether."

Sixteen of us stood at the edge, divided into four teams. Mine consisted of Cassian and two Royals: the sharp-eyed Delina and Elion, deceptively calm beneath a tousle of brown hair.

"Rules are simple," Ophira continued. "Fifteen relics will appear at random. Your cohort's collective score is your only measure of success. It is not a solo hunt. Let greed rule and you drown alone."

She gestured toward the vast Emberlock floor below. "The terrain will shift beneath you. If you fall, you're out."

"So...how do we win, exactly?" a Royal asked in the middle.

She arched a brow, not pausing. "I'm explaining, aren't I? Hear me out, then ask."

There was a pause. Then her voice rang clearer. "You have until the final bell. What matters is how many relics your team captures, how long each one is held, and how many of you are left standing when it ends. That means the early grab has the highest payoff. If one of you falls, the relic falls with you. But the game doesn't stop. You'll just have to find it again. Somewhere else."

With that, Ophira turned and walked out. The doors to Emberlock shut behind her, sealing the sixteen of us inside. A few moments passed, just enough for unease to settle, then the bell tolled.

The first platform shuddered. *Seems like preparation time wasn't part of the game.*

Cassian lunged before the echo faded, his boots skidding across shifting stone. "First relic's mine!"

"Idiot. He's going to die!" Delina hissed under her breath, but she followed him anyway.

The platforms crumbled and breathed, rising and falling with a hidden rhythm like the last time I was here. But this was different, too random to trace any kind of pattern.

Elion grabbed my arm. "We need a plan."

"We need to catch them first." I said and pulled him with me. We darted across the nearest platforms to catch up with the other two, judging the space between them, the tilt of the stone, the way the wind tugged at our balance. Then the first relic appeared, an orb of blue flame suspended over a crumbling ledge near the southern edge.

I turned instinctively to check our footing. Two teams had spotted it already and we had to rush.

"Those two tiles haven't moved yet," I muttered. But Cassian did not pause. "I will get it." He was already moving toward them.

"Cassian, don't—" Delina caught his arm just as the stone beneath his feet cracked, veering sideways with a grinding screech. He cursed and stumbled back, nearly dragging her with him.

"See?" she snapped. "Just think before you launch yourself off a—"

"We've got company!" Elion shouted from behind us.

Callen's team had already begun surging forward, aiming for

the same relic. Elion darted ahead, intercepting their path. He hurled a chunk of loose rubble at one Royal's knees, then spun sideways to elbow another square in the chest.

The four of us scrambled for the ledge. Elbows found ribs. A shove too hard. The relic, still untouched, wavered at the edge of the crumbling platform.

Elion lunged and I sprinted forward with him. He snatched the relic mid-slide, but the momentum sent him skidding across loose gravel toward a gap. The weight of the orb slowed him just enough.

He slid. Both legs dropped into the gap. I reached him just as his legs dropped over the edge, catching one ankle with both hands. My knees slammed against the stone edge of a nearby wall, but I shut my eyes and held on. I could feel the skin splitting across my knees and decided that was future-Mira's problem.

Cassian grabbed his other leg a second later and Delina looped an arm tightly around my waist, anchoring us both.

"You better thank me for this later," Cassian panted, straining under his full weight, arms trembling with the effort.

Elion huffed, teeth clenched. "Only if we win."

By the time we hauled him up, Lyria's shriek rang out across the arena. And Delina bolted toward the sound. I turned to see Lyria and Delina's cousin, Veyra, already grappling for a relic that had appeared near the middle column. Their hands clutched the same brass ring, a silent snarl between them.

"Break them up. Then maybe we will get it," someone shouted. But no one heard amid all the noises of shifts and shouts. Their feet slid over stone slick with dust. Veyra pulled hair. Lyria kneed her. The relic bounced free, spinning off the ledge into the dark, and all of them cursed colorfully.

The tiles shifted again, but we held onto the wall and started searching. It was really hard to spot these tiny relics in this vast space. The platforms moved unpredictably, but staying close to walls and anchored structures gave us something to hold on to if a tile slipped out from under us. I asked them to do the same.

We split up, weaving between crumbling paths, scanning for relics. Then I spotted one, glinting faintly in the far-left corner, half-hidden behind a fractured column.

Announcing it would draw the opponents. So I didn't. I moved casually at first, trying not to draw attention. But after a few steps, I could tell by the flick of her gaze, the shift in her stride, that Lorenza had seen it too. And she was doing exactly what I was doing.

So I ran. And a heartbeat later, so did she.

We collided midair. Her elbow jabbed into my ribs; my shoulder cracked against hers. The relic spun out of reach. The platform beneath us rumbled. Split.

We fell sideways, scrabbling. Her fingers caught my wrist, but not to steal the relic. She was trying to anchor herself. I should have let her go. But I had a very judgy spirit inside me who would absolutely frown upon me later.

So I dug my boots into a narrow ledge, heaved her up. She panted, pushing loose strands of hair from her face while I turned for the relic, opening my mouth to say something clever—

Pain exploded in my scalp. She'd grabbed my hair, yanked it back.

"What—" I hissed.

She plucked the relic from the floor with calm fingers.

"This is just a lesson," she said with a playful smile. "The Dissonance is not a game like this. Next time, do not hesitate."

And with that, she left. I seethed at myself. But beneath the sting, I knew she was right. What I'd done was foolish. Compassion has its place, but not in the wrong moment when kindness becomes a liability.

My knee was still bleeding and burning after this second stunt. I needed proper training after all. I was trading blows with warriors who had been forged in drills and battle since they could walk. If I didn't bridge that chasm, and fast, my epitaph would be a brief, unremarkable line in someone else's victory song.

CHAPTER 6
MIRABELLE

The Ring had begun to feel personal.

It had become a battlefield of panting, limping bodies. Dust streaked every tunic. Sweat slicked spines and forearms. Callen had a bruise blooming across one cheek, but still managed to blow me a kiss as he ducked beneath a flying boot and snatched another relic from Alden.

Overhead, the light had begun to dim, mist thickening at the edges of the Celestia, bruising the horizon with gold.

"Two," he shouted.

Nyric and Veyra were tangling with Callen and his squad, Delina driving one opponent toward a sloped platform that dissolved seconds later. Elion dove after a rolling orb, caught it, then almost pitched forward with the weight of it.

I reached him just in time to steady him. His hand squeezed mine once, and then he was off again. At this point, one would think I'd been appointed nursemaid to this entire exercise rather than a competitor.

Another relic sparked in the center and Delina ran for it.

"You have nothing to hold onto," I shouted and ran behind her, knowing I was already too late.

The platform had shifted wrong, just slightly, a hairsbreadth.

But she missed the ledge. Her hand flailed once, twice—and disappeared into the dark. I clamped my jaw tight, shoulders squared. "Keep moving. She'll want us to finish."

We did. The rest was a blur of pushing, pulling, slipping, and bleeding, more injury than grace. At some point, the back of my tunic tore clean through, and the only thing holding my tunic together was the stubborn binding of my cloth corset. But we made it. By the final second, we held three relics. We gathered again on the center disk as the platforms reformed into their original circular shape. Our cohort stood breathless. Dirt-smudged. Bloody.

Ophira reappeared atop the far terrace. Mavren turned the hourglass.

"Final tally," he said, and drew the standing on the board.

Team One, of Callen: Two relics. Four members remaining.
Team Two, of Lyria: Two relics. Two members surviving.
Team Three, ours: Three relics. Three standing.
And Team Four, the same.

Ophira lifted her hand. And Lorenza stepped forward, her tunic torn, her braid half-loosed. The relics at her hip still pulsed faintly.

"Your team secured one of the first relics," Ophira said. "Held the longest. And has three standing members."

She turned her gaze across the rest of us. "Which means they win. Because unlike the rest of you, they held what mattered." My shoulders dropped. The loss was mine to bear.

I glanced at Lorenza. She met my eyes and winked. *Damn her.*

"This was mercy," Ophira continued, her voice hard as tempered steel. "The Dissonance trials will not grant you second chances. Nor will your enemies wait for you to grow a spine, make decisions for you, or think for you."

Her eyes locked on Cassian. "And you certainly do not get to preen while your comrades bleed." Cassian said nothing. That alone told me how it landed.

The wind caught her cloak, billowing it around Ophira's body, and a cold droplet hit my cheek. Then another. The Celestia had been threatening rain all afternoon, and now it broke, fat, heavy drops splattering against the grounds.

She looked to me next. Her voice gentled. "It is not weakness to choose mercy. But mercy without foresight is just another form of recklessness." *So much for pretending it didn't happen.*

I nodded, rain sliding down my face, one droplet tracing the edge of my mouth. I fought the absurd urge to lick it away.

She turned back toward the gate, raising her voice once more. "We could try again in the coming days." A beat. "With more sense next time, I hope."

The moment her back disappeared beyond the terrace, Callen slung an arm around my neck. "At least your team got second place," he said, grinning as he ruffled my already drenched hair. "With all that bruising and bleeding, I was sure you'd be scraped off the tiles in pieces."

I shoved him off with a grunt, but the corner of my mouth twitched. The rain came down in earnest now, a deluge that had everyone scrambling for the covered walkways.

His forearm draped casually across my collarbone to tilt my chin up toward him. I pushed his arm off my throat. "Stop trying to choke me to death."

"Admit it. You're secretly in awe of my sculpted sinews. It's inevitable."

"What's inevitable is me pushing you into a puddle."

"Now, now," he murmured. "No need for dramatics. I fall. You jump after me. We are destined to plummet to our doom—"

His blabber dissolved into a sudden, sharp inhale. Cutting through the damp air was the aroma of roasted herbs. Tables had been set up beneath the stone archways, laden with steaming meat pies, crusty loaves of bread, and pitchers of something that smelled like spiced ale.

Cassian lunged for the nearest platter, earning a swat from Delina, who was already piling her plate. Lyria tossed a roll. I caught it one-handed, too hungry to care that it was probably meant for someone else.

We collapsed into the nearest long table, rain still slicking our sleeves, hair clinging to cheeks, tunics clinging to everything else. Callen slid into our bench with all the elegance of a soaked cat, followed by Lyria, two of his usual companions, and Delina.

Across from us, three other tables had filled. Lorenza sat at the center of one, a few women leaned toward her, laughing at something she said. She had already gathered a circle of Royals around her. She was easily likable, the kind of person who knew how to make others feel seen and welcomed.

At the far end, Irin settled in with another group of women. It was the first time I'd seen her since the Abyss.

My focus came back to our own table. "You eat like you fought for seven relics instead of two." I smirked at Callen, taking a bite of my roast.

He shrugged, a grin tugging at his mouth. "Looks like all it took was losing a trial along with me to bring back your charm."

I rolled my eyes, but he wasn't wrong. I couldn't even remember the last time I'd joined them for lunch. And before the Abyss, I usually ate alone.

"They should've given me a bonus round," he continued, biting into a fig with an exaggerated moan. "If only to witness the efficiency of my sprint *and* my commitment to team safety."

"You tripped over your own foot." Lyria snorted, tearing off a bite of her roll.

"I landed on the relic," he said. "You're welcome, Team Fourth Place."

Elion leaned forward, eyes fluttering toward Callen before darting toward me. "You got hit hard, didn't you? I mean..." He gestured vaguely at me. "You're...sort of showing.

I frowned, glancing down and immediately wished I hadn't. My tunic, still damp from the rain, had torn across one shoulder. The fabric clung in places it most certainly shouldn't. The corset covered most. Just...not entirely. I glanced around. The other women were in similar states. But I was the one teetering closest to indecency.

I flushed. Before I could think of a response, Callen leaned back with a wicked grin.

"Oh, she's showing alright," he drawled. "In fact, she looks entirely edible."

Delina gasped. "Callen!"

"What? That was a compliment."

I kicked him under the table. He yelped.

Callen teased anything that breathed and responded. And usually, I'd match him jab for jab. But now, I was too busy wishing my corset doubled as armor.

"Ignore them," Lyria muttered, handing me a fresh napkin from the stack. "He hits his head every time he lands on something."

"You're just jealous," Callen shot back. "No one's ever described you as edible."

She shook her head in exasperation and stole a fig from his plate in retaliation. I tore a piece of bread, dipping it in broth, when a hush fell over our table. I felt the brush of a heavy cloak being draped over my shoulders, still radiating the heat of whoever had worn it recently.

And I knew who had worn it.

Then Damien's deep voice, just behind my ear. "Join me at Hold when you are finished here." His fingers adjusted the fabric of his cloak, sending an unexpected warmth through me despite the chill.

I turned to look up into his blue eyes. A barely there nod was all I managed, my bread forgotten in suddenly clumsy fingers. I could feel an entirely unnecessary blush warming my cold cheeks, and I thanked the stars when he strode off before he could witness it.

"I didn't know Sovereigns gave out cloaks as trophies to losers," Elion said in an amused tone.

"Nor do I recall him offering *me* his cloak," Callen added, shaking water from his arms. "Clearly, my charms have faded."

I forced a laugh, but my appetite had vanished. I was hurrying to finish what was left in my bowl. Around me, the others began to disperse, and Callen pressed a loud kiss to my still damp cheek before darting off with the others.

Lyria leaned in, her voice low. "You know, don't be fooled by his kind gestures."

"Eh, what?" I asked, only half-focused, busy stuffing the food on my plate into my mouth.

Lyria toyed with her fork, her gaze distant. "I...sort of...fell for him." She laughed, hiding her embarrassment. "It's mortifying now, looking back. He rejected me, of course. Distantly. Like one would a child offering them a wildflower."

Oh. I stared down at my plate. "Really?" She'd been in love with Damien! That explained her furious outburst to me after the Abyss.

She raised an eyebrow at my awkward reply but continued. "Happens a lot to him, apparently. He sometimes oversees the training of Royals, and well...it's kind of hard *not* to fall for him. He is brave and chivalrous." She shrugged, though her cheeks flushed slightly. "But he said he was incapable of feelings."

I didn't know what to say. Every word out of her mouth clashed violently with the Damien I knew. So I said nothing, swallowing the last of my bread too fast, the crust catching hard in my throat. But my thoughts had already drifted to him. To whether he was still waiting or if I was already late, and he'd decided his time was better spent elsewhere.

Lyria, meanwhile, kept going. "Which is why I pity Lorenza. And why I'm warning you." She hesitated, then added, softer, "You're even more naive than I was, Mira." There was no venom in it, just concern. So I reached over and gave her hand a quiet squeeze. It was all I could offer.

Then I stood and left. Her confession should have stung or stirred something. But Damien had made me feel—*know*—where I stood with him. What I needed now was to see if I could bring that part of him back.

But what if that part of him was already gone?

CHAPTER 7
DAMIEN

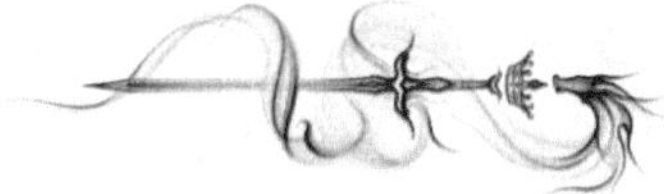

The lock on the Frost-tail's enclosure clicked shut with a sound like frozen stone. I let my hand linger for a moment on the chilled grill, feeling the hum of ancient power through the metal.

On the other side, the creature blew a soft, misty breath. His coat was the color of a winter moon, and the vast, feathered wings folded at his sides were traced with veins of gold that pulsed with a gentle inner light. Those luminescent markings swirled across his chest and legs, never still, like living runes writing and rewriting themselves. The ethereal flames that wreathed his elegant, antler-like horns crowning its head cast a shifting glow over its flowing mane.

Two. We had only ever managed to find two of these elemental spirits in all these long decades. Aethon, white and gold, and his counterpart, Hyx, whose coat was the color of a starless Celestia, marked with teal. Shy, elusive, and more valuable than a Sovereign's ransom. They were the reason we could cross the Realm in such a short time, shifting from a form large enough to carry a group in a cart to one small enough to be mistaken for a stallion.

I passed beneath their orbit without pause.

The Hold stretched before me in solemn vastness. The ceiling soared above, its arching glass panels transparent to the Celestia, though they could be darkened at will. Beneath my boots, the marble floor glimmered faintly, veined with pulses of soft light drawn from the ley-lines far beneath.

They were housed in deep, isolated seclusion, each a world unto itself. The space was immense, designed to keep them from feeling trapped and at peace. Once they Tethered, they preferred our proximity.

At the entrance of each stood a command aperture, a single opening through which their handlers, or those they obeyed, might summon the ones we required. A call of intent, and the creature within would stir, drawn forth by Tether.

The sound of hurried footsteps filled the Hold, and Mirabelle skidded to a halt beside me in a blink, winded. "I thought you'd left already," she said, voice half-swallowed by the vastness of the Hold.

"I said I would be here," I murmured. "Why assume otherwise?"

She didn't reply. Beside me, there was the faint rustle of fabric. I caught the motion from the corner of my eye, how the dark wool swallowed her frame, how her fingers brushed the edge.

Her hair fell out of her braid, still damp, clinging to her cheeks. Even her lashes were wet. I turned away before the image could stay.

"Who feeds them?" she asked, her voice still breathless from the run.

"Thralls," I said. "Trained for it. Each creature's needs are catalogued. Some prefer silence. Others demand scent markers before they will approach a meal."

She frowned, eyes narrowing as she peered toward a vast, dimly lit glass chamber to our left, the one where most of the Tameables' edibles were kept. The scent drifted faintly from within, warm and pungent, a tangy-spiced mix of root-fungi, dewthorns, and the pale, translucent algae that bloomed only in the shadowed pools of Etheris.

"We have stocked enough to last a full moonturn," I said. "As you know, Etheris has been sealed shut. There will be no resupply until after the Dissonance ends. The High-Fangs demand more."

She nodded slowly, still scanning the chambers. Her hand brushed the edge of the wall as though trying to feel something that wasn't there.

Her brow furrowed. "Flesh?"

"Life," I corrected quietly. "Dreadclaw doesn't consume carrion. Only what still breathes when it is brought before him. Same with NyxRathis."

They were the High-Fangs. The most dominant of the Tameables we possessed.

"I heard they're not exactly...friends," she murmured, gaze sweeping the arch where the Hold curved into shadows.

"No," I said, watching the edges of her expression. "They don't go hand in hand. Never have."

She tilted her head. "So why prefer Dreadclaw and not NyxRathis?"

"Because he is the strongest," I answered. "And the most predictable. With the right handler, he is easier to manage, at least by comparison." A pause. "Maybe you will be the one to make everything work," I added. "But you will need to get acquainted. Earn their trust and complete obedience."

I turned slightly to gesture toward the warded passage and stopped. She had discarded the cloak.

I blinked.

"Why are you—?" My voice stalled.

The dim light played tricks here, but not enough to soften the reality before me. Her rain-soaked tunic clung to her skin like a second one, and the tear along the shoulder had worsened. The fabric beneath had gone sheer with damp. She was holding the cloak, folded awkwardly, as if unsure what to do with it. Her corset had loosened beneath. She adjusted it again, fingers fumbling and achieving nothing.

A flush darkened her cheeks, visible even in the Hold's eerie light. My jaw tightened. I had only seen her drenched and shivering earlier. Had I seen how closely the cloth clung, I would never have asked her to come here straight from lunch.

I yanked at the clasps at my shoulder, unfastened my formal outer tunic, and gave it to her. "Put this on."

She mumbled thanks, then, without hesitation, began unlacing her own ruined garment, undressing where she stood. I turned my back with a snap.

A growl rumbled in my throat. "Do you always undress so freely in front of others?"

A beat of silence. Then the rustle of fabric as she pulled the tunic over her head. "I didn't think you'd look."

Unbelievable.

She muttered something under her breath, something resembling *not as if you haven't seen*, but too low to catch.

I turned, eyes narrowing. "What did you say?"

Her fingers tightened slightly around the hem of my tunic—black, a stark contrast against her pale skin and the damp strands of hair clinging to her face.

"I said... there isn't much to see."

A lie spoken too quickly. And an absurd one because there was far too much to see. I didn't respond. Instead, I turned and strode toward Dreadclaw's enclosure, my voice getting harsh. "I would prefer to field both Dreadclaw and NyxRathis together," I said. "Perhaps you will devise a solution where we have failed."

I paused at the threshold, hand resting lightly on the steel frame.

"Now?" Her low voice came from behind.

I turned. "For now, we see how Dreadclaw reacts to you." She opened her mouth, but her voice caught. Her hand had gone to her leg. Her step faltered.

I narrowed my eyes. "Why are you limping?"

She straightened, as if by force. "I... My knee got injured during the trial."

I stepped forward before she could finish, crouched low, and caught the edge of her trouser leg to roll the fabric up her shin. Blood. Stirred fresh again from her run to the Hold. *Of course.*

She always had scrapes and bruises because she hadn't been raised for this, hadn't grown up learning how to dodge an injury before it struck. She moved like someone who'd been taught to finish chores, not to fight.

I leaned in, pressing lightly near the bone to check for fractures. She inhaled sharply and tried to pull her leg away. My grip tightened.

"Stay still."

The fabric slipped higher as I lifted it, revealing her knee, swollen, discolored at the edges with that telltale bruise-purple. I swore beneath my breath. "And you came here like this?"

"I didn't know—"

"No," I snapped, sharper than I meant. "Clearly, you didn't."

She looked away. "I thought it would be fine. I didn't want to miss this."

Before she could say another word, I stood and scooped her into my arms. She gasped, startled.

"I can walk—" she began, then faltered. "Or maybe I can't...so you have to carry me." She grew still, her wide eyes holding mine.

Why in the Abyss was she blushing now?

"Quiet," I said, looking away from her flushed face. "Now keep this in your dutiful little head, Mirabelle. When someone demands something of you, you don't rush in like a stray set on fire. You pause. You assess. Like asking yourself whether answering that call on a half-ruined leg is worth what it might cost." I looked down at her, jaw set. Her mouth was shut. Wisely.

I carried her in silence down the corridor toward the infirmary, her breath warm against my neck, curling like a curse I hadn't earned.

I HAD SEEN to the final sealings before dusk fell, approvals stamped, logs checked and quill set aside. The envoy to Zarkon had been received with less resistance than I anticipated, their missive marked by a single stroke of assent. A success, as such things went.

The Tamer had been sent back to the Royal Chambers, ordered to her chambers to rest. She hadn't argued. Or if she had, it was swallowed by my footsteps as I turned away to visit my father before returning here.

The once-great Sovereign now took more interest in resting than in matters of rule. He spoke little, ate less, and repeated what few phrases remained to him with the tenacity of age. His only topic of enthusiasm was my betrothal, and even that had frayed into a dull recitation of Nyxarian bloodlines and Heir-producing propriety.

He hadn't mentioned the Dissonance once.

Now I leaned back in the chair of his study, fingers locked behind my neck, gaze fixed upon the vaulted ceiling. The candle-light danced across it like memory. The door opened without announcement. Only one person in Atlassian would dare.

"My Liege," Rowane drawled, stepping in as if he owned the floor he walked upon. "I do hope I'm not interrupting your nightly brooding."

"You are," I said without moving.

He dropped himself into the low-backed chair across from me, exhaling a sigh. "You see, it is a peculiar thing. You've filled your days with councils and scrolls and envoy flames, but you haven't let anyone past the perimeter of this chamber since the Abyss."

"I let you in."

"Yes," he said with a grin. "That's the part I find alarming."

We spoke of all the fragments we'd lost in Abyss, and how the coming battles would cost us everything that remained. His words were light, but his eyes held the sharpness of a man who understood too well. He remained the only one I ever trusted with my scars, after I learned how easily loyalty could be turned into a weapon in this wretched Realm.

"Your father asked about Nyxaria and the situation with Zarkon, by the way. Two days ago. Seemed to know the broad strokes of the Nathan situation before I'd briefed the council." He was quiet for a moment in a way that was not actually quiet—he was thinking, processing, filing. "How much does he know?"

"More than he should, for a man who no longer attends council or talks about politics with me." I kept my voice even. "I think he's been asking Mavren for summaries."

"Hmm." The sound had an edge to it. "And the council didn't think to mention that to you."

"Mavren did." I let that sit. "Eventually."

Rowane crossed an ankle over his knee. "You think he's meddling?"

"I think he is bored and restless and has spent thirty years believing he knows better than whoever is in charge." A beat. "Including me."

"Especially you," Rowane said, with the candor that was either his greatest quality or his most irritating one. "And the Tamer? He asked about her too."

I lifted a single brow. For him to inquire about the Tamer made no sense. "When?"

"Yesterday. He asked me directly whether the inquiry into her bloodline was proceeding."

He paused, drawing out the moment. "With her skills, I see why she's suddenly the jewel of the Clan. But I really don't understand why all you men are so...stirred. Is it her sensuality?"

I stood without thinking. Rowane leaned back instantly, laughing. "Stars, easy, Damien. I meant no disrespect."

"Well, stop speculating." My voice was harsh. "Her sensuality is none of your concern."

"Easy," he said, his brows lifting in surprise. "You'd best leash whatever that is. We both know you could take her if you wished."

"I do not wish," I said, returning to my seat. "And even if that were the case, I have no intention of pursuing it."

"Why?" His voice dripped with amusement. "Because you are not intrigued?"

"Because she deserves better," I said. "She is a rare talent, and the entire Clan is in awe of her Aether. To darken that with my own shadow would be a greater crime than you understand. And I have no time for distractions, even if it were not."

Rowane let the silence hold for exactly long enough to make his point without actually making it, which was the particular skill that made him both invaluable and insufferable. Then he leaned toward the desk. The candlelight caught the corner of the parchment there.

Without thinking, I reached out and flipped the page over.

Too late.

His eyes sharpened. "Is that what I think it is?"

"It is not," I replied flatly.

"Is that a Tameable alignment chart?"

"Yes."

"It doesn't look like one." He tilted his head, studying me with that slow consideration that always preceded something I wouldn't enjoy. "It looks like someone's background report. The kind with personal history rather than combat metrics."

"And?"

A slow smile. "The kind with details that have no bearing on Dissonance positioning. The kind a man reads because he wants to understand someone rather than—"

I shook my head at him. "Don't."

"—deploy them." He sat back with an expression of perfect innocence. "I'm just describing what I see."

"You are describing a strategic dossier on our most critical Dissonance asset."

"With her jaw in the margins."

There was nothing in the margins. He was fishing, and he was good at it, which was exactly why I'd never taught him to stop. I gave him a very unimpressed look, and he held up his hands, palms open, but the glint in his eyes was pure provocation.

"I didn't ask for this," I said. "It planted itself in my drawer. Her history. Mundane details that have no bearing on her role here."

"Is that so?" Rowane smile was a slash of white.

"And her bloodline matters," I said. "If we don't understand where it comes from, we can't predict what she's capable of. Or who will come for it."

"Of course it is." He uncrossed his legs and leaned forward, dropping the performance. "Look. I've been on it. The outskirts archives and the records the Abyss didn't eat. You'll have answers before the Dissonance if my reporters move well." A pause. "But I'd be careful, Damien."

"Of?"

"Of the fact that our council is already asking about her." He held my gaze. "You're not the only one who's noticed what she is."

That landed where he intended it to. "I am aware."

"Good." He leaned back again, the seriousness retreating beneath his usual ease. "Strange, you've kept no intimates. Even after the announcement of betrothal, most Sovereigns take Thralls—"

"I dismissed them," I cut in.

"Why?"

"I don't know."

Rowane tilted his head, a faint smirk playing on his lips despite the furrowed brows. "A cold bed leads to a cold mind."

"I didn't invite you here to discuss my bed."

"You didn't invite me at all," he pointed out.

I changed the subject. "We have barely four weeks left."

He leaned back against the wall, arms crossed. "Right. Two fortnights, and you are juggling Clan negotiations, Dissonance preparations, and twelve cities under your banner."

I gave him a look. "You're forgetting the forty-three villages. And the market reforms."

He clicked his tongue. "Ah yes, the glory of commoners' pool expansions and trade restructuring. Truly, your legacy will be carved in grain routes and construction stone."

"You would be surprised how close you can come to an uprising just by rerouting a trade path." I shook my head. "I don't even remember why I prioritized any of this so close to the Dissonance."

Rowane glanced at me. "You are not even overseeing the training yards anymore."

I exhaled through my nose. "Not since the coronation. Now, I am lucky if I get ten uninterrupted moments to draft a weapons requisition before someone's in my ear about Bonding ceremonies or border disputes."

"Hmm." He hummed, noncommittal. Then, after a pause, "Anyway, best get the woman out of your head."

I shoved Mirabelle's parchment into the drawer with more force than necessary.

"If you are quite finished," I said, fastening my cloak. For a fleeting, unwelcome second, I felt the sensation of adjusting it around her. Rowane's damned insinuations were planting seeds where there was only chivalry. I strode out without looking back. There were matters to attend. Those didn't ask questions I didn't want to answer.

And if my steps were quicker than necessary, if my mind lingered where it shouldn't, well. No one needed to know.

CHAPTER 8

MIRABELLE

It was a simple climb. Or so I thought.

I had managed to haul myself halfway onto the top, no small feat, given that the beast seemed determined to remain as uncooperative as possible. One leg swung over, and for a fleeting, triumphant moment, I thought I had conquered the creature.

Then my view tilted. I slid gracelessly toward the opposite side, arms flailing. A curse ripped through the air before Callen's hands clamped around my ankles and yanked me back with all the delicacy of a butcher wrenching meat from bone.

"Stars, woman," he growled, steadying the reins with one hand, "are you trying to break your neck before we've even left the courtyard?"

Lyria snorted from atop her mount, barely concealing her grin. A few paces behind, Cassian, Delina, and Elion were far less subtle, chuckling, trading comments like my flailing was their day's entertainment. Lorenza stood a short distance away, arms folded. At least she had the decency to pretend she wasn't watching.

In my defense, this was the tallest horse here.

"I was managing," I muttered, winded.

He gave a huff of a laugh. "Yes, like a water fish manages dry land."

The evening was ours to have a little fun. Originally, I had planned to train with Damien, but a summons from the council had pulled him away. Instead of getting disappointed and sleeping the time away in my chambers, I'd said yes when Callen suggested a ride through the Royal streets.

Lorenza had come to relay the change in Damien's plans, and now lingered, watching us prepare to leave. Her expression was difficult to place. Not envy exactly. She stood just far enough away to remain separate, to remind herself she wasn't part of this.

She would miss things like this. The simple, ordinary things the rest of us still got to do.

"You should join us," I offered out of kindness.

Her laughter was soft, airy, like wind chimes stirred by a passing breeze. "Sweet of you. But no. The moment I step into those streets, we'll be swarmed. We'd spend the entire evening fending off Majors instead of enjoying it."

She adjusted the edge of her cloak, already half-turned away. "Next time," she'd said with a smile that didn't reach her eyes.

I, on the other hand, was still wrestling with my saddle like it owed me a debt. My cloak kept tangling in my skirts, the reins slithered through my fingers like stubborn serpents, and the beast beneath me shifted its weight every time I tried to settle.

Callen finally sighed, muttering something about hopeless cases before hopping onto the saddle and hauling me up with far too much ease.

"You should've done that the first time!" I muttered under my breath. "You're dumb."

He only laughed and gave the horse a pat like he had done all the work.

And with that, we turned our mounts toward the palace gates, laughter trailing behind us as the streets waited just beyond. The horse lurched beneath us, and my grip on the reins turned desperate. Every jolt threatened to send me careening into the dirt. At one particularly spirited burst of speed, I did the only sensible thing. I flattened myself against the beast's back, arms wrapped around its neck like a drowning woman clinging to driftwood.

Callen's hand shot out, hauling me upright by the scruff of my tunic. "Stop trying to strangle the damn horse, Mira."

"I'm not strangling it!"

"You're lying on it like a corpse."

If this were as simple as Tethering, I'd have shown them who I was. But horses are not, and I was neither Royal, nor trained. So I went with my only remaining option, which was to cling on and try not to fall.

THE ROYAL STREETS were nothing like those I had known, a shimmering dream woven into the fabric of a city I had only ever known in shadow. The commoner's Dorms, with their rough cobbles and frayed edges, seemed a world away now. Here, the very air was laced with the scent of night blooming jasmine, frangipani, and the honeyed sweetness of ripening fruits.

Ancient trees arched above us, their boughs heavy with blossoms that caught the fading light like scattered shards of stained glass. Every building stood as a testament to legacy, their facades carved with the weight of centuries, their windows glinting like watchful eyes.

The wealth here was effortless, woven into the gilded filigree of lampposts, the seamless marble of the pathways, the quiet poise of a place that had never known scarcity.

I tried not to gape around me. But in truth, I was a bit light-headed with the simple thrill of it. I'd bought things I'd never allowed myself to even consider before, even though the guilt of spending nickels so freely gnawed at me, as if each coin carried the echo of every time I'd gone without.

A flared gown of midnight silk, its hem embroidered with golden constellations. Dried fruits from Etheris. A pouch of spiced pollen-candies. And a corset—oh, but it was so beautiful, its boning etched with delicate astral patterns. And a few things Amara had been obsessed with.

And I had bargained. Of course I had. Because in a commoner's market, buying without bargaining was practically an insult. It wasn't noble or elegant, so at first, those with me looked embarrassed, casting awkward glances as I haggled with a spice vendor over half a pouch of pollen-candies. But they caught on soon enough, likely because I rarely walked away without the better end of the deal.

The shopkeepers had laughed. Some raised brows. One even offered me a commission. The longer it went on, the more the others lingered behind me, watching with thinly veiled amusement. I glanced back at Callen over my shoulder, a small grin tugging at my mouth.

"Don't look at me," he said. "I want no part of whatever's happening."

"You're afraid I'll negotiate you into something."

"I'm afraid you'll negotiate me out of something and I won't even notice until I'm home." He watched me turn toward another stall. "Remind me *never* to negotiate with you. I'd give you my boots and thank you for the discount."

"Only if they're not scuffed." I said. "I have standards."

Lyria snorted, arms crossed as she leaned against a fruit cart. "At this rate, she's going to end the evening with three bags of goods and all of us sold off as part of the bargain." Delina chuckled from where she stood near Callen. It was strange how comfortable I felt now with them.

At last, we reached the stables. The horses were led inside, their coats brushed by attentive grooms who moved with the efficiency of those who served the elite. Our purchases were stored away, secured for retrieval.

"Now," Elion announced, stretching his arms, "we have actual fun."

Cassian's grin turned wolfish. "Let's see if you survive the night."

I swallowed, suddenly uncertain. "What does that mean?"

Delina smirked. "You'll see." And with that, they strode forward, leaving me to follow, into whatever waited.

THEY LED me around a corner and I paused. The plaza ahead was enormous, its center ringed by glowing stones and lined with small tents. Above them spun a slow arc of constellations, an illusion cast by mirrors and lightweaving.

"The Festival Arcade," Elion explained, stepping beside me. "They open it for tournaments, Bonding days, harvest feasts. Or when someone rich and bored throws a whim around."

"What are we doing here?" I asked.

Callen appeared beside me, holding a few skewers of something warm and steaming. He handed one over without asking. The first bite was a surprise: sweet, crisp, caramelized meat over something tart and smoky.

He grinned when my eyes widened. "Wild duckheart over windfruit. Don't ask more."

"Wasn't planning to," I said around a second, larger bite.

The plaza hummed with a kind of magic that had nothing to do with lightweaving. Elion nudged me forward. "They call it The Crucis."

I followed his gaze to the center of the plaza, where a series of raised platforms floated just above the ground, suspended by nothing but shimmering threads of energy. Between them swung pendulum blades, their edges gleaming under the illusionary stars.

"An obstacle course?" I asked, already knowing the answer.

"With stakes," Delina corrected, her eyes alight. A man in a silver-threaded tunic approached, his smile all teeth. "Three rounds. Fastest time wins. Fall, and you forfeit."

"Forfeit what?" I asked.

Cassian leaned in. "Whatever you wagered to enter."

"And what did we wager?"

Callen tossed a small, glittering stone into the man's palm—a soulmarker. The kind nobles used to seal blood-debts.

My stomach dropped. "You didn't."

"Relax," Delina said, though her grin was anything but reassuring. "It's just a game. And the marker's only makeshift. Your soul will—at least we hope—survive the night."

I handed Callen the rest of my skewer, rolled my sleeves, and walked toward the entry platform. Behind me, I heard Cassian say—not quietly, "Stars, she's actually doing it."

The platform under my boots vibrated, unstable. I took a long breath, looking around me. The first pendulum's arc was slower than it looked from below. That was good. It swung wide and slow, until it wasn't. I leapt, the blade whispering past my ankles, close enough to stir the hem of my skirt. The second platform tilted as I landed, forcing me to pivot mid-step.

"Not bad, rabbit!" Elion whooped from somewhere below.

The second pendulum was faster, and it swung toward me in a blur of silver. I'd clocked it wrong from the first platform. It moved in a shorter arc but doubled back quicker, the rhythm irregular enough that you couldn't settle into it. I let it pass once, gauged the return, then dropped low as it came back. I barely ducked. Wind sliced across my cheek as I dropped to all fours, the impact jolting through my knees. The blade passed a breath above my spine.

Gasps rippled from the crowd. I scrambled to the edge of the second platform, where a thin bridge of glowing runes awaited. It shifted as I stepped onto it, no wider than my foot and trembling as though it sensed my pulse.

This is madness, I whispered.

Ahead, the next floating platform dipped forward sharply, forcing a running leap. I hesitated. The rune-bridge beneath me began to tilt. Either I moved, or I fell. The next pendulum blade arced down toward the narrowing path.

Someone screamed below. And I ran. The edge of the platform loomed too soon. I pushed off—

And missed. For half a heartbeat, there was only air. Shadows appeared from me instinctively, not meant to save, only to soften the fall. I slammed into the edge of the next platform, ribs first, and clawed up with fingers scraped raw against stone. I nearly lost my grip.

"Mirabelle!" That was Lyria's voice now. Concern, but distant. *Too distant.*

I hauled myself onto the platform, chest heaving, limbs trembling. The final stretch spun ahead, three rotating disks, too slick for steady footing, and a final pendulum larger than the rest. I was not trained for any of these. Not in skirts. Not in these boots. Not with a bloody soulmarker on the line that didn't even belong to me.

And yet they were still cheering. I glanced back once. Elion had a drink in hand, laughing. Delina was perched on a ledge, waving his arm like a herald. Callen was nowhere to be seen.

The final pendulum swung low and fast, and I realized too late I was angled all wrong. I tried to shift, to twist, but the edge kissed my thigh. I limped forward the last few steps, teeth clenched so tight I thought my jaw might crack. My foot hit the final stone and cheers erupted. But it was all distant now. I felt only my pulse and the sting of blood pooling near my ribs and thighs, under my clothes.

The silver-tunicked man smiled as he approached with the soulmarker still spinning in his hand. "Well earned," he said. "Very few finish without breaking bones."

I nodded. Didn't trust what my voice would do if I used it. Callen reached me first, offering a hand I didn't take.

Delina looked vaguely sheepish. "Maybe not the best pastime, huh?"

Cassian appeared with sugared fruit in hand. "I was going to offer a dramatic slow clap, but figured your ribs wouldn't survive the echo."

"I could've died," I said flatly.

Elion blinked. "But you didn't."

"I'm not doing that again."

"Wouldn't expect you to." He grinned. "It's a one-time thrill."

My vision swam. I exhaled once, steadying myself. "We're going back home."

Callen frowned. "Already?"

"I said. We are going back." There must've been something in my tone, because no one argued.

We returned to the stables in silence. I climbed atop my mount with a little help this time, ignoring the persistent twinge in my thighs and ribs. The blood that had soaked through wasn't visible from the outside. I didn't want them to know I was not strong like them.

We rode through the dimming streets, the city softened by streetlamps, and I kept my thoughts fixed on one thing—how to slip into the infirmary unnoticed before tomorrow's training.

CHAPTER 9
MIRABELLE

None of us spoke.

The corridor outside the throne hall pulsed with silence. A heavy, bone-deep kind. We stood in a staggered line beneath the veined marble arches—Lyria, Callen, Cassian, Elion, Delina, every one of them visibly still, but taut beneath the surface. Even Cassian, whose mouth rarely knew peace, stared fixedly at the banners overhead, jaw clenched.

My fingers twisted in the fabric of my skirt, feeling again the sting in my thigh where the blade from The Crucis had kissed me. The healer had already seen to it, in a small antechamber off the corridor, murmuring as she salved the wound. It was shallow, she'd said. Barely worth fussing over.

And yet, the fuss had already begun. The moment we had returned from the Royal Streets, the courtyard had been a storm of motion. Horses snarling in their harnesses and Legion soldiers mounting. Damien in his formal attire astride that massive beast —Frost-tail—its hooves striking sparks against the stone. He had been halfway to the gates when he saw us.

The next, I was being hauled in a blur of movement I barely registered straight to him. His hands were already on me, scanning for injuries.

"Are you hurt?" he snapped, eyes blazing.

I shook my head, stunned. "No, I—"

Callen didn't even have time to react before Damien had him by the collar, dragging him down from the saddle with a force that sent his boots scraping against the cobblestones.

"What," Damien seethed, "in the name of every cursed House in the Realms, were you thinking?"

Callen opened his mouth, but no sound came.

"Dragging her into the streets like some common reveler? You know what prowls in streets. You know we have two rival Clans breathing down our necks, spies in every shadow, and you—" A shake, hard enough to rattle teeth. "You took the only Tamer this Realm has ever known straight into their grasp."

Callen winced, but he didn't defend himself. None of them did.

Lorenza stepped forward, her stance tempered with caution. "Damien—"

"Stay out of it." His words cracked like a whip.

"I insisted," I said, my voice barely more than a whisper. "It wasn't them. I wanted to go." I tried to reason, because I didn't want to lose the friends I'd finally made here. But Damien didn't even glance at me.

"All of you will wait outside the throne hall," he said, low and hard, "until I finish what you pulled me away from. And this"—his gaze swept over us all—"will not go unpunished."

He released Callen with a shove, motioned sharply to a nearby healer, and without looking back, he strode through the heavy doors and disappeared into the darkened hall beyond.

Now, we waited. Lyria stood with her arms crossed, her mouth pressed into a thin, bloodless line. Elion and Cassian leaned against opposite pillars, facing away from one another. Callen's knuckles were white where they gripped his arms.

We hadn't thought it would be this serious. Now, thinking about it, it was sort of foolish of us to think about it that way.

After the never-ending wait, a procession of Elders and Sages emerged first. Some spared us only the coldest glances. Others, pitying ones, which somehow felt worse. The guards stepped aside to let us in.

The throne hall was the kind of room designed to make you feel small, and it was good at its job. The ceiling went up farther than necessary. The pillars were black marble and too wide to put your arms around. Witchlights drifted between the stone columns, moving just enough that the shadows never fully settled.

And there, upon the dais, sat Damien—our Sovereign—his gaze fixed on my every movement. He was still in his formal attire; the dark black cloak pooled around his shoulders. The throne did not make him. He inhabited it, as though he'd been carved into it by the architects.

Lorenza sat off to the side of the court, in a high-backed chair of ashwood. Her gown shimmered with dark filigree, and she'd crossed one over the other. She tilted her head when she saw us. Her expression said nothing.

"You were warned," Damien stated.

I hadn't been, specifically. But I held my tongue.

"Atlassian stands on the cusp of a war," he continued, rising slowly. "And yet its warriors saw fit to parade through the capital unguarded, wagering soulmarkers, bleeding in public trials." He paused, looking at each of us in turn, his expression carved in restraint, his eyes burning with the effort of it. "I left negotiations with Elders from two allied Clans, each demanding terms that will determine who lives past the Dissonance. I left the command seat of our Realm's defense planning to be informed that the only Tamer capable of working with our High-Fangs was halfway through an illegal Crucis with a crowd cheering for her to leap off a moving platform."

My throat dried. He hadn't raised his voice. But his fury was a blade sheathed in ice. Callen opened his mouth and then snapped it shut again when Damien's gaze turned on him.

"This is not a lesson in etiquette," Damien said, each word a blade unsheathed. "It is your one and only warning." His gaze swept over them. "You will be stripped of ranks."

All flinched, but gasps were bitten back. Rank was not just a privilege; it was years of blood and sweat for Royals. But he wasn't done. "Blood debts will be taken from each of you before dawn," Damien continued, his tone chillingly matter-of-fact. "Paid directly to the Council for your recklessness."

Elion actually swayed on his feet. A blood debt was no mere fine; it was a physical extraction, and the oath sworn to seal the debt could bind their lives forever.

"I am not withdrawing you from Dissonance for now. If you repeat this kind of idiocy again, I will have you dragged to the prisons. Without trials."

None of us dared to respond. Then his gaze found mine. "You will remain. The rest are dismissed."

Callen took half a step forward, his voice rough. "She had nothing to do with—"

"Leave."

Callen moved to reach for my hand in a last gesture of solidarity. Damien's hand shot out, seizing Callen's wrist before his fingers could brush mine.

"I said leave," Damien ground out. "Not 'touch her on your way out.'"

Callen's face tightened. With a final glance at me, he turned on his heel and strode from the hall. The others followed in silence. Only Lorenza and I remained.

Damien didn't look at her. "Leave us."

She hesitated, then slowly slipped out.

"Did you think yourself untouchable?" he asked.

"No," I managed. My voice felt brittle. "I didn't think—"

"Exactly. You didn't think at all."

I lowered my eyes to the floor. He stepped closer. "You need time to reflect on the gift you have been given. On the responsibility that comes with it." A pause. "You will not be part of the Dissonance this time."

My head snapped up. "What?!"

"You heard me."

"You can't do that." The words came out sharper and edged with desperation.

"I can and I have." His voice left no room for appeal. "You lost that privilege the moment you chose a walk-away from your duty."

"It wasn't a bloody *walk-away*!" I fired back, knowing I was walking toward the edge of his patience. And I kept walking. "It was a breath of air when I thought I was free. And your schedule was tight."

A muscle in his jaw feathered. "My schedule is not your concern. Your safety is. And you risked it—and everything we're building—on a whim."

"A whim?" My tone was harsh. "You think I'd risk your wrath on a *whim*?" I held his gaze, daring him to see my point. "I didn't grasp the true stakes. I do now. That's a lesson I won't need twice. But maybe you'd prefer I never learn—that I stay the perfect, ignorant weapon." I knew I was provoking him. But the loss burned too sharply to swallow, and I refused to pretend it did not.

His eyes darkened. "Careful, Mirabelle."

"Or what?" The challenge hung in the silent air between us. "You'll sideline me *harder*? You've already taken the one thing that matters to me!"

"I said, you need time," he said, "to reflect on what you carry, and what it means to carry it." The finality in his voice was absolute. "I am a man very short on time. And you left me waiting in the Hold for an hour while you roamed the streets and risked yourself recklessly. It is better you take a break."

"You...waited for me? I only went because Lorenza informed me you changed your plans."

The doors parted and a delicate voice rang from the doorway. "You are mistaken, dear," Lorenza said smoothly. "The pressure must have confused you."

Wait. She had not left?

I blinked. "No, I'm certain—"

"I said he might have other things arise. That's all. I never told you he canceled." She offered a faint smile, gliding forward. That wasn't true. Or...had I assumed too much? No. I would never have let time with Damien slip away over a misunderstanding. Not willingly.

Her hand brushed Damien's arm, but he shifted away from the touch. "I will manage the rest of the preparations," he said, his voice clipped. "This break is for the best. Build your strength and resolve."

"I'm not broken," I murmured, but it barely carried. As if even I didn't believe it.

"How do you feel?" His tone had gentled, not enough to be warm, but enough to make me meet his gaze.

"Just...sore," I answered. "Minor scrapes, nothing worth the fuss."

He nodded once. "I will send a healer again in the morning." A pause. A flicker in his gaze, like he wanted to say more. Then he was gone. Lorenza followed without a word.

I stood alone beneath the vast, empty arch of the throne hall, the silence folding in around me. And it was a while before the guards let me out.

I still had the key.

That much, at least, had not been revoked. So I stepped into the Hold. Or rather, slipped through the side passage like someone sneaking back into a home they weren't certain still belonged to them.

The scent of moss-fed water and scorched salt lingered in the air. I moved with caution, every footfall soft, every breath shallow. I half-expected a guard to seize me by the collar and drag me back into my chamber. And perhaps I would have deserved it. I had disobeyed. Again. But what else was left to obey, when the only piece of myself that ever felt right had been stripped away without warning?

I hadn't slept all night. Every time I closed my eyes, I felt the weight of the key beneath my pillow.

At some point, when the night had stretched so thin it felt ready to snap, Callen had knocked at my chamber door. His apology had been awkwardly earnest, his eyes carrying more guilt than his words could shoulder. I had told him the same, that I was sorry too, though I could not explain what for. Sorry for being there? For accepting their invitation, or for letting it all unfold the unexpected way it had?

Now, I passed Zepharion's chamber. Empty.

The feeding tub had been scraped clean. Further down, the Whip-tail's chamber lay still and dark, its soft purr conspicuously absent. I paused. Whip-tail was a docile creature by nature. A healer. One who usually greeted my presence with soft clicks and a warm snout nuzzling against my arm.

I frowned and picked up my pace. The deeper I walked, the more certain I became that something had changed. The corridor bent, revealing the newly hewn entrance. I passed beneath it.

Beyond the threshold lay a vast range, unfamiliar to me. The space opened into a low amphitheater ringed by platforms, each shaped for training rather than containment. Lanterns hung from the iron lattice overhead, casting shadows through a haze of simmering mist. Two Legion Commanders stood near the outer ring, speaking in clipped tones. Tameables moved between them under command.

And standing beside them, her back to me, was Lorenza. The sight struck with more force than I'd expected. She was directing them and had been given a Tether, however shallow. So Damien had been swift in delivering his promise to replace me. My throat tightened.

Her fingers flicked in a sharp gesture at Whip-tail. The beast that purred at anything that moved now flinched, tucking its tail low against the ground. Something protective twisted in my chest. But I shouldn't have been here and I had no right to interfere. So I silently went back to the Hold.

To finally meet NyxRathis, if it was there.

CHAPTER 10

MIRABELLE

NyxRathis's chamber was far from Dreadclaw's, tucked into the deepest alcove of the Hold, a space that dimmed the torches with its very presence. Larger than the others, and colder too, though I couldn't say why.

Dreadclaw's unmistakable growl had sounded at my approach before, even in slumber. NyxRathis, by contrast, made no sound at all. I reached the threshold and paused. The chamber appeared empty. He might have been moved as well, perhaps to the inside range I had just left, though I had not seen him there.

I turned to leave, intending to check the main enclosure. But then—

Another puny, clueless being. The thought slithered into my mind at the same time I felt the Tether—dry, disdainful, and eerily feminine. I stilled. It was a female.

A slow smile tugged at my lips despite myself. *No wonder you don't get along with Dreadclaw.*

No answer followed. Only the sensation of being watched, intensely, as though I had stepped onto a stage without knowing the play.

I had heard that NyxRathis had been captured generations ago by one of Damien's ancestors, before the time of sealed portals. Of all the Tameables, it was one of the oldest housed in the Hold. A High-Fang with a temper.

And still, I saw nothing. Why was she hiding?

"Is this how you greet all your guests?" I asked aloud, crossing my arms and stepping into the hollowed stone chamber outside.

Nothing.

"You don't seem shy," I added. "Or maybe you just prefer glaring from dark corners. Very intimidating."

Still no sound. No growl. No glint of fang.

After a few moments, something in the ground moved. I scanned the ground, and there it was. Not a body, not quite. But the barest ripple in the lush grass. A shifting, like something displaced by invisible liquid.

I narrowed my eyes.

The stone just ahead of me had darkened slightly—a curve of shadow passing across it, though no light source moved.

She wasn't hiding. She was cloaked.

I crouched low and reached for the special key at my hip, one of the few that unlocked the reinforced enclosures. It slid clean into the keyplate, and the chamber's internal ward flickered once before fading.

I stepped forward, slowly, cautiously. My knees met the mossy floor. I kept my palms open, breath steady.

"I can't see you," I murmured. "But I know you're here."

The air shimmered in front of me. She moved again, swift and graceful, like water flowing in reverse. My fingers brushed against something cool, yet solid. Smooth as glass, but not completely liquid.

"You feel like starlight," I whispered.

Flattery? The thought came, faint and amused.

"Emm...observation," I said, still kneeling.

For a moment, she didn't retreat. Then a soft pulse of energy pushed at my hand, like curiosity.

"I came to meet you," I said. "Not to *tame* you, of course. That would be foolish."

Exactly. A pause. *Most of your kind begin with dominance.*

"I've learned not everything can be earned by force," I murmured, letting my fingers rest lightly against the invisible edge of her form. "Sometimes you need to wait. Or listen. Or bring wild duckheart skewers."

She snorted. Actually snorted—a gust of air that ruffled the loose strands at my neck.

"You don't like duckheart?"

Only when it's still screaming.

"Oh...charming."

Another ripple of movement glided around me. I turned slowly, careful not to chase the sound. She circled once, twice, studying. Testing.

"Tell me about Dreadclaw," I asked softly, glancing toward the shadows beyond.

A low, guttural growl echoed through my skull. Not angry, more like she was repulsed.

Too arrogant for his own good, she replied, the disdain practically dripping from her tone. *Always snarling. Cannot walk a straight line without flaring his tendrils like a fool.*

I laughed, quiet, but genuine. "You hate him that much?"

I loathe him.

My lips curled. "Well, I think all that snarling might just be his clumsy way of getting your attention."

The growl deepened, and something invisible shoved gently at my shoulder, enough to make me rock back on my heels.

"I'll take that as a no," I said, laughter spilling from my chest. She moved again, still cloaked, but more visible now in motion, her outline clearer against the flickering torches. There was something elegant in her gait, predatory and regal all at once.

I rose and turned to leave. Her form shimmered faintly beside me, just enough for one great eye—molten violet—to become visible in the shadows.

Return with duckheart, she said.

I grinned. "Screaming, I remember."

She vanished once more, and I stepped from her chamber with something fragile and unfamiliar blooming in my chest.

I LINGERED JUST outside the carved archway that led to the Sovereign's study, scowling at the two guards now stationed like ornamental stones beside it. Neither had budged since I first arrived.

"I need to speak with the Sovereign," I said again.

The taller one gave me a practiced smile, the kind offered to anyone clearly beneath the reach of decision. "Again, Lady, the Sovereign is not to be disturbed."

So much for subtlety.

I exhaled and glanced around the hall, feigned a defeated sigh, and turned as if to leave. Then doubled back and tripped dramatically against the guard's leg.

He cursed, trying to catch me out of instinct. I tumbled through the open doorway in a flurry of motion, arms flailing and voice pitched just right, somewhere between a gasp and a startled *oops.*

The guards gave chase, only to halt at the sound of Damien's voice.

"Let her in," he said from within. Low, but unmistakably clear.

The guards stiffened. One glanced at me in exasperation; the other muttered something like an apology under his breath and retreated. I turned and gave them both a smug little smile, brushing imaginary dust from my tunic before turning back to Damien, only to find him watching me with that infuriating, unreadable focus, his quill poised above a half-signed missive.

"Well?" he said, setting the quill down.

"I have a proposal," I said, lifting my chin.

He leaned back in the chair, fingers steepling beneath his chin. "Do tell."

I crossed the room, dragging a carved chair from the wall and planting it firmly near his side of the desk, feigning a confidence I didn't entirely feel. His brow arched slightly, as though unsure what game I was playing.

He watched this with a flicker of amusement in his eyes. "Comfortable?"

"Almost." I sat, smoothing my skirts. "Just waiting for you to come to your senses."

One of his brows rose higher.

"I will be working with the Tameables."

"That is not negotiable—"

"Just hear me out," I cut in, holding up a hand. "Please."

A breath passed. Then, slowly, he nodded. "Go on."

"Whether you like it or not, Atlassian needs me. I've heard how you value *the only Tamer this Realm has ever known*." I echoed his own words back at him. "So let's not pretend you actually want me out."

"Mirabelle—"

"Think." I leaned forward. "You want a cohesive force of Tameables on the first night of Dissonance. And you want them disciplined, loyal, and coordinated. Who else is going to manage that?"

His jaw flexed.

I pressed further. "I can work with NyxRathis and Dreadclaw. I think I can get them to cooperate."

His fingers tapped once against the arm of his chair. "And why would you think that?"

"Because." I sat straighter, getting more confident. "NyxRathis just asked me to bring her duckheart. And I think I can bribe her."

That drew a sound, almost a chuckle, from him. Then he reached out, caught the leg of my chair, and dragged it closer to his. The distance shrank to nothing. My breath tangled in my throat.

He leaned in, his voice low. "If you do something reckless again, I will lock you in your chambers. Is that clear?"

I nodded. Or thought I did. My whole body had forgotten how to move. His scent, the heat of him, the way his eyes held mine. His hand remained near mine, but not touching. A heat clung to the space between us. It was too much. And not nearly enough.

Then I swallowed. "I have one demand."

"And that is?" he said, his eyes still locked on mine.

I lifted my chin, steady. "I want Lorenza out of the Hold."

His expression shifted. "Lorenza was only getting to know them. She is not involved."

"Yet," I muttered.

He studied me for a long moment. "I thought you had accepted her offer of help."

"I did," I said, knowing full well how unreasonable I sounded. "But that was before I realized I require a certain...compatibility in my working relationships." It was a flimsy excuse, and we both knew it. This was pure pettiness, a deep-seated instinct that told me I could never truly walk hand-in-hand with Lorenza.

A pause. Then, to my surprise, he nodded. "Agreed."

Relief flooded me. "Thanks," I added, far too smug for someone who had just barged into a Sovereign's study uninvited. I stood and, emboldened by the way he looked at me, I gently patted his right arm—twice.

His gaze darkened, and he caught my wrist, tugging me back down. "Don't push your luck."

I stilled, feeling his skin against mine. His thumb brushed the inside of my pulse point, just once. A threat? A promise?

I pulled free, my heart fluttering. "Wouldn't dream of it, my Liege." And with that, I left, before he could see the flush creeping up my neck.

Mirabelle: one.

Suffering in silence: zero.

<hr>

THE REINSTATEMENT CAME WITH CONDITIONS. The first was that I attend council that afternoon, to be briefed on the Dissonance formations alongside the Elders and Legion Commanders. Damien's way of making sure I understood that getting back in meant getting all the way in—the parts that were useful to me and the parts that were not.

The parts that were not, it turned out, were considerable.

I had volunteered to attend the previous session because Damien was there and I could ogle him. Not because I had any interest in the formal way Elders threw jabs at each other or discussed something for an hour only to decide they'd discuss it further during next council.

Now that my briefing was over, I was trying not to nap on the table. The Council dragged on like a wounded horse. I kept my face calm, my hands folded, my head full of anything but political cadence—the way a foal flinched at thunder, the smell of spiced root soup, the ridiculous way an old Sage chewed his words like thick cud.

When it mercifully ended, I stood up too fast and the Sage beside me gave me a look.

"Good session," I said to no one in particular, then headed toward the western barracks to find the new Royals assigned to our Tameables. No one was allowed to face all three nights of the Dissonance. Damien would lead the second and third—one of Aether, one of weapons, while the first fell to me. To command the Tameables with the help of the Royals who had survived enough battles to be trusted.

My path took me past the old, secluded set of Royal Chambers, a place usually silent. Today, it was not.

A door down the corridor cracked. Voices—low, the kind you used when you didn't want the whole hall to know how ugly things are. Reckless curiosity was a sin, so I started to walk—

Then I heard that voice. Alaric. Damien's father. "...a simple decision, Damien. It costs you nothing." His voice was like grinding stone, devoid of any warmth.

I told myself to keep walking. But I heard Damien's name, and my feet rooted to the spot.

"I am aware it costs me nothing," Damien replied, his voice flat and utterly disinterested. "I can. But I won't."

A beat of heavy silence. "It seems the crown is making you forget the blood that flows in your veins. I should have had you vow-sworn to this decision before your coronation. It would have curbed this willfulness."

Damien's laugh was short and mirthless. "Willfulness will be the least of your regrets, I assure you."

"Look at you." Alaric's voice dropped, becoming crueler, more personal. "Sitting on a throne you inherited from your father and defying his decision. These decisions you make are a testament to my failure. You are everything I feared you would become."

I felt my own heart crack for him. To hear such venom from the man who was supposed to have been his first protector... No one, not even the unbreakable Sovereign of Atlassian, could be entirely immune to that.

Damien went silent.

The silence stretched, thick and suffocating. I could imagine his face, that stoic mask firmly in place, but I could feel the hurt radiating from the quiet, a wound being inflicted deep inside where no one could see.

When he finally spoke, his voice was ice. "The only disappointment here is the man who looks at his son and sees a reflection of his own inadequacy. Do not project your failures onto my crown."

I heard the sharp intake of Alaric's breath, but I didn't wait to hear more. Quick, light footsteps were approaching from the direction Damien had spoken. I couldn't be found here. I made it four steps.

The door opened.

I kept walking. Eyes forward, pace even, the full performance of someone who had simply been passing through and had somewhere to be and wasn't thinking about anything in particular.

"Mirabelle."

I turned.

He stepped out and pulled the door shut behind him. Whatever had happened in that chamber was entirely absent from his face. Jaw set. Eyes on me with the steadiness of someone who has already decided what to do with the next few moments and was simply moving through them.

The corridor was empty in both directions.

"I was heading to the barracks," I said. "West corridor goes through here."

"I know where the west corridor runs." A pause. He took one step closer, then stopped himself. "How long were you standing here?"

I held his gaze. "I heard some of it. I should have kept walking—"

"But you didn't."

"No."

He looked at me for a moment without speaking. "If you have thoughts about what you heard," he said, "keep them."

"I wasn't going to say anything."

The silence stretched. I didn't fill it. I'd learned that with him.

Then he crossed his arms, and the set of his jaw shifted slightly —still controlled, but underneath it something tight that hadn't been there before. He looked at the far end of the corridor instead of at me, just for a second.

"He's been like that a long time," he said. Low.

"I could hear it in the way he said it. Like he'd said it before," I said quietly.

He looked back at me then. Something moved behind his eyes —brief, barely there, and closed again almost immediately. But it was there. "It doesn't matter to me."

We both knew that wasn't entirely true. And we both let it stand.

I shifted my weight toward the corridor, giving him the exit. "I won't say anything. About any of it."

"I know you won't." Still flat. But less armored than he'd started.

He uncrossed his arms, looked at me once more with his closed, careful expression, and said, "Barracks."

"Barracks." I walked before I could make it into something he wasn't ready to give—those raw pieces of himself he kept locked away. He deserved better than my need to pull him open.

I didn't look back. But I carried it with me—that one unguarded second. I held it the way you hold something fragile that was handed to you by accident and wasn't meant for you and matters anyway.

The silent hurt I would now carry for him.

CHAPTER II
MIRABELLE

The envelope burned in my hands.

I never checked the mailbox because I never got anything. But this morning, as Lyria was thumbing through her pile, she had tossed one toward me with an offhand flick of her wrist.

"Yours," she'd said, already tearing into her own.

For a ridiculous moment, I imagined it was from Damien. A missive, folded into the common delivery so no one would notice. Something that said what he hadn't said out loud. Then I rolled my eyes at myself. If Damien ever wanted to say something, he'd barge into my wing and say it with that ridiculous certainty of his that left no room for anything except a response.

I ripped it open. Five words.

I do remember. Do you?

That was all it said. No name or mark.

My stomach pitched. I stared at the words so long they blurred. They could mean anything. Or nothing. The lost memory of Abyss, a thread from my past, or just a taunt, a riddle. I didn't know what to make of it.

Lyria glanced up from her own letter. "Good news?"

"Undecided," I shrugged, then folded it back up and put it in my corset, which was where things went when they needed thinking about and I didn't have time to think.

⁂

Royals had been assigned to me, when Damien stormed in, all urgency and sharp glances, to check if Dreadclaw was tolerating me. In truth, Dreadclaw had actually been scowling at Damien. I suspected it had less to do with me and more to do with his grudge against Lorenza.

I wasn't sure whether to be flattered; being chosen by a creature out of petty spite felt like the Realms' backhanded compliment. But I would take it.

I passed through the older enclosure, heading toward the new range where five Tameables would be chosen for the Dissonance.

When I reached the broad sandstone platform, all four of the Royals were already there, waiting for me. Three men. One woman. Each looked like they'd been chiseled out of duty and discipline.

I didn't know any of them yet, but I tried to read the room. The tallest had the stillness of someone who defaulted to patience rather than action. Good. The woman had earnest eyes. Also good. The broad one had crossed his arms in a way that wasn't hostile exactly, more *show me something worth uncrossing them for*. Fair enough. The fourth was already smiling, which meant he was either genuinely easy or wanted me to think he was.

"What an amazing...day," I said, injecting cheer into my voice like it might disguise the fact I had no clue how to command Royals who had likely been swinging swords since before I could afford boots. "Thank you for being here."

The tallest among them inclined his head. "Sovereign's orders," he said flatly. "We follow them."

"Ahh, splendid," I replied. "Let's make this painless, then."

The woman, graceful, with hair like river-dark silk, raised a brow.

"I'm the...Tamer." I resisted the urge to fidget. "The five Tameables from our Hold are part of the Dissonance's first night formation. I will be commanding the group. You will be linked to one of them through me."

There was a pause. "Through you?" one of the men echoed, dubious.

"Yes. I will anchor the Tether. You will act as the conduits."

Another pause. "Have you done this before?" the woman asked.

"No," I told her. "No one has. But we have a handful of days to make it work, which is enough if we start now." I looked at each of them. "Any problems with that?"

Nobody said yes. Nobody said no. The woman tilted her head slightly. "And if it doesn't work?"

"Well, I hope you're quick on your feet." I smiled at them. To their credit, no one outright scoffed or started whispering behind raised collars.

"We can do our introductions properly," I added with another smile. "I am Mirabelle."

Their gazes flickered, polite but unreadable.

"Vannor," said the first, tall and silent.

"Elsha," came the next.

"Rhane," the third muttered.

And lastly, "Tovelle," with a bow too theatrical to be sincere. *This one might be trouble.*

As Tovelle straightened, his arm brushed almost imperceptibly against Elsha's. She didn't look at him, but her posture, which had been ramrod straight, softened infinitesimally.

"Today's goal is simple: earn their interest. There are eight Tameables in total. But only five will be deployed for Dissonance. We will select the final five based on mutual compatibility and coordination."

They followed me in silence. Only Vannor had the decency to look faintly alarmed.

"I don't expect you to earn their trust today. That takes time. But walk beside them. Let them smell you."

"*Smell* us?" Vannor blinked.

"They are beasts. That's how they learn."

Rhane actually chuckled. "You're serious?"

"Completely." I pointed toward the row of gated enclosures.

I watched Tovelle tuck a strip of jerky between his fingers and feed it to Zepharion. The beast snatched the morsel. Then, with a grin that was all show, he held the remainder out as if offering charity; Elsha's hand shot forward, plucking it from his palm, and she fed it to another one. Tovelle watched. Grinned. This time, it reached his eyes.

Right, those two will be fine.

Below, Whip-tail coiled like a lazy cat, flicking his tail and blinking up at the new Royals with affection. When Rhane brought his hand near, Whip-tail leaned into the touch and made that soft sound of contentment that read, in creature-speech: *yes, yes, yes.* If he could've offered them sweet ale and a warm blanket in return, he would have.

"Pick one," I told the Royals. "Feed them. Just learn their tells."

Then I left them to it. The creatures knew me well enough by now. It was the others who had to earn their attention and survive it.

I RETURNED TO NYXRATHIS' enclosure, two duckheart skewers steaming in my grip. I'd convinced a Thrall to snag them from the street vendors before dawn.

The High-Fang lounged in her enclosure, her form half-there, half-dream, drifting like water through shade. Her presence was more sensation than sight, pressure behind the eyes, and a whisper against the spine.

The moment I crossed the threshold, her voice slithered into my mind. *You again.*

"I see we're still in a mood," I said, holding up the skewer like an offering. "Brought you a present."

A long pause. Then: *Bribery? Bold.*

"Hey, you agreed. And I'm not above it," I replied, dangling the skewer just beyond the silver-marked stones.

Her eyes gleamed violet, two orbs of molten dusk in the shadows.

Screaming?

"Unfortunately, not this time."

Silence stretched. Then the floor rippled. She flowed and poured into visibility, partially veiled by her camouflage. She revealed herself only in outlines: a curve of shoulder, the taper of a spine, a wing unfolding into nothingness. Tall as Dreadclaw but leaner, her wings sheer as stained glass when she chose to unfold them.

"You're...gorgeous," I breathed.

I know.

I snorted. "Modest too."

Stating the obvious, she mused, gliding closer. *You, however, have only one form. Average, by your standards?*

I scowled. "Thanks."

Her tail flicked, brushing my hair with startling gentleness. *You are also gorgeous. In a...mortal way.*

"Are you saying that for real," I demanded, "or just compensating for being mean?"

Both. She nudged the duckheart from my hand. *I am multifaceted.*

I shook my head and gave her the skewer. Then I watched her chew the duckheart with exaggerated delicacy, eyes closing slightly. When she finished, she gave a pleased hum in my mind.

"Ready for the field?" I asked.

Always.

She moved past me then, flowing over the stones like crystal liquid. I followed, boots scraping the stone in a far less graceful rhythm, trailing her shimmer toward the edge of the new inside training ranges.

The moment light struck her full body, her scales drank the

light and refracted it back like crushed amethyst. Then she vanished. As if she'd never been there.

I blinked. "Wait!"

I turned just in time to see Dreadclaw slither into view from the far side like a storm clothed in smoke, tendrils carving trenches into the stone as he approached. I had asked the handlers to open his enclosure so I could attempt something, whether coaxing them into cooperation and urging them to lay aside their ancient grudge.

Still playing ghost? he rumbled at her, his voice like boulders grinding together.

Stars, is this menace for real? I thought.

But before I could interject, NyxRathis responded loudly, without even looking at him. *Still mistaking arrogance for authority?*

I stared between them. Was this normal?

Dreadclaw's massive head tilted, his nostrils flaring as smoke curled lazily outward. *You are in my territory.*

NyxRathis was nowhere to be seen.

"NyxRathis...?" I called out, spinning, a prickle dancing down my spine. A shimmer pulsed beside me, and I turned just in time to see her reappear at my side, wings blooming into a half-translucent arch. A breathtaking veil of violet glass and shadow.

Your territory? she echoed, voice dripping with mockery. *You think you own every patch of dirt your claws sully?*

Dreadclaw took a step forward, claws raking deep furrows into the ground. *At least I don't vanish like a coward when challenged.*

You might consider trying it, she countered, fangs flashing. *It would do wonders for your scent.*

I winced. *Okay. So that's a no on friendly banter.* I tried to pacify one or the other.

Dreadclaw's snarl ripped the air. *I should've eaten you the day they dragged you in chains to this Hold, when you were untethered.*

Untethered after being tamed? Wait—what? I whipped my head toward NyxRathis. He meant that literally? She was brought here in chains? I knew she'd been captured decades ago, but he spoke of it as if it were yesterday.

You couldn't even catch me, she purred, lazily circling a pillar like he hadn't just threatened to cannibalize her.

I groaned, pressing my fingers to my temples as I searched for some way to mend this disaster. Before any thought could form, it worsened—Dreadclaw lunged.

A blur of black smoke and molten rage surged forward, jaws gaping. NyxRathis disappeared again a breath too early, and his bulk slammed into the stone pillar she'd just circled. It cracked from the impact, splinters of marble ricocheting into the dirt.

I stepped forward, every nerve on edge. "Enough!" I snapped, my voice pitched low and cold, letting the Tether flare beneath my skin. Dreadclaw halted mid-snarling breath. His head whipped toward me, smoke spiraling around my boots, but he didn't lunge again.

His tail lashed once, scarring the ground.

"If you so much as snap in her direction again," I said in stern tone, "I'll have you confined to your enclosure for a week. No range. No light." It was a threat I had no true intention of carrying out, but this immature menace didn't need to know that now.

He growled, reluctant and resentful, but he backed off, slinking toward the stone tunnel that led back to his enclosure. But not without parting gifts. As he passed NyxRathis, now reappeared on a stone plinth, he lazily dragged one tendril across her snout.

She hissed, every scale along her back rippling. I put my hands on my hips and exhaled hard. Now I understood why they said these two didn't get along.

And making them get along? That was going to be the death of me.

CHAPTER 12
DAMIEN

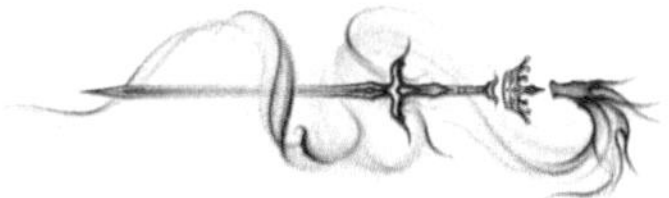

From the northern rise, the Dissonance formation resembled a breathing entity, cohesive yet ever-shifting, pulsing with potential beneath the frost-rubbed light. The ground below was stripped of wildgrass, flattened to hard-packed soil.

I watched our Legion align. Two hundred and thirteen.

We had narrowed them through days of preliminary trials, each tested under exhaustion, deception of illusion, elemental Aethers, and brute strength. Legion soldiers in their black-gilded mail, flanked by new Royals recruits and nine Majors, all of whom had survived long enough, fought hard enough, and proven useful enough to warrant inclusion.

At our command, the central diamond formation expanded, its outer edges forming into overlapping arcs, an evolving crescent meant to counter perimeter breaches. At a signal from Ophira, the flanks broke away, falling into staggered rip and coil spirals. Defensive lines within offensive ones.

Now, they shifted through formations in the dust bowl we'd made of the training field. It was hypnotic, in the way watching ants rebuild a kicked hill is hypnotic. Mostly, I was waiting for someone new to trip.

"Seventh quadrant is dragging its ass," Nathan said in his serious tone. At least sound carried here.

Alden, a Major with more heart than knee cartilage, flinched. His bad leg—a souvenir from a training mishap with an earth-mage—was trembling. He tried to hide it and failed.

"Fall out, Alden," I called, "before you take the whole line down. That knee won't hold in the third rotation."

Nathan grunted beside me. "He'll be ready?"

"He'll be dead if he's not." Cold, but true.

"Royce! You're up," Nathan called out to our back up recruits.

Ophira, scribbling on her cursed slate, muttered, "Third spiral's shadowed. Could be better."

"Noted," I said, though we were about to have much bigger problems.

The formation was coming apart. The complex, interlocking drill pattern, a replica of the War Plateau's defenses, was disintegrating into garbage. They were trying to hold the intricate shape while fighting, and the wild Aether surging up from the ground wasn't helping.

Patience, a resource I possessed in limited supply these days, ran out. I shrugged off my cloak and walked to the front of the formation. I looked at Nathan and gave a single nod.

"Full reset. Now," Nathan barked.

The sigh of relief from two hundred exhausted souls was practically a wind. They staggered back, lines dissolving into weary, confused clusters.

It began simply. A lateral shift. I moved, and the entire formation rustled like a great beast, adjusting its weight to follow. Then a pivot. A step back. A synchronized turn. I led them through the basic footwork, my body the point of the spear they were all part of.

The difference was immediate. The ragged edges smoothed. The collective breath began to sync.

. . .

IN A SMALL GAP BETWEEN ROTATIONS, Arthur from Zarkon appeared at my shoulder, his steps silent on the soft earth. Lightning flickered, unsummoned, in his dark eyes.

"A word?"

"Sure, speak."

"My lightning...and Lorenza's shadows. You have us on opposite flanks. We create two problems for an enemy. I understand the tactic."

"But?"

"But we are only half a threat *alone*. My Aether is a direct force. Her shadows are indirect control. Alone, they adapt. Together..." He let the implication hang. "They would not know what hit them. A storm they cannot see."

I stopped walking. The formation behind me froze mid-step. This was not a complaint. It was a tactical proposal, and he was right. I'd been thinking in terms of spreading threats. He was thinking in terms of creating a single, overwhelming paradox.

"Lorenza!" I called.

She jogged over, panting slightly, wisps of dark hair escaping her braid. She looked utterly spent. Her Aether was a deep well, but her endurance was shallow. A consequence, perhaps, of being the youngest, the most sheltered of them all. She needed to push herself harder.

"Damien?" she asked, wiping sweat from her brow.

"Are you tired?"

"No," she lied immediately. "I can continue."

"Good. You are with Arthur now. Consider yourselves a single unit. Your Aethers are not fire and water; they are two distinct ones. See what happens when shadow holds a target still... for a lightning strike that comes from within the darkness itself."

Arthur gave a grim, approving smile. Lorenza's eyes narrowed with fierce interest.

"Reset!" I commanded, returning to the head of the formation. "From the top. And this time, try not to let them scorch half the field."

I SHRUGGED out of my heavy formal cloak and dropped into the chair beside the desk, already covered in parchments inked with treaties, revised maps, and troop counts still awaiting final approval. Somewhere beneath it all was the formal summary of our latest meeting with the Nyxarian Royalties.

Half-hearted was the word for it.

Rhylen was reliable, but even his appointment had come bound in strings and veiled intentions. They wanted the alliance but they hadn't decided to trust us yet, which was their right, but it made every conversation a performance of cooperation nobody was quite committed to. And nor could I afford to trust them when every trail of evidence tied to the Abyss led both everywhere and nowhere at once.

The true price was the Bonding they'd demanded before the Dissonance. I had said no to the timing. But my father had to get involved, had to imply otherwise to the whole Clan, leaving me to break a promise I never made. Now their bitterness tainted every proposal.

I skimmed through the latest correspondence from the Sovereign of Nyxaria. Empty pleasantries wrapped in political perfume. Either he was being obstinate for the sake of it, or someone was pressing him to seize an upper hand by other means. And there was no mention of the Bonding, *yet.*

Lorenza's presence in Atlassian had become the symbol they required. She was managing her end of it well. She showed up when it mattered, said what needed saying, didn't complicate things publicly—even though she had been pushed into it much the same way I had. And she was carrying it with more grace than most would.

Even that careful dance was growing brittle beneath the weight of what we hadn't said. And it frayed more with each breath that bloody Tamer took in defiance. I couldn't place why.

I was informed the moment she stepped into the Hold,

blatantly defying my warning from the night before without a flicker of hesitation. And yet, I let it pass. I let her pass, because granting her one more chance wasn't indulgence. It was the wisest move I could make for Atlassian, and for the Dissonance to come.

She was just another name, still stumbling through the marrow of training ranges and masked Council rooms, trying to stand straight in a Realm made of sharp corners and pointed knives. Still bruised from training and raw from the responsibility she never asked for.

She wasn't supposed to become a variable. She was supposed to remain a tool. An asset. A rare one, yes. Unquestionably valuable, but ultimately manageable.

And yet—

I caught myself rereading her reports again. Rowane's old assessments from her first trials. Reports I'd read before. And annotated. And returned to like a man trying to divine the future from the scratches on a page.

She hadn't shown much of her true self then. Or so I thought. But the more I read, the more I began to see the corners of her personality that had escaped notice, buried threads of sharpness, quiet stubbornness, and moments where her instincts flared brighter than her fear.

Timid in court. Bold in the Hold. Fearless when cornered. And when alone with me? *Unpredictable.*

My study of her was clinical, necessary. If she held any tie to the Abyss or the rotting political gambles I was smelling the more I dug, I needed to understand it. If something from her bloodline or forgotten past left her vulnerable or dangerous, I had to know. It was the same reason I found myself watching her from the high alcove above the Hold as she moved among Tameables like a whisper given form. If she were injured or worse, we had no contingency plan in place. There is no second Tamer.

So of course, I watched her. Of course, I assigned four Royals to assist her with integration drills and asked them to protect her. Of course, I'd asked to be notified if she skipped a meal, if she limped too long on an injury, if she lingered too long practicing that unconventional archery past nightfall.

When she asked softly, just once, to keep NyxRathis in her care, I said yes. Not because that thread of uncertainty in her voice hooked behind my ribs and pulled, but because we needed her focused. Because emotional stability drove performance. A content Tamer was an effective Tamer.

I was being reasonable. That was all.

I picked up the dispatch. Read the same line twice without retaining it. Put it down.

A reasonable man should not bite down against the quickening of his own pulse at the sight of her hands trembling after training. And he certainly should not feel that hollow press in his chest when she flinched at another's words, only to lift her chin as though daring them to try again.

There was the corridor to add to it now. She'd heard. She knew she shouldn't have, said so plainly, didn't try to make it into anything. And I had expected—wanted, if I was being honest with myself, which I was trying not to be—a reason to draw the line cleanly. She'd been two seconds from giving me one.

Then she hadn't. She hadn't attempted anything. Hadn't pried, hadn't softened, hadn't offered me the particular brand of careful that I knew how to refuse. Something she said before she left had gotten under my guard in a way I hadn't allowed in a very long time. And I had almost said more in that corridor than I'd said to anyone in recent memory. The fact that I hadn't was the only small victory I'd managed where she was concerned. And still I stood in a corridor that felt emptier than it had any right to be.

Stars. I had sworn to keep the lines clear. To lead as Sovereign first. To serve the Clan above all else. And my focus could not afford to fracture. Battles and betrayals loomed over every breath we took. My days were a string of war councils, resource ledgers, and Legion rotations. I had to keep her separate. If not from the Dissonance, then at least from me.

A knock.

Then the door to my study opened without ceremony. *Again.*

"I have something for you," she said, far too brightly, as though she hadn't just barged into the heart of the Sovereign's study with all the decorum of a magpie crashing a funeral.

And she was smiling.

I exhaled slowly, setting aside the reports with deliberate care. "Mirabelle."

"I knocked," she added, with no small amount of pride.

"You did not wait."

She crossed the chamber anyway, her boots leaving faint traces of sand on the polished obsidian floor. From the folds of her cloak, she produced a grease-stained parcel, its contents emitting a scent that was equal parts savory and suspicious.

"Duckheart skewers," she announced. "Still warm. Well, lukewarm. But I had to convince Thrall Ga—" She caught herself. "Someone. To get this for NyxRathis. And you."

I stared at the offering. "You brought me street food."

She tilted her head. "Yes. You're welcome."

"I don't recall asking for duckheart."

She folded her arms. "Yes. But you looked like you haven't eaten anything but war in days."

That should not have affected me the way it did. "I have food," I said. "And in abundance. I do not require your charity."

"You require something interesting," she muttered.

"And you thought that was your job to provide?"

She just shrugged.

My jaw ticked. I had told guards to grant her open access to my study. At the time, it had seemed a simple and practical thing to do. But there was nothing practical about the way she stood here now, eyes bright in a way that no battlefield or contract could define.

And if I was wise, I would send her out. If I had a shred of discipline left, I would put her in place. Instead, I rose from my chair and walked around the desk until I was standing directly before her.

"You cannot keep doing this," I said.

Her brows lifted. "Feeding you?"

"Crossing lines that are not yours to cross. Speaking to me as though I am—" I broke off, the rest catching in my throat.

"Would you rather I pretend you're not someone who needs caring for, same as anyone else?" she asked, looking straight to my soul.

"I want you to remember I am not yours to provoke," I snapped, an overreach to mask what her words stirred.

Her breath caught, but she did not look away. "And what if I don't want to provoke you?" she said softly. "What if I just...care?"

Silence.

A long, dangerous silence.

And then I reached for the bundle she had brought. Untied it. Took a bite of the duckheart, warm and salt-sweet, smoky with spice. It was good. Of course it was.

She watched me with something like wary pride, and I felt the tightness in my chest give way to something worse. Something gentler.

"Fine," I said at last. "You have fed your *Sovereign*. Now leave before I decide that was an act of treason."

She stepped back toward the door with a grin that might as well have been a declaration of war. "I will bring dessert next time."

I hid the small tug at my mouth beneath a veil of indifference, unwilling to let her see that her insolence had not scraped my patience as it ought to have.

"And Mirabelle," I added, before she could vanish entirely.

She glanced over her shoulder.

"Next time, knock. And wait."

She winked. "No promises."

And then she was gone.

And I, Sovereign of Atlassian, stood there. Duckhearts in hand and losing battles no one else could see.

CHAPTER 13

MIRABELLE

By now, I knew the path well enough to walk it blindfolded. The way from the Hold to the morning meal took me beneath the gold-vined trees. Their canopies swayed above me in an unhurried rhythm, casting dappled green light onto the cobbled path.

Everything here shimmered in polished tones. Even the wind moved like it had been trained by an etiquette instructor.

I was late again because I was also surviving my strength drills with Ophira. I was lucky I remembered how to walk in a straight line. Ophira had a particular fondness for pushing me to failure, then glaring when I failed. Yesterday, she'd made me sprint half the grounds, then mount Zepharion without using my arms. I'd missed the beast entirely. Landed on my hip in the dirt.

My legs still ached from that fall.

The food tables were already half-empty by the time I arrived. Most of my cohort had left for their assigned trainings. Callen and the others to final Dissonance drills, Lyria to the armory, the rest scattered between battle formations and strategy sessions. Only a few remained, clustered at the far end of the long table: Lorenza and a handful of Royal women, their chatter and laughter soft as river stones.

One seat left. I noticed it even before I started walking.

I hesitated.

It wasn't that I longed to be part of their circle. Callen had already dragged me into his with all the subtlety of a summer storm, until even his friends had stopped groaning every time I opened my mouth. Even Royce, whose eyebrows seemed permanently sculpted in disapproval, had begrudgingly accepted that I was not, in fact, the worst company this Realm had to offer.

But this group was *a bit* different. They reminded me of the commoner kids from Dorms who wore better clothes than the rest of us, who still went home to family at the end of the day. When they sat together or laughed, sharing jokes, there was something about them that made them look unapproachable.

Still, I had to try here. I had to see if I was just being prejudiced. As I approached, Lorenza's gaze lifted. A flicker of recognition, the curve of a smile that seemed genuine, and I returned it.

"Is this seat taken?" I asked, with a brightness that barely concealed the nerves scraping under my ribs.

The woman seated beside the empty space, a dark-haired Royal, glanced up. Her tone was courteous. "I'm afraid so. Feyna will be back shortly."

"Oh. Of course." I nodded too fast. "No problem. I was just—"

They'd already turned back to their conversation. *Well...ouch.*

I pivoted neatly, if a little stiffly, and made my way to the far end of the adjacent table, one with benches still empty and bread baskets untouched. The awkwardness clung to my skin like damp linen.

Callen would've scoffed at me. *Since when do you give a damn about Royal seating arrangements?* he'd say, elbowing me aside to make space. *Sit. Eat. Stop being weird about it.*

But Callen wasn't here.

Oh and the bread was still warm.

I tore a piece with more satisfaction than necessary and stuffed it into my mouth. I had *warm* food. I slathered ashened butter on the next slice. What would I even have said if they'd let me sit there? *Oh, my strength nearly melted another training post this morning. How are your inherited sword techniques coming along? Need any help selecting embroidery patterns for your third estate's guest wing?*

I chewed my food in silence as I turned my eyes outward, across the sprawling sparring courts. From this distance, I could just make out the top of the Hold's arching roofline, rising above the edge of the training fields like a crown.

The scent of extra roasted meat drifted faintly from the kitchens behind me. Someone had bartered hard for that. Probably Cassian. He liked to claim his family's coin couldn't buy him charm, so he made up for it with overpriced poultry.

I smiled faintly.

NyxRathis had been chewing through my thoughts all morning, and not in the poetic way. After yesterday's mayhem with Dreadclaw and his ridiculous need to provoke her, I'd had to spend half the night reestablishing calm through our Tether.

She'd threatened to ghost out of the Dissonance Trial altogether.

I do not need to share a field with that lizard in heat, she'd declared, mid-coil, tail flicking a training post off its hinges.

We'd argued and she'd sulked. Then I had bribed her again. Duckhearts and petty paybacks against Dreadclaw were now my bargaining chip of choice. And then, the real surprise—she'd offered a suggestion.

Take Whip-tail with us, she'd said, violet eyes narrowed like she expected me to laugh.

I nearly had. "The healer?" I'd asked, blinking. "He purrs when Royals sneeze."

Exactly, she'd replied. *No one expects Whip-tail to survive on Dissonance grounds, let alone anchor the field. It's unthinkable. You could take advantage of that.*

We had traded a few arguments after that. And when I thought about it—really thought about it—it made a ridiculous amount of sense.

Whip-tail wasn't just docile. He was grounding. Calming. And yes, he healed, but more than that, he absorbed. Tameables lost control under pressure. They lashed out. Snapped Tethers. But Whip-tail soothed them, anchored them back to their Tethers. He might not scorch enemies or melt iron, but he kept the others standing.

Which, in a havoc-laced field of death, might be the most dangerous power of all.

So, I'd agreed. Whip-tail would join the trial. In return, I'd promised NyxRathis direct defense against Dreadclaw's next insult, and one single pass for minor bullying. *Only one.* I wasn't raising a menace.

The bench across from me shifted with a whisper of silk. I looked up, then stilled.

Irin.

Her long blond hair was pinned half-up today, neat in a way that didn't suit her usual look. I didn't meet her gaze as she sat, instead becoming very interested in the hard crust along the edge of my bread.

A second passed. Then three.

"I like the crust," I said at last.

"Hmm." She nodded, chewing one of hers.

We sat like that in silence. I kept my eyes on my hands because looking at her felt like standing too close to something I wasn't supposed to touch. *Did she know?*

Damien had killed her father. For me. Because of me. And now Haldric's daughter sat across from me, her presence humming like a plucked string. I shifted in my seat.

Without my thoughts to crowd the silence, the bright chimes of laughter and conversation reached me. The Royal women gathered around Lorenza, leaning in as she finished recounting something with her careful detachment. I glanced over. The vacant seat was still empty.

"...dismissed all his Thralls," one of them said. "Hmm...she must be *quite* the distraction."

Another leaned forward. "Didn't the Sovereign always keep two or three?" Tone tinged with intrigue.

The table hummed with amusement.

Lorenza offered a serene smile. "It's not uncommon for Sovereigns to shift their habits during Dissonance, dear." She lifted her goblet with grace. "Though, yes," she added, letting the word linger, "I suppose even Damien is not immune to fascination."

She paused just long enough to let the weight of her voice settle. "From what I've observed," she continued, "he's drawn to things that resist being known. That's the allure, I suppose. The riddle, not the person. But fascination is fickle."

A soft chuckle followed, just loud enough to be shared.

I didn't move. *Was she truly talking about herself? Or...*

One of the women leaned forward, her smile too wide to be innocent. "It's not just fascination with *you*. I think it's..." She let the words trail in a suggestive tone.

Lorenza turned her eyes to her goblet, but the corners of her mouth curled. Then she added, softer, but still audible, "He told me he liked the sound of silence in a woman. How rare that is these days."

That stung more than I wanted to admit. And I realized I was blatantly staring at them, listening as if I were entitled to their words, with no manners whatsoever. I looked back into my infinitely more interesting bread rolls.

Irin's voice suddenly cut through their murmurs. "That's strange. Sovereign told *me* once he preferred the ones who didn't lie when they spoke."

Lorenza's fingers stilled around the stem of her goblet. The conversation dropped into a brief, loaded silence.

Finally, Lorenza tilted her head, as though Irin were a child she'd momentarily forgotten was in the room. "Of course. But then everyone thinks they know Damien, don't they?"

Irin met her gaze. "But some of us have known him since we scraped our knees in the same courtyard. It's different from trying to imitate a history you don't have."

For a breath, the air between them crackled. Then Lorenza broke it with a poised smile. "I don't involve myself in these conversations, dear. It's rarely productive."

And she turned back to her dessert and berries, brushing Irin off like dust from silk.

I didn't breathe for a moment. I didn't know what I was supposed to think or how to react when they were calmly dissecting *my Etern* whom I now had no right to claim.

The man who killed for me.

Who dismissed his Thralls for the reason no one remembered.

Who looked at me like he was drowning, and I was the shore.

I swallowed a mouthful of bread I hadn't realized I was chewing. The crust scratched going down.

Then a sound broke through the quiet. Footsteps, urgent and uneven. A Thrall tore through the archway, breath ragged, face streaked with sweat. "The Sovereign's been injured—he shielded a boy—we need, he needs—" The words tangled in his mouth, caught between gasps and horror.

My body moved before thought caught up. I was on my feet. "Where?"

"What kind of injury?" Lorenza asked.

The Thrall swallowed. "Ward fracture at the eastern ridge. Combat drills. One of the Royals miscalculated a leap. It set off a domino. The wall snapped. Glyph shards went flying. He shielded a child who barged in midway—"

The rest blurred into a roar in my ears.

"Where is he now?" I asked in panic.

"The infirmary near the eastern ranges—"

I didn't wait for the rest.

I ran.

CHAPTER 14
MIRABELLE

"Lady," the unfamiliar guard repeated, stiff with formality. "It's not possible to enter. The Sovereign is stable and has asked for time to himself."

He looked young. Too new to know I'd never listened well to polite dismissal.

Behind him, the steps to the infirmary buzzed with murmured conversations. Elders, Majors, and Royals scattered across the courtyard like ants broken from formation. Lorenza had just arrived, and she quickly moved through them with the weight of her title alone.

"How is Damien?" she asked an Elder. "I rushed here as soon as I heard."

One of the older Sages replied. "The wounds are minor. A bit deep, but not alarming. Glyph shards. But it's already healing."

"He shielded a child?" she pressed.

The Sage gave a nod. "Foolish little thing wandered past the boundary. The wall fractured. Would've killed the boy outright. But the Sovereign acted first. Like he always does."

My chest twisted and warmed at the same time. He had shielded a child with *his* body while the whole Legion was there.

"Where is he?" Lorenza asked.

"In the inner chamber. The healer just finished."

I didn't wait for anyone to offer. As Lorenza swept toward the doors, I moved behind her, quiet and fast. The guards shifted to follow, then paused.

"She's with me," Lorenza said, not bothering to glance back. And I seized the opening, gritting my teeth against the bitter taste of owing her anything, yet ultimately grateful she'd let me slip in beside her.

Inside, Damien lay as before. Still, half-drowned in the faint green shadows of his self-healing. The bleeding had ceased. One arm rested beneath his neck, clean quilts drawn till below his chest, though the wrap across his ribs bore a dark stain where blackened blood had seeped through the edge.

His face was too calm for what I'd feared. I exhaled, the sound perilously close to a sob. I had half a mind to leave the chamber when Lorenza moved past me, crossing to his bedside. She laid a gentle hand on his arm, her fingers brushing along the bruise.

"I let you in because I dislike such scenes." She didn't look at me. "This is a palace, Mirabelle, not your old Dorm."

My nails bit crescents into my palms, but I held my tongue. From her perspective, I was exactly what she accused me of. She had no way of knowing how fiercely protective I was of him, or how much of that I buried beneath silence.

She turned then, her gaze a slow assessment. "You weren't raised to understand the delicacies of court. Yet your position as a Tamer grants certain...allowances." A pause. "But tolerance is not invitation."

Shame prickled hot beneath my skin, yet I kept my chin lifted, looking straight to her stern eyes.

"Damien is our Sovereign. Yours. Mine. And this"—she motioned delicately toward the bed—"is not the place to test the boundaries of that title."

"No. I—" I began, but she held up her hand.

"I know you came out of concern. I don't doubt that. But you cannot burst into private chambers, interrupt a resting Sovereign, and expect it to go unnoticed."

Still, I said nothing. Pride was a luxury I couldn't afford now. Whatever words crowded at the back of my throat would have to be saved for a time when I had ground of my own to stand upon.

"Let me be clear," Lorenza continued, pretending to ignore my burning ears. "This is not meant to embarrass you." She smiled faintly. "Think of this as a kindness. A word of warning from one who understands how delicate the court truly is."

I wanted to scream. That I hadn't come for politics or posturing. That I just needed to see, to know he'd wake up whole.

She stepped aside, her hand settled possessively over Damien's.

"I am staying with him," she added. Then, turning slightly toward the door, she called out, low but distinct, "Guards."

The doors creaked open once more. Two of them stepped into view, waiting just outside the threshold.

"You may go now. Return to your drills," she told me. "They will see you out."

❧

I WENT STRAIGHT to the archery range like a coward.

My bow was where I left it. Same notch, same string tension. But beside it, laid neatly on the stone shelf, was a new pair of archery gloves. Leather, finely stitched, still creased at the seams. But I didn't touch them.

I took the bow bare-handed and notched the first arrow. Drew. Released.

Again.

Again.

Again.

The thrum of the string burned across my skin. I welcomed it.

I didn't stop until my hands shook too badly to nock another arrow. The blood wet my knuckles and slicked the shaft of the final arrow. The sting forced my breath short. My grip slipped. I let the bow fall.

Only then did I let the ache settle in, the image that would not leave me. Lorenza slipping into his bed with the ease of one entitled to it, her hand trailing across Damien's chest as the door shut behind me. I cradled my ribs with one arm and turned away from the target, from the field, from everything. No one stopped me.

I reached my chamber in silence. The sheets felt too soft against torn fingers, too gentle for a body that wanted only to hurt.

I curled inward, hands throbbing, and told myself it was about the pain. But it wasn't only that. It was self-loathing. For how weak I felt, for not standing my ground, for failing to find a way forward.

I had known trials would come, but I had not known they would cut this deep. I did not know how to pretend none of it touched me, how to feign strength when I felt myself unraveling thread by thread. So I pressed harder against the wound, chasing the sting until it drowned the rest, until at last, sleep dragged me under.

⁘

THE INFIRMARY WAS empty when I arrived at dawn. No Damien or Lorenza. No guards. Just the lingering scent of healing fern and silence.

I shouldn't have gone to his chambers. But I did.

Damien's guards at the wing entrance let me through without question. Lorenza might emerge, half-dressed and irritated at my intrusion. The thought made bile rise at the back of my throat. Still, I could not stop myself.

I did not want to linger. I only needed to see him, just once. To be certain the wounds had closed, that his breath still came steady. Then I would leave and let my pathetic heart rot in silence until I could remember how to be strong again, how to think without tearing myself apart.

I needed to master this unrest before it mastered me, before I lashed out and made a spectacle of myself—some jealous fool clawing at the Sovereign—and shattered the smallest, most painstakingly guarded chance I had to reclaim everything I'd lost.

I crossed the polished stone hallway toward his chamber. The heavy door stood half-open, a carved wooden monolith etched with the crest of the Sovereign line, staring back like a warning. I rapped once. No answer.

"Damien?" I called softly.

Still nothing. So I stepped inside to check. The chamber lay quiet, dimly lit by the blue-white glow of a wardstone set near the hearth. His scent lingered in the air, edged with the faint warmth of his bath. And with it came an onslaught of our memories I could not stop.

But he was not here. *And I shouldn't be here.*

I turned to check the adjoining door to the palace infirmary, just in case. Maybe they'd chosen privacy to let the healers finish their work. And then I froze. Because the door to his inner dressing chamber creaked open, and Damien stepped through. His hair was damp, curling slightly at the ends, and a thin layer of steam still clung to his skin. He wore nothing but black tailored trousers that clung low on his hips.

My gaze went straight to the marks raking his torso, angry red lines, almost healed but still stark against his tanned skin.

"Are you alright?" I asked, before I could temper the way my voice cracked slightly on the last word.

He didn't answer immediately. Just stared. Water dripped from his hair onto his shoulders. "I thought I told you not to barge into my space."

I froze.

This time, the words stung more than they should have. I forced a faint smile, the edges brittle. "I am sorry. I just"—*needed to see you*—"wanted to make sure you were well."

"I am," he said simply.

I nodded, too quickly. "Good. That's...good."

I had already begun toward the door. My steps were slow; I could not afford to stumble. I did not look back. My face was burning with mortification, and to be met with cool distance, it was only fitting. I had no right to expect anything else yet.

"I will see to my drills," I said too brightly, too fast. "They've pushed sparring hour again, and I'm still behind. And the Tameables. Whip-tail's eating again, which is rare after he sulks. And I need to recheck the leather bridle since Dreadclaw gnawed through it. And I should—"

The words tumbled out in a rush, unconvincing even to my own ears. I turned to escape before he could see the cracks in my composure.

His hand caught my wrist.

The distance between us vanished in a single breath as he stepped forward, blocking the doorway entirely. "Look at me," he said quietly.

Before I could react, his fingers were at my chin, tilting my face up until I had no choice but to meet his gaze.

I did look. And he looked, truly looked, as if the rest of the world had vanished behind his eyes. Whatever faint curve had tugged at his lips faded slowly, drawn into something heavier. His thumb brushed the line of my jaw.

"Who told you that you weren't allowed to *stay*?" he murmured.

The words were too gentle to be imagined. But still, I blinked, wondering if I'd heard them right. I fidgeted under his gaze, unsure whether it was meant for me at all, or if I'd already drowned in my own illusions. Every bit of my hope had folded itself small and quiet since the moment I saw Lorenza slipping into his bed.

Still not convinced, I took a step back, just an inch, but he caught my hand before I could finish the motion. A low curse escaped him, barely audible.

"Mirabelle." His voice carried warning. His gaze had already fallen to my fingers. I tried to pull away, but he didn't let me.

His grip shifted as he took my hand fully in his and turned it over. The raw abrasions across my knuckles and fingertips were impossible to ignore. Some already drying in cracked crescents of black. Some still on the verge of bleeding.

His molars clenched so hard I could hear it. "Why didn't you put on the gloves?"

I stared at our joined hands, and the answer came fast and loud in my head. *Because I wanted to bleed.* But all I managed was a quiet "I will, next time."

His gaze flicked up to meet mine. "If you don't care enough to protect your hands," he said quietly, "there won't be another next time after that."

"I wasn't—" I tried, but the words didn't come. Shame sealed the rest in my throat. For what I had done to myself. I knew how pitiful it was to seek pain rather than face things with courage. But I had, and the cowardice of it hollowed me out until I felt both weak and hopeless.

He released a breath, still holding my hands gently. "You will come with me to the infirmary."

"No. No, I'll go myself," I said quickly. "You're the one who needs—"

"I said, I will take you," he cut in, soft but final.

I blinked. "I was just...checking in. I didn't mean to interrupt you."

He didn't argue. Just looked at me for a long moment. Then, quietly, "Have you eaten?"

"I will," I murmured. "I was going to—"

"Sit." He stepped back and pointed wordlessly to the edge of the bed.

I hesitated. He didn't repeat it. Just turned and moved toward the outer door. The moment he disappeared from view, I sat down. My fingers throbbed with every heartbeat. My chest did too, but in a far different way.

CHAPTER 15

MIRABELLE

A Thrall pushed the tray cart carefully past the threshold. The scent of grilled meat, root vegetables, and baked citrus-glazed fruit filled the chamber like an ambush. He inclined his head and left without a word, pulling the door shut behind him.

"The healer will come after we have finished this," he stated, turning back to the cart and lifting the domed lids one by one.

"Again, this is really unnecessary. I was only checking," I protested, my voice weaker than the first time, my gaze fixed on the staggering amount of food.

"Enough of the pretenses, Mirabelle." His tone was flat, even, too even. "We both know you are well past the point of etiquette with me."

I shut my mouth. *Well, wasn't that familiar.*

He didn't look at me as he grabbed a chair from his massive oak desk and turned it sideways before sitting, close enough that his knees brushed mine where I sat on the edge of his bed. The food trays clicked as he unlocked its remaining seals. Steam curled around the rim, rich and scented with clove, and something faintly sweet.

The spread was excessive. Glazed lamb haunch, seared stag marrow layered with sliced red fig, spiced root soup, fire-grilled strips of river fish wrapped in vine-leaf and pressed with crushed limeberries. Nestled between them were delicate crescent breads, still warm, and a bowl of pale fruit-glass segments, a rare frostvine melon that shimmered like citrine. And of course, a carafe of some dark, bitter tonic Royals drank with their meals to prove they were actually enjoying it.

He picked up the cutlery, carved a piece from the haunch, and held it toward me.

I stared at it. "I can feed myself," I murmured.

His eyes snapped to mine. "Tell me how you plan to manage that with those fingers." He exhaled. "Behave like an adult who values their own well-being, and maybe I will let you."

I am one, I wanted to snap at him. Already he treated me like some reluctant child, his brand of care a cage in itself. If he kept on this way, I would never win back the ground we had lost, never drag him into the Realm of partners, where I meant for us to stand.

Before I could retort, he pressed the fork gently but insistently against my mouth. "Open."

I opened my lips, more from surprise than surrender. The moment the meat touched my tongue, I hated how my stomach betrayed me. The flavor was incredibly rich, buttery, melting on my tongue. He watched me swallow, then turned back to the platter.

He carved a much larger bite for himself with the same cutlery, devoured it in two swift motions, then returned to slicing mine smaller. This time he paired it with a sliver of fig and a bit of crisped greens.

"Sharing cutlery now?" I couldn't help but remark, the intimacy of the act curling warmly in my chest even as I tried to sound flippant. "That's a bold breach of custom, Sovereign. Thralls might talk."

He didn't look up from his task. "Let them. I have already

broken enough rules for your... For what I deemed necessary." His voice was a low rumble. "And I have never cared about talks unless I could use it."

"Is that what you do?" I asked, tilting my head. "Use everything?"

"I could be assessing the advantage of every moment," he said, offering the next bite. "Even this one."

That stung a little, but I pushed. "And what's the tactical assessment of feeding me fig and lamb while looking like that?"

He finally lifted his eyes to mine. "Like what?"

Ah, brilliant. Just had to open that particular door, didn't you? "Like...you just walked out of a healer's trance and decided to...er... hold court shirtless." The words tumbled out in a rush. "It's... distracting."

A faint smile touched his lips before he sobered and shook his head, as if clearing his head. "The only relevant matter here is that you eat less when you are flustered. Now, finish this."

The next few minutes passed in awkward silence, filled only with the soft scrape of metal and the clink of crockery. I leaned slightly against his huge bedframe, watching him move as he cut. The gashes across his side had mostly sealed. It was better than when I'd barged in; his body was a testament to preternatural healing.

And his skin...was looking incredible now, the water-droplets long gone, leaving just a faint sheen and the defined landscape of strength. I was feeling a lot of things that shouldn't come to you when you visit an injured man. But the way his shoulders flexed as he cut was pulling my thoughts into a territory that was decidedly not about convalescence.

"Your drills with Ophira," he said at last. "How are they going?"

I blinked out of my own treasonous thoughts. "Oh, that. I'm getting better. I don't fall like the training dummies anymore. Not...much."

"Good." He offered me a sip of frost ale from his tumbler. When I reached for it, he made a soft *tch* sound and held it to my lips. I took a small sip. The cool liquid paired well with the warmth of food.

"You scared me," I murmured, after a moment.

He didn't respond right away, his movements stilling for a fraction of a second. Then, quietly: "Why?"

I stared at my hands. "I heard others were closer. That others could have reached the boy too. You could've—"

"He ran straight into the arc of the shatter. I was closer." His tone was matter-of-fact and final.

I shook my head, frustration and fear for him warring inside me. "You're the Sovereign."

He finally looked at me. "I am a man," he corrected. "And I had to choose. So I chose."

I could only stare, struck by the simplicity of it. He slid another bite toward me. Only then did I notice how he offered me again and again the morsels and spiced root soup I devoured with a sigh. The ones I wasn't much enjoying, he consumed himself.

The awareness of it melted the pain I held deep inside, just a bit. Maybe a lot. And it placed a new ache there, one with a softer meaning.

Something shifted after that. I don't know when it happened. Somewhere between the root soup and the fruit tart, the conversation grew easier. Laughter came easier to me. I caught him watching me when I smiled, and every so often, his mouth would slightly twitch, or his eyes would crinkle at the corners. It wasn't much, but I counted every crack in the Sovereign marble of him like they were stars in a chart I could finally read.

I found myself telling him about the petty squabbles in the Royal Chambers, an old Dorm story about a spoiled washing salts that turned Amara's hair bright blue, even a silly tale from Etheris he'd already heard before. He listened to everything, like he did the first time. Eyes half-lidded and focused only on me.

He shared bits and pieces when I nudged, offering small,

polished fragments of his own past I already knew about. And at some point, he started speaking more freely, a story flowing out of him, only to stop abruptly as if he'd crossed an invisible line. But I knew him. I knew how his mind worked, so I never pushed him past his limits because I knew him by my heart.

He stopped feeding me the moment he sensed my reluctance, reading my fullness as clearly as if I had spoken it. Our conversation softened until it became just the hush of words between breaths. The last bite disappeared from the platter, and for a moment we simply sat there, the silence between us no longer awkward, just full.

Then he stood, set the tray aside, pulled the chair back beneath the desk, and glanced toward the door.

"A healer will be here soon," he said, brushing his hands together as if that closed the moment completely. "Wait here until then."

I blinked. "You're going?"

"I have council," he said simply, already reaching for his cloak.

"But you're still not fully recovered!" I stopped myself. His side was better, yes, but not fully. I could still see the edge of the wound peeking beneath the healed parts. My eyes dropped to it instinctively. "Yes, you're not fully recovered."

He didn't even glance at the fading marks on his torso as he pulled on his boots. "If a few wounds are enough to stop me from my duties, then the Sovereign of Atlassian is weaker than our enemies believe."

The words were flat, devoid of arrogance. *There he is again*, I thought, a familiar sorrow settling in my chest. He was always like this. It was his father's doing.

Alaric the unbending had forged his son in a crucible of impossible expectations, where any sign of frailty was a failure of the bloodline. We had seldom seen the old Sovereign outside his private wing since Damien's coronation, but his ghost was a permanent resident in his space, in the set of Damien's shoulders.

He pulled the cloak around himself, just the dark black of

Atlassian royal weave, draped against his bare chest, no tunic beneath.

I opened my mouth, a stupid question forming...but Damien was already halfway to the door, booted and cloaked, the bare lines of his chest barely concealed by the royal fabric trailing at his sides.

He paused, hand resting lightly on the carved wood.

"You can rest here until the healer comes," he said over his shoulder, not turning back.

The question left my lips before I could cage it. "Did Lorenza sleep here?"

He stilled. For a heartbeat, the only sound was the faint crackle of the hearth. Then he turned his head just enough that I could see the sharp line of his jaw, the slight frown.

"No."

Emboldened by his answer, or perhaps made reckless by the remnants of fear, I pressed further, the words barely a whisper. "Has she ever?"

This time, he turned fully. His gaze was not angry, but intense, pinning me to the spot. He looked at me as if he was seeing the fragile, jealous thing I was trying so hard to hide.

"No."

Then he was gone, the door closing softly behind him, leaving me alone in the warmth of his chambers with the scent of him on the air.

NEXT MORNING, I woke drenched in my chamber.

Not in sweat, but in a slick, unfamiliar heat between my legs that had nothing to do with dreams. My sleep had been a black, dreamless void. Yet I'd woken with my heart beating a frantic, off-rhythm against my ribs, my skin too tight, and this...this dampness.

It had been days since I'd left Damien's chambers. The distance was intentional, a gift of air for him. But truthfully, I needed it too —my days and some nights were a blur of drills, setting formations with the Tameables, and the draining effort to get out of my shell and be present among others. There simply weren't enough hours to manage my own duties, let alone seek him out with my silly excuses.

I drank water, my hand trembling around the cup. Something was wrong. The air in my chamber felt suffocating.

And now I needed... *Stars,* I needed Damien. The urge I was feeling was a physical pull, a hook lodged deep in my gut, reeling me toward him. But I couldn't. He'd given me pieces of himself, and the last thing I wanted was to seem like a clinging vine.

So I needed to move, to feel the cool, damp stones of the Hold against my palms, to lose myself in the grounding presence of the Tameables.

Or...

I didn't even know what would cure this damning urge. I knew about Bloomwake. The time, every few fortnights, when a Bonded woman's body decided it was time to mate, and the only cure, whether offspring were the intent or not, was the proximity of her Etern. A cruel joke. My body was screaming for a man who, in his mind, saw me as some stray needing extra attention.

Pulling on a simple fitted tunic and trousers, I slipped from my chamber. The need was making me jittery and hypersensitive to every brush of fabric. I nearly collided with Lyria, Callen, and a few other Royals in the corridor. Their laughter felt too loud.

"Mira!" Lyria called.

I forced a tight smile, giving a quick wave. "Just...heading to the Hold." I tried to scoot past, but Callen fell into step beside me.

"You alright? You look flushed." His usual grin was tempered with genuine concern.

"I'm fine," I bit out in a sharp tone. I could feel a fresh, treacherous wave of heat pooling low in my belly. "Just tired."

"You sure? You're walking funny."

"I am fine, Callen." I needed him to leave. Now. The scent of his leathers, the sound of his voice—it was all too much.

He held up his hands in surrender. "Alright, alright. Get some rest, then." He reached out to ruffle my hair in a familiar, friendly gesture.

His fingers grazed my scalp and a jolt shot straight down my spine. I barely bit back a moan, my knees buckling slightly. I forced myself forward, my face burning with a mortification that had nothing to do with his touch and everything to do with my body's violent, unwanted reaction to it.

What in the Abyss was wrong with me?

I rushed forward, and turned a corner, seeking the sanctuary of the Hold's entrance, and there he was. Damien. Standing with Rowane, Nathan, Lorenza, and the new warrior from Zarkon—Arthur. They all were deep in some discussion.

The sight of him was a relief so acute it was painful. My treacherous mind didn't just want his proximity; it supplied a flood of vivid, lyrical filth. I wanted to feel the hard planes of his chest against my back, his teeth on my shoulder, his hands pinning my wrists, his low voice murmuring promises in the dark as he moved inside me—

I shook my head, trying to clear it. Just being near him, or hearing him, would have to be enough. I lingered by a pillar, waiting for their meeting to end. But when Damien finished his exchanges, instead of heading toward the palace or the Hold as I'd expected, he turned to the upper corridor leading to the war council chambers with Nathan and Rowane at his side.

My feet moved before my mind could reason. But as I slipped into the passage, a figure glided smoothly into my path, barring the way.

"And where do you think you're going?" Lorenza asked, her tone light but her eyes sharp.

"It's important," I managed, my gaze still fixed on Damien's disappearing back.

"Important?" she echoed, her head tilting. "What could be so urgent that it cannot wait for a more appropriate time?"

"It's... He would understand," I managed, hating the vague answer.

"Mirabelle," she said, her voice dropping to an exasperated sigh. "You look...unwell. So flushed. And the way you were watching them... It's giving *me* embarrassment."

My cheeks burned. My eyes flicked involuntarily toward the Zarkon warrior standing nearby, who was watching our exchange with open curiosity. Lorenza glanced his way and then back to me, a small smile biding time. "Just try to contain yourself. It's a bit undignified for the rest of us."

The weight of his gaze, combined with Lorenza's venom, was too much. My pride crumbled. I couldn't do this here, in this state. I turned to go, wanting only to escape. But in my haste and distress, my foot caught on the edge of a step. I stumbled forward with a gasp.

A strong hand shot out, grabbing my elbow to steady me. It was the Zarkon warrior. The touch was impersonal, but the impact jarred through my oversensitive body, a spark on tinder. A choked, half-moan escaped my lips before I could stifle it.

I wrenched my arm back as if scalded, mortified beyond words. I didn't even dare look at his face. Heat flooded my cheeks, fury at Lorenza, shame at my own reaction. "I—I am sorry," I mumbled to the ground.

"Don't mind her. She's just a bit overly responsive to any hot-blooded male. It's how Dorm-raised commoners are sometimes." Lorenza's voice was light, as if she were discussing the draperies, not dissecting a person's worth.

I ground my jaw hard and looked straight into her face. "You seem deeply invested in the *responsiveness* of commoners for an Heiress, Lorenza." I tilted my head slightly. "Is it the coldness of your own blood that fails to hold attention, or are you simply fascinated by a heat you cannot imitate?"

Her entire face went rigid. A flush crept up her neck, staining the tips of her ears crimson. "I—"

I did not stay to hear it. I turned and walked away before my composure could fracture again. I did not look back.

I kept walking until I reached my chamber. The door slammed behind me. I curled into a tight ball on my bed, the physical need a throbbing ache beneath the emotional devastation. I ignored it, forcing my eyes shut against a sleep that would not come.

CHAPTER 16
DAMIEN

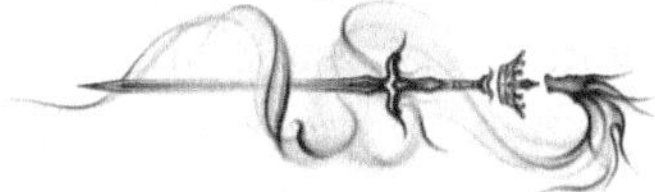

The clash of steel was a language I understood better than courtly tongues. Elsha and Royce did not circle like common recruits. They moved as one, an extension of shared purpose. Elsha's blade was a silver flash, high and direct, while Royce's came low and sweeping, a scythe of searing flame meant to cripple.

I flowed backward, letting Royce's overextended lunge carry him past me as I pivoted on my heel. The heat of Elsha's fire kissed my calf as I twisted away. My own blade came up to deflect Elsha's follow-up thrust, guiding it directly into the path of Royce's next arc.

Steel shrieked against enchanted fire. They recoiled, their rhythm broken for a single, vital second. It was all the opening required. I drove into the space between them. My elbow found Royce's ribs, a muffled crack of armor as my foot hooked behind Elsha's knee. I did not wait to see them fall. The flat of my blade snapped against Elsha's wrist, numbing her grip. A reverse strike caught Royce across the temple as he stumbled, not hard enough to fracture, just enough to daze.

Silence, then the clatter of a dropped sword.

"Your synchronization is your greatest strength," I said, my voice cutting the quiet. "And your most predictable weakness. You rely on it always."

Around us the vast courtyard thundered with shouts, grunts, the cadence of two hundred and more bodies driven to their limits.

I walked toward Rowane, who stood at the edge of the field, the din of combat fading into a backdrop. My skin was warm, muscles humming with the pleasant fatigue of exertion. Reaching his side, I took the proffered waterskin and drank deeply, my gaze sweeping over the sprawling training field.

Pairs and trios drilled across the stone expanse. I saw Callen moving against two opponents, his style all deceptive ease and sudden strikes. Lorenza was a whirlwind of controlled prowess, her movements ordered and brutal.

She had finally settled in well among the Royals and her cohort, much to my relief. She used to demand more of my time than was reasonable, and I had found it difficult to refuse her since she was here as our guest from another Clan. Now, she had found her footing with them, having adapted as I intentionally withdrew my oversight.

"Reports regarding your muse," Rowane murmured low, sliding parchment into my hand.

I gave him a look. He coughed. "I mean, reports of your Tamer. Your very promising, stubborn Tamer."

My eyes found Mirabelle amidst the fray. She was paired with a legionnaire twice her size, trading blows with tenacity that drew the eye whether one wished it or not. Her stance was still raw, her guard too high, but there was a new ferocity in the way she met his strikes and countered. She was learning.

I skimmed the scrawled words:

The subject was abandoned at the doorstep at three weeks of age. She was subsequently raised by the residents as their own child, and the circumstances of her abandonment were concealed from the subject till their death. Records indicate that some form of aid was provided during the initial months following the abandonment.

Investigation is currently underway regarding the deaths of the aforementioned resident parents.

I folded the parchment once, twice, until it disappeared in my fist.

"You brought this to the sparring ground?" I asked.

"Where else?" His attention was already wandering to the healers waiting at the edge of the courtyard. He smoothed his cloak, squared his shoulders, and set out like a knight to conquest.

"Rowane," I said.

"Hm?"

"Versa is here to treat injuries."

"I'm aware."

"You don't have any."

A pause. "I might."

He then set off across the yard at a pace that was carefully not hurrying. My gaze drifted over the training grounds, warriors falling out of line, correcting, trying again.

"Ever the observer," came a voice beside me. Lorenza moved to stand at my shoulder, her gaze drifting over the yard. "Now you seem to prefer studying them to sparring with them."

"Both have their place."

Her gaze flicked once toward the grounds, warriors still straining beneath blades. "Very well. From my understanding, the Realms will fully align in about a fortnight?"

I gave a single nod.

Lorenza continued, her voice curious. "Only then will we know the true pattern of this Dissonance. But we'll have three nights of battle, regardless. The first is for the Tameables. The second, for Aether only. The third..." She let the pause stretch, gaze unwavering. "The final battle. No Aether or Tameables. Only weapons and will."

"Yes," I said. "Still unclear? I thought you would have heard this since childhood."

"No. Why would I?" She shrugged. "It seems we were raised

differently. I have two brothers to handle such things. And this alliance wasn't a planned one."

"In that case, if you have questions, always ask them."

"Oh, I will," she said with a smile.

Her eyes slid across the sparring grounds in a quick, dismissive flicker. "So, the first night is for the Tamer. Though it seems your chosen one is currently trying not to expire on her feet."

My gaze was drawn to where Mirabelle struggled now against Ophira. She was near her limit, movements sluggish, shoulders heavy with fatigue. Dirt streaked her face. Yet she pressed on, deflecting a strike that should have felled her. An instinctive urge surged in me to tear the blade from her hand, lift her out of the ring, and see her fed, bathed, and sleeping in warmth beneath furs where distress could not touch her.

But the worst part wasn't the urge to protect her. It was everything else I wanted. And that's exactly why I never volunteered to train her. I made my hands fold in a conscious act of restraint.

"Damien." Lorenza's touch was light against the leather of my sleeve. "Spar with me. You haven't made time for it lately. Now that you are here, you have no excuse."

"You would do better focusing on the second night of Annihilation Trials," I said. "We will need your Aether then. The opposition might field five distinct Aethers if our worst calculations hold. We will have only three. The balance will already be against us."

"All the more reason to know how I fight without it." Her smile was faint. "Indulge me. Consider it a test. Let us see how I fare without Aether."

I studied her for a moment, then gave her a curt nod even though her reasoning made no sense.

We crossed to an open space and she drew her blade with confidence. The first few passes were clean. Her reflexes were good. She read the rhythm of my strikes faster than most. But that strength was her failing because of reliance on speed over power, a tendency to over-commit to the offensive, leaving her centerline vulnerable.

I deflected a thrust aimed at my throat, my blade sliding along hers with a shriek of metal. "You pivot on your back foot," I said, my voice loud amidst the clash. "It steals power from your swing. Plant and drive."

She adjusted, her next attack carrying more force. I met it, our blades locking. "Better."

We broke apart, circling. She feinted left and swept low, aiming for my legs. I sidestepped, using the flat of my blade to tap her exposed shoulder. "Predictable. Vary your rhythm."

She launched a furious series of attacks, each one met and turned aside. I saw the slight drop of her guard as she recovered from a wide slash. I stepped inside her reach, my free hand striking her wrist in a numbing blow. Her practice sword clattered to the stones.

The match should have ended there. But shadows coalesced around her fallen hand, dark, serpentine tendrils of Aether that snapped toward me like living whips. She had cheated.

I dropped my own sword. A blade was useless against this.

The first shadow snake struck. I pivoted, letting it hiss past my face. The second came for my legs, and I dropped into a roll, coming up inside her guard. She gasped, the shadows recoiling around her. I seized her wrist before the Aether could fully form, twisting her arm behind her back in one fluid motion. The shadows dissipated into nothingness as her concentration broke.

"The rules were clear," I stated, my voice flat.

I released her. She stumbled forward, turning to face me, her chest heaving. A slow smile touched her lips, and she took a step closer, one hand coming up as if to brush dust from my tunic, a gesture far too intimate for the sparring grounds.

I caught her wrist before her fingers could make contact. "Don't."

Her smile didn't falter, but it grew more pointed. "Is there a rule against that as well, my Liege?"

"I do not have time to waste here, Lorenza. You know this very well," I said, my voice low and harsh. "And if I have boundaries, you will learn to respect them. In every single aspect."

I let her hand drop.

"Focus on the second night," I said, turning to retrieve my cloak from the flagstones. "You know why your strength is best reserved for it. Cease deviating from what is required."

She rubbed her wrist with exaggerated effort and fixed me with a smirk, though my grip had been light, meant only to keep her from touching me. "Come on, that was a bit of fun."

"Did I look like I was enjoying myself?" I asked, sheathing my blade as I turned to leave.

She fell into step beside me, her breath still labored. "I find I am quite fatigued, regardless."

We walked several paces in silence before she spoke again, her tone shifting to one of thoughtful consideration. "Ah, I have a suggestion. I know it is not my place to tell this, but...I believe it would be wise to assign Whip-tail to the Tamer for the first night of Dissonance."

I glanced at her, intrigued despite myself. "Why would you think that?"

"No one expects him to anchor a field," she began, her words measured. "He is grounding. And yes, he possesses healing ability, but his true gift is absorption. Other Tameables lose control under the pressure of battle. Their Tethers could snap under the strain of their own fury. He may not be that aggressive, but he keeps the others standing."

I stopped walking. It was unorthodox, but sound. "That is an impressive suggestion. I will inform Mirabelle of the adjustment."

"Oh, there is no need," she said with a dismissive wave of her hand. "I have already mentioned it to her. She was initially resistant, but I managed to convince her. You know how she can be a bit possessive over everything."

She let out a light, understanding sigh. "You already know she did not like my presence the other day when I attempted to assist her." She paused. "But it is perfectly understandable. After all, she is new to all this, is she not? It must be overwhelming, coming from the Dorms to this—"

I cut her off before she could continue, my voice devoid of interest in her character assessment. "If she believes it is a sound tactic, it will be implemented." Then I met her gaze, ensuring my sincerity was clear. She shouldn't be discouraged from offering valuable insight. "Your suggestion is excellent. Offer those to her directly. If she proves difficult, bring it to me, and I will see that she hears it. But the final authority on all matters concerning the Tameables belongs to the Tamer."

Lorenza's smile tightened almost imperceptibly, but she inclined her head in acknowledgment. "Of course."

We finished the walk to the palace in silence. Daylight was fading, and the council I had postponed for training was still waiting.

CHAPTER 17

MIRABELLE

Days had begun to bleed into one another, marked only by the bruises along my arms and the scars the Tameables left across the outer fields.

I was nearly over cringing at my own foolishness. Following a Sovereign like that, driven by unthinking instinct... What had I even hoped to accomplish? Even the thought was mortifying. So I decided it never happened just after I had woken up from that lust-blurred haze.

What a stellar first experience. It felt like the Realm whispered in my ears: *Here's your first Bloom. Now go make a spectacle of yourself.*

The only thing I took from the encounter was a clear, clean read on Lorenza. She was the kind of woman who knew how to be vicious without trying too hard. And she seemed to hold a special grudge just for me—as if she could see right through my eyes and spot the half-formed plot to get Damien back.

Stars, I hated her for trying to humiliate me. And I hated that I wasn't the least bit sorry for hating her.

But this morning I didn't have room for any of it, because Dreadclaw and NyxRathis were fifteen feet apart and communicating entirely through hostile posture, and Elsha was still on the ground from the last attempt, and we had only countable days left.

For days, I woke at each dawn and swore I would keep all of them from tearing each other apart. Each dusk I found myself grateful to have survived another day with my bones still intact. Slowly, so slowly it felt like wringing blood from stone, I had brought them to the brink of tolerance. *Nearly.*

Now they stood in an arc around us. Five Tameables arrayed like living storms.

Dreadclaw's tendrils curled and uncurled in slow motion, coiling near NyxRathis, despite Draven standing between them. Draven, a Tameable with all sharp wings and beak, carved invisible lines through the air with each agitated stretch. And above us, the Choral Swarm shimmered in constant flux, a humming halo of fractured light and darkness, forming half-shapes that dissolved before they ever became whole.

I had anchored myself beside Whip-tail because putting myself at NyxRathis's side would have bruised Dreadclaw's ego further, and the other way around would have been just as bad. I had no wish to be trampled between them, *again.*

Elsha and Tovelle had been paired with the two High-Fangs instead, and they stood like sacrificial offerings at the altar of my terrible decision. Both Royals eyed their charges with a suspicion so sharp I thought they might pierce scales with glares alone. I had warned them repeatedly that the pair only baited for sport. That they would not truly strike. But I could hardly fault the Royals for refusing to believe me. Who would look at the creatures' smoke and teeth, then say, yes, harmless fun?

Elsha assessed her Tameable, her expression still cautious. Before she could plan her ascent, Tovelle moved behind her, his hands firm on her waist.

"Up you go, my heart," he murmured, lifting her toward the mounting stone beside the beast. She planted a boot on the ledge and pushed off, pulling herself onto Dreadclaw's back with effortless strength.

As she found her footing, Tovelle reached up, his fingers brushing her ankle in a caress.

"Try not to fall for me up there," he said with a wink.

A small smile touched her lips even as she shook her head in exasperation.

"Rhane," I called. Rhane was on Dravan's back, arms crossed, watching the Celestia where Dravan often kept diving at nothing. "He's going to take off again. Brace your left foot before he rises, not after."

Rhane looked at me. "How do I know when he's about to rise?"

"His tail goes flat and his wing roots tighten. Half a second of warning." I watched Dravan. "There—left foot."

Rhane shifted his weight. Dravan shot upward. The Tether went taut and Rhane absorbed it without stumbling, knees bent, the force distributing through his legs instead of yanking him off his feet. He let out a short breath.

"Better," I said with a smile.

We were in the range outside the Hold. Cassian lounged a few paces outside the Aetherium boundary, boots crossed at the ankle, and gave me a low whistle. "Finish sooner, Mira, and join us."

"Don't mind him," Lyria called from where she sat at his side. "He wasn't invited. This was meant to be a girls' gathering, and he refuses to leave."

The words warmed my insides. Since the Crucis, I had avoided most of them, certain their silence meant resentment. But they all had only been busy. And now she had arranged an evening with her circle: five or six Royals, and she had invited me. I had never been asked to such a thing before, and the thought stirred half thrill, half dread in my mind. *What if they don't like me there?*

Cassian ignored her entirely. "If they tear each other apart, can we at least place wagers on who survives longest?" he asked, pointing at our Tameables.

"Don't encourage them," I hissed at him, just as Lyria snapped his name. His grin widened.

What a loud creature, NyxRathis' voice slithered into my Tether. *Does that one ever hush?*

I could silence him for you, Nyxa, Dreadclaw rumbled, his tendrils writhing through the grass. *If you cooperate.*

Silence yourself for me, then, NyxRathis snapped back, venom dripping from every word.

I started to speak. "Would you two please just—?"

But before I could finish, Dreadclaw brushed a tendril against NyxRathis's jaw, a touch too intimate. She recoiled, then struck, biting down hard.

I sighed. "Never mind."

Dreadclaw was always touching, lunging, or poking—or simply shoving his weight against whatever stood in his path. Physical provocation was his rude language.

I ignored them and raised my hand, willing the threads taut to all around me. *Forward. Together.*

They obeyed, at first.

Dreadclaw surged ahead, smoke striking outward. NyxRathis slid past like a river current, her crystalline wings splitting his darkness into ribbons. Dravan dove low, talons sparking off stone. Whip-tail lumbered behind, lifting me higher as I climbed onto his broad back. He rumbled like a furnace. Above us, the Swarm spiraled downward, weaving light into a lattice that tethered the field in pale glow.

For a heartbeat, it held. Rhythm thrummed through my veins.

Then it cracked. Dreadclaw pressed too far, NyxRathis flared in contempt, and the line broke. Elsha slipped from Dreadclaw's flank, and he barely flicked a tendril to notice. I rubbed my temple.

It took several moments for us to reset.

"Again," I said, as my hand rose. "Forward."

Dravan shot skyward, wings slicing the air, dragging poor Rhane stumbling behind him as the Tether snapped taut. The Swarm dissolved into a rolling wave of light, then collapsed into a lattice again, desperate to match pace. Whip-tail, meanwhile, had strayed off course, tail twitching, nose buried in a glittering insect, some strange firefly that had drifted too close.

"Whip-tail," I called in soft voice, with what patience I could muster, though my teeth were clenched. *How many times have I told you to ignore the little things?*

He turned back at once, but the shame in his great golden eyes made me exhale in exasperation. I went to scratch behind his ears, to soften the scold. He was always easiest to guide, but hardest to keep steady. If the Dissonance grounds swarmed with flies, rabbits, or stars themselves, we were doomed.

I almost laughed at the absurdity of it, but my breath caught instead. Damien had appeared from the palace gates, Rowane at his side, heads bent in low discussion. His attention wholly consumed by the report Rowane carried.

It had been two days since I'd seen him last, two days since he had vanished from the training yard with Lorenza in tow. She'd whispered to her companions that she could hardly keep her hands off him, and then she'd gone to him. Then they'd sparred together, hard. He threw aside his sword and seized her bare-handed, as though his self-control had shattered against her will.

He never once offered to train me. Not that I expected him to; a Sovereign doesn't train just anyone. And I wasn't skilled enough to spar with him, or any of the Legions, for that matter.

The memory of them still burned behind my eyes. I'd lasted only minutes watching their intense combat before driving myself so hard in my own match that I knocked Ophira to the ground, twice. Rage had made me faster than any training ever had.

It was impossible not to compare us from Damien's perspective. Lorenza, with her perfect braids and sophisticated outfits. And then there was me: hair in perpetual disarray, hands calloused from labor unfit for court and endless hours of archery. When I caught my reflection that day, I flushed with embarrassment, covered in mud and dirt from the countless times I'd hit the ground.

Why so gloomy, little one? NyxRathis murmured, her thought like cool water poured over flame.

I slammed my mental shields in place, forcing all those ridiculous thoughts into a dark corner. My will surged through the Tethers, an order. *Hold. Form.*

The Tameables snapped into line. Dreadclaw stilled his tendrils, and NyxRathis flowed into his shadow without a fight. Dravan's dive was a precise counterpoint to the Swarm's ascent. Whip-tail surged forward, steady as a wall. And for the first time, the five moved as a single body. It was the faint, nascent ghost of coordination. The rhythm moved through the Tether in something close to harmony—not perfect, nothing was close to perfect, but connected.

Cassian's voice came from afar. "Well, look at that, They *almost* look like they know what they're doing."

Lyria's voice followed. "Ignore him. You're doing brilliantly, Mira," she said. "We've never seen anyone align so many at once. And certainly not those two."

We held it as long as we could. Then Dreadclaw decided the session was over, which meant the session was over. I released the Tether before NyxRathis could make a point about it.

"Ooh, magnificent," Tovelle declared, spreading one arm. "A triumph of the collective will. Songs will be written."

Vannor looked at Rhane.

Rhane looked at Vannor.

"Two verses, maybe," Vannor said. "Three if the Swarm picks a shape and commits to it."

The rhythm of the Tether still thrummed in my veins. A brittle pride tightened in my chest. For so long, I had tried to flee the path laid before me. Now, I would learn its every groove and weight until I deserved the right to hold it.

WE REMEMBER *the night they made us forget, don't we?*

The words were scrawled across a slip of parchment, folded neatly in an envelope that had been slid beneath my chamber door. I hadn't noticed it until now. I stood frozen, my eyes scanning the same words for the umpteenth time.

This was the second one.

The Abyss. They had to mean the Abyss. What else could these words refer to? But I had no clue who would send this. Was it a warning or an offer of alliance?

If I could find this person, gain their trust, and learn what they knew, I might untangle the Abyss myself. I wouldn't need to slowly, painstakingly build Damien's trust until it was so absolute he would believe the unbelievable. The idea was laughable because I was Realms away from that. Right now, he treated me as though I were some long-lost little sister incapable of protecting herself—helpless, hopeless, and apparently unable to stop making moon-eyes at him.

I scowled at that thought, the parchment crumpling slightly in my grip. The more I lingered in that space, the more he would grow accustomed to it. The more he would accept it. I needed to find a way out of that cage before it closed around me.

What would it take to shatter that perception? Strip myself bare before him and demand he see the woman, not the ward? He'd never made me doubt myself before. But that was before the proximity of a woman who looked like she's carved from moonlight—

Stop.

Just stop, Bellebelle. She's a just a viper clad in pretty smiles and perfect dresses. *Oh, and with a Royal lineage. Who cares. Not me.*

So. A new plan.

Find the sender. Unravel the Abyss myself. Use that knowledge as my leverage and my power. I wouldn't need to make Damien fall for me again; I would unveil the truth. Then I could win Izmer to my side, after the Dissonance. *Hopefully* before Damien was bound to Lorenza.

The midday horn had already sounded. I was a bit late for my daily trainings with Ophira. I'd slept in, thanks to last night's girls gathering. I liked them, and I hope they liked me too, but the conversation still felt edged with politeness. We weren't uncomfortable. But we weren't quite at ease either. But we'd get there... eventually.

Now I moved to fold the envelop again and that's when I saw it. On the back, nearly invisible against the cream-colored parchment, was a pattern. Not random scribbling, but an intricate drawing. A series of interlocking lines and symbols that looked like a star chart. I shoved the note into the drawer beside my bed, burying it beneath a stack of linens. Later. I would study it later.

For now, there were only the drills to gain strength. So I ran.

CHAPTER 18
MIRABELLE

By the time I reached the Hold grounds, sweat dampened my collar. Elder Mavren was already there, staff in hand, his expression as severe as the black-veined walls that loomed behind him. His face a mask of sternness that seemed to defy his relatively young tenure as an Elder. I could not recall ever seeing the faintest hint of a smile upon his lips.

"Learn to respect the time of others, Tamer," he said without greeting. "We all have matters to attend to beyond coddling your development."

I breathed hard, the words rushing out. "Apologies, it won't happen again."

"See that it doesn't." He turned, motioning me into the ring.

Ophira's training was a brutal dance of exhaustion. She would drill me until my muscles screamed, then fight me until I was familiar with the taste of dirt. But Mavren was different. He gave me no drills, nor did he make me run laps.

He simply began to fight me—it was a dismantling. He moved with a wise man's economy of motion, yet every shift of his weight and every flick of his wrist sent me stumbling. He didn't strike to hurt, but to unbalance and to demonstrate his utter superiority. After the third time he used my own momentum to send me sprawling onto the hard floor, my pride started to sting more than my hip.

He looked down, unimpressed. "You have no clue what you are supposed to do in this type of fight, do you?" he asked. "I am wondering why Ophira hasn't started with this already. Are you still too weak to bear it?"

I really didn't want to scowl at him, but I did anyway while I took his offered hand. He hauled me up easily with a strength that surprised me. "The first night of Dissonance is not a brawl between Tameables. *You* will face things that do not fight with fists and feet. So we're going to rectify your inability to adapt."

He stepped back, and the air around him shimmered. A ball of roiling orange flame bloomed above his palm, casting dancing shadows across the lines of his face. "We begin with flames, of course. Later, we will use Glyphs to simulate the others. Now. Dodge."

He didn't throw it like a pitcher throws a ball. He flicked it. The fire shot toward me, a comet of heat and light. I yelped, throwing myself sideways. The heat seared the air where my head had been.

"Do not leap," he corrected. "You waste energy. Shift. Aether moves faster than bone and blood. You must be faster in thought."

Another flick. A second fireball, lower this time, aiming for my legs. I pivoted, feeling the heat brush against my trousers.

"Good. Now, counter."

"Counter? With what?" I panted between breaths.

"With whatever you have."

I had so little. A sliver of shadows. Enough to save my backside when I hit the mud-floor or keep my teeth where they belonged when the ground came up to meet me. Nothing like the torrents I'd seen others command. But I reached for it, pulling at the well-spring inside me. A faint shield of force flickered to life around me just as a third fireball left his hand.

The impact was staggering. It was a concussive blast of will against will. My shield dissolved like smoke, and the residual force threw me backward. I landed hard, the breath knocked from my lungs.

For a split second, as I fell, I saw a ripple of darkness—thick, protective shadows—surge from within me. Mavren didn't seem to notice. He was suddenly there, his grip firm on my arm as I struggled to sit up, disoriented and gasping.

"Stop," he commanded, his voice cutting through my panic. "You'll die if you rely on my protection," he said sharply, stepping in. His hand caught my other arm, a swift tap against the muscle. "Don't thrash like a girl dragged off a horse-cart. Use the force, not your panic."

I nodded.

We began again. Fire after fire. I grew quicker, less frantic. My shields held for longer. I learned to block, to deflect, to let the energy skitter away into the air. Exhaustion settled deep into my bones as a heavy weight. But we kept going. Each failed block, each searing near-miss, was a lesson etched in pain and rush.

He was strict, his corrections blunt and unforgiving. But he was also...present. His entire world had narrowed to this moment, to my form, to the flow of Aether between us. And slowly, painfully, I began to learn the language he was teaching—the language of actions and reactions.

⊷⊱◆⊰⊶

"Please. I can't," I finally gasped, my arms trembling, the taste of soot and exhaustion thick on my tongue.

Mavren didn't lower his hands. The faint shimmer of Aether around them didn't fade. "No," he said, his voice devoid of mercy. "The Trials will not stop because you are tired."

He continued. My motions grew sluggish, my shadows flickering and dying before they fully formed. He didn't summon another fireball. But in the space of a heartbeat, he closed the distance.

I tried to block, but I was too slow and spent. He lunged at me, body against mine, striking with force. I tried to match, to push, but my arms trembled with fatigue. His grip corrected me, again and again, even as my knees buckled.

I fell hard once, then again. A raw sting flared down my forearm, the trace of a burn still smoldering from earlier. He had pushed me to my limits. But even then, he'd been careful with his Aether. The marks were few, just a scatter of faint burns here and there.

And still he pressed.

There was a strange thrill in it. He wasn't sparing me, wasn't shielding me. He was showing me how to fight when strength was gone, when power failed. He caught my wrist, twisted me around, and pulled me back hard against his chest, one arm locking across my torso, the other pinning my arms. I was trapped, utterly and completely. I twisted, but he shifted with me, his voice low. "Don't struggle like prey," he said. "Feel the weight. Anchor your hips. This"—his hand shifted mine against his grip—"is where you take the advantage."

He was breathing heavily too. I could feel the steady, powerful beat of his heart against my back. "You see?" his voice was low. "Aether fails. Strength fails. But leverage does not." His lips were close enough that I could feel the shape of his words. "You must *always* have a second move."

I felt him smile, a faint curve of his mouth near my temple. It wasn't cruel. If anything, I think he was...pleased. And I smiled too, quietly, at what I'd earned. He was seriously hard to please.

"Again," he said in a low voice.

"Mavren, get your hands off her." Damien's harsh voice cut through the air from behind us. We both turned. He was already halfway across the training yard, his expression a mask of frozen fury.

Mavren never got the chance to let go. A whip-crack of Aether slammed into his side, wrenching him from me with brutal force. He flew backward several feet before landing in a heavy heap on the stone. I gasped, stumbling forward from the sudden absence of his hold. My shock rendered me mute.

The smell of scorched cloth and flesh bloomed in the air as he hissed in pain, rolling to quench the dark fire eating at his tunic.

Damien scanned me with the same dark look, before snapping back to Mavren, who was climbing to his feet, his skin already blistering.

"I—" Mavren began, his voice strained.

"She had reached her limit. Why were you still *on her*?" Damien said, his voice hard and frigid. "Where is Ophira?"

Mavren looked unruffled, though a frown marred his features. "Ophira had matters to attend to. I thought I could take over the Tamer's training. She was not yet versed in fighting Aethers. But she is a quick learner." He gestured to his smoldering tunic. "Why did you—?"

"He's right. I was learning," I said, finding my voice. It came out hoarse. "That was the best session I've had. It was good."

Damien's eyes flicked to me, and the ice in them made me flinch. "Was it?"

I...didn't know how to respond to that.

He looked back at Mavren. "A quick learner is not an invitation to keep your hands on her past the point of use." He closed the distance in one step and took him by the collar, not violently—worse than that, calmly—and looked him in the eyes. "You knew exactly what the final moments were. Don't insult me by explaining them."

"That's not fair. You're mistaken," I insisted, trying to step slightly in front of Mavren. "He was really *helping* me."

Damien's eyes hardened further. A faint, dangerous flicker passed across them. Whatever it was, I knew only that he did not like my defense of Mavren. Not one bit.

But Mavren wasn't responding. Not to me, not to the accusation, not to any of it. He stood with his collar in Damien's fist and said nothing, and that was the thing that made my certainty waver.

Damien released him. "Leave." The word final and absolute. "And stay away from her. For good."

Mavren inclined his head, a faint, unreadable look in his eyes, and walked away without a backward glance, leaving the scent of fire and burnt skin in his wake.

Damien's gaze, which had been fixed on Mavren, slid to me, and the disapproval in it was potent.

"Why did you hurt him? He was a great partner. I was getting good with him!"

Damien's stride didn't falter as he moved to pass me. "Oh yes? Were you enjoying *everything* he was doing?" The question was laced with a cynicism that felt entirely foreign coming from him.

I frowned, my own frustration mounting. "Not *enjoying,*" I snapped, falling into step beside him. "But I was improving. He showed me things no one else has." I really didn't understand why he was making this into something that it was not.

He looked down at me, and the unspoken frustration in his gaze was a wall I couldn't scale. "This is not a negotiation, Mirabelle." His tone sharpened. "Be ready on the West grounds tomorrow at dawn. You will train with the rest of the Royals. Glyphs. Multi-Aether drills. Enough of this solitary one-on-one."

I grabbed his arm. He stopped, which surprised me enough that I lost whatever I was about to say. He was too close, or I'd stopped leaving enough distance between us. One of the two.

"Then why can't *you* train me? If you're so particular about how it should be done, do it. Why does everyone else get to but not you?" The words came out more direct than I'd planned, but I kept going because there was no graceful way back from them now.

He turned fully to face me, and the intensity in his eyes stole my breath. "I don't for the same reason I just stopped Mavren," he said, each word measured. "But with me, it would be much, *much* worse."

I stared at him. "What does that mean?"

He looked at me for a long moment, as if trying to read something written just beneath my skin. I had the feeling he was deciding something about how much of what he was actually thinking to let me see.

"Follow me to the council halls," he said, his tone brooking no argument. "There will be discussion of the first night of the Dissonance." Then he turned to walk.

"Damien, wait—"

He paused, but didn't look back.

"I was learning, wasn't I?" I said quickly, words tumbling out before pride could stop them. "That's all that matters here."

I desperately wanted to get to the bottom of whatever this was. Because I was beginning to suspect he was feeling something dangerously close to jealousy, and if that proved true, I fully intended to savor it later, when I was alone.

He resumed walking without bothering to look. "It is not all that matters."

I hurried to catch up, my frustration giving me a reckless courage. "Then what does it mean?"

He didn't break stride. "It means you are never to be alone with him. Or let him—or anyone—*touch* you."

I stopped short. "He—what? No. You're not seriously implying..." I'd spent three hours with Mavren, and he hadn't laid a finger on me in *that* way.

Damien stopped and pinched the bridge of his nose, exhaling a long, weary breath as if summoning patience from a deep, empty well. "Not everything is as straightforward as you see it. And when someone who has seen more than you tells you something, you would do well to accept it."

I crossed my arms. "Elder Mavren has also *seen more*. He is older than you. So, obviously he has more experience."

The weary patience vanished, replaced by a look so intense it pinned me in place. He closed the distance between us in one stride, his hand came up to cup the side of my neck, his thumb tilting my chin up. "Never even utter his name again," he said, the words a low, dark vibration. "Do you understand me?"

"But Mav—"

His index finger pressed against my lips, silencing the rest. "Don't test my limits, Mirabelle. I do not bluff."

My mind summersaulted into a giddy, breathless whirl. The intensity in his eyes was primal, possessive, and not remotely *brotherly* like I dreaded. So I did the only thing I could think of—I bit down on the tip of his finger. And I heard his sharp, indrawn breath.

In the next heartbeat, I was spun, my back flush against his chest. One of his hands captured my wrist, pinning it behind my back in a gentle, inescapable lock.

"You're going to be the end of my patience." His voice was a rough murmur against my ear. "Was that your idea of following an order?"

I forced a tone of casual defiance, though I was certain he could feel my heart hammering against my ribs. "I was clarifying the boundaries of said order. You were vague."

His chest vibrated with a sound that was almost a growl. "You know you are playing with fire."

"I've always liked the heat of it," I said, tilting my head to the side.

His hold shifted, his lips brushing the shell of my ear. "What are you doing to me?" he breathed, the question raw, stripped of all its usual control.

A shiver ran down my spine. "I could ask you the same thing," I managed, my voice barely audible.

For a long moment, he didn't move. Then, slowly, his grip eased. I stepped out of his hold, turning to face him. His expression was ravaged—a mixture of frustration and conflict.

I smoothed my tunic, clinging to the last shred of my composure. "In case you've forgotten," I said, my voice miraculously steady, "we have a council to attend."

I didn't wait for a reply. I turned and walked down the corridor, projecting a confidence I didn't feel, desperate to outpace the wildfire he had just set blazing in my veins. Still, my inner self did a silent, victorious dance, the ghost of a smile playing on my lips.

CHAPTER 19
MIRABELLE

I finally stole a moment alone, locking my chamber door before smoothing the parchment out on the bed. A web of interlocking lines sprawled across the page, some curved like constellations, others sharp as cages. It seemed nothing more than idle scrawl, but the longer I studied, the more deliberate it became.

A single, dark dot stood stark and alone near the edge. The parchment around it was slightly discolored, as if stressed by repeated pressure right there. My eyes traced the sketch, catching the same awful motif again and again: a small, square structure crisscrossed with harsh lines. A prison. Replicated across the drawing. And surrounding it all, a larger, fenced border...

These were prisons? I didn't know the exact location of the Atlassian prison, only that it was sealed off from the outside world. But some of the vacant spaces around these structures didn't match what I knew. I counted them. Eight cells in total.

Aetherium Hold!

Then the fenced areas must be its extensions. And the surroundings almost matched. I folded the parchment, shoved it into my pocket, and slipped silently from my chamber.

The hour was late, the corridors empty. I followed the mental map to the spot on the rightmost edge of the Hold's wall, near the fence. It was just...walls. Ancient, seamless stones, scarred by weather and time.

Nothing.

I ran my hands over the cold surface, pushing, pressing, searching for a hidden trigger or a loose stone. I slid my palms across it. There was literally nothing there. No hidden door or secret lever. Just unyielding rocks.

Frustration curdled into doubt. Was this a joke?

I leaned my forehead against the cold stone and exhaled an irritated exhale. If I had the option to write back to the owner of that stupid letter and its even stupider drawing, it would have been: *To the artist of the era: Thank you for the map. I especially enjoyed the part where it led me to a wall. Though, next time, a simple "meet me behind the third dusty tapestry at midnight" would suffice. It would save me a great deal of awkward wall-groping.*

Giving up on riddles and stone walls, I turned my focus to the only thing that made sense: control. I summoned the five Tame-ables into the grounds, their vast shapes emerging from the Hold's gloom. No Royals this time. Just me and them. My new aim was simple and born of necessity. Stop trying to conduct the symphony with an entire audience watching.

I poured myself into the Tethers. With Dreadclaw, I didn't force, just showing him the outline of the shadow I needed. With NyxRathis, I opened a channel, inviting her flow rather than restraining it. To my astonishment, they listened to everything. Dreadclaw's shadows no longer smothered NyxRathis's glow; they framed it. Dravan's dives were a counterpoint to the Swarm's ethe-real weaving.

Bringing Whip-tail to a fight felt like bringing a spoon to a sword fight. But I knew the probability of him holding the line if the others were injured made him worth choosing over an offen-sive Tameable.

Now, they all moved with a fluid grace, their individual power no longer a cacophony but a chord. Within minutes I had drawn out three, even four patterns, weaving them through forms I thought impossible. And each time, they picked it up faster, as though beginning to understand what I wanted before I even shaped the thought. Only when that rhythm held did I call for the Royals.

This time, when they stepped in, Tameables didn't see the Royals as extensions of the existing design. They were in motion, already aligned. The Royals had no choice but to fall into step, their movements tentative at first, then growing bolder as they realized the beasts were not just cooperating, but obeying. They were learning to dance in the eye of it.

The broken rhythm was gone. In its place was a song of Aether, a symphony of shadow, light, and force.

***

I WALKED the dimming corridors of the Hold. I had detoured to visit the other Tameables, the ones not chosen for the Dissonance, just to offer a scratch behind the ears and offering treats.

As I turned to leave, the memory of the parchment itched at the back of my mind. That dark dot. The impenetrable wall. I'd been so certain the mark indicated the exterior. But what if the drawing wasn't of the grounds, but of the Hold itself? The drawing had shown cells and ground border. The Hold was full of both.

Instead of heading for the main entrance, I veered deeper into the Hold's belly, toward the rightmost edge of the structure. The corridors here were older and darker, the air thick with the scent of moss. I found the section that somewhat aligned with the dot on the map. It looked no different from any other—same ancient blocks. I ran my fingers over the stones, feeling for anything, at least a heat change.

Nothing. *Again.*

Disappointment began to simmer in me. I leaned my back against the cold stone in defeat. As I did, the toe of my boot scuffed against the base of the wall, kicking up a small cloud of dust.

Something glinted dully in the faint light. I crouched down, wiping away the grime with my hand.

There, set flush into the foundation stone, was a small, dark metal plate no larger than my thumbnail. It was etched with the same intricate, angular symbols from the parchment. It wasn't a handle or a keyhole. It was just...there.

Hesitantly, I pressed my thumb against it.

One.

Two.

Three.

Nothing happened.

I let out a sigh. Of course. Just another dead end.

But as I went to pull my hand away, a faint, almost imperceptible vibration hummed through the metal plate. A series of the etched symbols glowed with a soft blue light, one after another. There was a deep click that seemed to come from within the wall itself.

Then, without a sound, an entire section of the stone wall, a door I would have never detected, swung inward a few inches, revealing absolute darkness and a rush of cold, stale air that smelled of dust and forgotten things.

My heart hammered like a frantic drum in the overwhelming silence. *What if it closes behind me?*

The thought was a spike of pure panic. This wasn't a training drill or a fun endeavor, but a secret buried deep in stones that might lead me to my doom. Still, the pull of the unknown was stronger than my fear. I knew, with a certainty that settled in my bones, that I would forever regret not taking this path.

Steeling myself, I stepped across the threshold.

The moment I cleared the doorway, the heavy stone door swung shut behind me with a final thump that echoed in the blackness. The suffocating silence that followed made me regret my choice. I couldn't even see my own hand in front of my face.

My breath came in short, sharp gasps that sounded obscenely loud in the cramped space. I spun around, my hands flying to the door, patting frantically across the smooth, cold stones where the seam should be. No handle, no groove, no hint of an exit. It was just a seamless wall.

Dread began to seep into my veins. I was trapped. Buried alive in the guts of the Hold.

Breathe. Just breathe.

I forced myself to take a slow, deep breath, then another, leaning my forehead against the unforgiving stone. As my eyes adjusted to the absolute black, a faint, familiar glint caught my attention. There, set into the wall was another small, dark metal plate. The same etched symbols were just visible.

With trembling fingers, I pressed it.

The same soft blue light traced the symbols. The same deep click echoed, and the door swung silently open, flooding the space with the dim, blessed light of the Hold's corridor. I stumbled back out, sucking in a great gulp of familiar air, my legs shaking with relief. I stood there for a long moment, just breathing, the relief of ensuring my escape path washing over me.

But the tunnel still waited. The mystery was still unsolved.

Taking another steadying breath, I stepped back inside. This time, I watched as the door closed behind me, sealing me in once more. The fear was still there, and a tight knot in my stomach, but it was tempered by determination.

I turned my back to the door and faced the darkness. As my eyes adjusted further, I saw it wasn't absolute. A faint, phosphorescent moss clung to the walls of a narrow, ancient tunnel that sloped gently downward, providing just enough ghostly light to see by.

Gathering my courage, I began to walk forward into the heart of the secrets. The tunnel turned once, then opened to a dark space.

I found myself standing on a narrow stone balcony carved directly into the upper wall of a vast, circular chamber. Below me, arranged in a perfect circle, was a large table, its surface gleaming dully in the faint, sourceless glow that permeated the room. High-backed chairs carved from the same dark wood were pushed neatly beneath it. The air was deathly still and carried a metallic tang, like old blood.

Despite the ancient feel, everything was impeccably clean. There was no dust on the table, no cobwebs in the corners. It felt not abandoned, but preserved. Waiting for something.

My eyes, now fully adjusted to the gloom, scanned the chamber. In one shadowy corner, I spotted a narrow iron ladder bolted to the wall, descending from the end of my balcony down to the chamber floor. I moved to it. The metal was cold and gritty under my palms as I climbed down. The soft scuff of my boots against the rungs the only sound in the oppressive quiet.

I reached the floor and approached the table slowly, each step echoing faintly. I ran my fingers over the obsidian surface. It was smooth, icy cold, and perfectly clean.

Then I heard a footstep. It came from a dark archway on the other side of the chamber.

Then another.

Someone was here.

My heart seized. There was nowhere to hide. No other exit. To run for the ladder or back into the tunnel would only betray me with the sound of my flight. I dropped into a low crouch behind the nearest high-backed chair and crawled in halfway, pulling my knees to my chest, making myself as small as possible.

The heavy door to the chamber groaned open. A glow of flickering torchlight cut through the darkness, widening as the door swung inward. A figure stepped into the room, the flame casting long, dancing shadows that writhed across the walls like specters. The door closed with a soft, definitive thud.

CHAPTER 20
MIRABELLE

I didn't dare breathe. The air in my lungs burned, but even the smallest sound felt like a death sentence. The figure crossed into the chamber, light spreading close when he walked. An Elder, perhaps, or a Sage.

He stopped directly opposite my hiding spot. Then his hand appeared under the table, reaching toward me. I flinched and clamped both palms over my mouth, stifling the scream that clawed at my throat. But his fingers didn't grab me. Instead, they found a hidden latch and I suppressed a sigh of relief.

A soft click echoed in the tense silence. His hand withdrew, and a concealed drawer slid smoothly open, one I never would have noticed on my own. Then the sound of shuffling parchment filled the tense silence. He was so close I could smell the faint scent of wool of his clothes. After a moment, he closed the drawer, the lock engaging with a final-sounding snick.

The footsteps retreated, the light faded, and the hidden door grated shut, plunging me back into the ringing silence. I waited another stretch of heartbeats, and when I was certain he was gone, I slowly, carefully crawled out.

My hands still shook as I felt under the table, finding the hidden catch he'd used. I pressed it. The drawer slid open silently.

In the deep gloom, its contents were veiled in shadow, visible only by the faintest ambient glow. One side was stacked neatly with parchments and ledgers. The other held an assortment of objects: smooth, translucent stones that seemed to drink the faint light, and a silver dagger in a leather sheath. And beneath them all, my fingers brushed cold metal—a key. I gently lifted it, careful not to disturb anything else. It was heavy in my palm.

I froze. It was *the* key.

The very one I had used to open the sigil, thinking it was for the portals to Etheris, the act that had unleashed the Untameable breaches and nearly got me killed. The key that had framed me.

I placed it back exactly as I had found it, my mind reeling. This key was useless to me now as it was, but its presence meant something. Something hidden and worth risking my life for.

So I kept searching.

I turned my attention to the parchments. I lifted the top one. Underneath lay a heavy, leather-bound book. I carefully opened it. The pages were completely blank. Frowning, I fanned the pages lightly. Nothing.

But then my attention shifted to the bottom parchment: days. Written in faint ink, set in repeating cycles of eight. Past days carefully tallied, the rest blacked out as though they were yet to come. The scribblings from past days were too ambiguous to understand, layered in symbols that refused to give up their meaning.

Carefully, I returned everything to its precise order, closed the hidden drawer, and locked it. My gut screamed at me to leave, a warning that had been ringing since the moment I slipped inside. The longer I stayed, the heavier the feeling became. It would be better to wait for another anonymous envelope to slip into my mailbox, to make sense of why they had shown me this hidden chamber.

I stumbled back the way I had come, up the ladder, through the narrow tunnel, my hand pressing the hidden plate until the stone door grated open. Cold, pale light from the Hold spilled over me.

The entrance sealed shut behind me as though it had never been there at all.

Fear was a familiar comfort, and hope felt like a trap. A part of me remained deeply, painfully skeptical. But they had the key. And I had a secret. And these days, I was *very* good with secrets.

I HAD BOOKED a formal appointment with the Sovereign of Atlassian to ask him to move my friend to palace premises. Standing outside the throne hall, I had the good sense to recognize how this sounded. I had done it anyway.

At last, the far doors opened. A cluster of Elders swept out, their robes whispering across the marble, followed by several Sages and a handful of Majors I didn't recognize. Perhaps from distant cities, their Supremes or Commanders.

The guard at the front door inclined his head. "You may enter."

I entered, my boots echoing against the polished marble floor. My eyes went immediately, inevitably, to the dais.

To our Sovereign.

He sat crowned today, the silver wrought with obsidian gems stark against the dark waves of his hair. His attire was all black as well. Deep, rich fabric edged in subtle silver embroidery, cut to sharpen the broad lines of his frame. It should have been severe, but the effect was...mouthwatering. Regal, untouchable, and so devastatingly handsome I forgot how to breathe.

And stars above, it was the most intimidatingly attractive thing I had ever seen.

His eyes found me at once, and he motioned to the guards and sent them slipping silently out. He began to rise.

"Don't," I said. My voice carried farther than I intended in the empty hall.

He paused, settling back onto the throne, his expression one of open intrigue.

"I need you to stay like that," I said. "Please. Just—for a few moments."

"Like this." He said it flatly, but there was curiosity behind it.

"Formal. I need you to be formal."

He looked at me for a moment. "I am always formal, Mirabelle."

"You know what I mean."

"I am not sure I do." He interlaced his hands in his lap with the deliberateness of a man deciding to find out where this was going. "Enlighten me."

Across the floor, stopping at what I hoped was the correct distance from the dais—far enough to look like I knew what I was doing, close enough to be heard without raising my voice.

"I've never presented a formal petition before," I said. "And I have a request that I think deserves the full"—I gestured vaguely at the hall, the throne, the general architecture of Sovereign authority—"weight of the occasion."

He was quiet for a moment.

"You booked a council appointment"—he leaned forward slightly, a ghost of a smile playing on his lips—"to experience the formal petition process."

"I had a real request."

"You could have sent a note."

"Notes don't have the same...gravitas."

"Very well," he said, and the shift in his posture was subtle but complete—the already straight spine finding its full authority. "Present your request."

I took a steadying breath. "Your Majesty," I began, my attempt at a formal tone coming out horribly stilted, "I am here to petition for the...formal relocation of one Amara—currently residing in Dorm Seven—to the palace quarters." I paused and added, "Formally."

"State your reasoning."

"She's—" I'd had an argument prepared. It was better than what came out. "She's exceptionally capable."

"In what regard?"

"Several."

"Name them."

"She's—" I thought of Amara. Loyal to a fault, warmer than anyone I'd met here. None of that was going to land well as formal testimony. "She has extensive knowledge of domestic operations," I said.

"As do the Thralls. As do the Royals assigned to estate management." He tilted his head, the picture of judicial attention. "What distinguishes her?"

"She is kind," I said desperately. "And loyal. She would serve better here than in a Dorm."

We went back and forth like this, him poking logical holes in my reasonings that sounded flimsier here in his presence than they had in my mind, me countering with increasingly desperate praises of Amara's character. I was running out of words, my well-defined plan crumbling into absurdity.

"She matters to me," I said at last. Plainer than I'd meant it, which meant it was more honest than I'd planned. In fact, this slip had never been planned at all. "She has no reason being in that Dorm when I have the means to change it. I'm asking you to let me change it. She can be helpful. I will take care of the arrangements. I have never demanded—"

"Petition granted." His words carried the full weight of the hall. "I will have arrangements made. See my advisors if you need to add anything specific to take care of."

"Your advisors are intimidating."

"And I am not?"

"You're different to me." I said it before I could catch the words and shove them back where they belonged.

But he just shook his head in amusement, the crown glinting. "Was the formal experience everything you hoped for?"

"Indeed," I said. "Your decision-making was impeccable."

His deep, rich laugh reverberated against stone walls, a sound so rare and wonderful it made my heart melt into a warm, helpless puddle. I had missed that sound.

"Good. But don't make a habit of it. My schedule is rather full." He was still looking at me, and the warmth in his eyes felt like it had nothing to do with petitions or formalities.

"I'm leaving, then," I said, attempting a formal curtsy that was more of an awkward leg dip. "Wouldn't want to waste the Sovereign's precious time."

HE DESCENDED the dais steps without answering and stopped when he reached me. He looked at me for a moment, then reached out and turned my hand over briefly in his, checking the knuckles, the palm. Finding nothing new, he offered his arm. "I will walk you."

"You have a scheduled evening to get back to—"

"I have an Advisor who is very good at rescheduling." He said it as we passed the man in question, who received the instruction with the practiced composure of someone who had heard worse.

"Come."

A giddy, breathless happiness bubbled up in me as I placed my hand lightly upon his elbow and walked out.

⊰•∘❉∘•⊱

WE SLIPPED INTO THE GARDENS, the dusk deepening into shades of violet and olive green. The air was enlivening with the intoxicating sweetness of night-blooming jasmine.

He guided me to the heart of the royal gardens, under a series of arched trellises heavy with dark red roses, their petals lush and spilling above us like a canopy, silver thorns glimmering faintly in the Celestial glow. Beneath our feet, the path was lined with smooth, pale stones that seemed to gleam.

We sat on a cool, gilt-inlaid stone bench. I hadn't expected him to bring me here, of all places. I tried not to stare but failed. I drank him in: the sharp cut where his jaw met the strong column of his neck, the corded strength of his throat, the faint shade of scruff he always kept like a secret he refused to tame.

When I finally lifted my eyes, I found his gaze already locked on mine. He'd been watching me watch him. Blush heated my cheeks, thankfully hidden by the dim light.

"The roses are...prolific this season," I blurted, desperate to redirect his attention.

Prolific? Prolific! Of all the words in the Realm, you picked prolific? Next, just comment on the gravel.

A Thrall approached silently before I could start rambling about gravel, offering a tray with two steaming cups. Damien took both, placing them beside him. The Thrall retreated.

He took a deliberate sip from one, then set it down and broke the silence. "Tell me of your parents."

A sad, small smile touched my lips. I told him the same story I had then, of common folk with kind hearts, gone too soon. He listened with the same focused intensity, the same shadow of pain in his eyes as before.

"The commoner outskirts are already being rebuilt," he said after a moment.

"I know," I said without thinking.

"How?"

"I mean..." I scrambled for the right words. "I assumed. You being Sovereign now... You're a good man. So I guessed you would."

He nodded unconvincingly, taking another sip of his drink, his eyes never leaving me. This time, he extended the second cup toward me. I accepted it, my fingers brushing his as I took it, and I brought it to my lips. It was perfectly tempered, as if he had kept it waiting just long enough to spare my throat.

He was filling some of the empty places the Abyss had carved out, places I didn't even know how to name. Even if I lost him in the end, I told myself I could keep these fragments of him—the small ways he still cared for me, even without knowing I was his.

"Seems you've been collecting companions. Busy as you are." His voice was a low murmur, closer than I'd realized.

A smile touched my lips. "And why do you sound surprised by that? Do I seem that unapproachable?" I asked, tucking a stray curl behind my ear, only for the night breeze to pull it free again. He watched the curl drift against my cheek.

"You are objectively bad at it," he said, blunt as a blade.

"Ouch." I smiled and took another slow sip. "So should I be flattered that you have been keen about my social failures, or alarmed you are skulking around me like a hawk?" The joke was soft; the question folded a dare into the space between us.

"Keen is a generous word for it," he said. "I keep track of what matters to Atlassian."

"And my social failures matter to the Atlassian's legacy?"

"Your stability does."

I set my cup down. "That's a very clinical way to say you've been watching me."

"Yes." He said it without apology. "It is."

Oh. That wasn't—I hadn't expected him to just—accept it. No version of *that's not what I said.*

I looked at the roses for a moment, gathering my thoughts. He didn't fill the silence, which was its own thing about him. He could leave it indefinitely, and somehow it never felt like distance. Like he knew something was coming and was willing to wait.

"Are you and Lorenza close?" I turned to find his eyes.

"No." He didn't hesitate.

"But you spent time with her." I tried to keep my tone as neutral as I could.

His eyes narrowed, a glint of danger and warmth appearing in their depths. "Have you been tracking my schedule, Mirabelle?"

"What if I have?" I challenged, holding the blossom to my nose just to have something to do with my nervous hands.

He leaned in, not much, but enough that his scent wrapped around me. "Then you would know my time with the Heiress is a duty. A public one."

"So you don't enjoy it?" The question was pure pettiness, and my mouth seemed to have a mind of its own.

A slow smile touched his mouth. "Do I enjoy councils, strategy sessions, and ledgers?" he asked, his tone feigning deep consideration. "I find them necessary, engaging. My enjoyment," he continued, his gaze holding mine, "is a much more limited resource. It tends to be reserved for pursuits that are...genuinely surprising."

I looked down, focusing on the white petals in my hand to hide the helpless, hopeful smile. When I finally looked up, he held my gaze for another moment. Then, he leaned back, deliberately breaking the intimacy, allowing the night air to cool the space he'd so thoroughly warmed.

I decided I'd burned enough questions on that subject for now. He was edging closer to the invisible boundary I'd drawn around him, answering more freely, less guarded by formality. But I needed to be patient. I had no wish to startle him.

The conversation drifted then. He asked about Amara, after my days, my past, my life, and though I had told him much of it before, it didn't matter. Because it was a balm to my soul. And the way he listened, the way his responses cut straight through my armor, melted me the same way they always had.

When I turned the questions on him, he gave more than I expected. A few things he avoided, slipping neatly past them, but even his evasions spoke louder than silence.

"Why is Rowane so...unwavering in his loyalty to you?" I asked softly.

Damien grew still, his gaze turning inward, fixed on some point in the distant dark between the rose bushes. "There was a kid," he began. "When I was a child. He was...kind to me when no one else was. He saw the Heir, but he kept offering companionship to the child trapped inside."

I know. *Rennard.* He'd told me about Rennard just before the Abyss took him from me. But I couldn't say it, so I simply nodded.

"And he lost his life," Damien continued, the words seeming to cost him. "To the treachery of other Clans. He was killed because he was my shadow." He didn't elaborate on the horror, the specifics of the siege or the body on the gates, but the hollowness in his voice painted a picture more vivid than any detail ever could.

"Rowane is his brother," he said, finally meeting my eyes. "I took him under my wing when he lost his parents during a Dissonance. Not out of pity, but because a part of Rennard lived in him. His loyalty, his spirit. And I thought it was the only way I knew to honor that memory."

He paused. "Rowane doesn't know that. He believes he wore me down all on his own with his relentless charm." He smiled, a small curve of his lips. "And in a way, he did. Just like his brother."

I smiled back, my heart aching and warming at once. "So you tolerate only the relentless, grinning nuisances who refuse to take no for an answer?"

His reply was a low rumble. "It would seem my preference is specifically *some* individuals who see a fortress and decide to move in without an invitation."

I laughed lightly at that. Still, the weight of his past settled around us. I reached out, my hand covering his where it rested on the cool stone of the bench. I let my touch say what I couldn't: *I see the boy you were. I see the man you became to protect his sanity. I honor it. And you are not alone with it anymore.*

He turned his hand over, his palm meeting mine. His fingertips traced over the rough skin and small cuts on my own from bowstrings. We lingered until the last of the Celestial light faded. The palace behind us bloomed into full illumination, its windows blazing like constellations, lanterns chasing the dark through the garden paths.

And when I rose at last, murmuring that I should leave him to his duties, he stood with me. His hand found the small of my back to guide me, as if it were the most natural thing in the Realms, back toward the Royal Chambers.

CHAPTER 21
MIRABELLE

A low vibration had shuddered through the ground hours earlier, a deep tremor that reverberated through the entire Clan. From the feel of it, and from the talks flickering through the grounds, it was likely the Realms aligning. But the palace was surrounded by high trees and taller structures, blocking any clear view of any visual signs.

The days bled into one another, a frantic preparation for a storm whose shape we could not yet see. I spent my hours drilling the new patterns until they were as natural as breathing. Around us, the Hold thrummed with a different energy: the powerful Aether-wielders selected for the second night honed their craft, while the Legions and physical combatants trained for the brutal final stand. A nervous dread had taken root in my stomach, tightening with each passing day. The Dissonance loomed, and nothing we did could fully prepare for what it demanded.

Damien had again become a ghost within his own Hold, swallowed by war councils, preparations, strategy sessions, the training of Aether wielders and combat units, and the honing of his already formidable skills.

Now the morning had come. The Realms aligned, the Celestia itself tore to reveal whatever pattern the fates chose this time. No one knew yet which Clans would face which, or what Aethers would be unleashed by them. It was different every Dissonance. Always unpredictable.

Damien had gone at dawn with Nathan, the Sages, and a knot of Elders, riding toward the Forsaken Lands where the first signs were expected to break. We had a fortnight to gather intelligence before the start of Dissonance Events. A tense truce where Clans could assess but not attack. I heard it was a dangerous game of spies, betrayals, and sabotages.

While optimism hung in the air like a fragile perfume, realism was a colder, sharper truth: this Dissonance could very well be the end of Atlassian's reign.

But it couldn't be. It wouldn't be. Not if we could help it.

⋯⟨⟩⋯

Now it was our turn for a final session of drill—the one postponed again and again for some unknown reason, finally starting. I had opted in, desperate to be included after being sidelined for so long. They'd busied me with Tameables and strength-building, but this was the last task we'd face together. With the Dissonance starting, survival wasn't guaranteed for any of us.

We moved quickly, though none of us knew where we were going. A long line stretched before me. Ropes of every hue hung in loops on the wall beside us, each marked with a copper band at one end. An Elder handed them out without explanation, tying one set around each person's belt. Mine was emerald-green, vivid even in the dim light.

At the far end of the corridor, the stone door pulsed with a rune of light. When the first person stepped through, the rune dimmed. The door rotated with a heavy click, and an entirely new entrance appeared in its place. The next candidate stepped into that one.

I glanced at the ropes, then at my cohort. All of us carried one set, but no two were the same color. Were we meant to tie one another or do something else? There was no instruction. And that was the catch. The Dissonance Trials would not announce some of its trials either. We were expected to react accordingly.

Behind me, Callen let out a groan loud enough to echo. "I feel like a trussed chicken marching to the spit."

"You smell like one," Lyria muttered.

I snorted. She wasn't entirely wrong.

Callen grinned, undeterred. "I smell like I had a productive morning. Very popular among women with taste."

Before I could roll my eyes, his forearm hooked over my shoulder from behind. He made a half-hearted attempt to ruffle my braid but only succeeded in grinding his sweat into it.

"Ew!" I twisted free, shoving him back.

"I know you missed me, Mira," he declared shamelessly. "But alas, Atlassian survival rests on my strength, and I had to offer it."

"I am not going to feel your forearm now oaf," I said flatly. "Shut up."

He waggled his brows. "Heartbreaking." Then his voice dropped. "Have you been to the archery range lately?"

The question was casual, but I knew what he meant. He was asking if I'd been hurting myself again. Shame warmed the back of my neck. I swore each time I wouldn't do it again, and yet, at the slightest tremor of heartache, I found myself walking those familiar steps, seeking that fleeting release. What a mess I was.

"No," I said quietly.

His posture eased. He gave my shoulder a quick shake before stepping back into line.

Ahead, another door opened and closed. The rune above it pulsed violet, then faded. An Elder stepped forward and secured my left hand tightly to my side with a strong thread, firm enough to immobilize without cutting off circulation.

Then came the blindfold, and a moment later, something sealed over it.

Darkness.

"Step forward," the Elder's voice said. I did. One step, then another. Stone shifted beneath my feet.

And the ground vanished beneath me. I fell without grace. Not far, less than a full body's length, but it was enough to make my stomach lurch. I caught myself on my free hand and breathed.

Silence.

Then, faintly—*drip...drip...drip.*

The air was warmer than the corridor had been, and the scent of damp stone was all I could sense for a few moments. My fingers moved instinctively to my belt. The rope still hung from it. I gripped it, breathing slow.

Something hissed. Not close, but not far either. I didn't know who or what was here. My ears strained. A soft scuffle to the left. Barely audible.

"Callen?" I whispered. No answer.

I turned slowly, one arm still bound, my steps small. The stone beneath my feet was smooth, too smooth. If the floor shifted, I would never hear it.

Another hiss. I dropped low just as something small and sharp *thwipped* past my ear. It struck my shoulder, not deep enough to wound, but enough to sting.

Then a fist cracked into my ribs, followed by a forceful kick that drove the breath from my lungs. My body hit the floor hard. The blindfold kept my vision pitch-black, but I could feel the presence, large and male, breath ragged with effort.

I blocked the next kick with my forearm, the impact vibrating up to my elbow. My free hand lashed out, catching fabric: a sleeve? A tunic? But they twisted away before I could get a grip. Another punch. I pivoted, taking it on my shoulder instead of my jaw.

I feinted left and let out a sharp breath like I was lunging, then dropped, sweeping my leg out. My boot connected with something solid. A muffled curse, and he fell heavily, hitting the floor with a grunt.

He was not using Aether. That meant the rules bound him not to.

Ropes. They gave us ropes for a reason. I lunged, my unbound arm snagging the rope at my belt. He recovered faster than I expected. An elbow slammed into my collarbone, sharp enough to send pain flashing down my side. I gritted my teeth, looping the rope around his wrist as he reared back for another strike.

I shifted, fast, legs snapping up around his neck, locking tight as I twisted my body. He staggered, choking, air cut off as I used the leverage to tie off his free hand against his torso with a yank and a twist. I wrenched his arm flat against his side and secured the final knot.

He thrashed, but I'd made sure of one thing: even if he broke free, the green rope would stay knotted around his arm as my marker. A claim.

A voice hissed in my ear, *Clever*, before it vanished into the dark.

I stayed crouched, listening. The stones were falling more frequently now. I crouched there for a moment longer, breath tight in my chest, waiting for the echo of retreating steps to fade.

I barely had time to catch my breath before a hand fisted in my hair and slammed me toward the wall. I twisted, throwing my arm up just in time to take the impact on my forearms instead of my skull.

I kicked backward blindly, connecting with something solid. A female grunt. It was either Lorenza or Delina.

She struck again, and I spun, catching her ankle with mine. She stumbled but didn't fall. Our feet slipped on smooth stone as the chamber roared with falling shards. She growled something wordless, and I kicked out, catching her knee. But she didn't fall. Instead, she ducked, yanked me forward by my injured arm, and slammed her elbow down over my shoulder. My knees buckled.

I tried for my rope. Too late.

In a single, practiced movement, she spun me, slammed me against the wall again, and looped her rope tight around my wrist.

I fought like a mad thing.

She didn't speak. Just tied. And then she was gone. The rope bit deep into my flesh. I wriggled, twisted. Stone chips continued falling, louder now. Angrier. My hands moved fast. I counted breath and friction, found the edge of one loop and twisted with every-thing I had. My arm throbbed. The skin split somewhere along the base of my thumb.

I ground my teeth and pulled again.

And finally—*snap*.

My head spun as I stood, blood dripping slowly down my palm. I couldn't tell how much time was left in this cursed trial, but the air tasted sharper. And I wasn't finished.

<hr/>

I was done.

Slumped in the lee of a jagged pillar, my legs curled beneath me, breath ragged and shallow, I clutched my last pair of ropes like they could keep me whole through this. I had managed to bind two more fast knots in a flurry of instinct and bruised muscles. I had no clue who they were. I no longer cared.

The storm of falling stone had thickened into something unholy. It shrieked through the chamber with a merciless rhythm, *hiss* then hammer, *hiss* then pain. A stone caught my shoulder, then another scraped across my thigh. I couldn't raise my arms fast enough to block them anymore.

I tried crawling, inching along the slick stone in the direction I hoped was out of this shambles. A hiss above—too late. Another volley of shards struck me, tearing skin with a cry I couldn't keep in.

There were others. I could hear them, three, maybe four, grunting low through clenched teeth, scuffling against the floor around me. Others would be out somewhere, fully tied. No one cared anymore to even raise a hand to one another now.

"Cover your head and lay down, Mira!" Callen's voice cut through the dark. "Something's wrong. This isn't supposed to pelt us with stone like this. Something has been tampered with."

Even I felt it—this reeked of sabotage. But who would do that, now, when we were finally gearing up for the battle for our survival?

Well. Turns out my ambition to participate in the final trial has been rewarded with a potential burial.

I pressed into the hollow between two broken stone ledges, curled tight, face buried into the crook of my elbow. During brief lulls in the stone rain, I could hear clashes and shouts from outside.

I hoped the ones who arranged this stars-damned, pathetic excuse for a trial were already finding a way to fix it before we were all slaughtered in here.

"If I die," I screamed back toward where I'd last heard Callen, my voice cracking, "give my gems and nickels to Amara!"

"Shut up, you idiot!" he howled back, followed by a grunt.

Stone storm continued until a creeping darkness began to edge into my consciousness.

CHAPTER 22

MIRABELLE

Then, as suddenly as it began, the rain of stones ceased falling on me. Not everywhere. I could still hear them pelting the chamber. But over me, there was silence. Warmth enveloped me, the scent of cedar and musk overtaking the iron tang of my own blood.

"How badly are you hurt, Bella?" Damien's words came out hard, a snap of terror he couldn't contain.

His hand tightened on my waist, while his other slid to the nape of my neck, guiding me down beneath the shelter of his body as the last of the shards rained around us. I smiled faintly against him, savoring the desperation in his voice when he called me *Bella*.

My blindfold was yanked off. Blinking against the eerie dim light, I found his face inches from mine. His eyes were dark with something fierce and unnamable, his hair damp with sweat, his gaze blazing with a panic I had never seen in him before.

His hand pressed me closer to him, inspecting my back. "Stars —answer me. How bad are your wounds?"

"I'm fine," I managed, throat raw. "No...I don't know. Just cuts. I—don't know."

He hissed something vicious under his breath, the kind of curse not meant for polite ears.

171

"I am getting you out now," he said, his voice low and soothing. "It is fine. It is over."

"Cover the rest!" Damien barked, seizing a shield and hurling it into place as he swept me into his arms. He moved, carrying me through the hail of shards, while the others scrambled to protect the remaining injured.

—————

I DIDN'T REMEMBER how we got there, only the brush of air against my skin, the searing pain, and the way Damien's arms never once loosened around me. He set me atop his desk. He was so gentle, like I was something that could break, which I was currently proving correct.

Being flat on a bed right now might as well be my end. The firelight flickered against the dark wood, casting long shadows over his face as he worked the knots at the wrist they'd used to bind me before the trial. Once free, he cradled my face, his breathing fast and shallow.

I held his wrists, my grip weak. "I'm fine. Not completely fine. Everything hurts. But I'm not that—"

"I know. I know," he murmured, his thumb stroking my cheek. "I will make it right." Then his lips touched my forehead. It was so sudden, so tender, I went utterly still, dumbstruck by the unexpected warmth of it.

"I will get this off first," he murmured against my hair. "Then I will see what damage that damned storm did." I nodded, though he wasn't looking at me, his focus entirely on the loosened knots.

Then his voice softened further. "Can I lift your top?"

I nodded with far too much enthusiasm for someone who'd just been pelted from every side. He pushed the fabric upward slowly, fingers barely skimming my ribs, until it caught. I looked like I'd lost an argument with a quarry. His mouth tightened. Blood had clotted along my side, soaking into the seams. The fabric wouldn't rise any farther.

He hesitated a heartbeat.

Then he tore the garment down the side with a sharp rip. He cursed under his breath before tearing the ruined garment completely and tossing it aside without looking. The sudden exposure sent a rush of awareness through me—absurd, given the circumstances.

I was bare above the waist, just a scrap of undercloth doing nothing to hide the damage. My skin was a map of shallow cuts and angry purpling bruises.

Not pretty at all.

Why, in *all* the Abyss, does *this* matter to you now, idiot? *You have a gash on your shoulder*, I reminded myself. *Focus on that.*

Damien's gaze was clinical as he inspected the damage, but his jaw tightened with each new wound he found. "There are a lot," he said hoarsely. "But most are shallow. You are almost alright." He was speaking more to himself than to me.

Then he took my hand and pressed a kiss to my inner wrist, his lips warm against my frantic pulse. Again. My heart fluttered wildly, a blooming hope taking root. If it took getting pelted with rocks for him to treat me like this...well, perhaps I should start volunteering for more stupid drills.

He turned away before I could say something dumb. He moved to his larders, returning with fresh linens, a soft tunic, and a basin of some sharp-smelling liquid. "A healer will be here anytime now," he said, dipping a cloth into the liquid. "Just hold still for me."

I was meant to be focusing on the sting, but I found myself watching the strength in his hands, the roll of his shoulders beneath his tunic, the gentleness with which those hands touched my nearly naked skin. *Stars, I was clearly deprived.*

I hissed when he found and removed a shard that had buried itself deeply, and his fingers stilled instantly.

"Shh," he soothed, his voice rougher than usual. "We are almost done."

When the last of the blood was wiped away, he exhaled

sharply. Then his forehead dropped to mine. Just for a moment. Just long enough for me to feel the tremor in his breath.

"I won't let you out of my sight," he muttered, so low I almost didn't catch it.

Then he pulled back, his mask slipping back into place as if it had never faltered. "You weren't supposed to be in there with the others."

I swallowed. "Because I'm fragile?"

"Because you're not expendable."

Ah. Of course. The Tamer of the Realm. His greatest weapon. If I died, he'd lose his edge. The fear was mostly for the asset.

And yet...he'd brought me here to *his* study. Why had he been the one to clean my wounds, to strip the blood-soaked cloth from my skin, to murmur consolation as he wiped the welts and bruises away with his own hands? He hadn't gone to Lorenza, who had certainly been tied up in that ring.

The door burst open before I could dwell on it further. The healer rushed in, followed by Lorenza herself. Damien moved in front of me, placing himself squarely between me and the open door where they stood. Before I could even reach for it, he took his tunic from the chair and handed it to me. I loosely draped it over my shoulders.

Lorenza's gaze swept the chamber. She was bruised, though nowhere near as battered as me. Her tunic was slashed at the shoulder, blood seeping into the pale blue corset. Her hair had come loose from its immaculate braids, but she still stood composed.

Damien asked her, "How are you feeling, Lorenza?" His voice was even.

"I am almost well," she said, her tone light but her eyes lingering on the way his body still partially blocked me. "But I suppose that wasn't a priority for you."

"I asked Nathan to look for you," Damien said, turning slightly away from me. "And arranged for a healer to see to you as well."

"That's…generous," she murmured, her smile not reaching her eyes.

"I heard we captured their Royal from the opposing Clan who sabotaged the drill," she said instead, shifting the subject with practiced ease. "You plan to execute him?"

"Yes."

"But no attacks are allowed during the Preparations. That's the rule."

"They started it, didn't they?"

"Mishaps happen during intelligence gatherings," she countered. "You know that."

"This was not a mishap." His voice dropped a register. "She could have died if we were late."

The healer was still waiting near the door and Damien moved toward her—low words, too low to catch. Lorenza's gaze finally settled fully on me.

"And how are you?" she asked in her usual polished tone. "I heard you and Delina took the worst of it. You really should have stayed where I tied you, outside the inner zone."

Her tone was perfectly pleasant. But I was too raw to let it pass. "Oh, I'm so glad you were conveniently tied up somewhere safe outside the final zone. Awfully lucky timing, wasn't it?"

Damien didn't so much as glance at either of us.

"See to her," he told the healer. "Let the guard know if she needs anything."

Then he turned to Lorenza. "Out. With me. We'll get you seen to in a different chamber."

He didn't look back. Lorenza shot me one last, unreadable look before following him. The door clicked shut behind them, leaving me alone with the healer.

Would he treat her wounds, too? The thought hit like a fist. Would he peel away her clothes with the same careful hands, wipe the blood from her skin with the same tenderness?

The healer cleared her throat, dragging me back as she stood beside me. "Let's see the damage."

I nodded, feigning an ease I did not feel, and let her work.

⟡

ONCE THE HEALER LEFT, I had slipped Damien's tunic back on and stepped into the hall. The guard outside the study straightened at my approach.

"Where is the Sovereign?" I asked, already knowing the answer.

"With the Lady," he said, gesturing toward the infirmary down the corridor. *Of course.*

Lorenza needed tending too. It was perfectly reasonable and expected that he should see to her injuries. What he did *for me* was the unexpected reaction.

I exhaled slowly through my nose, turned on my heel, and left, fighting the urge to retreat to the archery range. Reminding myself that I was strong.

Now, perched atop the coverlet in my chambers with my legs tucked beneath me, I watched Callen and Lyria bicker with the intensity of two cats in a sack.

"—like I wouldn't notice you going for the tickling maneuver, you child—"

"It worked, didn't it?" Callen sprawled across the window seat, having forgone his tunic, a lazy grin on his face. "You squeaked. *Squeaked.* Like a stepped-on mouse."

Lyria lunged for him. He caught her wrist, twisting her into a hold that looked more like an embrace than a restraint. I tuned them out, my fingers absently tracing the edge of the tunic sleeve.

Telmoria had aligned with Veldoria, and our opposing Clan was Kaldorix. Their Aether was tied to stones or rocks. The full extent of their power was still unknown.

Spies from our Legion, trained for such stealth, had been sent to the Forsaken Lands to learn more. The fact that Kaldorix spies had gotten so close to the palace grounds to sabotage our drill was alarming. Most Clans didn't risk such bold moves so soon after Alignment. Kaldorix was clearly an overachiever.

"You tied three of them, Mira," Callen said, suddenly serious as he glanced over at me, releasing Lyria. "Including Elion."

I shrugged, wincing at the pull in my shoulder. "Does it matter?" I said, mostly to myself. I was out of every Dissonance Trial except the first one.

Lyria gasped, straightening her tunic. "Of course it matters. You held your ground for longer than anyone expected."

"That's a very kind way to say the floor was the ceiling for what was expected of me."

"Oh, speaking of stories." Callen's grin returned. "Are we going to pretend someone didn't panic when he saw you bleeding?"

"Yes, we are." I threw a pillow at him. He caught it. Lyria laughed. I tried not to.

After a few more moments of half-hearted chatter, Lyria stood. "Final session," she said, already turning toward the door. "Try not to let him annoy you to death." Callen blew her a kiss. She rolled her eyes on her way out.

Silence settled, broken only by the distant clang of training yards and the rustle of parchments as Callen snooped through my discarded notes.

My body had begun to heal. There were two stubborn spots that ached deeply, and I'd been told to rest. Damien had arrived with a healer a few times during the night to recheck my injuries. I remembered only the sound of the door opening, the press of warm fingertips at my shoulder, and the scent of cedar before I slipped back into sleep. I hadn't bothered to open my eyes.

I knew the care he showed me was not platonic. And I knew he would check on Lorenza too. But I hated her, and I hated him for letting things blur the way they had. Maybe *hate* was a stretch, but I was damn sure I just needed to rest and heal, not be around someone who looked after the person I loathed. Clean air, clear mind, and all that bloody crap.

Now, I was simply expected to pass the day doing nothing. At least I had company.

Callen's voice cut through my thoughts. "You're zoning out again."

"What?"

He leaned forward, a mischievous glint in his eye. "So, your friend is coming and all, eh? Moving into the palace premises. Big step."

I grabbed him by the back of the neck, my grip weak but my intention clear. "I will end you if you try anything funny with her."

He laughed, holding up his hands in surrender. "Wouldn't dream of it."

Then he exhaled, shifting to sit cross-legged in front of me. The motion made the freshly healed burns along his torso pull taut, the skin still pink and tender. His gaze met mine. "Do you ever feel like it's not enough?"

I tilted my head. "What isn't enough?"

"All of it." He gestured vaguely toward the open window. "Training, ranks, whatever gets you praised that day. I don't even think I want half of it. But then my mother starts with her reminders and threats. And I remember I'm expected to become someone like Nathan."

"You'd make a terrible Nathan." I smiled, though it didn't reach my eyes. What was it with Royal parents and their gift for twisting free will into duty anyway?

"Obviously," Callen said with a grin, his eyes drifting toward the carved ceiling above us. "I'd at least make the drills more entertaining. Mandatory napping, for starters."

"And snack breaks," I added.

"See? You get it." He huffed a laugh, running a hand through his hair.

"You don't want to be him," I said quietly.

He shook his head. "No. But sometimes I feel like that's all they'll ever let me be."

"You could do better," I said, reaching for the ribbon beside me, attempting to pull my hair back from my face, but the motion tugged against the raw skin of my shoulder and I winced. "Even greater than Nathan, if that's what *you* want," I added.

"Here." He picked up the ribbon while he rolled his eyes at my comment, already shifting to his knees in front of me. A tangle of limbs and good intentions. "I've seen women do this. I think I can manage."

"You *think?*" I muttered as his fingers fumbled through my hair, pulling more than tying. "Stars—"

"I'm a fast learner, Mira."

"You're a disaster." I swatted his hand. "Stop offering things to others you're really bad—"

A knock rang sharply against the chamber door.

"Your hair looks like a bird's nest," Callen muttered, chuckling, just as the door burst open.

I only had time to get a glimpse of Damien's figure filling the doorway. He crossed the room in two long strides, caught Callen by the back of the neck, and wrenched him backwards, dragging him off the mattress.

I lurched forward, ignoring the flare of pain in my shoulder as I wedged myself between them. "He was just tying my hair!" I don't even know why I was explaining this to him. But I had to make Callen safe from this bull-headed rage.

Damien's grip on Callen's neck tightened. "Why were you half-naked on her bed?"

"Let him go," I snapped, shoving at Damien's chest. "He's injured, same as I am."

Damien's jaw clenched. Then he released Callen with a shove. "Out."

Callen steadied himself. His chest rose and fell in sharp breaths as he rubbed his neck, eyes flicking between us. "Mira, do you want me to...stay?"

Damien's look was lethal. "I suggest you reconsider that question, kid."

"Go," I said quickly, before Damien decided on some horrible consequence for his disobedience. "It's really fine."

I whirled on Damien the moment the door clicked shut behind Callen.

"What's wrong with you?" I snapped.

"What is wrong with *me*?" His voice rang sharp. "What was he doing bare-chested on your bed, his hands on you while you were still recovering?"

"He was just—" There was no point in reasoning with him now. "He's my friend!"

"And you are never letting him in your chamber again, dressed or otherwise," Damien snarled.

The command in his voice lit a fuse in my chest.

"Who are you to decide that?" I had to crane my neck to look into his eyes. "You can undress me and Lorenza in the span of moments, but I can't be with a friend in my own chamber? Sorry, Sovereign, I am a bit too injured to be taking your worthless orders."

I saw the flicker in his eyes, narrowing.

I didn't wait for him to reply. "So. Damn. You." I shoved past him, my shoulder screaming in protest, and stormed toward my bed to get some distance from his nonsense.

CHAPTER 23

DAMIEN

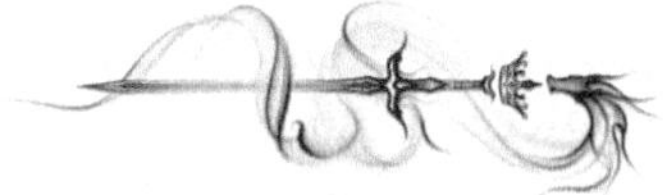

I turned the key in the lock, the metallic click sealing this space away. I was still in my formal court attire, feeling stifled by the warmth and the confined space of her chamber. Slowly, I began to shed the weight of it, but my gaze never left her.

She sat stiff-backed on the mattress, anger in every line of her small frame. Her hair was coming loose again from its hurried tie, and she looked breathtakingly beautiful in her fierce refusal to be anything less than defiant. And she was throwing daggers at me with her eyes, while clad in my oversized tunic.

"So you think only *you* can be in my chamber alone with me, but no one else can?" she challenged.

"Good that we are on the same page," I replied.

"Or perhaps you're delusional for a Sovereign," she hissed back.

"Perhaps."

"Leave, Damien. I don't want you here. Not when I need quiet and not confusion," she said, turning her face away. "I need rest."

"What you need is care," I stated, pulling the clasp from my mantle. I shrugged free of the velvet cloak, then unbuttoned the heavy coat with its silver trim and epaulettes, until I stood in just

181

my tunic, breeches, and boots. Her eyes tracked every movement as if she couldn't believe I hadn't left yet.

"If I wanted care or company, I'd call someone like Callen over you."

"Then by all means, call him," I said, not moving an inch. "And see how long he remains welcome in any room you occupy."

Her gaze snapped back to mine. "Who are you to decide who stays and who goes?" Her voice shook with rage. "You can decide if you want me on the palace premises or not. But if I have been given a chamber, *I* decide who enters it. Not you."

"You decide who walks through that door," I said, looking into those green depths to let her know I was not bluffing. "But you don't decide who walks back out with a still beating heart."

She looked back at me with the same intensity, her eyes full of a fury so potent I could almost feel it sear my skin. If she could have, she would have struck me.

A part of my mind, the part that was still rational, acknowledged how obscenely and wildly irrational I was acting. I blamed her petite frame and her impossibly expressive face for rousing the worst beast in me. And the worst of it was, I had no second thoughts, no regrets for the way I was reacting.

And I realized with clarity that I preferred her anger searing into me over her quiet belonging to anyone else.

I moved to her, retrieving a small jar of soothing balm I'd had the healers make for her. I sat beside her on the mattress, the space between us feeling both vast and impossibly small.

"Getting a bit cozy there, Sovereign?" she asked, her voice dripping with sarcasm.

"Could I not sit here?"

"What if I say no?"

"Then I will take you to *my* chamber," I said, my voice low. "Where you seemed to have no objection to being in the bed."

She narrowed her eyes, and I moved her shoulder cloth aside and began to rub the balm into the bruised skin there. She tensed, then slowly relaxed under the cool, soothing touch of the balm. My fingers worked carefully over the tender skin, and when I was done, I reached for the loosened ribbon in her hair. Gathering the tousled waves, I tied it back neatly, my fingers lingering only a moment longer than necessary against the nape of her neck.

"Don't you think you're doing a bit too much for me?" she muttered under her breath.

"I think I am not doing nearly enough," I replied in a softer tone.

She rolled her eyes at me. She really rolled her eyes at me—no one had ever dared before, but the insolence was strangely disarming. I smiled at her while I shook my head in disbelief.

When she caught me smiling at her, she glared deeper. I chuckled softly.

"If you are done here, you can go tend to other injuries," she said. "I'm sure there are eager candidates waiting for your attention."

I didn't forget her earlier mention of me undressing the Nyxarian Heiress. This wild one needed to learn to tame her tongue. Or else I would have to do it for her.

"Why did you assume I was undressing Lorenza," I asked, my tone dangerously even, "when I clearly told you my interest in her holds all the romance of reviewing inventory ledgers?"

"I don't know," she shot back, her sarcasm sharp enough to draw blood. "Maybe because you two are betrothed, and the whole clan is breathlessly waiting for you to have the most politically advantageous union with the most strategically fertile Heiress. A perfectly arranged ending."

"She is not my betrothed," I said, deciding to address her plethora of questions one by one. "It was an implied possibility after this alliance."

"But your father announced it to the whole Realm!"

"My father was eager for that Bond for a while," I replied, reaching out to gently trace the line of her frown with my thumb. "When the opportunity came, he seized it without asking me."

"Then why did you not deny it? You went with it!" Her voice was rising with frustration.

"Because I thought it beneath me to embarrass both my father and Lorenza before the whole Clan," I said. "She is our guest, and she had already sworn her presence for the Dissonance."

She was still mulling something over. I shook my head. "Ask it, Bella."

Her throat bobbed as she swallowed, and when she spoke, her voice was small with a vulnerability she tried to hide. "Did you treat her yesterday?"

I held her gaze, letting her see the truth in mine. "What do you think?"

She searched my face, but I knew deep inside she understood. I wouldn't touch another woman that way now. Her grudge against me wasn't for my actions, but for my silence—for not putting this truth into words and making things clear for us both. And I had shattered that silence yesterday when I'd finally drawn the lines clear with the Heiress and turned my back, leaving her to a healer's care.

"I haven't so much as looked at anyone that way since I noticed you," I said, my tone steady and sincere.

"So you like me, huh?" she teased, fluttering her eyelashes with an exaggerated coyness.

"Let's just say you have single-handedly crippled my rationality. Congratulations are in order, I suppose," I replied dryly.

Then I exhaled. I had not wanted this conversation to be like this, but it seemed inevitable. "Let me start by making one thing clear." My voice dropped. "You belong to me, Bella. And I want you to let that reality sink into your soul." I let the words hang, so she would understand I meant every single word of it.

Her head snapped up. "I do?" Then, "Wait, as in your Thrall or some sort of arrangement? Or do you mean it as a proper...I mean, an exclusive...affair?" She surged forward, her hands gripping the blanket as the questions tumbled out in a storm of confusion.

"As in *mine*," I said. "Because I intend to ruin you the way you have ruined me—my senses, my reason. You have occupied every single breath of mine since the moment I saw you in that crowd, looking at me like I had stolen your stars."

Her lips trembled into a smile so radiant it struck me like a blow.

She breathed in, a shaky, ragged sound, and then breathed out as if releasing a weight she'd carried for lifetimes. Her hand came up, and she pinched my arm, then my chest, as though testing the solidity of me and assuring herself I was no dream.

I pulled her into me, my arms wrapping around her so tightly it was as if I could press her into my chest, make her a part of me, where she would always be safe. She buried her face in the crook of my neck, her tears hot against my skin, her small hands fisting in my tunic. I held her through it, one hand cradling the back of her head, the other splayed across her back, feeling each shuddering breath she took.

"I have you," I murmured into her hair. "I have you." Her tears gutted me, each one a tiny wound, even knowing they were not born of sorrow. But I also knew they carried more than just happiness.

Slowly, her sobs subsided into hiccupping breaths. She pulled back just enough to look up at me, her eyes red-rimmed and swimming, but clear. And then she smiled. It was the first real, unguarded, soul-deep smile I had ever seen from her, and it was blinding. I had seen her amused, I had seen her pleased, but I had never seen her look like this, utterly, incandescently happy. It struck a place I didn't know was vulnerable.

"You were just made for me, weren't you?" I traced the curve of that devastating smile with my knuckle.

Oh, Damien, you have no clue, her eyes seemed to say.

"And you're mine." A statement, not a question, and I found I liked the sound of it.

"Completely and without negotiation."

Her smile widened even more, a sight so disarming it felt like it was tearing something new and fragile open inside my soul.

"I love that you are incapable of hiding your feelings from me," I murmured and guided her to straddle my lap, careful of her injuries but needing her closer. She came willingly, her hands settling on my shoulders, her smile never dimming.

My mind flashed back to the cold conversation in the infirmary after I'd left her with the healer. I had informed Lorenza that there would be no Bonding. She had no objections, and had listened with her usual composure. Only answering with the reason that had long been her weapon.

We needed her Aether, her strength, her Clan's alliance. And she was not wrong. To sever the arrangement now would imperil the fragile accord binding Atlassian to Nyxaria. It was my father, who had made the proclamation before the Realm, binding me with words I had never spoken.

Yesterday she had pressed our case once more. For the sake of both our Clans, she said, we would table the matter until the Dissonance was finished. We would speak neither of confirmation nor cancellation to Nyxaria. It had been reasonable. Necessary, even. Nyxaria had only just consented to renewed cooperation, sending Rhylen as proof of fragile trust. To turn from them now would have been nothing short of folly. They knew too much of our walls and our weaknesses.

Even I could see the pragmatism in patience.

Lorenza had asked me only this: why I cared so much for this one girl and whether she was the reason for my decision.

Care. I had realized in that moment that *care* was a pathetic, insufficient word. It was a cheap summation of what I had felt when I saw her under that rain of stones, folded in on herself beneath a ledge, helpless, bleeding and mine to protect. I had simply told Lorenza not to concern herself with matters that didn't involve her, before leaving the chamber.

When the sabotage at Emberlock struck, we were already locked in battle, cutting down the infiltrators who had slipped past our defenses. I was directing Legions, shouting orders to secure the perimeter and evacuate the trapped. Nathan had urged me to search for Lorenza when I got inside the Lock, when the words sliced through: *"Get the Tamer from inside the zone!"*

I hadn't known she was there. And clarity struck as I rushed through smoke and crumbling stone, my mind reeling, my gut twisting itself inside out. It was my fault she wasn't the priority, my fault I was bound by the fiction of alliance.

And one thing had become brutally clear last night: I was no longer capable of choosing reason or tradition when the safety of this reckless girl stood on the other side of the scale.

The moment she hurt, I could not think. I could not lead.

I could not even breathe when she was not safe.

Now she clung to me from the front with the tenacity of a raptor, her face buried in my neck, arms and legs twined about me with not the slightest intention of releasing me in the near future. And I—*damn me*—was liking it way too much for a man whose Clan was on the verge of doom and whose schedule was a tapestry of impending battles.

"So," she murmured against my skin, "no more implied Bonding?"

"No," I replied. "But we won't be mentioning it to Nyxaria until after the Dissonance."

She nuzzled deeper. "I can live with that."

Reluctantly, I coaxed her arms loose and placed her back on the bed, giving the tip of her nose a soft kiss. I eased out of the bed, pretending not to see the pout that formed on her lips that threatened to melt my remaining resolve.

"I am arranging a chamber for you," I said, straightening my tunic. "Closer to mine."

She sat up, her eyes sparkling. "Oh? So you can keep a better eye on me? Planning to tie a bell around my neck too?"

I shot her a look as I fastened my coat. "If I thought it would work, I might consider it."

Her fingers reached out, tracing the silver embroidery on the edge of my cloak. "Or is it because you get to watch who comes and goes?"

"Because it lets me know I can reach you first, *always*."

"That is not how doors work, Sovereign," she murmured, a smile curling the edges of her mouth. And I shook my head at her.

"Your friend will be settled into our premises by tonight," I said and moved to the door, my hand on the latch. But I paused, glancing back at her. She sat there, bathed in the soft light, her hair a mess, her smile both defiant and tender. My resolve crumbled completely.

I turned and strode back across the room in swift strides. I bent and slid one arm around her waist and lifted her effortlessly from the bed. She let out a small, surprised gasp, her hands flying to my shoulders.

And then I sealed my lips on hers.

CHAPTER 24
DAMIEN

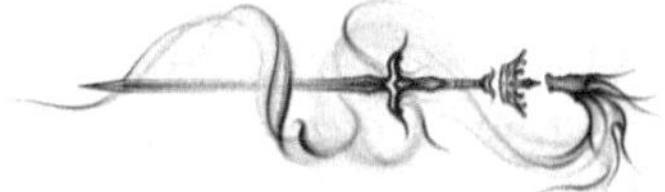

The first brush of her lips unbound every restrained desire I had buried within me. I claimed her mouth with mine, drinking her in like a man starved. It felt like coming up for air after a lifetime of drowning, a desperate, gasping salvation that tasted only of her. She met me with a hunger that mirrored my own, kissed me back like she knew every plane and contour of my mouth, her fingers tangling in the hair at the nape of my neck, pulling me closer.

I deepened the kiss, my grip on her waist tightening as I held her flush against me, the other hand tangling in her hair to tilt her head exactly where I wanted her. I could feel the quickening of her breath, the slight tremble she tried to hide. Her lips parted further, inviting, and I devoured them with a low growl that vibrated between us. She tasted like defiance and wildflowers, and her soft sigh as she melted into me was a victory and a surrender all at once.

I tasted the salt on her skin, felt the wild beat of her pulse where my thumb pressed against her throat. She arched closer, her fingers digging into my shoulders with desperate need. And I would never relinquish her command. Every movement was mine to guide, every gasp mine to draw forth. I was the storm, and she was the wild, willing sea rising to meet me.

I wanted to stop, to slow this down, to let her breathe, but she was clearly not letting me. She devoured me back with a hunger that felt years in the making, as if she had been dying without this, without us. Then she whimpered against my mouth.

I walked us back to the bed, laying her down without breaking the kiss. The stiff embroidery of my attire dug into my shoulders, but I didn't care. I could have been wearing armor or thorn. I wouldn't have stopped.

My tongue swept into her mouth, tasting her, and she moaned, a soft, breathy sound that went straight through me. I groaned against her lips. One hand cradled her jaw, angling her head to deepen the kiss, while the other slid further under her tunic, seeking the warmth of her bare skin. The moment my fingers found the soft curve of her waist, a shudder ran through her. She was so warm, so impossibly soft, and the feel of her like this under my touch undid me more than any battle ever could.

I pressed my palm flat against the gentle heat of her lower back, squeezing firmly as I pulled her tighter against me. Her body curved into my touch, her own hands roaming my back, pulling me down until I was half-covering her, her body aligned with mine in a way that felt devastatingly right.

Finally, I pulled back, just enough to rest my forehead against hers. We were both breathing heavily. I looked down at her. Her lips were swollen, her eyes dark and dazed, her cheeks flushed. I brushed a thumb over her bottom lip.

I had no name for this feeling that stole through me, that left my hands trembling. An onslaught of emotions I had never known existed. It was a terrifying and exhilarating vulnerability, like she had found a crack in my armor I never knew existed and poured light into it.

It was like discovering a new color. One so vivid no language could ever hold it, no voice could ever describe its depth to another soul. And it was mine alone to see, to feel—only in her.

I kissed her again, soft this time, to test whether I had been trapped in some desperate delusion.

I was not.

But she deepened the kiss, until I smiled helplessly against her lips. She was making it impossible to take this slowly. Or to leave.

"You are a menace," I murmured, my voice a rough whisper against her lips.

"You started it," she whispered back, her fingers tracing the line of my jaw.

"How do you feel?" I asked, pulling back to search her face, my hands gently checking her tender skin. "Did I hurt you?"

She shushed me with another soft peck on my lips. "Stop fussing. You're worse than some grandmothers."

I chuckled, the sound feeling strange, yet delightful. "Then let me fuss. I've found my calling." I pressed one last, lingering kiss to her forehead, breathing in her scent. "Rest. I mean it."

Her only answer was a slow, dazed smile. I forced myself to stand, to walk away, leaving her there in the rumpled sheets, looking thoroughly kissed, clad in my tunic from last night. I paused at the door, glancing back. Her eyes were already drifting shut, but her fingers were curled tightly around one of the coronation medallions she'd stolen from my coat.

I left her there, mine in truth if not yet in vow.

Closing the door softly behind me, I felt the unfamiliar sensation of a smile still lingering upon my face. My stride carried me down the corridor, and for once, I did not master it away.

⌖

THE KNIFE SLID in with a wet, grating sound. I twisted it sharply, and blood spattered in a dark arc across my sleeve, flecking the cold flagstones beneath us. A thick dark pool began to spread slowly around my boots. The body gave one final twitch before falling utterly still.

I yanked the blade free with a clean pull and turned. "Clean it,"

I said to the executioner who lingered nearby. He gave a curt nod and started toward the body.

The Royal had confessed enough for me to know he'd crept onto Emberlock grounds with the intent of taking the *Tamer's* life. Yet even under the knife, even as his own breath grew ragged and blood soaked the stone between us, he refused to speak of who had aided them. And it could have been any Clan who leaked the information moments after the Alignment. Now all of them knew about the nature of her rare Aether.

My father's proclamation after the Abyss about Mirabelle had made her name, and her Aether, the Realm's most interesting talk. She was a target, and the knowledge was a live coal in my gut.

"Will Dominion accept this?" Rowane's voice broke through the thick silence. "An execution without their judgment, on palace grounds? This could be seen as a breach of the Accord."

"I don't believe it is," I said, already walking toward the stables. Rowane fell in step behind me.

He let out a sharp breath. "We were meant to hand him over for judgment, not—"

"I did it now because I won't risk him slipping free if they press for release," I cut in, wiping the blade clean on a rag offered by a nearby guard. My voice was final. "Or for some well-meaning fool here to start pleading diplomacy."

Rowane opened his mouth, thought better of it, and closed it again. "Hmm...never heard of a Sovereign daggering someone himself in his own hall," he muttered under his breath. "We have men for that. You're meant to keep your hands clean."

I gave him a stern look. "I've never had much talent for delegating when it comes to traitors."

Rowane let out a soft huff. "Stars, you really do love making things simple."

I ignored him. He shook his head but said nothing more.

"Triple the guard on Mirabelle," I ordered. "Two outside my wing at all times. On the Hold, and on her archery practice."

Rowane gave a crisp nod. "It will be done."

"See that it is."

MY STALLION STAMPED IMPATIENTLY against the cobbles, snorting white plumes into the dim light. Behind us the carts rattled as the Thralls secured provisions and the instruments of the Sages who would spend the night measuring ley-lines at the ridges. Another carried Lorenza and Arthur, bound for the ridge to pay their blood debt. We would not return until next dawn.

Nathan swung into his saddle beside me. His eyes moved over the slow procession behind us, then flicked my way. "We cut it close. The last day. If their patience falters—"

"The Dominion has little interest in our timeliness, only in the weight of what we surrender." I loosened the reins, letting the stallion fall into an easy gait as the column formed behind.

He gave a low sound in agreement.

The ridges rose in the distance as we left the palace walls behind, towering up in the air like mountains of glass fused with ancient forest. They gleamed pale green where the light struck them, but their cores were shadowed, opaque. No one alive could see their inner workings from below. They stood fused to the Forsaken Lands as though dropped by stars, crystalline crowns against the horizon.

We passed under their long shadows, the carts creaking, wheels cracking over stone. I let my gaze linger on the ridges' sharp edges, where glass and root interwove. No door was visible until one knew where to strike.

Nathan broke the silence again. "I know what they say of the Accord Keepers. That they hold the power to tilt the scales themselves. Delay wars or accelerate them. End them before they even begin."

"It is not rumor," I said.

This was his first Dissonance as part of the Legion, and like the others, he was hungry for every scrap of knowledge about the Dominion. The Accord Keepers they sent to oversee each Dissonance—imposing, silent figures who stood as both judges and executioners under their own merciless laws. Until the Dissonance ended, their word was absolute. If they sensed imbalance, they acted. If they judged a Clan unworthy, they could, and would, scour its entire population from existence.

I kept my eyes forward. "That is why we obey them. They do not care for crowns or Aether."

Nathan grunted. "And if we fail—"

"Then they will rip the Aether from our dead, bind our Clan to the victor, and hand over our lands."

The Dominion ensures the transfer is final, with no rebellion or resistance. Etheris will be absorbed into the victor's Realm, and those of us left alive will be cast to the outskirts, reduced to Commoners under their rule.

We rode until the ridges loomed directly above, their walls glittering like frozen waterfalls. At the base of one sheer face lay nothing more than smooth glassy stone, veined faintly with green light.

I dismounted, pressed my palm flat against the surface, and knocked once. The ridge shuddered, the green veins flaring brighter. With a groan like mountains grinding together, a seam split open, forming a narrow archway into nothingness. The carts rolled forward first, their wheels sinking into the luminous threshold and vanishing as though swallowed. Then the horses.

We passed through together, and the world bent.

Ledgerdeep opened before us, the Realm carved of endless plateaus and stone tablets that burned with lines of light. Each tablet etched itself ceaselessly, writing down the actions of our world: the debts paid, the lives lost, the Clans risen and fallen.

And waiting for us at the threshold were the Keepers.

Figures of mirrored armor stood tall as towers, faceless, their reflections bending every light into something distorted. Behind them drifted the masked seers, robed in shadow, their faces hidden by porcelain veils painted with constellations. They did not move.

Nathan's stallion tossed its head, uneasy. The Accord Keepers had come to collect the blood-debt, to etch Atlassian into the stone of the Dissonance.

CHAPTER 25
MIRABELLE

A dramatic groan echoed through the chamber, followed by the sound of a body flopping onto the plush mattress beside me. "I'm dying. Actually...deceased. Tell the Sovereign his luxury is murderous."

I grinned, not opening my eyes. "The pillows too soft for you?"

"These pillows are clouds sent from the Celestia and I never want to leave," Amara sighed, sinking deeper into the bedding. "But my muscles are staging a rebellion. I think I should scrub a century's worth of grime from every corner of this...this...majestic rock pile." She said the word with a kind of reverent horror. "Do you know they have a separate soap for polishing silver? A *separate* soap."

I finally opened my eyes to see her staring at the intricately carved ceiling, her expression one of utter bewilderment. "It's a lot to take in."

"A lot?" She propped herself up on an elbow, her eyes gleaming. "Mira, your bath alone is bigger than our Dorm room. I half-expected to find a miniature boat in there for getting from one end to the other." She threw an arm across my waist, giving me a tight squeeze. "Thank you. For...all of it."

The sincerity in her voice made my throat tight. "Hey, lady, you don't have to thank me. You deserve it. You deserve safety, warm meals, and those ridiculously specific soaps."

"I deserve you," she corrected, her grin returning. "My favorite Tamer who pulled strings with the apathetic Sovereign himself. A little nepotism never hurt anyone." She wiggled her eyebrows.

A light laugh escaped me. "I'm the *only* Tamer, Amara. Your options are somewhat limited."

"And yet, I still chose the best one." She winked and pushed herself up onto her elbows. "I assume you're heading to the Hold to check on your beasts. Try and stop me from joining."

I shook my head at her, the smile still etched on my face. I had been missing this and I hadn't even known how much until I had her here.

When she'd arrived in a palace carriage, she'd stepped out as if she were descending from the Celestia itself, soaking in every opulent detail. She had made a spectacle of the journey before her foot even touched the ground, groaning dramatically about how she would never endure a common cart again now that she'd had her taste of luxury.

Half the day had been spent helping her settle, unpacking what little she owned into cupboards three times too grand, showing her the paths through the palace grounds, and listening as she filled every breath with news from the Dorms and streets.

And then, later, I'd told her about Damien, about his confession and the kiss that melted my core. Amara had stared, then groaned into her hands like she'd been keeping her delight bottled up for years.

"*Finally!*" Then she'd screamed, before throwing a pillow at my head and demanding every detail.

Even with her joy warming me, my thoughts twisted on themselves. Because I needed to tell Damien about the Abyss, and the cursed Crown that had cleaved our lives apart. I knew it was reckless, foolish, dangerous even to delay it. But some selfish part of me had clung to the need to see him choose me—Mirabelle, someone with an ordinary lineage, and not some obligation to a

Bonded partner he felt chained to protect. I needed to see him want *me* when the alternative was a woman like Lorenza, who embodied everything Atlassian needed in an Empress. Now I needed to find the right time to tell him everything.

We left Amara's new chamber in the Argent Estate, the name she insisted on saying in a terribly posh accent, and made our way through the bustling palace corridors. The change in her was immediate. Her limp, usually pronounced after a long day, was barely noticeable as she marveled at everything, from the towering arched windows to the silent, efficient Thralls gliding past.

Together, we walked towards the Hold, the echo of *our* friends, *my* friends, talk fading behind us.

⟡

I GUIDED her through the inner corridors of the Hold. She was here only to help with feeding the Tameables, and familiarizing herself with the other chores meant observing and seeing what suited her best. But I already knew where her preferences lay. She wanted to meddle in the daily lives of the Thralls.

I steered her into a quieter alcove, the sounds of the Hold muffled around us. "I'm not here only to train the Tameables," I said quietly as we walked. "There's something else."

Amara's brows arched high. "Oh? Tell me already."

I produced the folded envelope from my inner pocket of my cloak. Her eyes widened and she snatched it from my hands.

"Amara—"

She already had it unfolded, reading in a hushed whisper.

What you lost still waits for you. Be there on that day.

Her head snapped up. "What day? Like...what? Does this make any sense to you?"

"No," I admitted, my voice low. "But I want to make it make sense."

Amara clutched my arm, her theatrical instincts fully engaged. "I'm getting such a mystery energy. This is so—"

I pressed a finger to her lips, glancing around. "Shhh! I need to go somewhere to figure this out. It is risky and dangerous." I gestured toward the section of walls that concealed the door.

"Where is that?" she breathed, her voice muffled by my fingers.

"A place you need to stay out of. Wait here."

"Absolutely not," she declared, pushing my hand away. "That place looks shady as a willow tree at midnight. We live together; we die together. Mostly live, hopefully, but you're not going in there alone."

I wanted to argue, but the stubborn set of her jaw told me it was useless. "Fine. But you have to be quiet."

We slipped through the hidden door into the consuming darkness of the tunnel. The air was cold and still, the only sound our soft, nervous breaths and the quiet scuff of our boots on stone. The faint phosphorescent moss provided just enough light to see a few feet ahead.

This time, when we reached the chamber, *it wasn't empty.*

Shadows moved. Figures, cloaked and indistinct, were rising from the chairs around the obsidian table below. We froze, pressing ourselves against the cold tunnel wall, hearts hammering.

"...will end this once and for all next night," a low, gravelly voice said.

The figures began to move toward the exit. As one passed through a sliver of faint light from a hidden vent, I saw it. The insignia embroidered on the cuff of his cloak. Royalty. Only two men in all of Atlassian were permitted to wear that: the Sovereign...and his blood.

Damien. Or his father.

The sigil key I'd found in the drawer... Did it mean the old Sovereign was involved in the Untameable breach as well? The figures filed out through another hidden exit, their footsteps fading. The chamber was silent once more.

"Stars," Amara breathed beside me. "They all looked terrifying in this light."

I didn't respond. Moving on pure instinct, I climbed down and crossed to the obsidian table. My fingers found the hidden catch by memory, and the drawer slid open with a whisper. Inside, the parchment stack lay as it had before. The topmost page, with another day marked. The final night of the Dissonance. So that's what they meant by *ending this once and for all.*

The heavy leather-bound book lay where it had been. As Amara peered over my shoulder, I flipped through it frantically with a desperate prayer for a clue, or *anything* to manifest. But still, nothing. The pages were still infuriatingly blank.

I closed it—

And Amara let out a choked gasp, then a full-blown, muffled scream. I spun around and clapped my hand over her mouth, pulling her tight against me.

"Hush!" I hissed in her ear, my own panic spiking. She was trembling violently, her eyes wide with terror, fixed on something in the darkest corner of the room. She frantically tried to point, her breaths coming in ragged, silent sobs against my palm. I didn't look. I didn't dare. I just held her, my heart thundering, until the urge to scream seemed to pass out of her.

We didn't speak. We just fled, stumbling back through the tunnel, not breathing until the hidden door sealed shut behind us, leaving us safe in the familiar, well-lit corridor of the Hold.

Amara slumped against the wall, her face pale. "I remember, Bella—I remember."

I blinked, stunned. "Remember what?"

"All of it," she breathed, her eyes wide with dawning clarity. "The way Damien looked at you the day he asked you to oversee the new recruits. He asked you to call him by his name. The conversations about him. I didn't even know those memories were gone until just now. It's like...a veil lifted in there. *Oh, stars.*" She pressed her hands to her temples. "So many things make sense now. Your confusion about...my terrible advice...your visits...all of it. All of it."

The blank ledger. It didn't hold written truth. It stole them.

And being near it, perhaps even opening it, was what restored them.

"So the binder steals memories, and gives them back," I mumbled to myself. My eyes snapped toward the sealed door. "I should have stolen it."

But Damien wasn't here to create a diversion. If I took it now, they would know they'd been discovered, and whatever they were planning for that night might vanish, replaced by something worse and unpredictable.

Amara watched my face, reading the silent war raging behind my eyes. She placed a hand on my arm. "I don't know what to say, Bella," she whispered. "But think and do. Don't risk your life."

I nodded absentmindedly. My mind raced, spiraling through a dozen outcomes and half-formed solutions, but I couldn't afford to waste time here with the Dissonance this close.

So I sent Amara to the west cell to get acquainted with a somewhat-friendly Tameable, and I turned to face my own task, moving quickly toward the training grounds to drill my Dissonance crew.

CHAPTER 26

DAMIEN

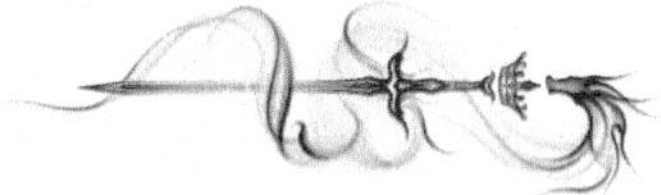

We were not led to the House of the Owed, where blood-debts were recorded and markers given. Instead, the mirrored guards ushered us into the House of the Tribunal. That means we were here to receive our verdict for the killing of the Kaldorix Royal.

No one spoke.

We simply followed, leaving the carts behind as we walked in silence behind the cloaked figures guiding us. The narrow passageway widened gradually until the jagged ridges gave way to a vast hall.

We were shown to a balcony overlooking the proceedings. Below, a verdict was being delivered. And we were next.

The grievance was between the Sovereign of Aquaris, the Fourth Clan of Telmoria, and the Heir of their Dissonance rivals. The Aquarian Sovereign stood rigid, flanked by his two Heirs and his Heiress on the defender's stand. Opposite them, the rival Heir stood alone in the stand of the accuser. He was a figure of imposing stillness, a contrast to the seething tension radiating from the Aquarians.

The charges had already been made. The balance had tipped. The Justiciar's voice reverberated, each word a hammer strike on the silent air. "The imbalance is plain. By decree of the Accord, Aquaris has forfeited blood, and the verdict is execution," he declared, his voice devoid of all inflection. "A life for the lives taken. The debt will be paid in the blood of the Aquaris Heir, Haelen."

A scream tore through the chamber, anguished and shattered. The Heiress lunged forward, but her father and brother held her back, their faces masks of grim, helpless acceptance. "No—please! Take me, not him! He didn't do it."

The Justiciar lifted one rune-carved gauntlet. "The Heir."

Haelen nodded to his father and a silent understanding passed between them. He then pulled his sobbing sister into a fierce, final embrace, steadying her as her knees gave way. He turned and walked calmly to the center of the dais.

A masked executioner, a silent specter we hadn't even seen, materialized from the shadows. In one fluid motion, a blade was plunged into Haelen's heart. He didn't cry out. He sagged, his eyes wide with shock, then empty, as his life drained onto the polished obsidian floor.

The Heiress's scream dissolved into broken, ragged cries of grief, her body collapsing against her father's restraining arms. Then her tear-rimmed eyes, blazing with a hatred, found the rival Heir. "I will make you pay for this," she shrieked, her voice cracking. "By stars and stones, you will—"

"Threaten me again"—his gaze slid to her with impassive disdain—"and I will give you something worth crying about forever."

She lunged for him against her father's hold with renewed, feral strength, her grief twisting into something more. Her father caught her fully, both arms locked around her from behind, his mouth close to her ear—murmuring something—while her brother braced her from the other side.

The Heir regarded her for a moment longer. "The verdict was blood for blood. If you demand another drop—from me, from mine, from anyone connected to me—I will drown your entire line in it. Your father. Your remaining family." A pause. "You."

He then turned without another glance at the shattered family and strode from the chamber, his retinue falling in behind him like a shadow given form. The Aquarians remained, broken, the Heiress half-collapsed in her father's arms, their men gathering them with hushed voices.

A mirrored guard stepped forward, faceless helm tilting toward me. The voice of the seer carried into the chamber:

"Atlassian. Kaldorix. Step forth."

And it was our turn.

WE DESCENDED FROM THE BALCONY, Nathan at my back. The obsidian floor seemed to leech the warmth from my boots as I led my contingent to the center of the dais. Opposite us, Arion Vexmar, Sovereign of Kaldorix, stood with his council. He was a middle-aged man with a hawkish nose and eyes that held the gleam of polished flint.

The Justiciar's faceless helm turned toward Vexmar. "State your grievance."

"Atlassian captured one of our Royals, Hiltser Weyn." His voice ringed with accusation. "It is a clear breach of Accord. We demand justice."

The Justiciar's helm swiveled to me. "Sovereign Azarios. State your reason, if any."

"The Royal was not merely captured," I stated. "He was caught manipulating our Aether-channels. His intention was to overload our Emberlock during a drill. He was an assassin."

"An allegation!" Vexmar spat. "Where is your proof? Where is the accused? Let him speak for himself!"

The Justiciar's head inclined slightly. "Do you present the accused to stand trial?"

The chamber held its breath. I met the Justiciar's unseen gaze. "He was executed for his treason."

A ripple of shock went through the watching balconies. Vexmar's face flushed with triumph. "He admits it! A clear, unjust killing. No one from Atlassian was harmed by our man's actions. We did what is permitted. We gathered intelligence. Atlassian committed murder. We demand a life for a life."

The Justiciar's gaze turned to our side. "The law is clear. A life taken without Tribunal sanction requires a life in return. Do you have irrefutable proof of his intent to kill?"

Vexmar spread his hands, the picture of righteous victory. "If he has no proof, then the scales tip in our favor. We will take one of his. The Legion-Commander, Nathan, perhaps. A fair trade."

My blood ran cold, but my expression remained the same. "I acted with just cause. The absence of casualties is immaterial here because the intent was there. And the target was our Tamer. This was not intelligence gathering. The Royal sought to unmake our defenses before the Dissonance."

Arion's mouth twisted into a bitter smile. "Intent? Intent does not kill, Sovereign. Acts do. And no life was taken by his hand. By yours, however, one was. Our Commander." His voice rose, raw with indignation. "You bring excuses in place of proof."

"The evidence," I said, my voice dropping into a deadly calm, "was his confession. Extracted before witnesses. He named his co-conspirators within your hidden Sages council. He detailed the plan, the timing, the specific resonance of the shards meant to trigger an accident."

Arion's nostrils flared, his face darkening. "Lies. Fabrications. This court will see what it is: Atlassian's Sovereign covering his own crime."

"Shall I share those names?" I countered, my gaze locking with the Justiciar's unseen one. "The Tribunal can verify the accuracy of the measures I describe against the resonance records kept in its own vaults. If you hold us both here, the verification cannot be tampered with. I assume that is agreeable?"

Vexmar's face filled with palpable tension, a muscle in his jaw twitching.

The Justiciar's faceless helm tilted. "If proven, both Clans would be found at fault. For Kaldorix: you sought intelligence and turned it into an act of war, striking not at knowledge but at life. For Atlassian: you shed blood without bringing the accused before us." The voice was final, weary of our feud. "With the Dissonance this close, we are not starting the full inquiry into the depths of your scheming."

He paused. "Therefore, I propose this: both Clans are hereby prohibited from gathering any further intelligence on the other. You will enter the fray blind. And judging by the silence from Kaldorix, the fault lies heavily there. Losing your Royal Commander will serve as your balance."

A hush fell among us. On parchment, it seemed like an even punishment, but the effect was brutally one-sided. The order would cripple us alone. Kaldorix had already found allies in two Telmorian Clans, while our own diplomacy was a tattered remnant with them. And almost all the Veldorian Clans stood tightly bound together.

His rune-carved gauntlet lifted, cutting off any protest. "The record will show this imbalance. Any further violation from either side will result in lives taken from your very lines. And they won't be soldiers."

The sentence hung in the air like a guillotine blade poised above both our necks. We would fight the most important battle of our existence blinded. The Justiciar's voice deepened. "Now, the blood-debts."

Another door opened. From the shadows emerged the pale-robed figures of the House of the Owed, their hands blackened by ink and ash. They carried knives etched with runes and tablets of obsidian already waiting to drink the marks.

"Sovereign of Atlassian."

I stepped forward and laid my hand upon the stone. The knife slid across my palm, blood welled. It fell into the etched channel of the tablet, searing as it touched. The words that bound us were spoken by the Owed: "By this mark, you grant us the right. Should Atlassian fall, all lives sworn to you will be ours to decide or forfeit. Their Aether will be stripped or shackled, their souls tallied. Do you swear this oath?"

"I swear it."

The blood hissed in the grooves, searing the stone black.

Arthur of Zarkon stepped next. His massive frame bent over the stone, voice gruff but steady as his blood joined mine, swearing the oath upon his life. Then Lorenza. Her lips moved with the same oath, her blood seeping black as ink upon the stone.

The Owed straightened. Their masked faces turned. "And asylum?"

"Yes," I said at once. "It has been agreed. Atlassian will shelter Arthur Louis of Zarkon and Lorenza Ashbourne of Nyxaria, should their Clans fall."

The Owed nodded. "Then let the terms be entered by night."

The tablets sealed, glowing faintly with the blood that bound us. The Owed withdrew. The Tribunal did not speak again.

We were led away, down into the narrow antechambers where rituals of sealing would be completed before dawn. And I had laid down the lives of my Clan upon the stone.

CHAPTER 27

MIRABELLE

NyxRathis flowed in her watery form in a motion that coiled around a crumbling pillar.

You flow too close to me, Dreadclaw's voice was a low rumble in my mind, velvet and dark and coiled with intent.

NyxRathis's form solidified just enough for her crystalline wings to catch the dying light. *Is the great beast unsettled by a little proximity?*

You mistake my patience for unease, he purred, tendrils of smoke stretching toward her.

Oh, do I? she chimed, her voice dropping to a whisper that seemed to vibrate through the very air. *Perhaps you are not as insightful as you pretend.*

You wish to test that premise? The threat in his tone was undercut by a dark, intrigued curiosity.

Hmm...I wouldn't dare. But her form dissolved, flowing around him in a sinuous, impossibly intimate circle. She wove through the spaces between his tendrils, her shimmering light gliding against the core of his shadowy form. It was a deliberate, tantalizing invasion. He growled a sound of vibration, and a tendril of shadow lashed out to grasp her. But she was already gliding through him, passing through his tendrils like light through smoke, leaving a trail of tingling cold and radiant energy in her wake.

For a heartbeat, he went utterly still, his form seeming to shudder and coalesce more tightly, as if savoring the sensation, his own darkness seeming to lean into the shimmering intrusion, enthralled.

"Er—" The sound escaped before I could catch it. Heat flooded my face as I glanced about, praying no one else was witnessing this spectacle. "Might we...preserve some measure of decorum? It is, after all, a shared training ground. Very much...shared."

NyxRathis slipped free of his grasp with a sound like chiming laughter. *You see? All menace. No follow-through.* With a final flicker of her wings, she glided swiftly toward the other end of grounds.

Dreadclaw let out a furious, frustrated growl and took a step to follow.

I moved quickly, placing myself in his path. "Please don't," I said firmly, meeting the swirling voids of his eyes. "You earned that. Let it be."

He growled at me, a cloud of dissipating smoke, but turned and stalked toward his own enclosure with a sulky air that was almost comical.

My thoughts were interrupted by a suspicious rustling near the Hold's entrance. I crept closer, peering around the corner to find Amara, a guilty look on her face, attempting to sneak a honey-glazed pastry into Whip-tail's eagerly waiting mouth.

"Amara!" I hissed, stepping out.

She jumped, whirling around and shoving the pastry behind her back. Whip-tail let out a low, pleading whine, nudging her hand with his massive head.

"We're almost done! Just...rehearsing!" she said, her voice a little too high.

"Rehearsing his digestive rebellion?" I crossed my arms, trying to look stern. "I heard from the Thralls he's been wasting his proper meals. Now I know why. It's because of you!"

Whip-tail had the decency to look ashamed like always,

ducking his head, but one large, soulful eye remained fixed on the hidden pastry. He let out another soft, rumbling purr that was clearly meant to be persuasive.

Amara sighed, her shoulders slumping. "Oh, come on, Bella. Look at that face. How can you say no to that face?"

"Easily! He's a several-ton healing beast, not a stray puppy! That honey-glaze will wreak havoc on his Tether-balance."

But even I was weakening. He nudged her again, this time with a little more force, almost knocking her over. She giggled, stumbling, and brought the pastry back out. "Just one last bite? For morale?"

I rolled my eyes but couldn't suppress a smile. "You are a very terrible influence." I watched as he delicately took the offered treat from her fingers, consuming it in one happy gulp before nuzzling her shoulder in gratitude.

"Alright, you big softie," Amara said, scratching under his chin. "Time to go in." She began leading a very content-looking Whiptail toward the Hold's great doors, throwing a cheerful wave back at me.

Shaking my head, I turned to round up NyxRathis when a familiar, drawling voice cut through the twilight.

"You know...you have become a threat to my profession and reputation."

I turned to see Izmer leaning against the archway, arms crossed, a familiar smirk playing on his lips. "How am I supposed to play the charming, indispensable advisor when you keep stealing all the aura?" he continued, pushing off the wall and sauntering toward me. "First you tame the Untameable like it's a mere parlor trick, then you make pets out of nightmares. Leave some glory for the rest of us, would you?"

NyxRathis, who had been observing the exchange, let out a sound like tinkling, mocking bells. Izmer glanced at her, then back at me, raising an eyebrow. "See? Even the scary, crystalline Lady agrees with me."

A sudden wave of emotions washed over me at seeing him. He

was someone who knew everything, who saw what I went through. The only one who had seen the truth of my past with Damien, who understood the silent sorrow I carried. Without thinking, I ran forward and launched myself at him, wrapping my arms around him in a tight hug.

He staggered back half a step in surprise, then let out a soft chuckle, patting my back awkwardly. "Easy there, kid. Don't crumple me."

I laughed, pulling back. "It's just...good to see you."

"The feeling is mutual, though perhaps expressed with slightly less force," he said, straightening his tunic. His gaze softened minutely. "You're holding up?"

The question contained a world of meaning. I glanced around us, ensuring we were truly alone. "Well," I began, letting out a slow breath. "A lot happened. But I'd say...I'm happy with the *progress*."

Izmer's smile returned. "Sounds like a not-so-happy situation for my Clan, but let's see how this goes." He leaned in slightly, his voice dropping to a conspiratorial murmur. "So, a simple question. Are we back to the lay *a hand on her and I'll rip your heart out* territory?"

A small smile touched my lips while I shook my head at his remark. "I'm afraid so."

His eyebrows shot up in mock surprise, followed by a low chuckle. "Good for you, then. Unfortunately, I can't stay to bask in the glow of your happiness. Duty calls me back to the council hall."

He turned to leave, but then his eyes snagged on a movement near the Hold's entrance. Amara was walking back out with her cute little limp, having settled Whip-tail, her cheerful expression shifting to curiosity as she spotted us.

Izmer went perfectly still. His smirk faded into something far more genuine, his eyes widening slightly as they tracked her approach. Amara slowed, her own steps faltering as she met his gaze. A faint, rosy blush crept up her neck and into her cheeks. She tucked a strand of hair behind her ear, a gesture I had never, *ever* seen her make. She was always so brash. Now, she looked almost... shy.

Izmer recovered his composure with a slow, dazzling smile that reached his eyes. He executed a flawless, slightly exaggerated bow. "Well. It seems my departure can be delayed after all. Izmer Castellane, at your service," he said, his voice a warm, inviting rumble. "And who do I have the immense pleasure of addressing?"

Amara's blush deepened. "Amara," she said, her voice softer than usual.

"Amara," he repeated, as if tasting the name. "A lovely name. Tell me, Amara, would you do me the honor of showing me the way to the outer gardens? I find myself quite turned around in this magnificent Hold you know by heart."

He offered her his arm. Amara, looking slightly dazed, slipped her hand into the crook of his elbow without a moment's hesitation.

"I...yes. Of course. This way," she murmured, letting him lead her away.

I stood there, completely forgotten, my mouth agape. Izmer threw a quick, triumphant wink over his shoulder at me before turning his full attention back to a blushing, smiling Amara, who was already laughing at something he'd said.

My heart did a funny, melting sort of flip at the sight of her giggle. It was a strange, beautiful thing to witness, because it was not the usual harmless flirting I just saw in her eyes. Still, my protective instincts warred with a surge of hope. Let him see how incredible she is and treat her like she deserves. Else I'll reintroduce that flirtatious Nyxarian Royal to NyxRathis.

Personally.

CHAPTER 28

MIRABELLE

I stared into the walk-in wardrobe, a space larger than my entire old room, and felt a familiar wave of overwhelm. Dresses. So many dresses were on the left side. I had not worn a single one. In fairness, showing up to Tameable drills in floor-length silk would have raised questions I wasn't prepared to answer.

I'd seen them worn, of course. Glimpses of Royal women gliding through the streets like swans on a lake, their gowns flawless, their hair intricate works of art. I'd always admired the artistry of it all. I'd wondered what it might feel like to wear something beautiful just for the sake of beauty, to feel for one night like I belonged to that world of soft light and chords. I had wanted, once or twice in secret, to blend in with them. To look even a fraction as composed, as elegant, as untouchable.

Tonight was different. An invitation to the ballroom lay in waiting for me.

I had no experience with such affairs. The only grand event I had brushed against was Damien's coronation, and then I had been too busy struggling to keep afloat to notice whether an invitation had ever reached me. I told myself I had not cared. Perhaps I had been too frightened to care.

But this time, I cared.

After what felt like a lifetime of rifling, I settled on a gown that didn't scream *I stole this from an Empress's closet*. My fingers finally brushed against a gown the color of a winter sunrise, fading into a soft, mossy green that almost matched my eyes. Delicate white embroidery of flowers trailed down the skirt, and the sleeves were sheer and flowing. It looked ethereal.

I wrestled myself into it alone. Then came the hair. *Stars, the hair.* I attempted a braided updo, something I'd seen a Royal wear. It ended up looking like a bird's nest attacked by a very angry squirrel. I tried pulling it half-up. Worse. I sighed, my shoulders slumping. *So much for feeling flawless.*

Giving up, I slipped into a pair of slippers and hurried into the hall, looking for help, the skirts swishing around my ankles. I found her in a quiet alcove, tidying linens, the kind, older Thrall who always had a warm smile for me.

"Let me, Lady," she murmured, guiding me to a stool.

Her hands were sure, weaving my hair into an elegant, loose twist that somehow managed to look both simple and stunning, with a few delicate strands left to frame my face. When she was done, I looked...different. Softer. I pulled her into a quick, grateful hug that made her smile, then gathered my skirts and rushed toward the ballroom.

The guards at the immense double doors checked my engraved invitation with a nod, and then the doors swung open.

The sight that hit me was overwhelming. The ballroom was a sea of glittering light, swirling silks, and the low hum of conversation and music. I hovered on the threshold, suddenly feeling incredibly exposed in my gown. Everyone looked so sure of themselves. So at home.

I hovered on the threshold for a moment, taking it all in, my stomach fluttering. I took a deep, steadying breath and stepped inside. Now I just had to figure out how to not stand in the corner like a potted plant.

I PLUCKED a cool ale from a passing Thrall's tray—if only to keep my hands from twisting in my skirts—and drifted into the swell of the ballroom. The chandeliers cast light like falling stars, and everywhere I turned were Elders, Royals, and Royalties. More than I had ever seen gathered in one place. Faces I did not recognize, accents sharper, silks brighter. Some must have come from other Clans.

Why hold an event like this with the Dissonance looming so close? I could not guess.

I fidgeted, my palms damp despite the cool glass in hand. A few strangers smiled as I passed, but I had no clue how to smile back without looking like I was being strangled. Relief washed through me when I finally caught sight of Callen and Elion near the edge of the floor.

"Look who braved the gilded nest," Callen said with a grin, slinging one arm around me in a side hug. "Didn't expect you here."

"What is all this for?" I asked, lowering my voice.

Elion laughed, his eyes running over my gown with a quick, appreciative glance. "From the look of your appearance, I thought you already knew."

Heat rushed to my cheeks. "I got an invitation, but it didn't say—"

"No need to explain," he interrupted kindly. "You're not sore on the eyes, Mira."

My blush deepened. He gestured vaguely toward the heart of the hall. "This is for the Royals—Nyxaria and Zarkon are here. The Dominion overseeing the Dissonance has forbidden outright intel gathering, so this is...a subtler way to firm the existing alliances. And asylum terms."

I tried to follow, but his words slid past me like water.

"Look there," he said, pointing toward the clustered, secluded section of the ballroom where plush settees were arranged. "Royalties, Sovereigns, Heirs, Commanders. See?"

My gaze snagged on Damien. He sat beside Lorenza, speaking to a Sovereign. Lorenza's hand lay idle on her lap. My stomach tightened at the sight of them together.

"That is Lorenza's father. I heard Nyxaria is here to finalize the Bonding with Damien," Elion said from beside me.

"What?" The word slipped out of me in a disbelieving tone.

"Top secret, from my family's place on the Council," Elion confirmed, his expression playful. "They're discussing granting Lorenza asylum and being Altassian's Empress if Nyxaria falls," Elion continued, oblivious to the growing fog in my head. "Damien would host her, strengthen the alliance. Nyxaria has leverage now, after the Dominion's latest verdict."

No. He wouldn't.

I forced a smile that felt like glass cracking on my face. I wanted to flee, to retreat to the archery field or somewhere. But leaving without a proper understanding of this felt like surrender. So I stayed, draining my ale in one go. I looked once more toward the settees, and this time I caught Izmer's eyes. He gave me a sad smile. I looked away before it could crush me.

A stranger approached, tall and broad-shouldered, with charming eyes and an easy smile. "May I?" he asked, extending a hand. I looked at it for a moment. I had nowhere else to be, and standing alone at the edge of a ballroom holding an empty glass was its own kind of statement. I tipped back the rest of my ale, then placed my hand in his. "Yes."

On the dance floor, his steps were sure, guiding me into the rhythm. "Your name?"

"Mirabelle."

"Zarkon speaks often of you," he said. "I confess I expected someone more—" He paused, searching.

"Feral?" I offered.

"I was going to say imposing."

"I'm working on it."

He turned me smoothly through a step. "You dance well."

"I took a few classes," I said, nearly tripping on my hem, "but not enough, it seems."

He laughed, low and smooth. "I had heard tales of your beasts, of your Tether with them. But no one told me the Tamer had eyes like emerald flame. Entrancing."

Oh.

Before I could find words, a hand caught my wrist, and I was pulled back against a solid chest I knew too well. "I would advise you to keep your fascination and hands to yourself if you want to keep living." Above me, Damien's voice was cold.

He didn't wait for a response, turning me away from the stunned commander and steering me firmly through the crowd with his hand pressed into the small of my back.

I resisted, digging my heels into the polished floor. "Get away from me. You don't get to touch me either."

His grip only tightened, his breath at my ear. "I will solve every single one of your problems after this. I swear it. But let me figure this out in peace. Just this once, cooperate. I won't get another opportunity like this again."

I gave in to the desperation in his voice. He was the Sovereign, after all. His duty was to his Clan, even if it felt like it was shattering my heart. But that didn't mean I should be here to witness it. He could have his peace and calm alone here with all of them.

I tried to pull my hand from his iron hold, my voice tight with a pain I couldn't fully conceal. "I was beginning to leave—"

"Is that what I just saw?" he bit out as we passed into the secluded seating area.

"Oh, no. You have no right—"

"Ah, this is our *Tamer*." Lorenza's voice cut me off. She addressed the gawking Royals from her Clan. "Always requires a guiding hand. Come along, dear." She smiled at me, and I ground my teeth so hard my jaw ached.

A Commander from the Nyxaria stretched a hand toward me in a welcoming gesture. Damien pulled me back a step and guided me to a settee, pressing me down onto the cushion. His posture shifted seamlessly back into that of the diplomatic Sovereign as he resumed his conversation with someone from Nyxaria. I sat stiffly, trapped, the ballroom swirling around me in a dizzying, nauseating blur of gilded light and polished lies.

The urge to flee was a physical ache, but a darker part of me wanted to see this play out. I needed to understand the game. I might be a masochist for punishment, willingly stepping into the snare. But I'd always had a curious side that overrode my primal instinct to flee and stop gambling with my emotional sanity.

The bitter truth was I was a fool to think Damien had invited me. It was someone else—someone who knew I'd see exactly this. Someone, perhaps, behind those letters.

After a moment, he leaned down, his voice a low murmur. "Do you need anything?"

I shook my head, not bothering to look at him.

"Let me have this conversation. Then we will talk." He squeezed my shoulder once, a gesture that felt more like a dismissal than a comfort, and then he was gone, swallowed back into the circle of power.

Lorenza followed him like a shadow in silk, and my eyes were helplessly drawn to them as they were joined by some Royalties from Zarkon. They stood together—Sovereign, Heiress, and allies —a picture of political perfection. Anyone with eyes would see a future etched in their proximity. They looked like they belonged together.

I had agreed to let them hold back revealing the truth about us until after the Dissonance, but I never agreed to stand by and watch them play at being a couple. I started to rise when a man lowered himself into the seat across from me. "Sit, young Lady" he said, his voice like gravel. "You are the Tamer, are you not?"

"Yes."

He was older, with sharp, severe features and eyes that lingered on my face with an unsettling, analytical intensity. I realized that this was Aramak, the Sovereign of Nyxaria, Lorenza's father.

"You have some...unique features," he said. His gaze was admiring; and it was also dissecting, stripping me down to my bone structure. I shifted uncomfortably, my eyes dropping to my feet, and realized I was wearing my frayed slippers I had forgotten to change. *Oh, how fitting.*

"A rare combination," he continued.

The Empress of Nyxaria, a graceful woman with kind eyes, quickly intervened, placing a hand on his arm. "That's enough, Aramak. You've set her fidgeting like a cornered doe."

She gave me an apologetic smile. "I am so sorry, dear. He can be a bit...enquiring." She looked at me for a moment longer, her gaze softening. "You are a very beautiful young lady, I must say. Tell me, how are you finding the festivities?"

Before I could stammer a reply, the Sovereign leaned forward again. "Where exactly are your origins from?"

The Empress sighed. "*Please*, my Liege."

I felt a pang of sympathy for her. "It's alright," I managed, but my smile wavered, awkward and brittle.

She placed a hand over his. "Aramak," she said in a low, firm tone. "Why don't you conclude your earlier conversation with Damien? After all, this may be our chance to finalize a day for the Bonding since he is also showing interest."

The words landed inside me with a sickening thud. I'd hoped it was all just rumors spun from political half-truths. But hearing it here, now, from the Royals themselves... Was Damien courting their alliance with lies? Or had the lie been the one he'd told me?

Fine. Let them have him. I was done with this pain, the stolen moments, the agony of hoping. I'd fight this war for my own honor, then take my saved coin and gems and disappear into the outskirts with Amara. I didn't need a Sovereign. I needed my pride.

"You are right," Aramak grunted, rising with a weary sigh. His slow steps carried him back toward the inner circle, leaving me with the Empress.

She leaned closer, her tone conspiratorial. "How long have you—?"

"Mother, what are you doing over here? Monopolizing the guest of honor?" Lorenza reappeared, her eyes glinting like frost.

"We were only getting to know this young Lady," the Empress said, unruffled.

Lorenza's smile was a knife's edge. "I think all there is to know of her is already known to the Realm. Quite exhaustively."

I met her gaze, forcing a fake smile like hers. "Oh, at least there was something worth knowing. How terribly sad for you that the most interesting thing about you will always be your father's name."

The Empress let out a soft, surprised chuckle. "Well, wasn't that neatly delivered?" She turned a reproachful look on her daughter. "And I'm sure that's not the case, Lorenza. She clearly has depths yet unseen."

"My apologies for the insult to your daughter," I said to the Empress, my tone not sorry in the least. "But she isn't very kind, is she?"

The Empress's eyes held a flicker of something like respect. "Kindness is a currency she believes she can't afford."

Lorenza sank onto the settee beside her mother. "A moment, mother?" she murmured, though her eyes shot a venomous glance my way.

The Empress inclined her head, and their voices dropped to hushed whispers. I didn't want to hear. *Stars, I didn't.* But my traitorous heart, desperate for a contradiction, strained for every fragment.

"...are we pushing to confirm the Bonding?" Lorenza's whisper was taut with a hope so raw it felt violent.

The Empress shook her head minutely. "Patience, darling. Let the man breathe. Damien has already spoken to your father. He's promised it will be settled just after the Dissonance."

I smiled at the cold hurt, freezing me from the inside out. It didn't matter what explanation he could possibly conjure now. How could he let this narrative stand? How could he parade her before the whole Realm, let her family—let everyone—believe this, while I...I would only ever be the outsider, the woman who stole him from someone who deserved him? There was no dignity in that. No future.

Hurt was good. Hurt was clarity.

Then the Empress's next words, so low they were almost lost: "As you said, if you could convince him to share his chamber last night in Ledgerdeep, you can easily make him agree—"

I stood up too fast, the settee rocking. A passing Royal paused. "Are you well, my lady?"

I ignored the man. I was already moving, a specter in silk, pushing through the crush of bodies. My skirts tangled with slippers. My shoulders brushed against embroidered coats. I moved past the soaring chords, past the curious stares, out of the secluded alcove and into the blinding, suffocating glare of the ballroom.

I hadn't even known she'd accompanied him to the Dominion. I was grateful, now, for whoever had slipped me this invitation. Better to see the truth than to be blindsided.

Once I was free of their sight, I ran.

I didn't know where. Only away. Away from the light, the lies, and the deafening, shattering thunder of my own breaking heart.

CHAPTER 29

MIRABELLE

I ran, the sounds of the ballroom fading behind me, replaced by the frantic rhythm of my own footsteps and the ragged pull of my breath. I didn't know where I was going, only that I had to get away from the pain I felt inside.

A hand shot out of the darkness, catching my arm just as I reached the archery range. I whirled, ready to fight.

"Let me go!"

Callen's face was grim in the faint moonlight. "Mira, stop."

"I said let me go!" I tried to wrench my arm free, but his grip was like iron.

"No." His voice was low, stripped of its usual teasing edge. "I stood by. I watched. I gave you space, didn't I? I never interfered. But it's been too long. It's time to snap out of it, out of whatever this is that's eating you up inside, whatever makes you think you need to do this. It stops now."

Frustration welled inside me. "You don't understand! Let me go, Callen. One last time. I promise, I won't—"

"Your promises are worthless on this," he said, his voice cracking with irritation I rarely heard from him. "I'm not an idiot."

A dark figure stormed out of the shadows toward us. Damien. His expression was a thundercloud, his gaze locked on Callen's hand gripping my arm. I instinctively moved in front of Callen, but he shoved me behind him, putting himself squarely between me and the Sovereign.

"Back off," Callen snarled, his body tense and ready for a fight.

"Callen, don't—" I pleaded. He couldn't risk his life, his future, over something like this. Not for me.

"Unhand her." Damien's voice was deadly quiet.

"Or what?" Callen shot back, not budging an inch. "You'll have me thrown in the dungeons? Strip my remaining rank? I don't care. I have a conscience, which is more than I can say for you. I knew it was because of *you* she's been hurting herself. I won't let you take her and break her more. So go to the one you just promised your Bonding to."

Damien flinched as if struck. His furious gaze snapped from Callen to me, the anger draining from his face to be replaced by dawning, horrified comprehension.

"You were hurting yourself?" The question was a whisper, raw and disbelieving.

I froze. Callen had exposed me. Just like that. Humiliation rose in my throat, and I had to clench my jaw against the sudden, hot press of tears. "I just need space. Please."

Callen's jaw clenched. "What do you think she was always doing in the archery range for hours? Playing with her own blood for fun?"

Damien closed his eyes, a wave of agony washing over his features. When he opened them, they were bleak. "Thank you for telling me," he said to Callen in a rough voice. He reached out and briefly squeezed Callen's shoulder.

Then he moved, ignoring Callen's protest.

"Don't you dare—" I spat, backing up a step.

When his hands came for me, I swung. My fist connected with his jaw with a solid, satisfying crack. He didn't even grunt. He just took the blow, his head turning slightly with the force, his expression unchanging.

"Get lost!" I shouted, shoving against his chest. "I told you I need space!"

He took another step, and as I spun to flee, he simply bent and scooped me up into his arms.

I kicked, I cursed, I told him exactly what he was—a liar, a heartless bastard—but he didn't even flinch. "I am sorry, love," he murmured into my hair, his voice thick with an emotion I couldn't name. "I can give you anything you ask for. Anything in this world. But I will never give you distance from myself. I am sorry."

And with that, he turned and carried me away from the range, away from Callen, and into the dark, leaving the echoes of our shattered peace behind.

ONCE THE RAGING anger dulled into helplessness, all that was left was shame.

He knew. They knew. That I was this weak, pathetic girl who couldn't face pain head-on, who had chosen the coward's way of self-harm instead. Who was too scared to face the reality. I cut myself. I healed. Then I did it again. I needed a reason to stop, but all I had found were reasons to keep going.

"Please," I whispered, my voice muffled against his chest as he carried me through the silent palace corridors. "Let me go. We are better off without each other in every way, Damien. I can see that now."

He didn't respond, didn't even try to argue. He walked, silent, up the stairwell's endless stairs, carrying me as though I wasn't just thrashing against his chest.

When I realized where he was taking me—his chamber— another wave of panic crested. I clawed at his arms in a final, desperate attempt to escape his hold. I couldn't hide my rage or my shame anymore.

He was the source.

Lorenza's voice cut through the dim hall from the entrance to his chamber. "What are you doing? You know they all are waiting for you to conclude the terms, and here you are..." Her tone was incredulous, blade-edged with disbelief. "Playing nursemaid with this Tamer—"

Damien didn't even break stride. "Shut up and get out," he said flatly, devoid of any emotion. He shouldered past her, into his chamber, and kicked the door shut behind us with a force that made the walls shudder, slamming it in her stunned face.

The moment the lock clicked, I wrenched myself from his arms. "Let go of me!"

He gripped my waist, halting my stumble as I lurched away. "You can have your space here," he said, as he stepped back to lean against the closed door, blocking the only exit.

I took a sharp step back, fury and indignity still brewing in my veins. "How generous of you," I scoffed, but the sound was brittle. "To grant me space in your cage. Just. Let me go."

"Never."

"Damn you."

He looked at me with a pained expression. "I am giving you time," he said, his voice strained. "Time for yourself. To—"

"Damn you and your giving time! I don't need it here!" I spat, the words lashing out. "I want space from you. You are the one who bears the blame for this!"

"I know."

He said nothing else, just watched me as I stalked to his heavy oak chair and collapsed into it, breathing in and out, in and out, trying to get air into my starved lungs. I was circling the fact of the hurt, then circling the more horrifying fact that I had been about to hurt myself again, badly this time. I wanted to erase it all, to go back and be someone stronger.

I braced myself, my mind already scrambling for excuses and justifications for the weakness he'd discovered. But when I looked at him, he was looking at me like I had broken something precious of his.

"Why are *you* looking at me like *I* was the one who hurt you?" I seethed.

He closed his eyes for a moment, a pained expression deepening into his features before he met my gaze again. "You hurt yourself...because of me."

"Yes!" I shouted. "Yes." And instantly, I regretted it, because I knew it was my fault, my own failing that I hurt myself, and no one else's. But I didn't care. I wanted to make him hurt for the pain he'd caused me.

"I should have been your shield." His breath hitched, the words struggling out. "I should have seen you. Stars, Bella. I should have seen you."

I shook my head and buried my face in my hands, rubbing at my eyes to stop the treacherous tears. I was good for Damien, and I knew that in my soul. But being just his Eternis was not enough for the Sovereign he was. I was too illiterate in the language of courts and politics. I wasn't bred for their twisted lies and betrayals, and I certainly wasn't fit to be the Empress of Atlassian. Because no true Empress would ever resort to self-harm when faced with a painful situation.

"I won't do it again. I won't hurt myself," I whispered, looking straight at him, at the raw pain in his eyes. "I promise. But not for you. For myself."

He searched my face. "You are speaking as if you will do this only for yourself. And I love that for you, precious. But do not, for one moment, think there will ever be a life for you where I am not breathing down your neck until I draw my last breath."

"Then don't make me draw that last breath out of you," I hissed, the words a venomous promise. "If that's what it takes to be free of this, I will."

A dark, humorless smile touched his lips. "I can think of worse fates. But let me make myself perfectly clear to you before you make that choice."

"Make what clear?" I shot back. "Oh, or was that your strategy all along, Sovereign?" I asked, my voice dropping to dangerously calm. "To let the entire Realm believe you and Lorenza are a couple? Oh, and I caught a rather interesting detail. You shared your chamber with her last night." I let the accusation hang, watching for any flicker of denial. "You were finalizing your Bonding with Nyxaria today, weren't you?" My voice turned to corrosive acid. "How foolish I was. To dress up and go like a naive little fool, believing I could belong by your side. While you paraded Lorenza as your future Empress among the Royalty, I was just the Tamer. Your Clan's useful weapon."

His eyes widened with something akin to horror and disbelief.

"Ah stars, what a mess." His words were barely a whisper.

"Yes, a mess *you* created!" I shot back. "You have lost me. Congratulations are in order, I suppose." I threw his own words back at him.

He shook his head, a sharp, frustrated motion. "No—No, I meant—"

Then he moved, crossing the room to kneel on the floor before my chair. He took my injured hand in his before I could pull it back. His thumbs were gentle, caressing the skin around the old cuts.

"How can you not know," he said, his voice rough with emotion, "that I would lay my body over burning coals so you could cross without so much as singeing your hem?"

"Well, I got burned anyway, didn't I?" The bitterness in me was a shield I was getting far too good at wielding. "Seems like the coals are everywhere, and you are spectacularly bad at laying your body anywhere but where it causes the most damage." I tried to pull my hands back from his grasp, but his hold was strong. "And again, stop looking at me like I'm the one who wronged you!"

He exhaled, the sound ragged. "I assumed you were secure enough, that you would never question your place in my life. That was ignorance from my part."

"Yes, maybe it's because you haven't ever felt the hurt you cause," I said, pulling my hand back, this time successfully. "Perhaps we should go back to the ballroom. But this time, maybe I can be with that handsome Royal. The one who likes my eyes, just like you—"

"His death sentence is half written in my mind, and you are etching it deeper with every syllable." He eyes went cold.

I exhaled in exasperation. This was going back and forth and I was getting tired. "I think," I said, standing up, "we are better off without each oth—"

"Don't." His eyes blazed with a ferocity that shook me to my very bones. "Don't you dare finish that sentence. We are not better apart. We are *nothing* apart."

"I cannot be your secret mistress!" I cried, trying to step around him toward the door. "Not anyone's! I have pride, and you are a poison to it!" I made a move to run, but his hand shot out and gripped my waist. Then he turned me to face him.

"A mistress?" he growled, his eyes blazing with a mix of fury and hurt. "Is that what you think this is?"

"What else could it be, if it feels like it?" I shot back, twisting in his grasp.

"Stop running, Bella." His voice thundered low, filled with a desperate command. "You've had your rage. You've made your accusations. Now it has to be enough." He took a ragged breath. "Let me speak. I feel like an absolute fool for not seeing this. Let me —please just let me speak."

He broke off, revealing a tormented man beneath the Sovereign. "I will explain it again, and again, and again, until you believe me. Until you know you are my destiny. That even if you see me with your own eyes doing some dreadful thing to you, your faith in me will rouse you from that fevered dream. You will know me well enough to understand that I would never hurt you. If I have failed to make you believe that, then the fault is mine, and mine alone."

I didn't respond. I just stood there, letting the words wash over me.

He drew in a long breath, his forehead pressing to mine. "Let me begin instead by telling you how breathtaking you were tonight. And it tears me apart that you even let someone else have the privilege of dancing with you before me. But I am taking it as my punishment for my blindness." His voice dropped, roughened by anguish. "I did not think I needed to narrate every political maneuver to you. That is clearly my mistake. If I had known you would internalize it like this, that you would see it as a reflection of your worth rather than the necessity of my duty, I would have tied you to a chair and explained every damned detail."

"Then explain, Sovereign," I whispered, the fight leaving me, replaced by a need to understand. "I think I have all the time in the world now that you've trapped me here."

"We have never fought a Dissonance without intelligence," he began, his voice grave. "Kaldorix—our rival Clan—would have it indirectly from other Telmorian Clans, while those Clans of Veldoria share nothing with us. We are at a disadvantage. I am not so arrogant as to deny the chance that we could lose. We will fight. We will win. But there is always a what if. And I could not bear the what ifs that involved you being harmed, or alone, or vulnerable in a Realm where I no longer exist to protect you."

The air left my lungs as if he'd punched me. "Stop." I reached up, pressing my palm gently over his mouth. Threatening him was one thing, but hearing him speaking about his death was a wound I was not prepared for.

He slowly took my wrist, turned my palm over, and pressed a soft kiss to its center. He then brought my flawed fingertips to his lips, kissing each one with a tenderness that spoke louder than any vow.

His voice was rugged. "I went straight to that event from the Dominion so I could trade a vow from the Sovereign of Zarkon himself that they would grant you asylum, that they would keep you safe and sound, cherished and protected, even if I fall. Even if Atlassian falls."

He continued, "Do you honestly think I care to even notice that Lorenza exists in this Realm? She was there as the Heiress of Nyxaria, and as the exchange ally for the Dissonance, just like

Arthur of Zarkon. With all of that to consider, and while speaking to them both, I hadn't even realized she was beside me until she was. I warned her away the moment I noticed she was following me."

"I don't—I thought I heard you were discussing a Bonding with Lorenza's father," I whispered.

"I was," he said. "And I made it unequivocally clear that I would not be pursuing Bonding with Lorenza before I left." A pause, something moving briefly through his expression. "There is more to that conversation than the Bonding. When I have clarity, you will have it." His jaw ticked once. "Until then, do not accept something as true unless you hear it from my own lips. Those ballrooms are a breeding ground for vipers." A muscle ticked in his jaw. "And it was my father who invited that entire flock of gossips while I only needed to speak with two Sovereigns."

The guilt was a crushing wave. I had been so consumed by my own pain, I had never considered he would have his side of this story, like I did every other time. And yet, something still didn't feel right in all of this. Because what I'd seen and heard—I had enough reason to believe it was real.

I reached for him, my hands framing his face, and leaned forward and pressed my forehead to his, closing my eyes, trying to pour every ounce of my understanding, my remorse, my devotion into that single, silent touch.

He carried me to his bed, and I straddled him.

"Why did you hurt yourself, Bella?" he asked. His face was a map of agony, and I was drowning in a sea of guilt.

"I...I couldn't breathe," I began, the words torn from me. "When it pained me, it was a pressure, building and building inside with nowhere to go. The...the sting...was a way out. It made all the other pains dull." I squeezed my eyes shut. "It was weak. I know it was weak."

His breath hitched hard, his forehead pressing to mine. "No," he said. "No. That was not yours to carry. And if you had no out but that, then the fault is mine. Mine, not a soul else's."

He shifted then, his hands coming up to cradle my face, forcing me to look at him in the dim light. His eyes were dark pools of intensity.

"Do you have any clue," he began, his voice low, "how bloody *precious* you are?" He gave a few breaths to let it float between us. "Every single part of you. The strength in your hands that calms beasts that would level cities. The fire in your spirit that challenges me at every turn. The kindness that sees worth in an unfeeling wretch like me." His thumb traced the line of my cheekbone. "The light in your eyes that is the first thing I search for in any room. You are a miracle I do not deserve but will fight the stars to keep. The thought that you would harm a single, precious inch of yourself…" His voice broke. He leaned forward and kissed me, slowly, deeply, before pulling back just enough to look into my soul. "It shatters me."

"I won't do it again," I whispered against his lips.

"You are my soul made whole, Bella," he said, his thumb brushing a tear from my cheek. "Even if I die, they will not harm a single thread of your hair. I have seen to it."

I shook my head against his, my eyes still closed, my own tears now mingling with his skin.

"And the chamber." He let out a long breath, his thumb stroking my wrist. "I shared a chamber with Lorenza. And with Nathan. And with six other members of our Legion. It was a strategic meeting point, not a rendezvous." A faint, weary smile touched his lips. "Nathan snores, by the way. Loudly."

A choked sound, half-sob, half-laugh, escaped me. I slumped against him, all the fight gone, replaced by a weary shame.

What a mess, indeed. I would have kicked me out if I were him. Good thing that he wasn't me.

I had thought he was ashamed of me, that he couldn't bear to talk to Royalties with me by his side. And in that moment, a crystalline realization settled deep into my bones. I had been looking at my lack of breeding as a weakness, a reason to hide, an excuse to escape. It was easier to let doubt gnaw me hollow than to claim the place fate had thrown at my feet.

The Dorms didn't raise me to be an Empress. But it was a blank slate. I wasn't bound by centuries of stifling tradition. I could learn. I could grow. I could become strong, not by pretending to be like the women born to this life, but by forging my own kind of strength.

I was standing at the edge of something greater. Fate had sprinkled me into it—no, hurled me into it—and if I was to remain, if I was to walk beside Damien Azarios as anything more than a self-harming girl, then I had to be worthy of it.

Of him. Of myself. Of the title.

I lifted my head from his shoulder and met his gaze. "Meet me in the training yard after your duties tomorrow. I need to show you something." There was no more delaying it. He had to descend into *the Abyss*.

Without waiting for a reply, I leaned into him again, tucking my head back under his chin, my arms winding around his waist. I let out a long, slow breath, the last of the tension leaving my body.

————⋘⋙————

THE ORANGE LAMP guttered low and the chamber softened into a pocket of dark and heat. It took me a few dazed moments to realize I had fallen asleep on him, and he had succumbed as well, both of us still in the same pose—me straddling his lap, his arms locked tightly around me.

He stirred first. I felt the deep intake of his breath, the shift of his form. Then his voice, rough and graveled with sleep, shattered the quiet in the most beautiful way imaginable.

"I am in love with you."

Of all the things I thought I might hear from him in the deep of night, this was the one I had never truly allowed myself to expect.

The words were so simple. But they landed as if my soul had turned itself inside out until it bore his name at its center. Every struggle, every moment of pain, suddenly reoriented itself into a path that had led directly to him. It felt as though nothing else mattered anymore.

I pulled back my face and looked at him.

"Truly?" I whispered. The question was a thread of hope spun from disbelief. This was the least expected revelation in the deep of night, after...well, after the very eventful evening.

"Yes. I love you." He looked down at me, his smile a little pained, a lot awed. "My soul recognizes yours, Bella," he said, his voice low and certain. "I had already accepted that it was futile to fight it. I loved you even when I had no words for it. I'm only saying the words now because I did not know this was what love felt like." His thumb dragged slowly across the corner of my eye, wiping away the tears gathered there. "I have never loved anyone. Ever. Until you."

I took his face in my hands and kissed him slowly. It was my answer, my surrender, and my trust, all at once. I tasted the salt of my own tears on his lips and felt the shudder that went through him as his hand came up to cradle my neck.

I pressed my forehead to his, my thumb tracing the line of his jaw, feeling the slight roughness. I couldn't speak. The words had lodged somewhere in my throat, too large and too sharp to swallow past.

"Rowane asked me once what *I* wanted," he murmured against my skin. "I never answered then, because I didn't know. I have only ever taken what was necessary and left the rest. But you—you I want with a selfishness I'm not ashamed of. All of you. The parts that are soft and the parts that bite. The grace and the wreckage. I want to be the only one who knows the difference between them."

I pressed closer, my fingers curling into the fabric of his shirt, holding on like he might dissolve if I let go. His hand moved to the crown of my head, fingers threading through my hair, and he held me there.

"Sleep," he whispered, breath warm against my hair. "I will begin repairing the world for you in the morning."

CHAPTER 30

MIRABELLE

When I woke again, it was to the hush of morning light and the cocoon of warmth around me, soft quilts, deep furs, and the steady rhythm of peace I had almost forgotten existed. The first thing I was truly aware of was the gentle tracing of Damien's fingers over my fingertips.

"Awake, precious?" His voice was a soft rumble.

The memories of the previous night washed over me, my accusations and theatrics. A hot blush instantly flooded my cheeks. He chuckled, his thumb stroking the heated skin. "I hate waking you when you look so untroubled. But I wanted to see if you would join me for breakfast."

"Yes," I said, my voice still thick with sleep, and yawned, stretching like a cat. I blinked, finally taking in the sight of him, fully regal in his formal attire, while I was swimming in his tunic. The contrast was absurd.

"You look..." I started, gesturing vaguely at his pristine state.

"Like I didn't have my soul rearranged by a tiny, furious Tamer?" he finished, a smile playing on his lips. "Appearances are deceptive."

"Why you are already awake?" I asked, noticing the faint shadows under his eyes.

"I had a few things to finish that I had left behind," he said.

A sudden thought came. "Did you change my clothes?"

"I didn't think you would be comfortable sleeping in your gown. So yes."

A more mischievous thought followed. "Did you steal a touch?"

His smile shifted to a look of disbelief. "If you seriously think that I have patiently suffered through all these days of wanting you, just to *steal a feel* while you're asleep, where you don't feel it, where I get no reaction, no sight of your eyes going dark, no sound of your breath catching when I touch you for the first time, then you underestimate both my patience and my greed."

The intensity of his response made my stomach flutter.

"About the first time. I have something to tell you," I began, my tone shifting.

His expression shifted, misreading the shift entirely. A dark, cold edge entered his gaze. "If you are about to speak another man's name—"

A giggle burst out of me before I could stop it. He was jealous. And he was jealous of himself.

His eyes, which had been cold, softened in confusion at the sound. He stared at me, and the longer I giggled, the more the rage drained from his gaze, replaced by a bewildered fascination.

He suddenly caught me against him and kissed me, hard enough to steal the laugh from my throat. I smiled against his mouth, but that only coaxed him to deepen it. His hands roamed with a hunger that left me weak, and I moaned against him, kissing him back with equal fervor.

His lips left mine, trailing a line of fire down my jaw. He buried his face in the curve of my neck, his breath hot against my sensitive skin. Then his mouth found a spot that made me arch my back. A low, throaty moan escaped me, my fingers tangling in his hair to hold him closer. His hands slid down my back, pulling me flush against him, and one came up to cup my breast through the thin linen of the tunic, his thumb brushing over the peak in a way that made me gasp against his shoulders.

I broke the kiss, nipping his skin. "The breakfast," I whispered, breathless, though my body begged otherwise.

He sighed, resting his forehead against mine, his breathing ragged. "What were you going to say?" he asked, his voice a low rumble.

I smiled, tracing the line of his jaw. "I would rather show you after your duties," I murmured, and pressed a soft kiss to the corner of his mouth.

"Hmm." His hand still cupped me, his thumb tracing lazy, maddening circles. "There is still time for a first course," he murmured, his eyes closed, savoring the feel of me. His other hand slid from my back, his fingers splaying low on my hip to pull me firmly against the hard ridge of his desire. "We are not late."

I pushed his hand away gently. "Yet. You are not going to be able to stop this if you keep doing that."

He opened his eyes, a challenge in their blue depths. "You don't know the extent of my self-control."

"Oh, trust me. I do," I said, smirking and leaning in to press a soft kiss to his cheek before sliding out of his arms.

With obvious, painful effort, he regained his composure and released me. He muttered something that sounded like *a very cruel Tamer*, but there was a warm amusement in his eyes.

I padded over to freshen up and then to where he'd laid out clothes for me. I slipped into the dress similar to the one from the ball, cream fading into green. Simple yet lovely. When I emerged, smoothing the skirts, Damien was reaching for me with his hand at my waist, and twirled me once in a dizzying, perfect spin.

"You owe me a dance," he murmured, his mouth curving faintly.

The orchestra was only a memory, but he hummed under his breath, low and sure, guiding me with practiced grace.

"You can sing," I blurted, astonished.

He raised a brow. "That surprises you?"

"Yes," I said. "You can't be good at everything."

"Apparently, I can," he replied with maddening calm, before spinning me into a dip.

His face hovered so close that all I could see were the storm-blue depths of his eyes. My heart fluttered like a captured bird against my ribs, and I felt the curve of my lips answering the warmth he ignited inside me. His gaze melted into that rare, unguarded smile he reserved only for me.

"Better," he murmured, his voice low and intimate as he righted me but did not let go. Then he led me out, his fingers laced with mine, into the corridor where the early morning light streamed through the windows, painting everything in gold.

I HAD ANTICIPATED a quiet meal with a few Elders. So I stiffened under Damien's touch when we entered the dining hall to find a veritable battalion of Royalties gathered at the long, curved table. Sovereigns, Empresses, Heirs, and Heiresses sat beneath the glittering crystal lanterns, their low conversations doing nothing to help my nerves. Thralls moved soundlessly between them, filling goblets and laying out platters of steaming food.

He paused first before an older couple robed in Zarkon's deep indigo. "Sovereign Karzul, Empress Eyra," Damien said, his voice smooth but firm. "This is Mirabelle."

A look of recognition passed between them. The man studied me with a quiet, assessing curiosity that quickly warmed. "There is pride in your voice when you speak her name, Azarios. You hide it poorly."

"Who said I meant to hide it?" Damien answered unbothered.

They both chuckled, and she reached out and gently squeezed my hand. "You will always find sanctuary in Zarkon."

With a final, respectful nod, Damien guided me toward the head of the table. But there, two chairs stood, and one was already occupied. Lorenza sat there with her back straight, her black hair intricately braided in a thin glossy coronet. The rest of the table was a sea of unfamiliar, regal faces, all engaged in murmured conversation. They offered nods to Damien, who returned them with curt ones.

From the far end, Damien's father, Alaric, spoke without looking up from his plate. "The Legion are breakfasting in the next hall. A Thrall can accompany her there. We have matters to discuss that do not concern a Tamer."

Lorenza tilted her body toward Damien's empty chair. "It would be more appropriate. We are rather tight on space as it is." Her smile was a razor's edge, and she was not hiding it anymore.

My cheeks burned. Damien's jaw tightened as his glance touched the chair Lorenza sat in, perhaps meant for me. I would not have him make a scene over bread and broth.

"I will take my breakfast in with the Legion," I began softly.

But Damien had already moved. He simply sat in the empty chair beside Lorenza, who immediately angled herself toward him to say something, when he clutched my wrist and drew me into his lap.

A shocked gasp escaped me, echoed by the sudden silence that fell across the table. Every gaze snapped toward us. I flushed crimson, squirming in his lap—utterly unaccustomed to being the center of such intense, collective scrutiny. But Damien was the picture of calm. His arm settled around my waist, steadying me.

Into the silence, his voice rang out clear, leaving no room for doubt. "To avoid any future confusion, let it be known that Mirabelle is the one I shall set upon Atlassian's throne. As my Eternis and Atlassian's Empress."

A wave of astonishment swept through those gathered. My own heart beat a frantic rhythm. To make such a declaration here, among this company, was beyond bold. I should not have been surprised that he had not seen fit to give me a warning. How perfectly like him, to shape my future with such unshakable certainty, never doubting for a moment that I would stand beside him.

"There is another matter to rectify," he continued, his gaze sweeping them before settling beside him. "Lorenza is our honored guest for the Dissonance, as part of the alliance with Nyxaria, which we very much value." He gave a nod toward Aramak, her father. "However, we are not arranged to be Bonded. The declaration was a misunderstanding from my father's side, made prematurely. My intent is to make the truth clear to all present."

Lorenza stiffened as if struck. She stared directly into his face, her composure dissolving into a visible, silent squirm in her seat.

Then reactions rippled through the assembly. The Sovereign of Zarkon offered an approving nod. An Heir smothered a grin behind his cup, while others murmured tributes. Lorenza's face went pale, then into a frozen mask of fury.

From the far end of the table, Alaric muttered, his voice a low growl of displeasure, "This is not a matter for the breakfast table."

Damien's gaze didn't even flicker in his father's direction. "On the contrary. There is no more important matter for any table I preside over." He adjusted his hold on me. "Now, let us begin, shall we?" he stated.

The spell broke. The low hum of conversation cautiously resumed. Cutlery chimed against porcelain once more. Thralls resumed their silent, efficient ballet around the table.

As if the declaration had been a simple passing of the salt, Damien reached for a silver casserole dish and began filling the plate before us with foods he knew I favored—honeyed fruits, roasted meat, soft cheeses, even a few pieces of duckheart.

He caught the eye of a Thrall and signaled with a slight nod. The woman hurried over with a small, steaming bowl of the spiced root soup I was hopelessly addicted to. He ladled a generous portion into his bowl, the rich, fragrant steam rising between us, and then placed it before me.

We ate like that. I cut into a duckheart. His hand—resting on my thigh—gave a slight, approving squeeze. He took a bite of his own portion while listening to the Heir of Zarkon, his hand idly tracing circles on my thigh.

The Nyxarian Sovereign leaned forward, his gaze fixed on me with the same intensity as the day before. "And the Tamer? Where does her...unique lineage place her in your strategies?" A thin, probing smile touched his lips. "One hears such unusual things—"

"No." Damien's voice was flat. "I am not entertaining inquiries about her history here."

Beside him, his Empress gave a soft, dismissive laugh. "You have been ill-served by your own curiosity, My Liege. There are questions fit for the negotiating table, and questions fit for courtly gossip." Her eyes glinted, cool and unamused. "You have chosen the latter."

A few low, tense chuckles breathed out around the table. And I felt a pang of sympathy for the Empress.

Then the Heir of Nyxaria, a handsome young man who looked strikingly like Lorenza, turned a disarming smile toward me. "It is fascinating, though. Your Aether. How does it feel to wield it? Was it something you always knew?"

I found my voice, aiming for a tone of cool politeness. "It feels... quite natural. I don't know how to explain it. It is simply there in my mind."

He leaned forward slightly, his curiosity undimmed. "And do you hear what they think?"

"When I am Tethered to them," I said, "yes, I do."

"Oooh, that's really fascinating," murmured an Heiress from Zarkon, her eyes bright with intrigue.

Another Heiress clasped her hands together lightly. "Would you mind showing us? Just a small demonstration before we depart after the breakfast."

"If the field is free after the board, I will," I said with a smile. Surprisingly, I wasn't feeling uncomfortable being at the receiving end of their attention. In fact, I was enjoying it—even though I truly hadn't been feeling all that settled in his lap in front of every-one. But that awkwardness had faded into a distant corner.

"Aren't you going to ask permission from your Sovereign, girl?

Or do you make a habit of performing like an untrained one without command?" Alaric's cold voice cut in from the end of the table. I felt Damien stiffen behind me.

I met Alaric's gaze and spoke before Damien could. "Contrary to popular belief, I am not anyone's beast to be commanded. I am a weapon to be wielded—and only I decide when I am drawn."

I turned back to the Heiress, my smile sharpening. "I would be pleased to show a few of my tricks."

Damien's hand gave my thighs another approving squeeze.

It was then that another Heir of Nyxaria, perhaps emboldened by wine, gestured between Damien and the seethingly silent Lorenza. "And this...change of heart regarding the Bonding? This is because of the Tamer?" He nodded toward me.

Damien's voice was unruffled, a study in diplomatic calm. "The discussion of a Bonding was never a promise. It was mutually dissolved later. That is the beginning and end of the matter."

Lorenza nodded at him and smiled, a careful expression that did little to conceal the bitterness tightening the corners of her mouth.

I squirmed faintly in his lap until his arm tightened around my waist, settling me firmly in place. I took no pleasure in her public discomfort—well, perhaps a little. Fine. A little too much. She had created all these rumors circling Damien herself. So this was the only way to put an end to them that she would understand.

Damien spared me the cuts he knew I disliked and claimed the rest, his hand steadying the dish while mine worked the knife. And when I had almost finished the sweet, glistening grapefruit, he asked, "Had enough, precious?" and I answered with a satisfied nod.

Apparently, Alaric was not finished. "Sentimentality is a luxury a Sovereign cannot afford. It makes you weak. Just like your mother's soft heart. I see you've inherited it." He took a sip of ale. "I thought I had made you harder."

I was dumbstruck. To question Damien so openly, so callously.

It was a desecration. And he'd done it without a flicker of hesitation.

Damien's reply was glacial. "You made me hard enough to endure your inability to be anything like a father. A pity you still mistake loneliness for strength."

"A ruler is alone," Alaric shot back. "That is the first and last lesson. I should have imprinted it into you sooner."

A protective heat rose through me. I turned in Damien's lap to face the far end fully. "You are not just a useless Sovereign who nearly ran this Clan into the ground before his son took the crown. You are a spectacularly useless father. The whole of Atlassian knows that, if not for Damien, it would be ash and ruin. You mired yourself in making the Royals richer while he learned the value of every life in his care."

My palm was sweating, but the tremor in my hands stilled when I felt the faint press of Damien's smile against my hair.

I leaned forward, my anger a hot, bright flame. "He carries the weight of this entire Clan on his shoulders, a weight you placed there without a shred of the guidance or care he deserved, because apparently you knew how to make an Heir but had no clue how to raise a son. He never asked for *you*. I mean, who in their right mind would ask for a father like you?"

Someone choked on their drink.

I was seething with rage. "And the greatest failure in this hall is not Damien's capacity to show affection, but your inability to do anything but criticize and belittle the one person who saved this Clan from your neglect."

A stunned silence fell.

Alaric's face purpled with rage. He slowly rose to his feet, his knuckles white on the table's edge. "You insolent—"

"Utter one word against her," Damien said, his voice like a blade drawn in still air, "and you will learn exactly what kind of a man you never bothered to raise."

Alaric stared at his son, and for the first time, I saw a flicker of genuine fear. With a final, seething glare, he turned and strode from the hall without another word, the great doors thudding shut behind him.

Then, I felt Damien's lips pressed gently against the crown of my head, a soft, lingering kiss that spoke of gratitude. I knew that no one had ever stood up for him. He didn't need it, since he'd learned to stand alone as a child. But even a child who learned to stand alone should have had someone to stand *for* him. The thought was a lance of piercing pain through my heart.

I turned back, my hands trembling only slightly now. I cut one last piece of the sweetened fruit from the plate, then held it toward Damien's lips. "Do you want a taste from mine?" I asked, my voice softening. "This is really good."

A smile ghosted across his mouth. "Sure, love," he said, and took the bite from my fingers. Lorenza's spoon clattered sharply against her porcelain plate. But the breakfast continued like normal. The conversation buzzed with a new current.

Then a low, vibrating hum began, so deep it was felt more than heard. It shuddered through the floor, up through the legs of the table, rattling the cutlery. Damien's arm tightened around my waist like a vise.

The hum intensified into three distinct, seismic waves, each stronger than the last. Goblets of ale shivered, their surfaces rippling. Every conversation died mid-sentence.

A sudden, pitch-black darkness swallowed us, as if night had fallen in an instant. The grand windows showed nothing but a void. Only the faint glow of the overhead lanterns remained, suspended high above like dying stars.

When the light returned after a few dreadful moments, it was tinged with a faint red hue that painted every face with dread. The first face I saw clearly was Sovereign Karzul of Zarkon across from us, his expression grim and knowing.

"It is not possible—" the Sovereign Aramak whispered, his knuckles white where they gripped the table's edge.

The Heir of Zarkon was the first to move, slowly pushing back his chair to stand. "Well," he said, his tone cutting through the stunned silence, "if we move now, we might at least be fashionably late for the end of our Realm."

It was the start of Dissonance.

A week early.

CHAPTER 31

MIRABELLE

I rushed to grab my boots from Amara's chamber. I shoved the door open without knocking.

And froze.

Amara was pressed against the wall, and Izmer was...well, he was kissing—or swallowing—her. Thoroughly. Her hands were tangled in his hair, his arm braced against the wall beside her head. I was too dumbstruck to turn back, still grasping the scene in front of me.

They broke apart at the sound of the door, both breathing heavily. Amara's eyes went wide. "Bella! It's not—it's not what you see! He had...a crumb? On his lip? I was just helping. You can help too if you want—"

Izmer reached out and covered her mouth with his palm, his eyes closing in exasperation. "Stars woman, stop talking." He then looked at me, his expression shifting to wary assessment. "Well?"

I finally turned around, certain I was beet red.

"Canoodling now?" I burst out, my voice strangled. "Did you not feel that? The Dissonance has started! Your Clan has probably already left! They might be reaching the front lines as we speak!"

"Turn around little Mira," Izmer drawled. "It's not like you haven't done considerably worse and had the audacity to look innocent about it after."

I turned to see a very crimson Amara, who was looking at me with adorable mortification.

"Well, I said the Dissonance has started."

"Oh. That's what that was," Izmer continued without missing a beat. "Even I was confused. The chamber shook. I thought it was just...us." He gestured vaguely between himself and a still-flushed Amara.

Typical Izmer Castellane.

Amara closed her eyes. "Izmer."

"I'm being honest."

"Please stop being honest."

He considered this. "No."

He ran a hand through his already disheveled hair. "I thought we had one more week. This type of inconsistency should be..." He muttered a vivid curse under his breath.

"Apparently, if more than half the Clans breach the Accord, the Dominion pushes both Realms," I said, the words tumbling out in a rush. "I mean, the Sages think that might be the reason."

Izmer's face darkened. "These bloody warriors and their inability to keep their swords or tempers sheathed." He turned back to Amara, cupped her face, and gave her one quick kiss. "I will be back in four nights. Don't do anything recklessly brave without me." He squeezed her shoulder and walked out, grabbing my arm on his way and pulling me with him.

"One moment!" I said, shaking him off and darting back to Amara.

"Bells," she hissed in a whisper-shout. "He just...he kissed me. Do you understand? Izmer Castellane kissed me!"

Despite the fear clawing at my mind about our existential crisis, a laugh slipped out. "Yes, I just *saw*." I caught her hands, squeezing. "And you'll tell me every detail later, when you're capable of standing upright without swooning sideways."

She grinned, dazed. "I might actually swoon."

I laughed and hugged her tight. She pulled back and grabbed my hands, her eyes wide with a panic she was trying hard to mask. "Wait, you're leaving?"

"Of course I am," I said, forcing a lightness I didn't feel. "Who else is going to tame the big, scaly things?" I poked her side, making her jump.

She managed a wobbly smile. "Be careful. Promise?"

"I promise. I'll see you tomorrow morning, alright? Save me a honey-cake." I gave her a final, fierce hug.

"Wait!" she said as I pulled away and shoved a sealed envelope into my hand. "This came for you."

I grabbed it, gave her one last, reassuring squeeze, and bolted out the door.

Once we were in the hall, striding quickly toward the main keep, Izmer's demeanor shifted entirely. "Listen," he said, his voice low. "I tried to have a word with Damien, but the problem is there are incidents, and properly sourced reports, about the Abyss." His jaw tightened. "They state it didn't just erase memories. It also planted a few false ones. I'll admit, even I'm starting to question what's real. Are you absolutely sure you are Bonded to him?"

I stopped in my tracks. "Of course I'm sure. It's not in my head. Falling for someone isn't one event you can tamper with. It's a hundred moments, a thousand. That doesn't vanish. And he'll trust me over the reports."

Izmer rolled his eyes, rubbing his throat. "Oh, I know all about you falling. And about the everything that came after." Then his tone softened. "But maybe don't tangle him with all these now. It might not be wise, not when he's balancing an entire Clan on his shoulders. Do it after the battles."

I pressed my lips together, the protest rising anyway. "We have a ledger as proof."

"I know," Izmer said grimly. "Amara told me. Look, just take the ledger and hide it somewhere safe when you can. But do not give anyone the slightest hint that you know about it, or about their meetings. The ones behind the Abyss will react the moment they realize you're on their trail." He nodded toward the envelope in my hand. "And these letters—you need to speak to whoever is sending them and gather more evidence if you can, before they suspect you're digging into their schemes. Otherwise, they'll bury everything deeper."

"Of course they will," I muttered. "Easier said than done." The ledger would have to wait until after tonight. Assuming I lived long enough to make it through the Dissonance.

He sighed. "And I am sorry about Lorenza. She's always been... intense about Damien. It is a bit embarrassing that she tried to make it seem like they were a couple. We'd thought it was just an infatuation. She's cunning, but ultimately not a real threat. Still, jealousy can be lethal."

"She's nothing but noise," I replied. "But thank you for the warning."

A grin flashed across his face. "Good. Now, take care of my girl until I get back."

I scoffed. "*Your* girl? Did you just ask me to look after my own friend? If anything, I should be the one threatening to rip your balls off if you try anything funny with her heart."

He clutched his chest in mock horror. "A vicious protector. Perfect. She'll need that." With a final salute, he peeled off down a different corridor, leaving me alone.

I looked down at the note in my hand.

I lost my father because of you. And I needed you to do this for closure. Nothing more.

Irin. She had always been strange with me after the Dissonance, trying a few awkward talks here and there, but never crossing into the obvious. I'd always suspected she needed to talk about her father, but I was too much of a coward to initiate that conversation. After all, I was the reason he was dead. But this, a *closure*—how?

I needed to find her, to see if she truly wanted to be an ally, or if she was just another player in this game, sharpening a knife for revenge.

But there was no time to unravel it now. I was told to grab my gear and rush to the Hold. I had to move before Damien decided the safest place for me was locked in his chamber, guarded by a battalion. He was a protective bastard like that.

Stuffing the cryptic note into my pocket, I broke into a run, my heart hammering against my ribs for an entirely new set of reasons.

I PUSHED OPEN the heavy oak door to the preparation chamber, the scent of cold metal filling my lungs. Inside, the four other Royals, Elsha, Vannor, Rhane, and Tovelle, stood already clad in identical crimson and steel. The sight sent a nervous energy coiling in my stomach. I had already changed into the fitted leathers and engraved steel plates I'd owned since starting at the Hold, with the Atlassian's crest against my chest.

Ophira and Mavren were there, murmuring in low voices. "...when it starts, we won't know the half of what we're facing..." Ophira was saying, her eyes scanning each of us in turn as I fastened a pauldron. "But there will be an indication. A signal from the Dominion. Look for it. Watch for shifts in the light, a change in the arena's energy, a sound. Everything is a clue. Your survival depends on reading them faster than the other side."

I fumbled with the final strap on my vambrace, my fingers clumsy with the rush. The stubborn piece of metal refused to sit flush against my wrist.

"Having trouble, Tamer?" Damien's voice came from the doorway.

I didn't look up, focusing on the buckle. "Just ensuring everything is perfectly inconvenient, my Liege. Wouldn't want to be too comfortable out there." A beat of silence, then the soft shhh-click of the vambrace finally securing.

His gaze swept over my attire as he crossed the space between us. His fingers went to the gorget at my throat, adjusting its angle where it sat crooked against my collarbone. "Who are you going to be with?" he murmured, his breath a warm caress against my temple as his hands moved to the slipped clasp of my cloak, settling it back onto my shoulder.

"Whip-tail, as you well know by now," I breathed, my skin tingling where he touched.

His hands moved next to the cinch of my breastplate, his fingers brushing the metal as he found the loose strap. He pulled it taut with a firm tug that brought me a half-step closer, close enough to feel the heat radiating from his body, to smell the clean scent of cedar that clung to him. "Could I take Dreadclaw and come with you?"

I shook my head, a small, fond smile touching my lips. "That's not going to happen, and you know that. You need to lead the next two. Besides, you didn't even get a chance to rehearse with us. You wouldn't know the signals—"

"I know them," he interrupted. He reached up, his fingers brushing a stray strand of hair from my cheek, tucking it securely behind the gorget. "Every single command. Every shift, every feint, every counter-pattern you created in the outer field."

"How?" I asked, already knowing the answer.

His gaze locked onto mine. "One learns these things when he's spent every spare moment of the last fortnight watching the most captivating sight in the entire Realm."

The riot of warmth through me at his confession was entirely inappropriate for the brink of battle. I forced a lightness into my tone I didn't quite feel, wanting to soothe the worry I saw in the depths of his eyes. "Well, if you're that good, maybe you can give me notes after. But for now, you'll have to trust that your captivating sight knows what she's doing."

His smile held the unguarded look of admiration. *Perfection*, he murmured, so low I almost missed it. Then his expression softened. "We know you are so damn brilliant," he said, the words a solemn vow. "Lead them for us, my precious."

Then his hands moved to my hip, and I felt the cool weight of his own dagger as he slid it into an empty sheath on my belt. Then he framed my face with his hands and kissed me with desperation and passion and intense sweetness. It said everything words could not: *Come back to me.*

He broke the kiss, resting his forehead against mine for a single, breathless moment. Then he closed his eyes, exhaled as if releasing me to the fates, and stepped back, clearing the path.

His gaze swept over the other Royals. "I expect the ballads will do you all justice." He gave a single nod, a gesture of finality and faith, then turned and left the Hold, Ophira and Mavren falling into step behind him.

"Now," I said, turning to face them all, my voice taking on the clear, steady tone I used with them. "Let's begin. Shall we?"

A ripple of straightened backs and sharpened focus went through the group.

Moments later, we mounted. The great gates groaned open, revealing a world bathed in the red hues of the storm-wracked Celestia. Cloaks billowed crimson in the wind. I felt Whip-tail's grounding hum vibrate up through the soles of my boots. NyxRathis shimmered beside Dreadclaw's smoky form, Dravan clicked his beak impatiently, and the Swarm buzzed a harmonious note.

And at the center of it all, surrounded by their immense, wild strength and hard-won harmony, I felt not fear, but a terrifyingly exhilarating rightness.

CHAPTER 32

MIRABELLE

The wait was making us all nervous. The Dominion's masked ones had led us here, their porcelain visors gleaming faintly in the glow of the sealed crust I had shown them. Beyond that, nothing. We were stranded here, jittery and tense, knowing the storm was coming, though not when it would finally begin.

Only the dark, gaping mouth of an entrance stretched before us, a tunnel that seemed to breathe shadows. Somewhere within, it opened into that enormous crystalline globe we'd seen from afar—dark and opaque, like a blind eye. A world where everything was going to happen tonight. It hung suspended like a heart waiting to beat with us inside.

I hadn't imagined the audience would be this vast. In truth, I had not imagined there would be an audience at all. From the high ridge where we stood, I could see them passing, a sea of faces. Clusters of Royals, Majors, and even a few commoners, all flowing into the towering observation levels that curved around the immense, dark openings around us. It was a spectacle, and we were the main event.

Visitors streamed past us on a separate stairway. I could hear my name shouted, voices rising above the noise, some waving when they caught my eye. *My* name. But I didn't register much, only the deafening rush of my own blood in my ears.

Whip-tail shifted at my side, his tail curling anxiously. *Can we walk?* he asked in his enthusiastic voice through our Tether.

Not yet, I answered, reaching to rest my palm against the scales of his neck. *We'll know soon enough.*

I could feel it through all five Tethers. This wasn't like facing Legion drills or even the Abyss. They weren't just going to war; they were being sent into an unknown against Tameables born of a different Etheris. They felt the wrongness of it, the violation. As if they felt the metallic taste of impending death.

Then, the world went black to an absolute, suffocating absence of light. The ground beneath our feet tilted smoothly, a quick motion that sent us sliding forward into the void of the tunnel.

A scream lodged in my throat. There was no air to make a sound. It was a fall through nothingness, a nauseating plunge that stripped all sense of direction. My stomach lurched into my throat. This is it. We're just going to smash into the ground—

The fall ended with a sudden, silent cessation of movement. We had fallen somewhere inside the opaque globe. I blinked—not seeing the green crystal and light I'd expected from the look of the risen ledge, but an oppressive gloom. I stumbled, my boots sinking into something soft and wet. The air that hit my lungs was stale, cold, and carried the gruesome scent of dampness and decay.

Titan's Graveyard. The words echoed as though someone had whispered them straight to my skull.

I was standing in a graveyard. Leafless, twisted trees clawed at a bruised, twilight Celestia. Fog coiled around crumbling headstones and sagging mausoleums like grasping fingers. It was utterly silent, yet the silence was alive, watching.

Whip-tail pressed against my side, a low whine escaping him.

"Elsha?" I called out, my voice a pathetically small thing swallowed by the heavy air. "Rhane!"

Only the echo answered. The fog shifted, and for a heart-stopping second, I saw a skeletal figure standing by the crumbling skull of a long-dead beast, pale, still, and watching.

I blinked, and it was gone.

The ground gave another wet squelch under my boot. I looked down. A coil of innards, half-dissolved and half-calcified, slid greasily between the cracks of the dark soil. It was too warped and alien to be whole. The pungent scent of decay hit me with the next gust of wind, and my stomach lurched violently, trying to empty its contents.

These were the remains of Tameables. Rotten pieces and parts of beasts left behind.

We moved forward with urgency, searching for the rest of us who might have been scattered across this fractured place. But the fog grew heavier. And it felt like a tangible force that resisted our movement.

Think.

I had to think.

But my thoughts dulled, every step like wading through treacle. The longer we stayed, the more the oppressive fog seemed to sap our strength, slowing our steps, making my head swim. We needed to find the others and get out.

Let's find high ground. My thoughts were sparked through Tether. *I had to see.*

There was a brittle crack, and the land beneath my boot gave way. A plume of acrid, black fume erupted from the shattered carapace hidden beneath the muck. I screamed as searing pain shot up my leg, the bottom of my boot sizzled and melted, the heat biting into my sole. Whip-tail also stumbled back with a pained yelp, the corrosive spray splashing across his forepaw. He shook it violently, whining as the flesh there reddened and blistered.

Gritting my teeth against the pain, I forced myself forward to take a look at his wound. A soft, green aura already began to emanate from him, washing over my injured foot and his own wound. The pain dulled to a throbbing ache as his healing started to knit the worst of the damage.

"Don't tire yourself now, love bug." I gasped. "We'll need it later." The healing faded. The relief was temporary, but enough to keep us moving.

If I were with Dravan, I could have taken to the air, seen above this cursed fog. I looked around to search for a way to find an escape from this. Sensing my thought, Whip-tail gave a sad, understanding whine, nuzzling my hand. He couldn't fly and he wanted to do it for me.

It's alright, buddy, I whispered. *You're exactly where I need you to be.*

I hoped so.

Then my sight hit on a massive thing that looked like a tree trunk, lodged at an angle in a split in the ground, its top half raised just above the roiling fog. I ran for it, my boots slipping on the gruesome terrain, and began to climb. The bark was slimy and brittle, but I hauled myself up, hand over hand, climbing out of the suffocating mist.

I broke through the surface. The air was still cold and stale, but I could see. And what I saw made my blood run cold. The grave-yard and fog stretched out in every direction. It felt endless, a wasteland where we could wander until the Dissonance consumed us, until we collapsed and died.

Suddenly I saw a movement, and I squinted. In the distance, Dravan was flying around with Swarms. He flew in a ragged pattern, diving out of the choking fog, his wings tearing the mist apart. The Swarm clung to him like a restless cloak, surging and folding with his every movement. Diving in and out of fog, they were searching for us.

"Here!" I screamed loudly, waving my arms.

His gaze snapped toward me. With a screech, he banked and arrowed toward my perch, the Swarm flowing with him. As he drew closer, Elsha shouted from his back, "We found an edge to the west! A cliff face in the middle!"

"Then guide Whip-tail. Take him there!" I called out to the Swarm. The Swarm detached from Dravan and shot downward, disappearing into the fog to find him.

Vannor reached a hand down from Dravan's back to help me up. I shifted to jump, but my boot slipped on the slimy bark. I fell.

I landed wrong in a coiled nest of sinew and shattered bones. My leg twisted beneath me with a wrenching snap. White-hot, nauseating pain exploded from my ankle, shooting up my leg. I bit down on a scream, blood filling my mouth where my teeth cut my tongue. A grunt of agony was all that escaped.

I couldn't let them know now. They didn't need me as an additional problem.

I pushed myself up, hiding the way my leg buckled. Dravan swooped low. Vannor's hands seized my arms, dragging me up, half-hauling me onto Dravan's back. I clutched at Dravan's jagged horns, swallowing hard against the rising pain.

We flew, diving in and out of the fog, my mind screaming through the Tethers, searching for the others. And finally, I felt it, a faint, fading pulse from NyxRathis. It led us to a cluster of massive, decaying rib cages piled together like a macabre hut. In the shadows between them was a dark, narrow opening.

"Tovelle," I yelled, my voice tight with the effort of masking my pain. A weak, chiming sound echoed from the darkness into my Tether. *Inside...the air...*

Dravan landed and I slid off his back. I caught myself on a sharp rib bone, my vision swimming with black spots. Elsha and Vannor rushed to the narrow opening. A rotten scent poured from it. Elsha gagged, clamping a hand over her nose and mouth.

Vannor peered in, then his face went ashen. "They're in there! They're not moving!"

My vision blurred at the edges; the toxic air was leaching our strength. We had to move. Every moment we stayed here, our chances of surviving this plummeted.

"That bone!" I gasped, pointing a hand at a long, curved rib fallen out of the rotten ribcage. "We can use it to pull them out!"

Vannor braced himself and wedged his shoulder against a rib the size of a tree trunk, veins bulging as he forced it upright.

"Help!" he rasped. Elsha and I grabbed the other side, the bone groaning as it scraped across stone.

Dreadclaw surged from the shadows beside us. Rhane slumped across his back, barely conscious, his leg armor melted away, revealing burned and blistered flesh beneath. Through me, his Tether snapped taut, and I screamed what my voice could not. *NyxRathis and Tovelle.*

"Grab on!" Vannor's voice tore through the fog.

Dreadclaw lunged forward, his half-form bleeding into the void. For one heart-stopping moment, he was gone. Then he returned, tendrils of living shadow enveloping NyxRathis, pulling her clear of the foul air. Tovelle was next, dragged out, limp and still. Dreadclaw laid him gently on the ground, one dark tendril gently brushing NyxRathis's head as she stirred.

My heart stopped. Tovelle. His skin was a horrifying, mottled black, his lips a terrible blue. He wasn't breathing.

"Come back!" Elsha's voice cracked into something broken. She fell over him, clutching his body, sobbing so hard it shook her. "Don't you dare leave me—" Her screams tore through the choking mist, raw enough to shred the silence itself.

My heart stuttered. "Breathe!" I dropped to my knees, shaking his shoulders.

"Breathe, damn you, breathe!" Elsha cried out. Nothing.

Dreadclaw's thought cut across my mind. *Leave him. He is gone.*

My legs gave. The fog pressed in, heavy, hot. My vision narrowed, then warped, grey edges creeping inward. If we didn't move now, we would all collapse here, into the same pit that had swallowed him.

"Elsha," I rasped, gripping her wrist, but she clung to Tovelle, sobbing into his still chest. I could barely hear myself over her cries, my own cheeks wet, every breath tasting of rot.

"No!" The denial was ripped from Elsha, a raw, guttural sound of pure agony. But even her strength was failing, her own consciousness slipping away into the same darkness.

I slumped against Dravan. The toxic air was winning. "Elsha..." I croaked. "We have to go...now...or we all die here..."

Vannor, his own face a faint purple, finally moved. He wrapped his arms around Elsha's waist and physically hauled her away from Tovelle's body. Her screams were echoing through the fog.

We stumbled, half-carried by our Tameables, away from the deathly hollow. As Dravan launched us back into the foggy air, I looked back one last time.

Shapes emerged from the mist around the rib cage hut, pale, skeletal things with too many joints. They converged on Tovelle's still form. One looked up, its hollow eyes seeming to meet mine just before it bent its head and tore a strip of dark fabric and flesh from his arm with a sound that didn't reach my ears but echoed forever in my mind.

They were eating him.

CHAPTER 33
MIRABELLE

We were trapped. The only path was the one we'd come from, and it led back into the heart of the horror where pale, feasting things still crouched. I stared into the endless gorge that opened before us. It was a cliff-like jagged edge in the middle of the graveyard. On the other side was only a swirling void of deepest black that seemed to swallow the faint light from the glowing moss.

My pain began to ease to a manageable throb the longer I stood pressed against Whip-tail's warm, solid flank. I could stand without biting my tongue raw.

This was it. This was the choice. The Dominion didn't design trials with no exit. They designed them with exits no sane person would ever take.

"I think we have to jump," I said, my voice surprisingly steady.

They all stared at me as if I'd finally gone insane.

"There's nothing there!" Rhane protested. "It's just...nothing!"

We were gaining a bit more clarity from Whip-tail's proximity, but it only made the abyss in front of us look more real and final.

"It's the only option that is not going back there to die," I argued, gesturing toward the graves behind. "The trial is a test of will. Not just strength. This is a leap of faith."

"There has to be another way. Maybe a path in the mist we missed," Vannor insisted, his eyes desperately scanning the fog.

But we were running out of time. The air itself was growing heavier, more putrid. And the Tameables—I could feel their confusion through the Tethers. They saw the void with a primal clarity we lacked. They saw a rocky, certain death. But that was the point. The trial was testing our faith in a logic beyond the physical.

I turned to Whip-tail, placing my hands on either side of his great, gentle head. I poured every ounce of my certainty, my desperation, down the Tether. *I need you to trust me. I need you to jump with me. I sense a path you cannot.*

He looked into my eyes, and I saw his deep, instinctual fear of the precipice. Then, he gave a slow, rumbling purr through my palms and nudged me toward the edge.

I looked at the others, my resolve hardening. "The Tethers are still open. You can feel my intent. You can feel his trust. Trust it. We are not staying here to be eaten alive."

I didn't give them another second to argue. I climbed onto Whip-tail's broad back, wrapped my hands tightly in his single horn, and urged him forward.

For one terrifying heartbeat, we teetered on the edge of everything and nothing.

Then we jumped.

A scream tore from my throat, lost in the rushing wind. I saw Elsha, moved by some sudden spark, leap after us on Dravan's back. And through the Tethers, I felt the lurch as the others—Rhane on Dreadclaw, Vannor with NyxRathis, and Swarms—followed us into the void.

Darkness pierced my eyes. I saw the jagged, rocky bottom of the chasm rushing up to meet us, and I braced for the shattering impact. I didn't want Whip-tail to die before me. I threw my arms around his neck, hanging from his front, burying my face in his neck, trying to shield him with my own body.

But the impact never came.

The rocks felt like mist, like cool, heavy snow. We glided through them, and a sudden, blinding white clarity erupted around us. The world dissolved and reformed in a heartbeat.

I could see everything at once. The spectators high above in the Dominion's arena, their faces frozen in various states of shock and awe. I could see my own Clan's deck, see Lyria's hand clamped over her mouth, Callen leaning so far forward he was almost over the rail. The cheers were a distant, muffled roar. It was like looking through a hundred panes of glass, each showing a different angle of the same moment.

Then, with a sound like a thousand shattering crystals, that layered vision tore open. We fell through the rupture, tumbling out onto the soft, damp moss of a dark, wild forest. We landed in a small, perfectly circular clearing where a shaft of pure light pierced the canopy, illuminating us. The transition was so abrupt. Yet calm. The only sound was our ragged, collective breathing and the gentle hum of the woods.

⸻ ❦ ⸻

Too alluring. Too calm. Too perfect.

The forest that stretched outward was impossibly serene, slender trees arching upward, their canopies filtering light into silver beams. Crystals of every clear, geometric shape thrust from the ground and hung from branches, scattering the light into faint rainbows.

The air tasted crisp and clean. It was so beautiful that for a single breathless moment, I thought the trial was over.

That peace lasted for about three heartbeats.

"Welcome, late ones." A figure cloaked in shifting darkness and sewn from shadow itself coalesced into existence before us. It was draped in a cloak of blackness. Where a face should have been was only a swirling, featureless void.

"To claim the *Quartz*, you must bear more than half the

Shields." Her voice was low, devoid of warmth, a mere statement of fact. "*They* have gathered many. You have not."

As suddenly as she appeared, the darkness blinked out, leaving only the serene, mocking beauty of the woods behind. The orb blinked from existence, and silence returned.

I turned to the others, urgency a live wire in my veins. I opened my mouth to shout a command: *Move forward, fan out, find the remaining Shields!*

Nothing.

A silent scream caught in my throat. My lips moved, my cords strained against an invisible barrier, but the only thing that escaped was a choked, soundless gasp.

The plateau of Silence, echoed in my mind.

I saw the same panic reflected in Rhane's wide eyes, in Vannor's frantically moving lips. Elsha just stared with her hollow, red-rimmed eyes. I couldn't speak to the Royals. But the Tethers... The Tethers were still there, humming with life. I slammed my will down the connections to the five Tameables.

To me! Form a perimeter around the Royals! Now!

The response was instantaneous. Dreadclaw's shadows coiled protectively around Rhane, NyxRathis flowed in front of Vannor, and Dravan took to the air with Elsha, a screech that made no sound tearing from his beak.

We need to find the Shields! I pushed the thought-image of a glowing, disc-like object toward them. *Search!*

The Royals mimed shouts, useless and voiceless, then moved to the open space. But the beautiful clearing was a trap. The moment we moved to search, the forest itself seemed to attack. A pulse of scorching heat hit us first. From behind a thicket of ferns, a nightmare of black volcanic rock and pulsating violent energy emerged on six crab-like legs. Its two hammer-like forelimbs slammed into the ground, and the ground shuddered.

It was a Kaldorix Tameable.

Then it began to give *birth*. Globs of molten rocks dripped from its undercarriage, hitting the moss with a hiss and immediately taking shape. Smaller, skittering versions of itself, each with a single, burning eye and claws that scraped furrows in the ground. They scuttled toward us in a wave of menace.

Dreadclaw met the large one's charge with a roar, the two titans colliding in a shower of rock and shadow. Still, the impact was deafeningly silent.

The smaller ones were everywhere. NyxRathis became a whirlwind of light and edges, slicing through them with deadly grace. Each one she cut down dissolved into a puddle of sizzling slag. But for each one she eliminated, the large beast seemed to pulse and another two dripped from its form. They weren't strong, but they were endless, and they were fast.

One latched onto Rhane's leg with searing claws before he could kick it off, its touch leaving a smoldering gash in his armor.

They're just distractions! I screamed the thought down the Tether. *The big one is the source. We can't play defense till they win!*

It would tire us out, burn us down to nothing with its infinite, expendable children while the rest of them hunted for Shields.

Dravan, strafe the big one's back! Make it look up!

Dravan shot into the air with a silent screech, banking hard before diving toward the monstrous crab's spiny back. Talons of Aether scraped across its volcanic shell, drawing a shower of sparks and a silent bellow of rage from the creature. Its hammer limbs swung upward, trying to swat the flying nuisance out of the sky.

Now, Dreadclaw! Its underside! Now, now, now!

Then I left them there to do what they had to, left Whip-tail with them, and I moved through the mayhem they were creating. I whispered a breath of thanks to NyxRathis for her presence—without Whip-tail, I would have been crawling instead of moving at all. I ran as fast as I could toward a cluster of vines hanging from a massive tree, certain I had seen a glint of something there. Our Royals fanned out, as they desperately searched.

My fingers brushed against the vines. Just as I moved to push them aside, the ground at my feet began to ooze. A horrific amalgamation of mouths, eyes, and tentacles slithered toward me. A whip-like tentacle shot out and grazed my arm.

Agony seared through me. I clutched my arm, stumbling back as the flesh instantly blackened and began to necrotize. I screamed a voiceless gasp.

A Royal, one of the Kaldorix, saw me vulnerable and lunged. He shoved me hard, sending me crashing to the ground atop the oozing Amalgam. But before its mouths could find purchase, an invisible force wrapped around me and yanked me backward. NyxRathis. Her form shimmered into visibility for a split second before vanishing again, dragging me clear.

The Amalgam thrashed, confused, lashing out at empty air. NyxRathis struck, a flicker of light, a deep slice from an invisible blade, then faded before the creature could retaliate.

But the Amalgam was not mindless. Its many eyes swiveled, not tracking NyxRathis herself, but only the subtle signs of her passage and the faint crush of moss under an unseen weight, the slight shiver of a leaf as she brushed past.

It stopped its wild thrashing and began to move slowly, feigning confusion while positioning itself to strike where she would be, not where she was. I saw the intent through my accidental Tether with their beast.

A cold spike of understanding shot down my Tether to NyxRathis. *It's tracking your footsteps! It is faking! Move now!*

NyxRathis flowed sideways just as a massive, pseudopod-like limb slammed down exactly where she'd been standing. The Amalgam let out a silent roar of frustration, its many mouths gnashing at the air.

The creature's central eye cluster swiveled from the empty space where its prey had escaped and locked directly onto me. Unfortunately, it had also felt the warning I'd sent. It knew. A wave of hateful recognition washed over its form. I offered it a bloody, pained smile and a small wink.

The insult was all it needed. With a soundless shriek of rage, it forgot the invisible opponent and surged toward me. I ran. But NyxRathis was already there behind it. Having used the distraction I'd given, she solidified behind the creature. Both of her crystalline wings extended like twin scythes, and with a powerful, sweeping motion, she cleaved through the core of the oozing mass.

The Amalgam shuddered, its form collapsing into a dissipating, foul-smelling puddle of black sludge.

Gritting my teeth against the pain burning up my arm, I scrambled to my feet and ran toward where I thought I'd seen the Shield. But it was just a trick of the light, another glowing crystal.

The scene was descending into mayhem. Royals from both sides were now brawling blindly amidst the battling Tameables. I saw Vannor trip, the hammering beast descending toward him. Dravan swooped from above, talons wrenching him skyward just in time.

Shields! I screamed down the Tether to my Tameables, pushing an image of something similar to a glowing disc. *Don't try to kill them all! Help our Royals search!*

Whip-tail surged toward us. His healing energy flowed into us, a cool wave that staunched the necrosis just enough to keep me from fainting.

Dreadclaw rose from his clash with a furious snarl, with his shadows twisting into jagged spears that harried the beast. He was buying us time. NyxRathis and the Swarms moved in a coordinated blur, creating diversions, blocking lines of sight, giving our scattered Royals moments to search.

I saw another Shield while I tried to mount Whip-tail, half-buried in the moss near a giant, gnarled root. I pointed frantically for Elsha to see, but the one who actually caught my gesture was as a Kaldorix Royal. He tackled me, sending me sprawling from Whip-tail's back. We hit the ground hard.

He flipped me onto my stomach and his hands closed around my neck from behind. I clawed at his arms, kicking wildly. My vision was already starting to spot at the edges. Then the pressure shifted—not gone, but distracted by something—and I drove my forehead back into his nose with everything I had. The crunch was satisfying.

He grunted, blood hitting the back of my neck, grip loosening just enough. I wrenched forward, kicked him hard—once, twice—making sure he wouldn't grab me again. Rhane, who was already running toward us, veered for the Shield instead when he saw I wasn't dying.

Just as his fingers closed around it, the ground opened under him. A three-headed serpent surged from the soil, venom spraying from three mouths. Rhane threw himself into a roll, the venom sizzling on the moss where he'd been a second before.

In front of me was a symphony of disarray. We were losing control.

Dravan, fly high! The Serpent is still down there!

Dravan dove with his talons raking, his body colliding with the serpent in a flurry of wings and scales. They grappled, a cyclone of fury and shadow, before the serpent twisted. One venomous maw clamped down on Dravan's skull with a sound that froze my blood.

Help him! I screamed through all the Tethers while I moved towards him.

Dreadclaw and NyxRathis rushed together with me, but the serpent struck again and again. I screamed, soundlessly, until my throat ached, and I somehow ran toward him. The serpent backed away into the gloom, escaping just before any of us could reach it.

Dravan convulsed once, wings flaring wide in a final spasm of agony, before his body went limp. The Tether snapped, the void of his absence tearing through my chest so sharply I screamed.

"No—" The word ripped uselessly from my lips, swallowed by the silence of the plateau. I don't know how long I stayed there. Long enough that NyxRathis came and pressed her snout to his flank.

With a sound like a great lock turning, the entrance to the next plateau of Shields shimmered into existence above us. I looked around to see the Shields we collected had vanished. Rhane had somehow gotten two Shields.

I looked at Dravan one last time. His wings were still spread. I wanted to fold them, to do something, but there was no time and no way and the plateau waited and he was already gone.

We moved forward toward it. I ignored my aching body and screamed at my mind to go numb.

CHAPTER 34

DAMIEN

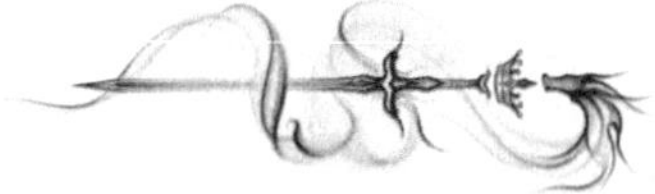

The obsidian platform was a butcher's block under the Celestia of dead stars. And on it, she commanded them without her Aether, without her Tethers this round. With nothing but her screams and shouts. The whole scene was amplified and magnified for the viewers. Whatever we needed to see, we saw it up close. We could hear it all. And all I heard, all I saw, was her prowess.

The love of my life.

She was a sketch of pain etched in blood and smoke. Every line of her was wrong, the arm hanging too loose, the leg buckling with a weight it couldn't hold. I could see the fine tremor in her hands, the way she favored her side with a subtle hitch in her breath. She was bleeding from a dozen places. She hid and held her spine straight and swallowed her own agony so it wouldn't drown them. But I could feel even the splinter beneath her nail from this distance.

The sight of her that gutted me to my core was the very proof of her strength. But I shackled it with a credence deeper than fear, more absolute than rage: my faith in her. My absolute conviction in her ability. A handful of fortnights. That's all she'd had to forget

275

how to be someone who simply existed and become someone who led.

And now they all stood against a perfected reserve force. Kaldorix's strategy was one of calculated preservation for this round. They held their strongest warriors back, conserving their strength for later, a luxury granted by their initial advantage of time. We entered this fight already broken. But they were rewriting the numbers now. We were witnessing a clash of minds and a war of commands she forged in days and nights. And Kaldorix certainly had nothing to match the seamless control Mirabelle wielded over our Tameables. Their handlers could only do their best and face inevitable defeat.

Our Royals, the absolute finest of the Legion, those who were trained to bind Tameables and Tethers, were digging. They were searching for Shields as if they were born and raised to do it, despite already losing a warrior and a beast. Mirabelle's voice was ragged, but it still cut through the plateau. A flick of her wrist, and the Swarm became a living veil, shielding those digging for the Shields.

Her eyes—*stars, her eyes*—were a constant, flickering assessment. She saw Elsha's grief and gave her a purpose to blunt its edge. She saw the blood on Rhane and Vannor and maneuvered them back toward Whip-tail's fading light, taking over their position.

Then the net fell over Mirabelle. The creature they'd preserved only for this. A living, multiplying lattice of energy did its work perfectly. The more Tameables destroyed it, the more the net thickened, trapping her in a prison.

NyxRathis understood before any of them did. She stopped fighting it from the outside and let herself go fluid. Then oozed into the net's very structure, and from the inside, she pushed outward. She expanded it, stretching its fibers until they grew thin and translucent.

In that moment of their struggle, the serpent struck on a Royal's command. Whip-tail made a wet, broken cry. Mirabelle moved the moment the creature's structure broke around her. She turned her protective fury into a weapon. As the Serpent surged from below, she pivoted, letting the force of its own lunge carry the middle head past her, and in that heartbeat, she was on it. One arm hooked around its thick neck, her body twisting mid-air as the other two heads struck like thunder. She swung herself beneath its jaw, evading fangs that could pierce plate, her legs scissoring around its throat as it tried to drag her under.

The beast vanished beneath the ground, taking her with it. Dreadclaw lunged after them without hesitation, smoke trailing as the ground swallowed him whole.

The crowd above went silent.

Three heartbeats. Four. I stood at the balcony edge without realizing I'd moved there, both hands on the rail, every muscle in my body locked against the very specific torture of having no influence over what was happening. My breathing had gone shallow.

I watched the ground.

The fifth heartbeat stretched longer than the others.

Then the ground shuddered. A deep heave that sent cracks spidering across the plateau floor, and Dreadclaw erupted from the dust in a burst of smoke and displaced stone, and Mirabelle came up with him. The middle head of the Serpent was clutched in her grip, its eyes dulled, its neck torn raw. She threw it at the feet of the wounded Whip-tail, then turned back toward the fight with uneven strides. That coldness with which she did it was the most terrifying and beautiful thing I had ever witnessed.

I never thought I would consider killing an art, until I saw her do it.

The gallery around me was a roaring ocean, but I was at the bottom of the sea. The sound found me then. It began as a whisper, a single name caught in the throat. Then another. Then a thousand.

Tamer. It was a chant of recognition.

From the Kaldorix section, hisses of fury, curses, drowned in the tide of her name.

My hands were still fused to the railing. I could not move. I could only watch the woman limping and running amid the wreckage, looking like someone who had looked into the abyss and found it lacking.

She was blood and bone and breathtaking courage. Oh, and she was so *mine*.

And the feeling that broke over me was so vast it had no name. It was pride, it was terror, it was love, and it was everything I didn't have a name for.

And as the gateway to the final plateau shimmered open behind them, Mirabelle's eyes scanned the roaring thousands until they locked squarely on mine. Her face was a mask of dark, drying blood. And in the midst of a thousand voices crying her name, it was her eyes on mine that felt like the rarest of privileges, a staggering honor that stole beats from my heart. She owned that thing. And she knew it.

CHAPTER 35
MIRABELLE

There was no Quartz. Only a shifting shadow of one, hanging in the center of the plateau like a mirage. A ghost of itself, hanging in the void just out of reach. One last Shield flickered along with it.

The ground beneath my boots groaned, and we were tilted in a full, nauseating rotation. The obsidian platform was fracturing, great chunks of it splitting away and spinning off into the void. We were on a dying, rotating rock.

"What are we supposed to do now? Hold on?" Vannor cursed, bracing himself as our section of floor listed sharply to the side.

"The Dominion said we have to get the Shield, then the Quartz," Rhane panted, leaping across a newly formed gap. "We have equal Shields, so?"

"So?" a Kaldorix Royal with lank brown hair spat from his own fracturing island of stone. His eyes raked over me. "It's because of her. The pet of Azarios. The Dominion loves a spectacle. They'll watch us all struggle just to see her perform."

Someone behind him muttered, "That bloody Hiltser. Fool couldn't even finish this vile girl."

Rhane told him to shut up. I didn't even look at them. I didn't give a single damn about them. My mind was racing, scanning around us. The Quartz was visible but untouchable like a reflection. Which meant... "There must be something binding this, right?" I murmured, the pieces clicking into a whole.

"Something anchoring the real thing apart from us. We break that; we bring it back," Elsha muttered, her voice still raw and her eyes dull.

A massive fracture opened up in the center of the plateau, a yawning chasm. And there, at its heart, pulsing with a sickly light, was a twisted spire of obsidian, an Anchor. And before it, a perfect, circular hole carved into the rock, deep and dark. *A sacrifice hole.*

The Kaldorix Sovereign was already pointing. His Royals moved. Just as we started moving towards it, the ground under Dreadclaw gave way. It happened fast—a section of rock that had looked solid simply wasn't. He plummeted into the darkness, his roar of surprise cut short as the shadows swallowed him.

"No!"

Screams ripped from all of us. I was at the edge before I knew I'd moved, the others shouting around me, Rhane grabbing my arm to stop me going over with the crumbling rock. The Swarm drove near the edge, its light downward, deeper, trying to find him, and in the Tether, I felt his presence.

A blur of amethyst light. NyxRathis dove after him in the next moment, her form a streak of desperate hope against the swallowing dark. We watched, hearts lodged in our throats, as she vanished into the gloom after him.

I couldn't lose them all. I didn't come here to sacrifice them all. N— No—

Then, a haunting sound: Dreadclaw's roar from the depths. Of agony. Of world-ending grief.

Had she sacrificed herself for him? *Stars.*

I rushed to the edge, my own grief a sharp stone in my throat. "NyxRathis!"

A weak, chiming sound echoed from the darkness, followed by a low, pained rumble. Then, slowly, painfully, NyxRathis hauled herself over the edge, her crystalline body cracked and dim, one wing hanging uselessly. Dragging himself behind her, her tendrils wrapped tightly around him, was Dreadclaw. He was battered, smoke leaking from his tendrils, but alive.

He collapsed beside her, his massive head nudging her broken form. A broken, questioning sound escaped him.

NyxRathis managed a faint laugh. *Do...you truly think it's that easy to be rid of me...beast?* she choked out, her voice a faint whisper in my mind. He rumbled, a sound that was almost a purr, and curled his body around her, shielding her with what remained of his strength. Whip-tail, bruised and exhausted, limped over. A soft, pained green light emanated from him, washing over them both in a feeble attempt to knit the worst of the damage.

The Kaldorix were in no better state. Their great stone-beast was now a crumbling pile of rubble. Another of their Aether-wielders clutched a bloody stump where his arm had been, his face pale with shock and pain. This was no longer a battle of strength, but a test of who had anything left to give.

And the solution was now horrifyingly clear. The Anchor pulsed, waiting. It needed a sacrifice. A life to bridge the gap between the realms.

The Kaldorix were still arguing amongst themselves, voices sharp with panic.

We need to move, some part of me registered. *We needed to move thirty seconds ago.* The plateau was crumbling from the sides.

"We can draw lots!" Vannor yelled over the grinding rock. "Randomly!"

"No, calm down," I said, quiet but absolute. "Let me first try and see if we have another solution. We should—"

"I've been trying to figure out what I'm for," Elsha said, almost to herself. Then she looked at me, her eyes clear of the grief that had haunted them before. They were filled with a peaceful resolve. "I think I know now. It was my privilege to fight alongside all of you. And I am at peace...*Atlassians will prevail.*"

My blood went cold in realization. "Don't! Elsha—" I ran, my hand stretching out. But she was already stepping off the edge. A perfect, graceful arc into the fissure, aimed straight for the pulsating Anchor. She didn't scream.

The impact was silent. The effect was not.

A violent, silent shockwave erupted. It hit us like a wall, throwing us to our knees. The ghostly Quartz, the mirage, shattered and then reformed, solid and blindingly real, hanging in the air before us.

The plateaus had merged.

The Kaldorix, who had sacrificed nothing, were already moving, scrambling for the real Quartz.

"Run!" I screamed and ran, fury overriding my grief.

They were already in motion, scrambling on hands and knees as the ground beneath the Quartz dissolved. Vannor launched himself, his fingers closing around the crystal just as the obsidian beneath his feet turned to dust.

He had it.

A deafening chime echoed through the void. The voice of the Dominion was a thought seared into my mind. *"The trial is concluded. Victory is accorded to Atlassian."*

Light flooded the platform, solidifying it beneath our feet. The relief was a physical pain.

And then I heard a wet, choked cry.

I turned.

Whip-tail was on his side, his beautiful eyes wide with shock and pain. Protruding from his neck was a dagger.

Standing over him was the brown-haired Kaldorix Royal with the cruel mouth, wiping his hands. "Finally," he spat. "I've been spotting this nuisance since the first level. The little crap had to go, or its memory would have spoiled my sleep."

The world narrowed to a single, red point. I was on him before he could blink. Damien's dagger was in my hand. I stabbed him, his dark blood splattering everywhere.

Again. And again. And again.

There was no thought, only a rending, tearing, silencing anguish.

Hands grabbed me, masked Dominion figures pulling me off the bloody ruin. But I was already done with the pieces of his butchered meat. They threw me. My view went dark, and I landed hard on the cold, familiar ground of Telmoria, the staging ground. It was nearly dawn. The crowd roared around me, a cacophony that meant nothing.

I scrambled, ripping through the press of bodies. "Whip-Tail! Where is he?"

I found him. The healers were gathered around, their faces grim as they worked. He was fading, his light guttering out like a dying star. I fell to my knees, my hands hovering over him, afraid to touch. "No, no, no—please, my gentle little light," I begged, my voice shattering. "You're fine. You're going to be fine."

He turned his big head toward me. His purr was a ragged, broken sound—and still, he was trying to comfort *me*. He nuzzled my bloody hand, his eyes holding mine, telling me it was alright, even as the light in them began to fade.

The pain came in waves. An onslaught that crashed over me all at once. The searing pain in my leg, the blinding ache in my ribs, the throbbing ruin of my arm. Injuries I hadn't felt till now. Wounds he had been soothing without my even knowing. Now they screamed into being, raw and vicious and utterly merciless.

Because he was gone.

He was gone.

And my world went black.

⟨◊⟩

I woke to the familiar scent of fern and dried blood. Dawn light streamed through the high window of the infirmary. Two healers sat in the corner, their murmurs soft as the rustle of cloth. I sat up too fast. My ribs ached, tender but no longer broken; even my legs, raw from burns and bruises, felt almost whole. Almost.

Memory came back like knives. My chest constricted, the grief pressing down before I could even draw a steady breath. Grief doesn't make me strong. It never made me strong; it made me hollow.

"Where is Damien?" My voice was a rasp, scraping against my raw throat.

One healer stepped forward. "My Lady, you should rest. The Sovereign was quite clear—"

"Where is he?"

"Sovereign was here until dawn," the other healer said softly, "then summoned to urgent matters. We have been ordered to ensure you are well rested."

"Can we bring you something to eat?" the other asked gently.

I was famished. But it was nothing compared to the need to see Damien and anchor myself in the one solid thing left in my shattered mind. I ignored their protests, swinging my legs over the side of the bed. A sharp wince shot through my calf as my feet hit the cold floor. Not fully healed—but I didn't care. I walked out.

The corridor beyond was hushed, lit with the gold of early light. And there, just as I turned the corner, was Lorenza. Emerging from Damien's chamber.

Her nightgown clung like silk to her figure, the faintest smirk playing over her lips before she smoothed it away. Her breaths came just a little too hard, a little too visible in the quiet hall. She startled upon noticing me in the corridor, then smiled coldly as though she had been waiting especially to see me all along.

My heart beat wildly against my ribs, an instinctual drumming of surprise. But beneath that initial rush, a steady certainty was there. I knew with clarity that I had nothing to fear when it came to us.

"Oh, my sweet little Tamer," she murmured, gliding toward me. "I am sorry you had to see this." She reached out to pat my cheek.

I caught her wrist in mid-air, my grip like iron. Her eyes widened in shock. "Don't," I said, my voice hard and final.

"Our Sovereign is a bit tired. And rather aggressive. I suggest you give him the rest he so desperately needs. Especially before the big battle today." Her tone was dripping with vile implication.

My grip tightened. I twisted. Her gasp broke sharp and her composure fractured in a flash of pain. "Get in my way again and I will break your bones." Then I released her, wordlessly, and walked past on aching legs.

Behind me, her soft laughter followed.

I shoved open Damien's door. He was sitting on the edge of his bed, head in his hands, elbows on his knees. His whole body was a tense line of anguish.

"Get out," he snarled without looking up. I flinched at the sound.

"It's me," I whispered, stepping closer.

He stood so fast the furniture rattled. "Get out of my chamber!" he shouted. I could see him now. Rumpled tunic, disheveled hair. And on his neck, stark against his skin, four faint, crimson scratches.

My heart stuttered. "Damien? Look at me. What happened?"

He moved away from my reaching hand as if my touch would sear him. "I said leave!"

The rejection hurt and I took an instinctive step back. Then my eyes caught the glint beneath the edge of his bed: a knife. The ornate hilt. The ceremonial blade. And on the blade, a smear of fresh blood.

My vision blurred. I stumbled toward it, my trembling fingers closing around the cold hilt. He was there in an instant, his hand wrenching the knife from my grip.

"Enough," I snapped, my voice cutting through his panic. "I am not leaving until I get answers. You do not get to shout me out of your chamber when there is blood on this knife and scratches on your neck."

He stared at me, his chest heaving, and his pupils were wildly dilated, swallowing the blue almost entirely.

"Did you Bond with Lorenza?" The words were a harsh whisper.

He recoiled as if I'd struck him. "No." The denial was immediate and violent. "Stars, no."

He searched my eyes, as though trying to read every truth hidden there, then closed his own and drew in a shuddering breath. When he opened them again, his gaze locked on mine with more clarity.

"It's you—" His voice broke. His hands lifted, trembling, hovering just inches from my face. Every line of his body strained with the effort of restraint until, at last, his fists curled tight at his sides so he would not touch me.

"I am sorry, Bella," he choked, his breath ragged. "I can feel it's you. But I am not myself. My mind is veiled by a brew. I've been seeing things...hearing things." He faltered, his chest heaving. "And I will not take the chance. Even if it's only one breath in a thousand that it isn't you, I would not risk it. I would not touch even a fingertip when I know my mind is not my own. So, please."

My vision blurred with unshed tears, their burn mingling with the cold rise of rage toward Lorenza.

"Why is there blood on this knife?" I asked.

His gaze burned into mine. "I know the wrong scent before the wrong touch." His jaw clenched, pained, furious. "It is absurd that you even think—" He shook his head.

"I didn't ask you to—" I shook my head. "Are you hurt? I will get a healer—"

"No." The word was final. "No one comes in here. No one. I will ride this out alone, I will be fine. *You* need to heal." His eyes pleaded with me, even as he guided me backward. "Go back to the infirmary. I will come to you the moment this passes."

The knife clattered to the table as he shoved the door open, his body rigid with a self-loathing restraint that was somehow more heartbreaking than anger.

"Did she try to force—?" I started, the question a knife twist in my own gut.

The look he gave me was answer enough, a storm of fury. He

finally reached the door and held the door open in a silent plea for me to go.

I stepped forward, grabbed the front of his tunic in my fist, and pulled his face down to mine. He stiffened, a low sound catching in his throat, but he didn't pull away.

I pressed my lips to his forehead. "You're mine," I said against his skin. "You protect what's yours. So do I." I released him. His eyes remained closed, his breath held. I turned on my heel and walked out.

The door slammed shut behind me, the lock clicking into place.

The fire in my legs forgotten, I ran.

CHAPTER 36
MIRABELLE

I slammed Lorenza's chamber door wide enough to rattle its hinges. She was at her vanity, brushing her hair, and she jumped, the silver brush clattering onto the polished wood.

"Have you lost all sense of decorum?" she hissed, rising, her composure cracking for a split second before smoothing into icy disdain. "Ah, I forgot you even—"

I crossed the room, and my hand caught her cheek in a hard grip. "If you ever go near Damien again, it will be the last thing you do," I said, my voice deadly calm.

Her eyes widened, then narrowed to knives. She tried to jerk free, but I tightened my hold until her skin flushed red beneath my palm. When she finally yanked back, rubbing the mark, her glare was poisonous.

"Sorry to disappoint you," she sneered, "but I can't stay away from my Etern."

My hand flew, cracking across her cheek with a force that snapped her head to the side. "Shut your filthy lying mouth."

For a moment, there was only stunned silence.

Then a feral snarl ripped from her throat. She moved faster than I thought possible, shoving me back with surprising strength. My head slammed into the stone wall behind me, stars exploding in my vision. Thick, liquid shadows erupted from the corners of the room, pinning my arms to the wall, holding me fast.

She stepped closer, a cruel smile twisting her beautiful face. "Hopeful little thing...so rationally assessing if he is my Etern." She rubbed her cheek, and then her own hand flew out, slapping me so hard my ears rang. "We don't have proof, do we? He's going to remember nothing tomorrow in detail except the fact that I was there, knife and blood were involved, and you made a scene."

My shadows stirred as a protective fog seeping from my skin, trying to push back against hers. But her Aether was stronger, older and deeply rooted in a power I was only beginning to understand. They held fast while mine were only defensive.

Still I smiled back, equally evil, through the pounding in my head. "Shame. He's harder to deceive than you seem to think."

Her laugh was a really ugly sound. "He was delirious. He'll wake with the memory of a Bonding struggle, the scent and mark of *our* blood, and the satisfying conclusion that his betrothed is finally, *truly* his." Her gaze slid over me, cruel and cold. "And you will be back to nothing. A jealous, necessitous nobody."

Her fog pressed harder, trying to crush me. My ribs screamed.

I lifted my chin, let the pain sharpen me. I had to provoke her to break her hold. "You're right about one thing, Lorenza. I am a nobody." My smirk cut like glass. "But I'm the only nobody Damien will *ever* want."

Rage snapped across her face. She lunged and the chamber erupted into disarray. Her shadows whipped out, but I twisted, smashing my forehead into her jaw. She hissed, staggered, but recovered fast. A kick slammed into my injured calf. White-hot agony tore through me, my leg crumpling. Her hand clamped a handful of her own silk bedding over my mouth.

She kicked again, her boot connecting directly with the half-healed wound. I screamed into the cloth. She ground her heel into the injury, twisting, trampling it against the floor.

I fought blindly, head-butting her shoulder, evading her grasping hands. But her fingers tangled in my hair, yanking my head back before slamming it down hard against the solid wood foot of the bed. I choked on my blood.

She produced a length of cord from her bedpost and tied my wrists together. I was panting, with blood smeared on my face.

She leaned down until her face was inches from mine. "Listen to me, you vulture," she hissed, her hand closing around my throat. Not enough to cut off air, but enough to promise it. "I have had him before you even learned to walk properly. We *own* each other, and he is going to remember it soon. I am done with you rubbing your indigent, whorish self against him...confusing his mind with your innocent act and sensuality." She squeezed harder. Her eyes glittered. "I am disgusted by you touching him...disgusted with you even breathing near him."

Her voice dropped to a venomous harsh whisper. "All I required was a credible excuse and a suitable pawn to get rid of you. But you came so willingly to me. That's so sad for you. Now I can sacrifice a guard or two to frame this... This was a very bad mistake, Tamer."

Then, she turned, confident I was broken.

But I wasn't. I couldn't.

I swung my good leg out, hooking her ankle, yanking hard. She fell with a shocked gasp, hitting the floor. I rolled, ignoring the pain tearing through me, and crushed my injured leg down on her throat. Her eyes bulged, her shadows convulsing as she gagged under my leg. I leaned on top of her, my tied hands finding her throat. I pressed my bound wrists down, crushing her windpipe with all the strength I had left.

She choked, her eyes bulging, hands clawing at my arms.

"You are so wrong," I snarled, my voice ragged, my teeth bared in defiance. "You have no clue what I've hidden under this"—I coughed, a spray of blood darkening the air—"indigent skin."

Her struggles grew weaker, her face turning purple. I loosened my grip just enough for her to drag in a wheeze of air. "Terrible timing, Lorenza," I hissed, leaning closer to her ears. "When I say I will end you if you lay another finger on him...I will. And I will savor every single moment of it."

Her snarl twisted into a strangled sound, and I drove my leg back onto her windpipe, watching her own darkness flicker and collapse around us as if it knew its mistress was losing.

I held on until her eyes rolled back and her body went limp beneath me. Gasping, I rolled off her. I used my teeth, sawing at the knots on my wrists until they gave way. Then I used the same cord to tie her securely to her own bedpost, gagging her for good measure.

Fair's fair.

I crawled toward the door, my legs useless, my head pounding, vision blurring. I clutched the key, after locking her doors, in my bloody hand. I didn't look back.

I dragged myself out into the corridor and across the hall, collapsing against Damien's door. I could barely see, barely breathe. I needed to make sure he knew about her, truly knew, before they took her into battles tonight.

THE FAINT LIGHT of the solitary lamp hit my face. I took in the familiar surroundings for a moment, and I jerked upright. I was in Damien's chamber.

I'd fallen asleep. No way I had fallen asleep this long.

Hours had bled into the deep night.

No. No, no, no...

I cursed myself and swung my legs from the bed. My leg buckled, and I caught myself against the bedframe with a sharp hiss. At least the rest of my wounds had mended well enough. I forced myself upright and hobbled toward the door.

It was locked. I slammed my palm against the heavy wood.

It swung open to reveal two guards. "My Lady? Do you need a healer?"

"No," I said, trying to push past them.

They shifted, blocking the doorway smoothly. "Our apologies, but we have strict orders from the Sovereign himself. You are to remain here for your own safety until he returns from tonight's Trials."

The Dissonance battles. He was already gone.

"You don't understand, I need to—"

"The order is absolute, my Lady." Their faces were apologetic but immovable. They closed the door before I could argue further, and I heard the lock click into place.

I sat on the bed, frustration and fear felt like a live wire under my skin. My eyes fell on the tray of food by the bed. And beside it, a piece of parchment in Damien's script.

I snatched it up.

Precious,
I need you safe. Truly safe.
Forgive me for confining you to our chamber. I swear I will make it up to you.
There is too much to sort through, too many words I need to confess that cannot be spilled into your drowsy haze. But for now, I need you to eat. And rest.
Call the healers if you have even a flicker of pain. Spend the night in our bed and know that I am fighting my way back to you.
Only *yours, D*

THE WORDS WERE a balm and a torment. He'd written this before he left. But did he remember what happened? Does that *only* imply he remembered Lorenza's spectacle? Did he take her with them without knowing?

The fear was a cold knot in my stomach. Just like she said, he might not remember what she did fully, the poison in his mind twisting the truth.

I ate what I could, swallowing enough to give myself strength.

The juice went down too fast, sparking the faintest echo of a memory: Damien gently insisting I drink something while I slept. My eyelids had been so heavy then. But it was gone as quickly as it came. The only memory was the faintest impression of falling asleep in his bed, wrapped in the safety of his arms. Even that felt distant, like a dream.

Cursing myself for my exhaustion, I tested my leg. Painful, but it should work. I couldn't stay here. I needed to get that ledger before tomorrow.

With a guilty pang for disobeying him, I climbed onto his desk. The window was half open. I swung my legs over the sill, ignoring the protests from my calf as I lowered myself onto the narrow stone ledge outside. The drop was two stories into the lit courtyard below. My legs wobbled, but I pushed the fear down.

I inched along the ledge, my back pressed to the cold stone of the palace wall, until I reached a drainpipe. I shimmied down, my arms shaking with the effort, and dropped the last few feet into a secluded courtyard.

Then I carefully made my way around to the side of the building where Lorenza's chambers were. Her window was slightly ajar, a faint sliver of lamplight escaping into her chamber. I found a trellis, biting my lip as I climbed, my fingers scraping on the wood. I hauled myself up to her windowsill and peered inside.

The chamber was pristine. Perfectly made.

And empty.

The door to her chamber stood open. They had already taken her out. They might have found her tied up—or perhaps she'd freed herself; she had the shadows to help. I was too injured to prevent this from happening.

Despair washed over me. I knocked my forehead lightly against the cool stone wall in frustration. I didn't even have her door key anymore. If Damien woke imagining he'd Bonded with her... No.

Now I had to get to Irin. I had to gather whatever I could about the Abyss, and I had to be ready when they returned.

I climbed higher, onto an open terrace, then shimmied down

the large tree on the other side. The old cypress reached like skeletal fingers, its branches scraping my arms as I descended. My feet had just touched the damp, night-chilled ground. I yelped with pain.

And then—

A hand closed hard around my wrist.

MIRABELLE

I whirled, my free hand coming up, ready to strike.

"Stars, Bella! What were you doing, babbling on the palace roof in the dead of night? I thought you were supposed to be resting!" Amara's voice was hushed. Her eyes were puffed from crying and that sight alone ripped the grief wide open inside me. Whip-tail's loss hit me anew, a fresh wave of grief seeing it reflected on her face.

I just pulled her into a hug. She clung to me just as tightly, her shoulders shaking for a moment before she drew a ragged breath.

"You can't keep running like this," she whispered against my shoulder.

"I don't have much time," I murmured, pulling back. "They'll check my chamber soon. I need to get things done. Lorenza is—"

"—a snake? Tell me something I didn't already guess," Amara cut in.

"Not only that—but—I have to find Irin. And then I need to get the ledger before tomorrow night." I glanced around, my eyes straining against the deep gloom, scanning the shadows between the trees and the dark windows above, half-expecting armed figures to already be descending on me. "I hope it's still there," I muttered under my breath.

Amara's eyes narrowed with calculation. "I'll get the ledger and meet you."

I shook my head. "Wait... It's too risky—"

Amara cut in, her voice dry. "Your limp is three times more prominent than mine. I think I have better odds if something goes sideways."

I closed my eyes briefly, frustration and fear warring within me. "I mean it. If you find someone there, anyone, just get out. We will find another way later."

She grabbed my face firmly, kissed my cheek. "Wait for me in my chamber. It's safer." Before I could argue, she was gone, slipping back into the inky shadows of the garden like she'd never been there at all.

I FOUND Irin in the Royal wing, speaking quietly with a group of older Royal women shuffling through silks. Her eyes met mine over a stack of folded cloths, and she excused herself.

"Let's walk?" she asked, her tone neutral, falling into step beside me. We moved in silence toward one side of the Royal garden, where a shallow stream gurgled over smooth stones in the darkness. The sound was deceptively peaceful.

I didn't wait. "Can I skip the introduction and just ask what you remember?"

Irin let out a soft, humorless laugh. "That's a weighted question, isn't it?"

"I know we both know more than we should. And I'm not your enemy."

She stopped walking and turned to face me, her expression unreadable in the low light. "And you're certain I'm not yours? Pretty confident for someone who remembers *everything*."

I flinched, the memory her father's death flickering in my mind. "I—"

"Anyway," she interrupted, her gaze drifting to the flowing water. "I'm not looking for revenge. Not anymore. And I know my father deserved what he got because…" She looked away, her jaw tightening, then forced her eyes back to mine. "He deserved what came to him. He had…appetites. He even tried to convince *me*…just before the Abyss." She scoffed, a bitter, broken sound, and shook her head.

My heart ached for her. I reached out and squeezed her arm. We had always known her as a rebel, someone armored in confidence, both liked and feared by the other Royal women, perhaps because of her history with Damien.

"Why are you here?" she asked, her voice softer now, wanting to steer the conversation away from her own wounds. "To ask how I remember?"

"Yes. And anything and everything you know."

She let out a slow, measured breath. "You see, I have…history with Damien. You might know."

I kept my expression carefully neutral, though an unwelcoming knot tightened inside me. This was a path I had no desire to walk down now.

"As much as I don't want to talk about this with you," she continued, "I just need to tell someone. I have no one else to share this with." Her smile was brittle, a fragile thing that didn't reach her eyes. "It was my father tricking me again. He told me if I convinced or even manipulated Damien to Bond with me, he would release my half-sister, my only remaining family. He was keeping her under—" She looked away, too hurt to complete the sentence. "Yes, I had feelings for Dam—the Sovereign, back then, but I also knew his interactions were…transactions. Devoid of feeling."

I said nothing. I didn't want to hear it, to dissect it with a woman who had been used as a pawn by her father. But I held my tongue, giving her the space to speak her mind.

She continued, her words spilling out now. "I tried to trick him into more with me, and I was the reason he stopped engaging with other women at all." She must have seen a flicker in my expression because her brittle smile returned. "Oh, I worded it wrong. What I mean is, I made him realize his transactions with us weren't guaranteed loyalty, so he limited those...transactions, to Thralls, who are formally bound to the agreed terms." Her smile was thin. "It's absurd you even made that face."

"It is—" I started, but she cut me off.

"All you feel is his affection and care." Her voice turned analytical, almost cold. "But you have no frame of reference. You never knew the man who was forged without a heart for anyone. What you have now isn't a change of heart. It's a miracle. I don't know what kind of sorcery you pulled there, but"—her mouth quirked into the ghost of a joke—"let me know when you have time to teach me a trick or two."

My smile was small, tight at the edges. What was I supposed to say here? *Thank you? Yes, he was a monster, but I'm glad I could help?* Or maybe, *Some hearts aren't missing, they're just waiting?*

I'm sure he always had it in him?

Eww.

I cleared my throat and shook my head.

Then her expression sobered again. "I was accidentally there when they regained all the memories from the Abyss. I had access to the council chambers—" Irin's focus snapped back to me. "There's a ledger. And it has—"

"I know about the ledger. But who was there to regain the memories?" I asked, my pulse quickening.

She frowned, a line of suspicion forming between her brows. "I'm not sure. I was there without their knowledge, hiding. I wanted to get my father's journals, to know the extent of my sister's torture, to help her." Her eyes narrowed. "How do you know about the ledger already?"

"I have seen it, from the drawer. In that place."

"What place?"

"The place from the letters you sent me."

Her frown deepened into genuine confusion. "What letters? Mirabelle, I have never sent you any letters."

"What?" My blood ran cold. "You—what? You didn't?"

She shook her head slowly, her eyes searching mine, now filled with a wary confusion that mirrored my own. "No. Never. I was shocked you even guessed I knew about any of this."

The ground felt unsteady beneath my feet. "I...I have to go," I stammered, the words faint. "Amara—!" I didn't finish. I turned and limped away as fast as my leg would carry me toward the Hold.

Someone else was playing this game. And I felt like we were playing the moves they had already predicted.

⬥

DARKNESS and the silence of the hidden chamber wrapped around me like a cloak. Still, a thin wave of relief washed over me. Everything was normal. No signs of a struggle. No Amara. She might have successfully taken the ledger and slipped away...or she might have seen or heard something and fled.

I slowly climbed down the ladder, wincing with each step. But my focus was entirely on the obsidian table. I pulled the hidden catch. The drawer slid open with a whisper.

The ledger was still there. So she hadn't taken it. Or couldn't.

The breath I didn't realize I'd been holding rushed out of me. I reached for it, my fingers touching the worn leather cover.

Click.

The sound was soft, but it echoed like a thunderclap in the silent chamber. A footstep on stones outside the door.

Panic seized me. I took the ledger and slammed the drawer shut, too fast. The sound was a sharp crack in the silence.

Idiot.

I dropped into a crouch behind the large chair, just as I had the first time, every nerve on fire. The footsteps paused right outside the chamber door. I held my breath, every muscle tensed.

A long, agonizing moment passed. Then, the footsteps began again, fading down the corridor. They hadn't come in. I released a shaky exhale, my body slumping with relief. I stayed there for a count of ten, listening to the silence. Nothing.

A shaky exhale escaped me, relief rushing in. I turned to rise, clutching the ledger close. And my eyes crashed into a pair of dark ones, staring directly into mine.

They were mere inches from my face, from behind a featureless porcelain mask.

A suffocating scream locked in my throat. I froze, paralyzed, my blood turning to ice.

The familiar eyes behind the mask gleamed with cruel, terrifying amusement.

And the ledger slipped from my hands.

DAMIEN

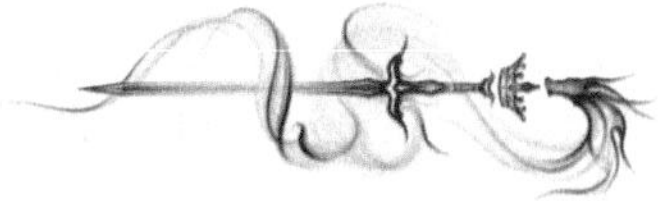

Darkness. A breathing entity that swallowed sound and thought.

The only illumination came from the flickering, unstable flames that wreathed our arms and the faint, sickly glow of the War-Golem we were shepherding toward the gorge. Halfway through the storm of fire and stone, we were already spent.

The construct lumbered ahead of us, a monstrous being of stones and flaming Aether, its surface etched with runes that glowed faintly in the black. It was a mountain of stone, with dreadful lava oozing out of it, walking toward one of the sunken altars.

If it reached ours, Atlassian fell.

If it reached theirs, Kaldorix fell.

Each death fed its stride, pulling it toward the side of the fallen. And too many had already died on both sides.

"Push him back!" Nathan bellowed to Draves, our Elder who wielded blue flames.

My own flames surged in a wall of heat, halting a Kaldorix Royal who had come too close. I was still half-veiled, my vision blurring at intervals, but there was no choice except to wield the

Aether and fight as though my life depended on it—because it did. The soldier's armor blackened, cracked, and he fell, lifeless. The Golem shuddered, its runes flaring, and lurched another step toward their altar.

The battlefield spread across shifting plains, three concentric rings alive—fire in one, stone in the next, healing in the last. Step into the right ring and Aether magnified, roared through your blood. But linger too long and it twisted you—hallucinations, weakness, your own emotions weaponized against you.

And the cure also came with a cost. We had learned this the hard way, when one of ours lingered too long in healing. He laughed as the rock bent for him, then laughed some more as it calcified his legs to the knees. We had to cut him free while Kaldorix struck.

Beside me, Arthur fought as if born for this cursed field. Fire burst around him, and he surged forward with his lightning. Stone slid aside, wounds knit on his flesh before blood fell. He was at home in the mayhem, balanced where others faltered. Because this was a trap for Atlassian and Kaldorix, not for alliance soldiers like him. For every drop of our blood, he shed three of theirs.

"Keep Arthur in the center!" I roared. "Don't let them drive him to the edges!"

His curved blade split open a Kaldorix soldier in a single stroke. The Golem lurched, its runes flared. Another step toward their altar.

But we were bleeding too much. Kaldorix had three Aether-wielders from allied Clans. We had only Arthur with us.

My chest burned with fury. Had Lorenza stood with us, had she not wormed her way into my chamber while I lay mind-veiled, then fled before I could bind her in chains for what she did, and demand answers, perhaps Nyxaria's strength would be ours. Instead, she was out there somewhere, conspiring more, and I needed to find her, to end what she had begun. She had made a ruin of us.

I shoved the thought aside. I could not afford distraction. Ash and copper coated my tongue as I ducked a surge of stone spikes. My flames roared in answer, clashing against Arion Vexmar's relentless advance. The Sovereign of Kaldorix who wanted to see me dead since the Ledgerdeep.

He fought like a storm, his stone-armored form hammering toward me. And someone—someone I had not yet seen—was driving him closer, cutting off every retreat.

Then I noticed Nathan across the battlefield, locked in the fire ring. His body shook with the heat, his flames too wild, too vast. His pupils blown wide, his grin manic. Infernos burst from him indiscriminately, half striking Kaldorix, half striking *us*.

My head throbbed with veil.

They had forced him too deep into the fire's pull until it owned him. "Nathan, pull back!" I shoved through the ring, stones slicing my skin like searing nails. "You're feeding off it too long—"

He snarled like a beast. His strike nearly grazed me. For a heartbeat, I thought he had turned his blade on me. Then clarity flickered in his eyes, barely.

"They're everywhere," he rasped, sweat pouring down his face. "I can't—I need it—"

"Damn you," I hissed, catching his wrist as he swung again. His fire crashed into me, flames devouring my armor and searing more flesh. I locked my arm around him, forcing him back as Kaldorix soldiers surged in, their stone pelts hammering against my back, while Nathan's fire strikes slammed into my shoulders.

"Fight with me, not against me!" I roared, hauling him across the ring. My nails tore against the stone as I dragged him, his flames continually lashing at my skin. Another pelting blow—my ribs crunched. Stone crushed into my spine. Still I carried him, locking him over my shoulders, staggering beneath his weight.

I reached the healing ring, collapsing to my knees as water poured from my hands over his face, steam rising where it met the fire consuming him.

"Wake up, Nathan," I shouted over the noise, shaking him hard. "Don't make me bury you here."

For a breath, nothing. Then he gasped, his hand clamped my shoulder in fierce gratitude. In the next instant, he was a blur of motion—shoving himself upright, his free hand lashing out to kill two Kaldorix in a single rush before he fully gained his feet and leaped back into the fray.

The Golem slowed, its runes dimming, now pulling back toward their altar.

I scanned the battlefield. Our Royals fought in tandem with the Elders, their forms cutting arcs of fire and steel. Royals clustered with Mavren, Ophira, and other Elders' chants rising. We were recovering, slowly, terribly.

I surged toward our fire ring. If I could anchor there, even briefly, before losing myself in the delirium, I could drag the Golem farther toward their side, reclaim what we had lost till now.

Stone armor gleamed red in the firelight. I struck low, my blade carving through his thigh, and when he faltered, my flames poured into the wound. His scream turned raw as the fire consumed him from the inside, spilling molten cracks through his stone shell until his chest burst apart in a fountain of slag and blood.

A second wave of soldiers surged in from the side, hurling slabs like siege stones. One caught my ribs, and another cracked across my back and forced me to one knee. He advanced, stone hammering at my skull. I answered with flames, in a torrent so hot it peeled their armor in curling sheets. Another one staggered as molten rock dripped from him in ropes. I closed my hand, sending water waves slamming through their lungs, then ignited it. Flesh burst apart in a geyser of steam. The stench of scorched meat filled the air.

The Golem answered by lurching harder toward their altar, fed on the slaughter.

A laugh. High, girlish, sweet. I snapped my head to the side. Mirabelle stood at the edge of my sight, untouched by the wreckage around her. Her eyes were wide with a kind of joyful wonder. A single, perfect crimson tear traced a path down her cheek, like a jewel of life. She giggled as it dripped onto her tunic, her body trembling with uncontainable delight.

She reached out a hand toward me, her smile radiant, an oasis of impossible peace in the heart of the hell we'd made.

For a heartbeat, the world wasn't ending. It was perfect.

"Bella—" I reached for her, and she was gone. Only scorched ground remained.

I tore myself free from the apparition's grasp, stumbling across the threshold into the stone ring before it further consumed my mind. The weight of the haunting was lifted, the madness purged in a painful wrench, though the echo of her laughter still clawed at the back of my skull.

I spat blood, raised my hands again, and faced the next wave.

"You cannot hold forever," Arion growled behind me, his eyes black with contempt. "Atlassian is already bleeding out. All it takes is their Sovereign to fall."

His Aether heaved like jagged spears, driving me to my knees. I melted them with a blast of flame, turning the shards to glass, stepping into his reach. I was about to end him when—

Flames struck my back.

Not stones.

Flames.

Enough to stagger me into Arion's waiting blade. Pain tore across my side. My vision tunneled, battlefield dissolved into a ringing silence painted fire and blood.

I never gave my back to anyone. But I had begun to trust my Legion a little too much. Because in a logical world, no one digs their own grave. They will fight for their own Clan's survival. But someone had turned traitor. And with their grave, dug ours, unless—

Another blow. My warriors roared for me, but their voices dimmed. I saw the Golem nearing our altar in my blurred vision.

I tasted iron. Dark, black blood ran from me in sheets. The attacks rained down. Arion's voice followed. "So this is the end of Atlassian's Sovereign, brought low by his own. How fitting."

Beneath my pauldron, my hand reached to find the vow-stone. But it had already soaked with my blood. A faint smile touched my lips. At least Mirabelle would be safe. She would live. She had to.

Darkness closed in, swallowing the world whole.

Pity I had to go without a chance to demand answers from the Eternis thrust upon me today.

CHAPTER 39
MIRABELLE

The ropes bit into my wrists where they looped above my head, tiny stars of white fire flaring where skin met hemp. For a long moment I only measured the weight of my hands, the small lift of fingertips and the ridiculous economy of motion that let me trade pressure for a breath of air.

My shoulders screamed when the tendons stretched to their limit, my weight suspended from my bound wrists. My toes scraped for purchase on the cold stone, my legs trembling with the effort of keeping the full agony at bay.

A single lambent flame sputtered to life above, casting a jaundiced glow that did little to push back the shadows, only made them dance and leer.

Lorenza sat across from me.

Tied to a high-backed chair, her posture as rigid as if she were at a formal dinner. Her hands were bound behind her, the silk of her gown rumpled. A strip of dark cloth sealed her mouth, but her eyes—wide and furious—were fixed on me.

"Ahh, dear. You know why I loathe the *good ones*?"

The voice was a melody of cultured cruelty, smooth as polished glass and just as cold. It came from the shadows beside the obsidian table with the secret drawer. The Empress of Nyxaria—

Lorenza's mother—stepped into the light. Her battle attire clung about her in a way that made her look like she had stepped from the field straight into this scene. She smoothed a sleeve with slow, exact fingers and watched me with curiosity.

"Because they are not trustworthy," she continued, her tone conversational and polite, as if we were taking a walk through the evening gardens. "At some point, their tedious morality will always, always choose what they deem right over simple loyalty. It makes them so terribly unpredictable."

My mind scrambled like a frantic animal in a cage. Revenge? If this was for Lorenza, why was she trussed up like a prize goose? This scene made no sense to me.

The Empress sighed. She gestured vaguely toward me. "In this situation now, see. You are living this extra life because of my mistake. I chose my *good-minded* Thrall for a specific task," she said, amusement soft as velvet. "Oh, I suppose he no longer loves me for it, because he no longer lives."

She was talking about asking someone to kill me, but I didn't understand when or why.

"And now I trust no one," she said, her gaze sweeping over me with clinical disinterest before landing on her daughter. "Not even my own daughter, whom I raised to be rational and wise. Not moral." She reached out and stroked Lorenza's perfectly coiffed hair, a parody of affection.

I had a thousand questions burning my tongue, muffled by the gag.

"My little lamb," the Empress said to Lorenza in a tone that was indulgent.

"You always find the most inconvenient moments to follow your feelings," the Empress mused. "And you found an awful time to do impulsive things. Wasting my time and spoiling my carefully constructed plans." She rounded the chair and sat, crossing her legs.

Lorenza's eyes flashed. She tried to speak through the gag, vain, mute words scraping at the fabric. The Empress made a small sound, as though disappointed in the interruption, and pulled the cloth away from Lorenza's mouth long enough for one sentence to tumble out.

"I love him," Lorenza said, voice raw and strained. "We have been close since childhood. He—"

The Empress snapped the cloth back over her daughter's mouth. "Ah, please," she said to her in patronizing fondness. "I had hoped you might add something more useful to this conversation. But alas, no."

Then she looked into my eyes. "Between you and me," she said to me, "it's all in this child's head. Because this Sovereign gave her his dagger once to protect herself during her visit here. A political courtesy he doesn't even remember. My emotional little lamb has built an entire fantasy upon it. In Nyxaria, we give a dagger to those we wish to Bond as a promise. She's been carrying that hope like a wound since then."

The Empress's hands were clasped so calmly that I could see every bone in them.

"You must forgive my frankness," she went on, as Lorenza shook her head, straining against her bonds to muffle more words against the gag. Her mother ignored her.

"Now, coming back to the relevant matter. I have this pent-up frustration. Two decades of it. I've had no one suitable to share it with, you see." She smiled, a thin, bloodless thing. "And I've always regretted disposing of lives without giving them the reason why they deserved it. I would say it is really unsatisfying." She exhaled and continued. "I usually do it with proper care. But in your situation, Mirabelle, I couldn't. I was in such a rush before."

She spread her hands, indicating the dark chamber. "But now that I am seeing to matters with my own hands, I have time to offer you the reasoning. This conversation is getting so much more...substantial this way, don't you think? I do so believe in clarity."

A tendril of shadow, summoned by a flick of her wrist, slithered through the air and loosened the cloth from my mouth. It fell away, and I drew a sharp, ragged breath. My throat was dust-dry. I said nothing. I just watched her, every sense screaming at me to look for an escape.

The Empress waited, her expression one of polite expectation. When I remained silent, she turned to Lorenza. "You see? Already better composure. Still wonder why that Sovereign chose her over you?"

Lorenza's answering glare could have scorched stones.

The Empress turned her placid smile back to me. "But I have a rather large issue. That is my Etern. Who, apparently, *smelled* you." Her voice sharpened a fraction, the first crack in her polished veneer. "Ahh, you just *had* to come into that secluded space reserved for Royalty in the ballroom, didn't you? And flaunt your... uniqueness. Then, of course, there was my stupid daughter, sending out invitations with her own petty little plan to make you jealous. To achieve what, even she didn't know. If she weren't my blood, I would have had her disposed of for that idiocy alone."

I was too confused to form a clear thought, so I decided to stay silent and let this woman untangle her own meaning.

She leaned forward, her eyes glinting in the low light. "So, My Etern had started to become obsessed with you. Intrigued. And I had no option left but to kill you. It's simple arithmetic, really. Power is everything. *Everything*."

The feeling of disgust curdled deep within me. Yes, the Sovereign made me uncomfortable. But choosing to go this far over that incident was awful.

She continued in her melodic voice. "I was raised well, bred well. I have fought and struggled tremendously to become the lawful Empress of Nyxaria. And yet, a petite, red-haired tramp had to do nothing but flutter her eyelashes at him to get the same? No, I—"

"Aren't you ashamed?" Rage finally broke through my shock. "To go to such an extreme over this? I have no interest in your throne or your Etern—"

She tsked. "Let me finish, child. Don't interrupt. It's terribly common." She tilted her head, studying me with renewed intensity. "The red-haired, petite tramp in this case...wasn't you. Although I can certainly understand why you'd mistake it for yourself, given how he was so enthralled with you the last time we spoke."

My rage evaporated, replaced by a sinking confusion. *What?*

"It was your mother," the Empress said, her voice dropping to a conspiratorial whisper.

I could only stare. My mind went blank, then filled with roaring thoughts.

The Empress sighed, as if explaining something very simple to a very slow child. "Come now. Even an infant in a cradle would understand you were not born of a commoner. You think you just *happened* to Tame the beasts of Etheris with your little finger? It is a wasteful shame, actually, to kill you. Such a useful tool gone to waste. But a necessary pruning."

My thoughts still spiraled. My mother? The woman I'd known was gentle, quiet, her hands worn from work, her eyes always a little sad. The Empress's words were a key, turning in a lock I never knew existed, threatening to open a door to a past I didn't recognize. The foundation of my entire life shuddered beneath me.

"Who...was she?" I whispered.

The Empress's face twisted with a fresh wave of distaste. She ignored me completely, lost in her own bitter history. "My Etern chose your enthralling mother over me every single time, even after I locked his fate with mine. He met her during some Hunts and fell in...love. My daughter somehow inherited his awful trait—very, *very* bad for her." She shot a venomous glance at Lorenza.

"We thought your whorish mother was dead when he finally Bonded with me. Ah, even I believed it. But no. She'd simply been hidden away in that wild Realm. So I had to get rid of her myself, successfully this time. But you...you slipped away because of that virtuous fool I killed very recently. He was supposed to kill you, not fake you as a commoner of another Clan."

All my life was a lie.

I was the daughter of the Nyxarian Sovereign and a woman from Etheris. A woman he'd loved. A woman this monster had murdered. The grief felt like a ghost inside me, haunting the hollow where a mother's love should have been. I ached for the tenderness I'd never felt, the care I never received. Because the parents who raised me never truly felt like parents. I was grateful, I never complained, I loved them fiercely—but I always knew something was missing. I just never dared to acknowledge it, not even in my own mind, until now.

"My children have the rightful place in my Clan," the Empress continued. "And my Etern would sacrifice his entire legacy to give it to you, since he Bonded that creature first. And you could say I happen to have a soft spot for him." She smiled a pained, terrible smile. "It's not *only* the greed."

"I don't want anything from your Clan!" I cried out. "How did you even—?"

Again, she talked over me as if I hadn't spoken. "Ah, that said, I have my blood here to assist me. I didn't have another choice because of my dull-witted daughter. Your Sovereign," she said, meaning Damien, "if he knew something was amiss. He would not let us live, would he? He is a bit impossible to convince, unlike his father. So, your Sovereign should already be dead by now. With the perfect backstabbing and all the—"

"No!" I shouted. "He wouldn't—" *No, calm down.* He's too strong. He knows how to fight. He just simply couldn't leave without me. They could try, but they would never succeed in defeating him. I knew it.

Lorenza, with a desperate, furious effort, finally tore the gag from her mouth with a wrench of her head. "Mother, why?" she screamed.

The Empress moved faster than thought. Her hand snapped out, squeezing Lorenza's throat, cutting off her cry. "You deserved this for being so reckless!" she hissed, her composure shattering. "You had to try Bonding with him in the middle of the Dissonance? You spoiled everything!"

Then she released her, as suddenly as she'd grabbed her. She straightened, smoothing her attire, the mask of calm slipping back into place. Lorenza gasped, sobbing.

"But," the Empress said to me, her voice returning to that horrifyingly polite tone, "as much as I want to teach her a lesson, she is my daughter. And now that we are clear of all things, and you know why you are going to die...think of it as revenge on my behalf. I killed my daughter's love, or whatever nonsense that was. I wish to do something in compensation for her, right, dear?" she asked Lorenza, who could only weep.

I hope she tries to *choke* me to death, I thought wildly.

The Empress stood and picked up the ledger that had fallen from my hands when she'd caught me. "We had suspected that you didn't forget anything, being the Tamer with all your specialty. The letters were just a trick. And we love that you fell for it." *Alaric. The Elders.* I'd known they were involved. But with her confession, the conspiracy yawned wider, swallowing faces I couldn't even comprehend. If I died here, who would tell Damien? *Stars*, it was all my fault. I'd thought I had time to gather proof. I'd been so catastrophically wrong.

She held the ledger over the flame of the single candle on the desk.

I screamed, "No! Don't!"

"Hush, stop being dramatic," she chided, as the first corner of the precious book blackened and curled. "You are dead. Your lover should be dead by now as well. It is of no use to you anyway." The pages caught, flames licking hungrily at the truth within. With a dismissive flick, she tossed it into the hearth, letting the flames consume it completely. "But I am burning this so that no one in Atlassian will ever remember our failed plotting. I promise, we didn't intend to get that far with the Abyss. We didn't know what we were doing—just some tests from that dead Elder Haldric to rule the Clan, and I needed his cooperation."

The past, the proof, the only thing that could have cleared my name and damned hers, turned to ash before my eyes. And with it, any hope of anyone ever knowing the truth. A faint smell of burning leather and old paper filled the small space. The Empress watched the flames consume the last of the ledger with a satisfied smile.

Then, without a word, without a change in her expression, she flicked her wrist.

Shadows detached themselves from the corners of the chamber. They were not an absence of light, but a solid, lively darkness. They moved with terrifying speed, coiling around my throat like icy serpents.

The pressure was instant. It felt like the ocean depths closing over my head. A cold force that blocked my windpipe and stole my breath in a single, vicious squeeze. I couldn't even gasp. My eyes bulged, straining in their sockets.

The Empress watched, her head tilted, her expression one of mild curiosity.

My vision began to tunnel, blackness creeping in from the edges. The lamplight haloed around her head, then started to dim. A high, thin ringing filled my ears, drowning out the faint crackle of the dying fire and Lorenza's muffled, frantic sounds.

My lungs burned and screamed for air that wouldn't come. Then I felt a terrifying warmth spread through my body in a desperate protest. Spots of brilliant white light danced in the narrowing circle of my sight. The pain in my shoulders, the ache in my legs, it all faded, replaced by this one, overwhelming, final sensation of ending.

I hung there, a puppet with its strings cut, my body twitching with useless, dying reflexes. The darkness wasn't just around me anymore; it was inside me, pouring into my skull with a calming finality.

I waited for it. I welcomed it.

CHAPTER 40

MIRABELLE

Through the final narrowing tunnel of my vision, the last thing I saw was the Empress's face. Calm. An artist observing her finished work. Satisfied.

Just as the darkness threatened to become permanent, I called upon the deepest, most instinctual part of myself.

To protect.

Shadows lived in my blood. The ones that had always been my silent guardians stirred. They wept. A thin film of darkness seeped from my pores, from the skin of my neck beneath the Empress's crushing tendrils. It was a subtle expansion, a thin cushion, forcing a hair's breadth of space between the killing force and my throat.

It wasn't enough to breathe. But it was enough to not die.

I choked on a single, minuscule gulp of air and stopped myself from the extreme urge to gasp for more. The need to suck in a huge, ragged breath of salvation was a torment worse than the choking.

Then I let my body do what a dying body would do. I had to make it real.

My legs gave one last, involuntary twitch against the empty air. A faint, guttural sound rattled in my crushed throat, the very actions of a life shutting down. I let my head loll to the side at a broken angle, my mouth falling slack.

My lungs screamed for more air, but I only let in the tiniest amount necessary to sustain a flicker of life. My body convulsed with the need. I had to brace against the spasm in my lungs as they clawed for even a sliver of air, while outwardly forcing myself to remain utterly, perfectly limp. I had to endure the sensation of drowning while a phantom lifeline held me just below the surface.

I let my body hang like a dead weight. A sack of bones and extinguished life.

For one heartbeat. Two. Three.

Then, I felt the slight relaxation in the oppressive force around my neck. A whisper of thought, a mental shrug from the Empress. Done.

The shadowy tendrils uncoiled from my throat with a sound like slipping silk and retreated, slithering back into the corners of the chamber. The absence of their pressure was a new kind of agony, a rush of fire back into strangled tissues.

I hung from my bonds. My ears roared with the strain of listening over the frantic, silent screaming of my body for survival.

Silence. Then, a soft, rustling step.

"Such a waste of potential." The Empress's voice was a murmur, still devoid of triumph.

Lorenza's sobs tore through the quiet. "How could you do this to my—?" The sound of her thrashing against her bonds followed, the chair legs scraping frantically against stone.

"He is dead. Get over it." The Empress's voice was dangerously soft. A sharp intake of breath from Lorenza suggested a grip, a warning. "If you continue to make a scene and get us all killed, I will rip you apart myself before their blades ever reach me."

Damien *is* alive. He swore to me. It was that simple.

Lorenza's sobs were reduced to silent, hitching tremors.

"Now," the Empress said, her tone shifting back to business, "I have one unfinished thing to do before we slip back to Nyxaria. Gather your composure. Find our guards. I need to have a...discussion with that limping commoner friend of hers. She has a rather large mouth."

Amara. My blood ran cold.

"And we cannot risk two bodies rotting here. We'll take them with us."

I heard the door open and shut. Lorenza was gone.

I sensed the Empress's attention shift, a faint rustle of fabric, the click of a hidden door opening into an adjacent chamber.

My eyes slit open a fraction. The room was empty save for me.

Now.

I called again on the shadows that were my birthright, the Aether I now knew came from my father's blood. They pooled at my wrists as a tool. I focused every shred of will, forcing them to expand, to exert a subtle pressure against the rough hemp. The fibers groaned in protest, stretched to their limit.

From the other chamber, the Empress's voice slithered through the stone. She had left the door opened. "—you know why you are going to die?"

A weak, muffled sound was the only reply. *Amara.*

I twisted my wrist, a minute, agonizing movement that sent fire through my shoulder. A single strand of rope snapped with a faint ping that sounded as loud as a thunderclap in the tense silence. Then another. My wrists were slick with my blood, making the ropes slippery. With a final, gut-wrenching twist, I pulled one hand through the loosened loop.

I hung by one arm now, the strain immense, but I was partly free. I immediately began working on the other knot, my fingers fumbling, slick with blood, my ears straining to catch every sound from the next chamber.

A weak, but defiant cough. Then Amara's voice, strained but clear, "Let me guess... You've run out of loyal subjects to bore to death?"

My brave, foolish friend.

The Empress's voice came again, a polite taunt. "Now, that's not how you speak to a—"

Amara didn't let her finish. "To a what? A coward who ties up girls in dark chambers? Oh, I must have missed the lesson on etiquette for that."

I stifled a smile and continued picking at the knot, my breath held tight in my chest.

"You should know," the Empress continued, her voice dripping with faux sympathy, "your friend just died. She—"

A beat of silence. Then a raw, shattered scream tore through the wall. "No!" The sound of a struggle, a chair scraping against stone. "You lying snake!" I heard the sound of spit, followed by the sound of a sharp, sickening crack of a slap.

"Insolent gutter rat." The Empress's voice was cold steel now.

"You're a monster!" Amara cried out, her voice thick with tears and fury.

"It was my fault, I suppose," the Empress mused, as if to herself. "Allowing a commoner rat to speak—"

I redoubled my efforts, my bloody fingers tearing at the final knot, fueled by a terror for Amara that eclipsed my own pain.

Finally, the last loop gave way. I dropped the last few inches, my legs buckling instantly beneath me. I crashed onto the cold stone, biting my tongue hard to stop the cry of pain that fought to escape. I had been hanging for too long; my muscles were leaden, shrieking in protest. My good leg, the one I'd used to balance for hours, was completely numb like a dead weight.

I crawled toward the ladder.

Then, the sound I dreaded. Boots. Many of them. The squad of guards were already down the corridor outside.

No. No, no, no.

I hauled myself up the ladder; my body felt like a useless, painful weight. I was too slow. The main chamber door burst open.

"She's not dead. She is free!" Lorenza's voice rang in shrill panic.

I didn't look back. I scrambled up the last few rungs into the dark tunnel above, my limp a grotesque, stumbling run. I could hear them giving chase, their heavier footfalls pounding on the stones. My legs gave out.

I fell, skinning my palms, and pushed myself up again, running, falling, running. The door. I had to reach the door.

There it was. The dark metal plate with its etched symbols. I slammed my hand against it. The door began to slide open with a hiss.

A hand, encased in hard leather, closed around my ankle. It yanked with brutal force, pulling my legs out from under me. I crashed onto the tunnel floor, my chin snapping against the stone, the air driven from my lungs in a painful whoosh.

Before I could even gasp, they were on me, dragging me backward through the dark passage. I was a sack of grain hauled back to the Empress for slaughter. They threw me down the ladder into the chamber I'd just escaped. I landed in a heap, biting back a scream of pain.

The Empress looked down at me from what felt like a great height, her expression one of almost bored annoyance.

"Well, well, well," she sighed, as if I were a persistent insect that had flown back into the room. "I must say I am impressed. You've just tainted my impeccable history of clean kills." She pulled a slender, wicked dagger from her belt, its edge glinting in the low light. She tested the point with her thumb. "This time, we do it the good, old-fashioned way. A blade through the heart. It lacks finesse, but it has a certain...undeniable finality."

Lorenza hovered behind her. Her eyes were wide, fixed on my face. "Mother," she whispered, her voice trembling. "Why is she smiling?"

I was.

A slow smile spread across my lips. I pushed myself up, leaning heavily against the cold, damp wall for support. I cocked my head to the side, a trickle of blood from my split lip tracing a path down my chin.

The Empress froze, her perfect composure faltering for a split second. Her eyes narrowed to slits, darting toward the dark mouth of the tunnel. "Did anyone follow her? Did anyone enter the tunnel?" she snapped at the guard who had dragged me back, her voice sharp with a sudden sliver of fear.

The man rushed to check, returning moments later. "No one, My Lady. I had sealed it. She's alone. She's just playing for time."

The Empress's gaze snapped back to me, the fear evaporating into undiluted contempt. "You finally went insane from the lack of air, I see," she hissed, her voice turning venomous, her elegant facade cracking to reveal the ugliness beneath. "A fitting end. Babbling and smiling like a fool."

"Seems like you're not that composed when you lose control of a situation," I said, my voice a raw scrape. "All it takes is a smile to unravel you. How pathetic is that?"

With a snarl of rage, the Empress lunged, the dagger aimed unerringly at my heart.

It never landed.

A blur of motion. A sound like ringing crystal. The dagger was wrenched from her grasp and flung across the room, clattering into the darkness.

The Empress stumbled back, falling onto her hands, her eyes wide with shock. She scrambled backward like a crab, true fear etching lines on her perfect face.

I shook my head in disappointment. "It's a shame," I said, pushing myself up straighter. A pair of brilliant, molten violet eyes gleamed in the shadows beside me, and a form of liquid night and crystalline fury solidified out of the air. "That you chose to try to end a Tamer in her own den."

CHAPTER 41
MIRABELLE

NyxRathis hissed out a sound that promised annihilation. Her form surged upward, shifting from invisible fluid into the full, terrifying majesty of her wyvern form. Her wings, sheer and sharp as stained glass, stretched to the corners of the room, scraping against stone.

I had left her cage unlocked in anticipation of exactly this brand of treachery. And she waited beyond the sliding door I had just opened, listening for my Tether.

The Empress could only stare for a few moments with an expression of stunned disbelief. Her reign of control built on composure finally met a force it could not manipulate, could not strangle, and could not outrun.

Bloody stars, my body was screaming in agony. Still—*Oh how I want to savor this.*

The Empress's shock lasted only seconds before hardening into a viper's focus. "Kill it!" she yelled at her guards.

Four guards lunged with shadow-wreathed blades. NyxRathis met them with finesse. A snap of her jaws took off an arm. A sweep of her wing sent two men crashing into the wall with the sound of shattering bone. She was death incarnate.

Two other guards—*pretty little traitors of Atlassian*—unleashed gouts of fire at her from behind. The flames washed over NyxRathis's scales, but she didn't even turn. The heat seemed to be absorbed, refracted, and then she moved in a blur. A tail, whip-like and tipped with a blade, lashed out. One fire-wielder was severed cleanly in two before his scream could fully form.

Lorenza's panic finally boiled over, and she attacked. She wielded her Aether and sent them lashing out like whips, trying to bind one of NyxRathis's massive forelegs. A jeweled dagger flew from her hand, end over end, aimed at NyxRathis's flank. It was a pitiful, desperate move. The blade clattered harmlessly off the wyvern's scales.

"Let's get out!" she yelled at her mother and ran towards the door.

NyxRathis didn't even take a break from her fight. One moment, she was eviscerating a guard; the next, a translucent, violet wing snapped out with a dismissive, backhanded swat. It caught Lorenza across the torso and sent her flying into a far corner of the chamber. She hit the stone wall with a thud and a sharp howl of pain before slumping into a heap, moaning.

While NyxRathis was momentarily turned, shadows shot out from the Empress toward her. But at the last possible moment, they diverted and wrapped around my arms like serpents, pinning them tightly to my sides against my ribs. She was on me in an instant, her hand fisting in my hair, yanking my head back. The sharp point of her dagger pressed against my throat.

"Enough!" Her voice echoed through the chamber.

NyxRathis froze, a guard's limp body dangling from her jaws. She dropped him with a thud and turned her full attention to the Empress. A low, continuous growl rumbled from her chest at the sight.

"One more move," the Empress spat, her breath felt hot and frantic against my ear, "and I open her throat from ear to ear. Stand down beasty, or I render your Tamer a corpse."

The dagger bit into my skin. A warm trickle of blood slid down my neck. NyxRathis's growl deepened into something that promised an excruciating end. But she took a single, hesitant step back. Her eyes burned with helpless rage.

This was the standoff the Empress wanted. I was a bargaining chip—a shield to get her to the door. But I was so done being weak-kneed.

My eyes met NyxRathis's. In that glance, I poured a single thought: *Trust me.*

With a strength born of intent, I moved. I didn't try to pull away from the blade. That's what she would expect. Instead, I slammed my body backward, driving into her, using my weight to force her arm. At the same time, my hands found the hilt of the dagger she held to guide it.

Her eyes widened in shock, her mind scrambling to make sense of my suicidal move. She thought I was panicking and trying to escape the blade. She tried to press it harder, to punish me.

I helped her.

With the last of my strength, I shoved the hand that held the dagger.

Down.

The sound was a sickening splat—but it wasn't my flesh that tore. *Fortunately.*

The Empress's body jerked against mine. A gushing warmth flooded my back, soaking my dress. Her grip on my hair loosened instantly, replaced by a shuddering clutch. Her shocked gasp was right in my ear, followed by a choked, gurgling sound.

I stumbled forward, pulling away. My hand was still wrapped around hers on the hilt of the dagger. Blessed, for the blade did not pierce my breast. It was buried to its quillon in hers.

Lorenza's scream was a raw, shattered thing from the corner. "No!"

I let go, and the Empress fell backward, collapsing onto the cold stone. She landed on her side, her eyes wide with incomprehension, staring at the ornate handle protruding from just below her ribcage. A dark pool began to spread rapidly beneath her, her mouth working silently as she tried to draw a breath that wouldn't come. A bubble of blood formed on her lips and popped.

I turned, my injured leg buckling, and had to catch myself against the wall. I looked at Lorenza, who was pushing herself up on shaking arms, her face a mess of tears and dust, her hands clapped over her mouth.

NyxRathis took a single step forward, her head lowering, her gaze now fixed on the sobbing Heiress. The growl had returned, lower, more focused.

"Please," Lorenza begged, scrambling backward on her hands and knees. "Please, don't! I didn't want this! I didn't know she would—I just wanted—"

"Shut up, Lorenza." The words left my lips as a bloody, exhausted whisper. I leaned heavily against the cold wall, the rush beginning to recede, leaving a graveyard of pain in its wake. Every part of me was yelping.

She kept babbling, incoherent pleas and excuses tumbling out between sobs.

"Just...shut up. Your regret is an insult. It came too late, and you didn't have another option."

But she wouldn't stop. A torrent of desperate excuses and explanations tumbled out between her sobs. "I'm so sorry! She encouraged me the whole time. It was all for her benefit! I just wanted to have Damien and to have a place... Damien never even let me near him! Not even the two times he was unconscious. He kicked me out both times! You have nothing to worry about, I swear!"

I pinched the bridge of my nose, a wave of dizziness washing over me. Her voice was a spike driven directly into my pounding skull. "I am not going to kill you," I said, the words slow and thick with pain. "So just stop. I don't have the strength to listen to it."

"I didn't Bond with him!" she cried out. It seemed like she wanted to get everything out of her, to stockpile sympathy or to plead her case in full.

"I know, Lorenza," I said, the heat of my anger cooling into something solid. "He is *my* Etern. And you are my sister. It was impossible even if you had wanted to."

She stared at me, her face a mess of tears and shock. "He Bonded you? Just like that, when—?"

"Yes." I cut her off, my voice dropping into a low hiss. Blood from my bitten lip coated my teeth. "And if you ever raise a finger against any of us, I will not be so merciful. I am sparing you only because your misery—living with what you are, knowing what you allowed her to do—is a better revenge than your death."

And maybe—just maybe—I simply couldn't bring myself to kill my own sister. Even if she was a damn viper.

The chamber door burst open. But it wasn't more Nyxarian guards.

These men had heavier armor, etched with stark geometric sigils. Zarkon. Their leader's eyes scanned the carnage—

"No," I whispered. This wasn't right. The realization was a second dagger, twisting deep in my soul.

"No," I said again, louder. "No, no, no...Noooooo!"

The scream tore from my ruined chest, a raw, animal sound of denial. He couldn't be gone. He promised. He was Damien. He didn't fall.

Eyra, their Empress, moved to me and crouched. "I am sorry, my sweet child. Atlassian fell. And—"

I barely heard her. I stopped listening. The world was blurring at the edges, darkening like ink in water. "I'm going to wait in *our* chamber," I mumbled, the words thick and clumsy on my tongue. "Can someone help me walk? I need a healer. Damien won't react well, seeing me like this," I mumbled, the words slurring. "He's just late."

Suddenly, Amara was there. She must have been freed by the Zarkonians. She threw her arms around me, sobbing into my shoulder. "Bella, *oh stars*, Bella."

Her tears were warm on my cold skin. I patted her back awkwardly with my clean hand. "Stop crying," I murmured, my voice distant. "Are you insane? We got the traitors. Can't you see? We're going to... Everything's going to be fine."

Rowane pushed through the Zarkonians, his face ashen, his healer at his heels. His eyes took in the scene.

"Rowane," I said, my voice light and welcoming. "Quite a mess, isn't it? Don't worry. We'll have it cleaned up—"

Rowane's jaw tightened. He nodded to the healer, a woman with kind, sad eyes. She approached me with a vial of milky liquid.

"Now, now," she said softly. "This will help with all the pain."

I shook my head, trying to push her away. "Just heal me. I don't want that. Everything is going to be alright." I took in their expression. "Why are you all looking at me like that? Why are you going this far?"

The healer's grip was firm. She uncorked the vial. "I know, I know. Just get some rest."

I fought it, a weak, struggling thing. "You are all...you are all being so..." The world was fading, the sounds muffled. The last thing I saw was Rowane's devastated face as the sedative pulled me under into a blackness where promises couldn't be broken and Sovereigns couldn't die.

CHAPTER 42
MIRABELLE

I woke and ran.

Straight to the locked doors, shoving past the final set of ornate doors of the Zarkon stronghold. The rest was a blur of stone corridors and the panicked, pitying faces of guards who knew better than to touch me.

My injured leg was a distant protest I ignored. My lungs burned from the whimper I was choking back. I didn't believe any one them. Not even Empress Eyra. I shoved away every hand that tried to pacify me, to pull me back, and kept moving. I moved towards the center. Torches flickered in sconces shaped like wolf heads. And there, on a bier of black granite, he lay.

He was so still.

So impossibly still.

Damien was never still like this.

But they hadn't been able to hide the waxy pallor of his skin, the lack of warmth. And they hadn't changed his clothes. His Sovereign's armor was rent and torn, blackened by fire and stained a deep black with blood. So much blood. It soaked through the leather and mail.

"The blood of a fallen Sovereign is sacred. We do not wash it all away," someone said from somewhere. "He wished to be brought here, should the worst happen. We honor our debts."

My hands, trembling violently, reached for him.

"Damien?" The name was a broken whisper.

I touched his face. And recoiled.

A wail erupted from me, a scream of unadulterated agony that scraped my throat raw. "He's cold!" The words hiccupped out between ragged breaths.

I pressed my forehead to his chest, where his heart should have been beating for me. Only cold, hard leather met my skin.

I looked into Eyra's red-rimmed eyes. "Why is he so cold? Someone, get a blanket. Please," I told them in urgency and turned back to him, my voice crumbling. "Please, please, wake up. Please. This isn't funny. Damien, please."

I was vaguely aware of a presence beside me. Eyra placed a hand on my shoulder. I flinched away from the touch. "He fought like a titan," she said, her voice low and resonant in the hushed room.

The words were like shards of glass shoved into my ears.

"He held the line at the gorge, mind veiled and alone, for an hour. He died a Sovereign's death. A hero's—"

"I don't care!" I screamed at her, shoving her hands aways. Then I shoved myself upright, glaring at her through tears. "I don't care about heroes! I don't care about stands! I want him! Give him back! Get him back to me!"

My voice broke into a thousand pieces. I turned back to him, my hands frantically patting his face, his arms, as if I could jump-start him back to life. "I'm sorry," I sobbed, the words pouring out in a torrent of regret and pain. "I'm so sorry. I was waiting...I was waiting for the right moment. I was such a fool. I thought we had all the time in the world."

A pain, sharp and physical, lanced through my chest, so severe I couldn't draw breath. I gasped, clutching at my heart, crumpling over his body. "We Bonded," I choked out, the words barely audible, meant only for him. "In every way that mattered, we Bonded. I am yours. I was waiting to tell you...to tell you prop-erly...I love you. I love your stupid, serious face in the morning. I love the way you smell of cedar and metal. I love how you fuss. You are my Etern. You are my everything. Please...please, don't leave me here alone. Take me with you. Please, take me with you."

I looked up, my vision blurry, scanning the stunned, silent faces of the Zarkonians. "Do I have any way to join him?" I begged, my voice rising into hysterical despair. "Someone tell me! If I die now, right now, can I go where he is? Somebody bloody help—"

They should have Sages with them. They should—

My hand was shaking violently, a useless, trembling thing against the cold granite. My jaw was locked, teeth chattering with a force that felt like it would crack them. I tried to form the words, to demand they bring every healer, every Sage, every mystic from every corner of the Realm, but my mouth wouldn't obey. It could only shape silent, ragged gasps for air that wouldn't come.

My body was wracked with great, heaving sobs that had no sound left to give.

The world dissolved into a suffocating blackness, the echo of my own silent scream still tearing at my throat. Then, a searing, white-hot pain behind my eyes.

Light.

It was softer. Gray. Dawn light filtering through a window.

The scent of blood and cedar was so vivid I could still smell it. I gasped a sucking sound, struggling to take breaths and failing. Tears were already streaming down my temples, soaking into the pillow.

I scrambled upright, my body wracked with tremors. I was in a bed. A large, unfamiliar bed in a room of dark wood, not a strong-hold or a tomb.

The relief was so violent it was nauseating.

But. No. No—

I flung the furs back and stumbled for the door. My hands, still shaking uncontrollably, fumbled with the heavy iron latch. I couldn't get it open. I started pounding on the wood, wordlessly hammering.

"Open!" I finally screamed, my voice hoarse and broken.

I somehow slammed the door open with one rough, hard pull, but before I could stumble through, it was suddenly shoved back shut. A strong arm slid around my waist, pulling me back from my frantic assault on the wood.

"Now, slow down, wildcat," a voice murmured, deep and rough with sleep, directly by my ear. "Let's not have them think I am mauling you in here."

Him.

And cedar.

And warmth.

He lifted me so my injured leg wouldn't touch the floor.

I went limp in his arms. Rested my forehead against the solid wood of the door and sobbed, shuddering in waves of relief that felt eerily similar to the waves of despair from moments before. I was taking him in—the warmth of his chest against my back, the solid reality of his arms around me, the scent of him.

I was afraid to turn around. Afraid this, too, was a dream, and I would wake up alone in the silence.

He held me, his chin resting on the top of my head.

Finally, I dared to move.

I twisted in his hold, and he let me, his arms loosening but not letting go. My tear-blurred vision focused on his face. Damien.

My hands came up, trembling so violently I could barely control them. I framed his face, my thumbs tracing the line of his jaw, the curve of his lip, the arch of his brow.

He was warm. So wonderfully *alive.* His hair was tousled, and his blue eyes were shadowed with concern. "Hey," he said softly, in a low rumble. "I am right here."

"How?" I managed, the question itself unbelievable, because he was so unbelievably *here.*

He tucked a loose strand of my hair behind my ear. "Nathan put his life on the line to pull me from death—"

I couldn't let him finish. I crushed him in a hug, pressing a fierce kiss to his forehead as a new wave of tears broke free. "I love you," I choked, the words tripping over each other, desperate to be said. "I love you past fear. Past the end of me. Past *everything*." I tasted my own tears with each word. "I love you, I...love you." My whole body was trembling in his arms, unable to draw a full breath.

His eyes closed for a long moment, his entire being seeming to still, to savor the words, to drink them in as if he'd been dying of thirst. When he opened them to look into mine, they were rimmed with red, the blue of them blazing with too many emotions.

My voice was a whisper of sobs. "Damien, I cannot live without you. I thought—I—" I couldn't finish.

He lifted me higher and I locked my legs around his waist, clinging to him, trying to dissolve in him. He held me there, my back against the door, his arms a fortress around me.

"Say it again," he breathed, his voice stripped of all its usual command, leaving only a desperate need. "Tell me you love me."

"I love you, Damien," I whispered against his forehead.

He made a low, broken sound in the back of his throat, half a groan of pure relief. It was the sound of a man who had been waiting an eternity, who had convinced himself he might never hear it. The sound made me feel foolish, selfish for all the times I'd held the words back, thinking I needed the perfect moment.

I had been deprived of him in ways that went beyond distance or silence—all while knowing that no one he cared for had ever told him they loved him. And I had done the same. I was late to realize that there was no perfect moment. There was only this. Him. Us.

I tightened my hold until I heard him grunt softly, but he only drew me closer, his face pressed into the curve of my neck as if anchoring himself to the truth at last.

"Stars, Bella." His voice was muffled against my skin, thick with emotion. "You are the only thing that has ever been real for me. Now I feel...whole."

He didn't give me a chance to respond. His mouth found mine like a brand of ownership and surrender. It tasted of salt from my tears and the honest truth of him. It was a feeling no language in this Realm could describe—his fear, his relief, the terrifying weight of what we'd almost lost, all channeled into that one, perfect connection.

When he finally pulled back, he carried me back to the bed, trying to lay me down gently, but I wouldn't let go, my legs still locked around him, my arms vise-tight around his neck. He chuckled softly against my neck and let his weight settle beside me instead of on me, propped on an elbow, one hand still cupping the back of my head.

"You're going to choke me, woman," he murmured, but there was only a dizzying warmth in that complaint.

"I dreamed you were cold." The words were a fragile confession in the space between us. "And I couldn't get you warm... I need to feel your warmth." A tear escaped, tracing a path into my hairline. "Don't ever be cold."

His expression softened, all traces of amusement vanishing. "Never," he vowed, his thumb brushing away the tear. He leaned in and kissed me again, slower, sweeter, in a silent promise that he would never leave me.

His chest was rising and falling against mine. He kept his forehead pressed to mine, his eyes closed, just breathing me in.

"Don't you ever," he whispered while his lips brushed mine, "wait so long to tell me something important like that again."

The plea was so vulnerable it ignited me from inside.

"Only if you promise to let me have you," I breathed against his lips, and closed the infinitesimal distance between us.

My hands slid from his face into his tousled hair, gripping tightly, holding him to me, and pouring every ounce of fear, every shred of relief, every moment of longing into his lips. He breathed out in a sound of shock that quickly morphed into hunger. His arms tightened; one palm spread over the small of my back, the other tangled in my hair like an anchor.

He let me explore the taste of him, the feel of his lips moving against mine. But the dam had completely broken for both of us.

He rolled, pinning me gently beneath him, his weight was a delicious pressure.

"Your leg," he rasped, even as his hips pressed against mine, the evidence of his desire a shock against mine.

"Shut up and come here," I gasped, arching into him, my good leg wrapping more tightly around his hip to pull him closer, my fractured one a dull, distant protest I gladly ignored.

He cursed softly and the sound turned into a low laugh. "Stars, wildcat."

The word, the name, tore through the haze of sensation. I went still beneath him. "Wait, Damien—" My voice was breathless. "Did you just call me wildcat?"

He hummed, the sound vibrating through his chest into mine. His hand, which had been tracing a path up my ribcage, stilled.

"Why?" I asked, my heart beginning to hammer for a completely different reason.

He pulled back just enough to look down at me, his eyes dark with passion but now also sharp with a sudden intensity. "Why do you think?"

The air left my lungs. He remembered.

Everything.

CHAPTER 43

MIRABELLE

I didn't know how to respond with words.

My hands framed his face. In a surprising motion, I used my grip and the strength of my good leg to roll us. He was too shocked to resist, his balance already compromised by the intensity of the moment. Suddenly, I was straddling him, looking down at the Sovereign of Atlassian, who was staring up at me with his wide, astonished eyes.

A slow, wicked smile touched my lips. I leaned down, my hair curtaining our faces. "My turn, your Majesty," I whispered, and attacked his mouth with a kiss, nibbling and biting. He groaned, his hands coming to my hips to hold on as I poured every ounce of my rediscovered strength into showing him exactly what his remembered endearment had unleashed.

I tore at the ties of the thin linen gown they'd dressed me in. The cloth fell away in a flurry, tossed to the floor. I felt ridiculous and ferocious at once—exposed, yet invulnerable.

I leaned down, letting him find the breast I offered, and his mouth closed over its peak. He hummed low in his chest, the sound reverberating through me, and I arched, meeting the motion with my back as if to press him deeper into that heat. The hum turned into a greedy sucking; his lips and tongue mapped me. I moaned, the sound ripping from me, refusing to be stilled.

Each tug of his mouth sent a quick shock of sensation along my ribs and down into a heat that went straight to my core. It was intoxicating—the way he focused his attention on me until nothing else existed. I pulled him closer, suffocating him with the press of my breasts, and he answered by drinking, by kneading, by the slow ferocity of a man who had been starved of this language for too long.

When his hand slid under my spine and cupped the soft swell of my lower back, I felt that whirling bloom that gathers before everything else breaks loose.

He moved, lips crawling down the valley of my sternum, breathing in the faint salt of my skin, trailing to the band at my hip. I adjusted, mindful but reckless: my leg pressed more weight into him, hooked around his hip. He clenched, a small grunt of warning. "Not so foolishly, precious," he breathed into my mouth. "Not on that leg."

"Sorry," I rasped, and leaned down to kiss him again, tasting cedar and the stubborn man beneath. "Now please, *please*."

I fumbled at my thin underclothes, but he tore them aside. He dragged me up by the hips until my hips hovered above his face and then his mouth was on *me*—hungry, reverent, devastating.

I buckled at the intense sensation, fingers finding the headboard, one hand tangled in his hair as he worked pleasure into frenzy. Waves pulled through me, each lick and suck building me toward that fathomless edge; my breath came in torn gasps, vision bright with stars. He hummed against me.

When I came, it spilled through me in feverish waves, my vision blurred and my knees unable to trust themselves. I could feel him tasting the rhythm of my release and savoring it. He licked me clean, his lips soft, refusing me rest until the tremor in my hands eased.

I tried to pull back, to steady myself—but he would not let me go. One hand captured both of mine and drew them behind my back, his other palm splayed against my hip. He lifted his face and kissed the inside of my thigh. "So damn sweet," he breathed, voice thick. "Just as you've always been."

Heat coiled upward again like a tide of want, of need. The longing for him had been a constant ache in my bones. I begged him, "I need you. I need you inside me."

He *tsked*. "Let me devour every inch I own," he said, slow and maddening, his fingers dragging like a dare. His mouth found all the tender nerves on my body, ignoring the way I pleaded. I felt him measure me with the precise cruelty of a man who had learned to make time an ally. He teased, licked, and then slid a finger into me, pressing with a rhythm that made me break and then rebuild on the same breath.

The sensation wracked through me in a shattering tide of bliss. I gripped his hair so tight the strands slipped through my fingers, tears blurring my eyes, and I tasted another thunder of release again.

When that hungering need swept through me and left me breathless and pliant, he rose. He slowly undid his tailored trousers, with a fervent look at me that stripped me more naked than any cloth could. He studied every inch of me with the intensity of a man scanning a map he planned to memorize. Heat rose at my collarbone and I glanced sideways.

"No," he said with a command that was simple but absolute. "I want to watch you watching me." He gripped my chin, forcing my gaze to his, and in that stare, I saw the raw need for me. "Let me see you see me claiming you."

He settled over me, aligning his body with slow exactness. One hand closed at the nape of my neck, tilting my head just so; the other bracketed my waist, fingers spreading to keep me exactly where he wanted me.

I felt the press of him, the delicious, inevitable closeness that had been waiting in the hollow between us for weeks of stolen glances and half-said things. His face hovered over mine, breath hot against my mouth, and his eyes dragged mine into a tide.

"Eyes on me." A command wrapped in plea.

A laugh—short, breathless—escaped me, equal parts incredulous and feral. I swallowed the rest and met his gaze.

Then he entered me in one single, hard thrust. Swift enough to steal my breath and slow enough that I could feel the entire length of him move forward, deeper inside me. The first moment was shock. The second was a bloom of the most exquisite friction. He filled me, pressing into places that had only ever been known by him.

He moved slowly inside me, and I felt the delicious fullness that made me cry out in bliss with each thrust. Every motion was intimate: I could feel the rub of his hip against mine, the way his length sat in me and brushed that impossible hollow. It was both invasion and homecoming. This was what I had wanted when I chased him through my first Bloomwake, when my body screamed for his and I didn't understand why. This. And everything beyond.

"You fit like you were created for me." His voice was rough and it flowed through my own veins. I answered by arching under him, drawing him deeper with the press of my hips, my fingers threading into the dark hair at his temples.

He moved so slowly, and I could feel him thrum in his chest with every motion, the vibration matching the building pressure low in my belly. The pleasure inside me began as a small, sweet curl. It was not merely physical; it was a map of all the nights we had lost and the days we would steal. He rode that line between tenderness and ferocity, and I matched him. Legs wrapped, hips rising, knees trembling.

"My home," he breathed once, looking straight into my soul. In it lived refuge and claim and a thousand small promises. The way he said it pulled a salt-hot sob from me. I kept my eyes on his as everything else blurred. In those blue depths I saw a mirror of my own emotions: fear, love, and relief that he was still here to meet me in it.

He shifted angle, the line of him changing so a different, deeper plane was reached. The new movement struck me in a way I had not expected. Fuller, hitting a place of deeper bliss that made my breath stutter and toes curl. Each stroke whispered of mornings and of fighting side by side and of quiet vows that bound us together.

I could feel that massive tide coil inside me, a pressure that gathered like a storm rolling closer with nowhere to escape. My breaths came in ragged little bursts; I whimpered because I did not know how else to face what was coming.

He kept watching me. The way his pupils darkened, the small catch at the base of his throat, told me he was there with me in this. His eyes were an open mirror of everything I felt: hunger, awe, a vulnerability I had never seen on him before. He was bare and unguarded. I drank him in with the pure animal need of it. We lost and found ourselves in one another's gaze, drowning in that clarity and clutching at it with both hands.

He bent and pressed the lightest of kisses to my mouth. It felt soft like petals and thick honey, warm and light on the tongue. When he pulled back a fraction, his voice was close enough to be felt. "Let go for me, Bella," he whispered. "Let it all come undone."

His command was my permission. I unclenched. And the wave that had been building slowly for an eternity finally broke—long and consuming, searing and tender—and I fell through it as if I had been unmoored. My body spasmed around him; tears rolled down my cheeks. His chest pressed hard to mine and the world narrowed to the cadence of his breath.

He followed me over the edge, his body answering mine with the same violent grace. When it was over, the aftershocks shivered down my limbs. I lay shaking, chest trembling, and felt the steady drum of his heart against my ear like an anchor. Tears left salty tracks on my face and I did not know what to do with them. So I let them fall.

He did not speak at first.

He kissed me—temple, eyelids, cheek, the hollow beneath my ear—each press of lips felt like an oath.

"I love you, wildcat," he murmured. "I have loved you in the dark and in the quiet and in the small moments I thought no one watched. I have loved you when everything else wanted me to be less than honest. I have loved you in ways that terrified me. I love you now with the steadiness that has survived demise."

His hands cradled my face, thumbs brushing my cheekbones with warmth. He kissed my chin, then the corner of my mouth, then met my eyes again. His were blue rimmed and impossibly open. "Do you understand?" he asked in a low voice. "You are not a story I will allow to be retold by strangers or rumor. You are mine. And we are keeping it that way. Forever."

My tears were quiet now. "I do not know why I am crying," I managed between breaths. I wanted to respond to him with more grace, to find the right words that could capture how the sheer force of my love for him made my soul suffer in a beautiful agony.

But the look on his face told me he was comprehending all of it from my tears alone.

His hand slid down, his touch infinitely gentle as he cupped my hip, his thumb stroking my bare skin in a soothing rhythm. With exquisite care, he eased his weight away and slipped out of me, but only to gather me closer. He took me into his arms, cradling me against his chest, tucking my head beneath his chin until all I could hear was the strong, steady drum of his heart.

We lay like that, tangled together in the quiet. His fingers found the place where my shoulder met the curve of my neck, drawing slow, hypnotic circles that unraveled the last of my tension.

I let myself drift into the safety of his hold.

And into the warmth of his life.

CHAPTER 44

DAMIEN

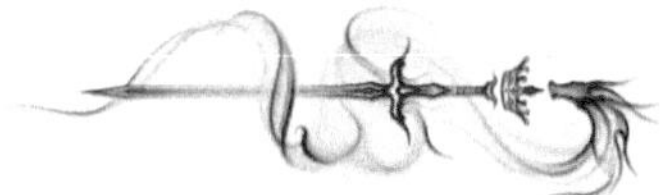

The fire in the study crackled, casting dancing shadows over the calm face of the Zarkonian Sovereign. To his right, leaning against a bookshelf with an easy grace that belied the tension in the room, was his second son, Elric.

Karzul leaned forward. "Your scouts report Nathan took the final blow meant for you. But what of your own condition? Are you well now?"

I leaned back against the highchair. I could see the shadow of the gorge in his question. "Two of your best healers and my Aether did what they could. I will be fine."

"And your Commander?"

Before I could answer, Elric chimed in. "Father's being tactful. He means to say, can we rely on you not to be assassinated by your own before the ink on any treaty is dry?" He flashed a grin that was more sharp than friendly.

"Elric," Karzul warned, but Elric continued as if he'd heard nothing at all.

"And while we're on the subject of alliances," Elric said, his eyes glinting with a smile, "the new winning Clans...father's already calculating. Thinks someone has to extend a hand first, break this cycle of decades-old enmity."

Karzul shot his son a look. "You are safe from such alliances as long as your elder brother breathes. My concern is practical. We all need to stick together now for our own sake."

"Ah, but I told this old man I don't want to be *safe*," Elric drawled, leaning back with a conspiratorial smirk directed at me. "Now that he's mentioned it, maybe I should see about stopping that particular breath. Free myself up for some good old-fashioned political alliance."

"Even if you succeed," Karzul said in a flat tone, "I will have you reassigned to latrine duty till the next Dissonance."

Elric shook his head in mock disappointed, mumbling something under his breath.

Then Karzul turned his attention back to me. "As I was saying, such betrayals as you suffered do not sprout in a day. This was planned, Damien—patiently, and over time."

"I am aware," I said, the words bitter as cinders.

Ophira. Her betrayal had come as an unexpected turn, though in truth I should have read it sooner. She was my father's trusted advisor, yet I'd been conveniently blind to the truth of her blood: niece to the murdered Empress of Nyxaria. Planted within our court after an old Dissonance, her family had bartered with the Dominion and my own father to keep her here. To what precise end, I still did not know.

And her most recent gambit—mind-veiling and then back-stabbing me during the battle. It was the neatest solution to the problems her aunt and her wretched cousin had begun. That cousin's effort to Bond me while my mind was veiled would almost be comical, if it had not been so contemptible. She saw the veiling as an opportunity and lunged at me with her ceremonial dagger, unaware she was trying to bind herself for eternity to a man already marked by her kin for the grave.

"About extending a hand," I said, pulling myself back to the present. "Even I agree to that, Telmoria needs stability, not more blades at each other's throats."

Karzul studied me for a long moment. "Insight," he rumbled, a note of respect in his voice. "It has been too long since Atlassian spoke with such sense."

"It is the only logic that serves our Realm," I replied, deflecting the praise back onto the simple truth of the situation. "And a Frost-tail will be delivered before the next moon."

Elric let out a low whistle. "A Frost-tail? Now, that's...very generous."

Karzul's expression softened. "It is a great help, son. Truly. Those beasts have been treacherous for our Hunters, and we have none. And it's too generous for what we have done." He smiled. "Let us know if you need assistance in return. Untangling internal politics—it seems you have a thorny patch to clear."

They had no clue, I thought, a cold wave washing over me. They had no clue how deep the nest went, or that the head of the serpent was my own blood. My mind flashed back, as a visceral memory...

Just before the second night of the Dissonance, I'd been in my father's study. On his desk, beside a half-finished missive, lay the heavy iron key to the West Chambers of the Hold. He *never* went there. He had no interest in the Tameables, especially after I'd taken over his duties. The sight was a wrong note in a familiar song.

I didn't touch it. Instead, I found Rowane. "Check the old infirmary in the West Chambers," I'd ordered, my voice low. "See what's left behind."

When he returned, his face was grim. In his hands was a ledger, its cover worn and dusty. "It was hidden behind a loose stone," he'd said, his tone hollow. "Damien...it's..." He looked upward, as if searching the ceiling for strength, then thrust the ledger into my hands. "I'll leave you to deal with this for yourself." He turned to go, pausing only to add, "I've replaced it with a similar ledger. So, they're still on the blind side."

The moment my fingers touched the aged leather, a dam burst into my skull. It felt like drowning. A staggering wave of memories —every glance, every touch, every argument, every moment of understanding. The first time I saw her at the trials, all fierce defiance and hidden vulnerability, and the sudden, unshakable certainty that I would keep her.

Our heart-to-hearts under the stars, the heat of her skin under my hands, the way she challenged me, healed me, fit herself into the cracks of my armored life until she became the only part of me I couldn't bear to lose. Our Bonding, the moment of bliss. It was like rediscovering sight after a lifetime of blindness.

Then, the crushing emptiness—the journey back to Atlassian after the Abyss, that was a hollow echo. The first conversation with my father...him probing the edges of my memory, feigning concern, strategically sowing panic about the Realm's stability until the alliance with Nyxaria seemed not just logical, but necessary. *Why not?* I had thought, but the ghost of a feeling for a girl I no longer remembered as mine still felt like a betrayal of something I couldn't name.

The memory made my heart tear apart for her. She had endured it all alone. She had tried to reach me, to break through the wall around my mind, and she had suffered for it in silence. The fury that thought ignited was a cold, focused fire in my veins. I would not be sparing anyone connected to this. Starting with my father, who now sat in the dungeon, awaiting an execution I would personally oversee.

Karzul was still speaking, but a raised voice sliced through the heavy door from a chamber down the hall. Even muffled, I could never mistake that voice. Mirabelle.

Karzul's eyebrows lifted slightly. I sighed. "It seems my reason for needing your vow is attempting to dismantle your fortress stone by stone."

I stood and began to leave.

"Secure your own borders first, Damien." Karzul's voice was sincere with genuine care.

"Sounds like a handful. Do you need another hand taming your *reason*, Sovereign?" Elric called after me, his tone light and teasing.

"Not if that hand values its bones unbroken," I replied without looking back and closed the study door firmly behind me.

A soft, low chuckle from the Sovereign followed me out.

━━◆◈◆━━

SHE WAS in the same chamber, a storm contained in a room, wearing my tunic after her own gown had torn and was facing down two flustered Zarkonian healers with the ferocity of a cornered hawk.

"—not a prisoner to be locked away!" And she was shouting.

The healers looked immensely relieved to see me. So did she, though her relief immediately morphed into a fiery glare.

"You," she seethed, pointing a finger at me. "Did you order them to lock me in here? Again?"

I closed the door behind me, leaning against it. "I ordered them to ensure you rested. We have a battle to finish, Bella. I need to win it. And to do that, I need to know you are here, safe, and not bleeding out somewhere because of the treachery that seems to dog our every step. So, yes."

"That is not your decision to make!"

"It is when the alternative could be your corpse!" The words came out sharper than I intended, fueled by the visceral memory of finding her here, leg twisted, ribs bound, a bowl of water beside her already stained black with her blood.

I was so damn proud of her for fighting, for surviving, for taking care of herself when I couldn't. But now was not the time to encourage her to break more bones.

She crossed her arms, her chin lifted. And that was not a good sign for me. At all.

"Then I will spend every moment you are gone finding a way out of this chamber. And if I manage it, I will limp straight onto that battlefield," she hissed.

I stared at her, at the stubborn set of her jaw, and the absolute certainty in her eyes. She meant it. She would break herself trying to follow me. The fight drained out of me, replaced by a weary, inevitable surrender.

She would always be my greatest vulnerability, and my greatest strength.

"Fine," I bit out, the word tasting like defeat and strange pride. "You can come."

I looked at the elder healer. "Her leg?"

The woman nodded slightly. "The injury is stable, Sovereign. It requires rest. Any significant strain or fall could worsen it."

I turned my gaze back to Mirabelle, grinding my jaw. A murderous rage toward everyone who had played a part in putting that fracture there: the Empress, the Heiress, the guards, the entire rotten scheme, curled in my gut. I swore to myself, *again*, that every single remaining one of them would all suffer for it.

"See?" Mirabelle said, a touch of triumph in her voice. "It's not *that* bad."

"It is bad enough," I countered.

"Please," she whispered.

I closed my eyes. *That was it.* She knew what to say, when to say it, and how to say it to make me helplessly comply. So I strode to the closet and pulled out a simple, sturdy dress and underclothes —dark wool and soft linen.

I dismissed the healers with a nod. The door clicked shut, leaving us alone. I was still angry at her ultimatum, but the battle was lost. "Lift your arms."

She did, a mischievous smile playing on her lips. I gripped the hem of my tunic she wore and pulled it up and over her head, leaving her standing naked before me in the gray light.

My gaze lingered for a heartbeat on the hardened peaks begging for my attention, a rush of heat rising despite the circumstances. But I steeled myself, shoving the urge down deep.

I worked quickly, my movements almost clinical. I dressed her in the underclothes, pulling the soft linen shift over her head. My thumb brushed—perhaps lingered a moment too long—against a puckered peak as I smoothed the fabric down.

She swatted my hand away, though her eyes were dancing. "I thought you were above stealing a feel while playing nursemaid."

A smile threatened to break through my stern expression, but I bit it back. "There was a wrinkle to smooth out," I said, my voice a low murmur.

Her laugh was a soft sound that brightened the dim room. "Oh, now, was there?" she teased, her eyes sparkling with warmth. A genuine smile finally lifted my lips, and my insides melted at the sight of her twinkling eyes.

I moved to the dress, easing it over her shoulders while she sat on the bed. I finished fastening the dress. Then I cupped the nape of her neck, my thumb stroking her jawline. "Please behave." I warned, my voice a low growl. I leaned in and pressed a long, warm kiss to her forehead.

She responded by leaning up and nipping my cheek.

I shook my head and swept her into my arms, careful of her leg, and carried her out to the waiting carriage. It was almost afternoon.

We had lost quite a few warriors yesterday. I needed to see the replacements from the reserves.

And all I could think, as I settled her inside, was how right it had felt to wake up with her in my arms this morning, even on the brink of war. She was my calm, the wound and the balm. So these moments with her counted as my much-needed peace before the storm of the final battle. I needed it. And if that made me selfish, then I was selfish. I'd been called worse for less worthy reasons.

⚜

THE CARRIAGE FASTENED to the Frost-tails was a small world unto itself, a cocoon of warmth and soft furs rolling through the Zarkon landscapes. I had chosen the largest, most comfortable one, with the intention of leaving it here for her—a mobile sanctuary for my Tamer while I fought the battles.

Now it carried both of us, the cushions piled high, furs folded into neat nests. The lantern hung tight to the ceiling, throwing a shallow glow of light. In that fast-moving room, she lay against me —small, stubborn, her leg propped on a rolled blanket. My arm rested across her waist because, for the life of me, my hands kept going there.

She'd been quiet for a long while, but I felt the question building in her like a storm. I knew exactly what it was. I was surprised she had waited this long, but the exhaustion from the battle and the more pleasant exertions had stolen her words.

Now, I saw the fidgeting of her hands, the way she'd bite her lip and then stop herself. She was trying to find the right way in. The last two times she had tried to circle the topic without landing on it, so I had feigned ignorance, letting her stew. She deserved a little torment for holding back so many things that mattered.

I understood the precise moment she decided to just ask. Her shoulders squared, and she took a determined breath. I kept my gaze fixed on the fast-passing landscape, giving her the stage.

"How do you...erm...you?" she began, her voice tentative.

I turned my head slowly, raising an eyebrow. "What, Bella? What do you want to know?"

She huffed out a sound of frustration. "I know you know what I want to know. And you are pretending otherwise."

"Now, why would I do that?" I asked, my tone deliberately light.

She mulled it over, the cart's gentle sway rocking us together. "Because you think what I did was..."

"And what did you do, exactly?" I prompted, turning fully to face her now, resting my arm along the back of the seat.

She looked into my eyes with those awfully big, earnest ones, and her voice was small. "I did something...bad." The sheen in her gaze carried her regret. Then her head snapped up. "Wait. How do *you* remember?"

I turned and reached into the narrow compartment built into the side of the carriage. The ledger lay there, bound in dark leather.

I had carried it with me since Rowane handed it over. I couldn't risk losing it.

Her face went pale. "But I saw the Empress burning it!"

My jaw tightened at the thought of her there, at that Empress's mercy, a flame waiting to be snuffed out. I forced the image down, along with the urge to kill them all with my bare hands. *Oh, the killing I will do all right—the captured ones are still breathing.*

I closed the compartment. "Rowane replaced it with something similar. She burned that one. Not this."

"Oh." A pause. "I think I'll have to express my gratitude to Rowane."

"Express it to me. I will pass it along."

She shook her head, then looked at me for a beat. Two. "So you knew."

"Yes, Mirabelle. I knew the same night I found you at my door —black and blue and unconscious. And that is why I locked you out of that damn chamber. Because I never, in my wildest imagination, thought you'd escape through that window with that injured leg of yours." My voice cracked at the edge. "Risking your life. What were you thinking?"

She flinched. The regret in her face struck me square in the chest. I softened instantly. Lifted my hand, very slowly, and took her jaw. Just to feel her there.

"What were you thinking?" I asked again, quieter now. "I would have taken care of it. I would have borne the consequences if every single one of them slipped through and escaped. I would have signed any treaty. Paid any price. There is no consequence I wouldn't have shouldered if it meant you stayed safe. How do you not see that?"

She looked at me, her eyes searching mine as if trying to find the edge of my patience, the place where this would finally break. She wouldn't find it. With her, that place had never existed.

"I could lay down every war I have ever won at your feet and it would still not come close to what I owe you," I said, my thumb brushing along her jawline. "You bled for something I could not even remember losing. Do you understand what that makes you to me? There is no word for it in any tongue I know. I live and breathe for you. You are the purpose of my life. And you were planning to sacrifice *your* life to give me back my memories? Can't you see the absurdity of it?"

"I...I thought it was my last chance to make everything right," she whispered.

I smoothed a hand over my mouth, dragging it down my chin, and closed my eyes for a beat before letting the breath out. When I opened them, my expression was soft, all pretense of annoyance gone. "And why didn't you tell me any of this before, precious?"

Now she looked utterly undone.

"I'm sorry I held back. It wasn't that I wanted to hide the Abyss from you. I just never found the right moment to say it. I couldn't risk testing whether you would believe me. I was just another soldier in your Legion. I knew no one in their rational mind would believe a story that absurd. Least of all the Sovereign of a Clan." She swallowed. "But after that..." Her voice faltered. "After that, maybe I did hold back, for a very little while." The rest of the confession caught in her throat, unfinished, as though completing it would strip her of something she could not afford to lose.

I exhaled hard, a sound of surrendered exasperation. "You are lucky I am physically incapable of denying you anything when you look at me like that."

I reached out and tucked a stray curl behind her ear, my fingers lingering on her jaw. "But I promise I will see to your torture, my precious, precious nuisance, later—for holding back." I paused, my gaze locking with hers, before my voice dropped, becoming serious. "What on Abyss were you thinking, hiding our Bond from me, Mirabelle?"

She tried to explain, her words tumbling out in a rush. "I just wanted to know you'd choose me if she...if someone like Lorenza was your other—"

The sound I made was halfway between a laugh and utter disbelief. "You should know by now that I would never, *ever* consider being with someone other than you. It pains me that you even thought I had another option when there is you." I leaned closer, my voice dropping to a low, intense murmur that vibrated in the small space between us. "When I said I don't choose you, it's because choosing implies I'm taking one from several options." I looked into those green depths. "You are not one of my options, precious. You are my only destination. And I meant it for all my lifetimes. Get that through your pretty, stubborn little head."

I shook my head, exhaling slowly. "I can't even fathom you were reckless enough to test my words with our actual lives."

"I know, I know, and I believed you then. Completely," she insisted, her eyes pleading for understanding. "But if you were in my place—"

"If I were in your place," I interrupted, "I would have dragged you back to my side, even if you were screaming and kicking."

She was wordless for a moment. Then a small smile touched her lips. "Well...you are not exactly easy to carry, even without screaming and kicking...and all that." Then she mulled something over, her brow furrowing. "But I know for certain now, but back then I thought...you hadn't actually been with an Heiress like that? So you hadn't seen—"

"I hadn't seen what?" I cut in, my exasperation returning. "You think that I haven't been offered Heiresses before?" I pinched the bridge of my nose, a headache brewing behind my eyes. "Stars, Bella. I was the only Heir of a long-standing Clan on this Realm. What do you think my life has been? I have *seen* enough to know the difference between a political arrangement and the woman who holds my soul."

She scrunched her nose at me saying *seen*, a gesture so endearingly irritated I almost smiled. *Well, she had asked for the truth.*

"And I was trying to gather evidence," she countered. "Because my explanation of the Abyss sounded insane, even to me. I needed you to know me, to trust me first." She sounded logical, yet guilt lingered in her eyes.

"And after I began to trust you?" I pressed.

"How was I to know you trusted me *enough*?" Her voice wavered between defense and plea. "Enough to believe a secret that huge without proof? It wasn't only that," she said, her voice gaining a little strength, trying to steer the conversation. "I told you, it was also about not feeling certain enough. But I'm over it now. I was talking about that time, not now. I am secure enough now—"

"Yes," I countered, my tone dry, "*after* you tested it and made sure."

She looked down at her hands, her shoulders slumping. "I am sorry, see? You were treating Lorenza well, and she was... gorgeous."

"Stars, woman," I said, my voice softening despite my best efforts. "Have you seen yourself?"

"I...yes. Again, I said I *was*, not am," she whispered, the word barely audible. "What I did was not fair. But I've been raised in Dorms, Damien. I had nobody except Amara telling me anything good, not a single soul. And Amara hardly counts, because she swears my skin shines even when I'm caked head to toe in mud."

She took a small breath, her vulnerability a stark contrast to the warrior who had ridden into battles and bathed in blood. "I have been bullied, called ugly, when I grew up in the Dorms. A scrawny, commoner girl with too-big eyes and weird hair. If someone looked at me kindly, I waited for the joke. And I didn't even know how attraction or physical intimacy worked except from small gossip stories from Amara. So I was...navigating in the dark."

The confession landed like a stone in my gut. For all the years I hadn't been there for her. And all the time I had been within reach, yet unreachable to her. Until now, I hadn't even considered her going through her first Bloom of desire. Her first real awakening to mating feelings, alone and confused, without me there to guide her, to cherish her, sliced through me.

I couldn't tolerate her guilt any longer. I reached for her, pulling her into my arms, holding her tightly against my chest. I felt her initial stiffness melt away as she buried her face in my tunic as if she could hide from her own past.

"I get it, precious," I murmured into her hair. "And I need you to know, you are the most breathtaking thing to ever exist in this world. I only understood the true meaning of desire when I first laid eyes on you. It even caught me off guard. So, you are not the only novice here."

She was still for a long moment. Then, she slowly took my hand from her back, lifting it. She pressed a soft, lingering kiss to the center of my palm. Then she looked up, her eyes meeting mine. And she smiled.

And it was a smile that cracked my heart wide open and filled the fractures with a golden, searing light. In that moment, every doubt, every moment of pain, was worth it.

DAMIEN

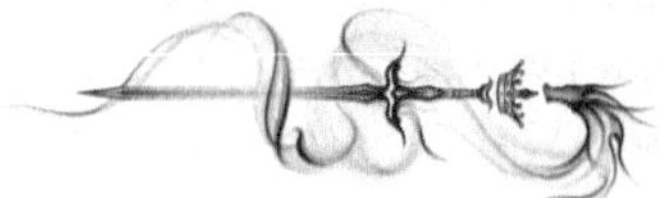

We had been playing this game of questions for most of the journey, and I found myself eager for more. And she steered it back to the one thing she longed to ask again.

"I have had your background figured out for a while. I just wasn't entirely sure. I had to talk to your father."

She pulled back slightly, her eyes wide. "You knew about my father and hid it from me?"

"I told you there was more to the alliance. I needed to be certain before I told you, before peppering you with something that could shatter your entire understanding of your life," I explained. "And I wanted to make sure your father didn't have ill intentions."

She began to protest, but I continued. "I knew something was missing about the Abyss, but not its full extent. I have never trusted the false courtesy of the Nyxarian Empress or her extreme interest in my private discussions with your father. So when I suggested a theory and he confirmed her jealousy over your mother, I didn't have to think hard to connect the dots. The timing, your age, some reports from Rowane—it all pointed to her. But I hadn't realized she was involved in the Abyss till she entered Atlassian in the middle of Dissonance, in secret."

"So you knew you had forgotten something?" she said, confusion etching her features.

"I suspected, but wasn't sure. You were one of the variables that fell out of place," I said, a small smile touching my lips. "I knew for certain that I would never have looked into your eyes and agreed to tie myself with someone else. I was not that weak-willed."

She tried for a cheeky response, a playful glint returning to her eyes, but it faltered under the intensity of my gaze. A blush crept up her neck, and I leaned in, capturing her lips in a lingering kiss.

When we parted, she was breathless.

"But...how were you sure about me?" Mirabelle's voice pulled me from the dark memory. "What if I knew nothing...I mean, I could have also forgotten—"

I chuckled, the sound low in my chest. "You were not subtle about your advances, or your mumbles under your breath, wildcat." I traced the blush that bloomed on her cheeks. "And Izmer's conversations with me, which made no sense at the time, suddenly became perfectly clear. And I knew by then you were not someone from Atlassian."

The way I fell for her was a revelation all over again. When my feelings were wiped away, there was nothing left for me but the cold duty of the Dissonance. But she was a blissful rebellion against that emptiness.

A splash of vibrant color in a world gone gray, a stubborn melody that insisted on being heard even when I was determined to live in silence. She hadn't just reminded me of my love; she had made me fall in love with her all over again, every single day.

⟶❧⟵

IF WE LOSE THIS, everything we have bled for will be ash.

In the heart of darkness, we waited. The silence was broken

only by the shift of hooves on hard ground and the soft chink of bit and bridle.

Nathan still lay abed, his body waging a brutal war against the killing blow that had been meant for me. We had lost Elders in the night, and almost all of the reserve soldiers had to be moved to the army to cover the severe losses we had suffered.

A sliver of light. Then another.

The dark mantle lifted.

The platform exploded into light, sound, and motion.

"For Atlassian!"

The roar went up from two hundred and thirteen throats, and we surged forward as one. I dug my heels into my horse's flanks, and we surged forward as one with the line. Across the field, the Kaldorix line did the same, a mirror of screaming men and glinting steel. This was the Binding Core. No Aether. No Tameables. Just flesh, blood, and the will to survive.

The two fronts collided with a sound like a mountainside shearing off. My sight narrowed to the arc of a blade, the grunt of effort, the spray of blood hot against my cheek—I moved on instinct.

Parry, thrust, pivot. A soldier came at my left; I sidestepped his wild swing and drove my blade up under his ribcage. He fell with a choked gasp. Another took his place, then another. They came in a relentless wave. I saw an opening, a break in their line, and pushed forward, my guard down for a split second.

My confidence in Atlassian's might was a hard-won thing, forged in real victories, and tempered by the bitter experiences of treachery. We had always fought the border skirmishes between Dissonances, regardless of which Clan prevailed in the grand trials.

A volley of spears arced through the air. I wrenched my horse's reins, guiding the beast into a tight, spinning turn. A spearhead grazed my pauldron with a shriek of metal. I leaned low over the neck, the second and third spears passing harmlessly over my back. My horse, a veteran of such battles, needed little guidance, its muscles coiling and releasing as it dodged and weaved through the deadly rain. He was more partner than steed, an extension of my will.

From my right, a Kaldorix horseman thundered toward me, his blade a silver flash in the murky light. I evaded a swing that was meant to decapitate, the wind of it whipping past my face. As he passed, another lunged from the fray, a huge spear aimed directly at my chest. I kicked free of the stirrups, throwing my weight sideways in the saddle. The spear tip ripped through my cloak, missing my flesh by a hairsbreadth. I righted myself, my sword already swinging to block the horseman's return strike.

A crossbow bolt whooshed past my ear with the sound of an angry hornet. It wasn't aimed at the one with the spear, who was already stumbling from my evasion. But the bolt took him in the throat. He toppled, gurgling.

I took a very deep, steadying breath, and my eyes found a pair of eyes. And I cursed. Those gleaming green eyes were smiling at me from across the battlefield.

Mirabelle perched lopsided on Callen's horse, a reloaded crossbow in her hands. Her smile deepened into a wicked territory, insolence in the middle of slaughter. I should have expected it. The little minx had stolen my spare harness the moment she thought I was not watching.

She was clad in her battle leathers, but the way she sat was all wrong, lopsided, favoring her injured leg. A sword whistled past my head, jerking my attention back. I parried, shouting orders to a unit of Royals to plug a gap in our line, trying to fill the void Nathan's absence had left. But my focus was irrevocably split. A part of me was now tethered to her movement across the field.

And that tether burned with outrage at myself. Because it was my fault. My fault she had chosen to ride with an untested boy instead of coming with me. I would never have allowed it, with her leg still weak. Yet she had truly wished for it, and I had failed her by letting her believe she could not come to me. Stars, if she had asked, I would have found a way.

And the fear for her was a distraction, making my commands

too sharp, my movements frantic. Metal clashed at my side, another Royal stumbling, and I drove my blade through an enemy's ribs in a forced thrust.

I cut down another advancing soldier, my eyes snapping back to her. I saw her claw her fingers in the air for balance as the horse jolted, and a visceral need to wrench her back and crush her against me nearly overwhelmed my sense of the battle.

I cursed under my breath and fought my way toward them, a scythe cutting through anyone who stood in my path.

She was not ineffective—I had to admit that. They weren't engaging in prolonged fights. They would ride close, drawing an enemy's attention, creating an opening for Callen to land a killing blow. She used her small size and precision with the bow to brilliant effect. But they were taking insane risks. Callen was fighting half the time to position the horse to protect her, and she was already sliding to the other side of the saddle, lining up another shot.

Then I saw it happen in slow motion. She leaned out for a shot, overcompensating for her weak leg. The horse shifted beneath her. She lost her balance, swinging dangerously sideways, only her white-knuckled grip on the saddle horn keeping her from falling under the hooves. Callen, engaged with a swordsman, couldn't help.

I reached them in three heartbeats. I rode straight at Callen's opponent and took the man down with a hard thrust. But not before the soldier's blade had found its mark; a deep gash on Callen's shoulder was already bleeding through his leathers. Without breaking momentum, I wheeled my horse and leaned over to hook my arm around Mirabelle's waist, then hauled her from his saddle onto my own, dropping her in front of me. The air left her lungs in a soft *oof* as she landed against my chest.

Callen's wide eyes flicked to me, but the glare I leveled at him froze him where he sat. "Fall back to the secondary line, and fight with Rowane. *Now.*"

My arm, still wrapped around her waist, pulled her back flush against me, adjusting her seating until her spine was aligned with mine. I could feel the frantic beat of her heart, the quick, shallow breaths she took.

"Hold the reins!" I called in her ear and shoved the leather straps into her hands. "And feel the movements!"

She fumbled for a second before her fingers closed. I immediately shifted my focus, parrying a blow from the left with my sword, my body curving around hers to form a shield. My hand covered hers for an instant, forcing her grip steady.

"Weight in your left stirrup!" I commanded, my free hand splaying across her abdomen to press her down into the correct position. "Your right leg is for balance. Don't grip with your knees. You'll unbalance him. Just feel his stride. Match it!"

I fought one-handed, steel continuously flashing in my right while my left closed around her waist, anchoring her. I shifted her hips with a firm press of my thigh, correcting her posture, dragging her into the horse's movement.

"Breathe," I ground out, defending one blow and cleaving through another aimed at her. The shock of it rattled my arm. "Stop fighting him, precious. Let him carry us."

I corrected her again and again—a squeeze to her shoulder, a tap to her hip—even as I deflected strikes. Her body was tense, but she listened.

And then I felt it. The moment her breath evened out. The moment the rigid line of her spine softened into our horse's rhythm. He was understanding her as well, stride evening out as she ceased to resist. She stopped fighting the animal and started becoming part of it.

A fierce satisfaction surged through me, even as I met another blade with a shower of sparks.

"Good girl," I rumbled in her ear. "Now stay with me." And I let her ride us toward the center.

CHAPTER 46
MIRABELLE

This was nothing like the Tether with the Tameables. That was a meeting of minds and a silent understanding. This was a conversation of the body. The shift of muscle, the flick of an ear, the way the great beast responded to the slightest pressure of my knees or the gentle guidance of the reins in my hands. It was a beautiful language, and I was clumsily learning to speak it.

A proud joy swept through me, cutting through the battle-fear. I was doing this.

And at my back, my personal wall of solid heat. Our *Sovereign*. *My* Sovereign.

He'd given me the reins, literally and figuratively. His trust was a shield stronger than any armor. His instructions were short, growled near my ear only when death was the other option. "Left. Now." "He's coming too high." "Shift to your left." It was all I needed. With him behind me, I felt invincible.

We plunged deeper into the heart of the battleground. Around us, the battle was a chaotic symphony of violence, but within it, I began to see the order we had forged. Atlassian was dominating. Mavren's troops held the left, a bristling wall of shields and spears that advanced with grim determination.

On the right, Rowane's soldiers moved like a school of deadly fish, flowing around stronger opponents, isolating and overwhelming them. They all moved with a shared purpose, their eyes flicking to Damien for signals, Elders barking orders that seamlessly integrated into the whole.

Screams of soldiers and horses. The clash of steel was a constant, deafening roar. Ahead, the Kaldorix Sovereign was a whirlwind of death, but his circle was shrinking, our soldiers pressing in like wolves.

"Slow circles, precious. Don't stop moving." Then Damien was gone, sliding from the saddle with a warrior's grace, his sword already singing as he rushed towards their Sovereign. Two Elders broke from their units, positioning their horses on either side of me.

I guided my horse as he'd taught me, a wide, careful arc that kept us moving, a harder target.

I'd convinced Callen and Mavren to let me take the spot of a last-moment injured Royal. My mind flew back to Callen's haunted face when he told me how Ophira had orchestrated Damien's fall. But Elion, her son, had been another poison. He'd carefully fed lies, selling twisted stories of Lorenza and Damien across the Royal circles, all while pretending to be a confidant. He had broken Callen's trust just as thoroughly as Ophira had broken our ranks.

And they had nearly succeeded. While I was fighting for survival, Damien had been bleeding out on this field, desperately trying to redeem his vow to the Zarkonians to protect me, believing in that moment that I was the one dying. The thought was still an ache, a hollowing out of my chest so deep. I blinked back the moisture every time I thought about it.

Their voices cut through the cacophony and my spiraling thoughts.

"I didn't know you were born with such ridiculous luck, Azarios," the Kaldorix Sovereign snarled, deflecting a blow from Damien. He was trying to bait him, to enrage him into mistakes.

Damien didn't acknowledge the taunt. His reply was a short,

brutal thrust that forced the Sovereign back a step. "Your babbling will be the footnote in your history."

A feint, a blindingly fast block that sent sparks flying, and then Damien's blade slipped past the Sovereign's guard like a silver serpent, punching deep into his chest with a hard crunch.

The Sovereign staggered, his eyes wide with shock and denial. He looked down at the sword protruding from his ribcage as if it were a bizarre anomaly.

"Nothing much to say?" Damien said, his voice flat and cold, devoid of triumph.

The Sovereign fell to his knees, then slumped to the side, his lifeblood pouring out to stain the churned mud.

It was over. The Kaldorix soldiers nearby faltered, their will breaking with their Sovereign's fall.

The man was dead or dying. That wasn't in question.

I raised my crossbow. Aimed carefully. Two inches from Damien's sword. My mark next to his. I released.

The bolt struck clean.

Damien turned. Found my eyes across the field without searching. I held his gaze and didn't apologize for it. I didn't care if the man was almost dead. I wanted my mark on him. I wanted there to be no version of this ending where I hadn't been part of it. He had tried to backstab Damien. He had tried to kill Nathan. I had to do it for Whip-tail, for Elsha, for Tovelle, for Draven, for all the life we had lost.

A slow, dark smile touched Damien's lips in a silent acknowledgment of my petty vengeance.

The Kaldorix line broke.

And Atlassian held.

⟡

THE SCENT of roasting herbs and simmering broth filled the kitchen, a comforting blanket after the cold scent of blood and steel that had clung to me for days. I watched Amara, a flour-dusted whirlwind, commandeering pots and pans with theatrical flair, knowing full well I was her only audience.

"So now your passion is for cooking?" I'd asked, leaning against the doorway.

"A passion for meddling with Thralls, Bella," she'd said, grinning as she brandished a ladle. "And it turns out, I am marvelously good at it," she said. "Cooking is a close second. Watch and learn."

I reached for the pot to sneak a taste of the rich broth she was stirring, but her hand snapped out like a cat's and smacked mine away with a *thwack* from a wooden spoon.

"Hey!"

"No, hey," she scolded, her eyes sparkling with mock severity. "That's for the Sovereign's table! Your fumbling finger in the middle is going to ruin its delicate balance of flavors. I'm an artiste!"

I laughed, rubbing my hand. "It was just a taste!"

She wiped her hands on her apron, then gave the pot a final stir. She shoved a warm, buttery roll into my hand as a consolation prize. "Here. We can go out. The bread needs to rest anyway, and so do you from bothering my art."

My leg was mostly healed, and I could walk slowly, though a persistent sting reminded me I wouldn't be running any races for another week. As we stepped into the lit courtyard, Amara nudged me.

"So. You're the new tittle-tattle of all Atlassian, you know."

"What?"

"The Sovereign sent out a proclamation to the whole Clan. Announced you are the *Celestial Light of the Entire Realm* and that anyone who looks at you sideways will have their eyes plucked out by himself."

"What! Really?"

She burst out laughing. "Of course not, you goose! But something similar, I'm sure. Knowing Damien's dynamics about you, it's not past him. Probably declared you the official Tamer-Sovereign-consort-heart-of-his-life or some other mouthful."

I punched her arm, laughing.

"Ouch, Bella!" she yelped. "Not so hard on the injured chef!"

My thoughts drifted. Damien had left for Ledgerdeep with Arthur to finalize the Dissonance tally. Lorenza was there too, presented as a prisoner of our Clan. I'd talked him out of executing her, much to his frustration. I'd even had to use *please*, which had made him scowl magnificently. Letting her father—*my* father, the thought was still strange and prickly—take responsibility for her seemed right to me. I had a soft spot for her, the flicker of a sisterhood I'd never had.

Telmoria had won. Our three Clans had prevailed. But the two new Clans elevated by the Dominion were unknowns. I just hoped they weren't as viperous as Kaldorix.

"I'm leaving for Zarkon with Izmer," Amara announced, slicing through my thoughts.

I blinked. "Oh? You've already settled everything?"

A blush crept up her neck. "No, not exactly. I will have to convince him. I don't know, give a kiss or two?" Her eyes got a dreamy, faraway look. "Oh, but it's...nice, Bella. I didn't know it was this nice." She punched my arm again, softer this time. "Why did you keep it from me?"

"Keep what? The state of your love life is hardly my secret to tell!"

"Not my love life! The kissing! The...feeling. It's very... delicious."

I chuckled. "*Delicious* might not be the word I'd use—"

"The former Sovereign is asking for you, my Grace."

I turned to see a guard had approached, clearing his throat.

I looked around, half-expecting to see someone else. *My Grace?*

Amara snorted. "Told you. Tittle-tattle of Atlassian." She wiggled her eyebrows. "Better get used to it, my Grace."

I ignored her, turning to the guard. "Where is he? I will meet him when Damien returns."

The guard, an older man with a weary but kind face, shifted uncomfortably. "I agree, my Grace. But he...he is in the dungeons.

Awaiting his sentence. And I have been guarding him since I was a boy. I...I tried my part to give him some measure of closure I thought he deserved." He paused for a few moments. "I respect your wish." He inclined his head and began to turn away.

Damien's father. The architect of so much pain was now broken and imprisoned.

Amara groaned loudly. "Oh, for stars' sake." She clapped her hands, stopping the guard. "Sorry for my manners, don't know your name, but she wants to meet him."

I turned to her. "I didn't—"

"Stop, Bella," she cut me off, her voice dropping to a pragmatic whisper. "This is the safe way. Otherwise, you'll end up sneaking down there by yourself tonight and getting trapped in some tragic, dusty conversation. I," she declared, placing a hand on her hip, "need to experience all the other...ehm...delicious things in life. And we don't want you spoiling it for me by getting yourself into trouble, do we?"

I shook my head, a reluctant smile tugging at my lips. She was impossible. And right.

"Fine," I said, turning back to the guard. "Lead the way."

Amara gave me a wave of her hand, already walking back toward her kitchen.

CHAPTER 47

MIRABELLE

The dungeons were not what I expected. They were cold, yes, and the air was heavy with the scent of stones, but they weren't the filthy, rat-infested pits of stories. A prison for high-ranking traitors or maybe pre-trial traitors. Light came in narrow bars from a slit high in the wall, slicing the dark floor into ribs of shadow.

The cells were spaced far apart, their doors solid grills of enchanted iron, and the torches burned with a clean, blue flame that cast long, stark shadows. I passed a few cells holding familiar Elders and a few guards, their faces pale and resigned in the eerie light. They didn't meet my eyes.

NyxRathis followed me as a shimmer of invisible heat at my back. I had been taught my lesson in hard ways. And if I was going to experience all of my life's...delicacies...as Amara put it, that included trying not to be stupid.

Alaric's cell was at the very end, larger than the others, more like a spartan chamber than a cage. He sat on a narrow cot, leaning against the stone wall, his posture still holding a shred of that pride, but the fire in his eyes was gone, replaced by a hollow exhaustion.

He looked up as I approached. His gaze slid over me, then past my shoulder to where NyxRathis's molten eyes gleamed into visibility for a heartbeat before vanishing again. He looked back at me, and an odd, almost wistful expression crossed his face. We were alone, the silence broken only by the drip of water somewhere and the low hum of the wards.

He did not greet me. His gaze drifted past, as if fixed on some other Realm only he could see, and then he began to speak.

"There was a young, vibrant Heiress," he said, his eyes locked on a point buried deep in the past. "A bright thing. You would have liked her—smiling all the time, hands never empty of someone's hurt to fix. And she was...achingly beautiful." A faint, pained smile touched his lips.

"But her Clan was thin and tired. They needed a healer more than a shield, so she gave them what they asked. Do you know what happens when we choose someone to be a healer?" He finally looked at me, his gaze sharpening. "We make them surrender their Aether. We strip them of their power, their potential for anything else. They become just that...a healer. Whether they were born a Sovereign or a Major, it makes no difference. Because no one can do both and survive it."

A faint sense of unease began to stir within me. I had an awful feeling where this was going.

"This young woman was so selfless," he continued, his voice gaining a bitter edge. "She did not surrender her Aether, and didn't let her Clan fight without her Aether, because she was the only child. And during a Dissonance...she went into the field and lost everyone. All of them. Everyone but her. Because the ruthless Sovereign of the opposing Clan found her too gorgeous to kill."

He let out a short, harsh breath. "He caged her, wanted to keep her as a toy. Until his interest grew into something deeper and uglier. Until she made him fall for her in the matter of a few nights. And he fell hard. As hard as a man like him was capable of falling, anyway." He huffed out a sardonic laugh.

I did not know what to say, and his story was digging into places I hadn't expected. It made me uneasy and nervous.

"She *loved* him," Alaric continued, and the word hurt him like a hand on bare skin. "She forgave him. She cherished him. Gave his wretched world meaning... She became his life, and his reason to breathe. Until she Bonded with him and was carrying his child."

His voice cracked. "The more the child grew in her, the less she was herself. The child was killing her. And he...the Sovereign... begged her to let the child go, to save herself. But this selfless fool, this love of his life, didn't care. She loved her child fiercely. She was determined to give it life, even if it cost her own."

My throat felt as if someone had tied a string around it and was pulling low.

"The night she gave birth to his child was the night he lost his love." Alaric's voice was a raw whisper now. "She didn't die, then. She fed her child, half-conscious, and then she collapsed into a stupor from which she never woke. The Sovereign lost her for good. She never opened her eyes again. And he had to press his ear to her chest every day, just to feel the faint beat of her heart, to know she was still...alive."

My throat was so tight I could barely breathe. He looked directly at me, filled with a bottomless pain. "And whenever he looked into the blue eyes of his son, all he could feel was the way the boy had stolen the life from the same blue eyes he lived for."

I shook my head, my vision still blurred. I wanted to scream— *how could any of this be the fault of an innocent child?* But I knew there was no reasoning with a man who had lived for one soul alone, who had carried this grief for decades. I knew I could not.

"He put the child away," Alaric said, his fingers worrying the hem of the blanket. "He could not father what he would not bear to understand. He didn't have the selflessness in him to be its father. So he gave the child to keepers who would tend and train and shape. He needed greatness more than he needed love. He thought it safer for the child, safer for him."

My soul wept for the child who had been left without love, without softness, without even the chance to feel. He had been expected to rule before he had even been allowed to be a boy.

Expected to endure the politics, the ambition, the endless deceit of a Clan of wolves, each hungering for power, circling him with sharpened smiles, conspiring in the shadows while feigning loyalty in the light.

All the tears brimming in my eyes, all the pain splintering through my chest, were for the love of my life—who had turned his heart to stone, not because he wished it, but because he would not have survived otherwise.

"Why tell me this?" I asked finally, my voice a strained thread. "Do you think dumping this on me makes your betrayal any better? This makes everything worse!"

Alaric's face was quieter than I expected. "To think a Sovereign who's sat on a throne through decades of treachery could be that naive is generous, girl," he said.

I glared back.

"I need something else. I need your help." He made it sound reasonable.

"Then that decades-ruled Sovereign should know I hold no sway for a heartless monster who broke my other half."

He completely ignored my venom. "I chose you because you are my son's only weakness. And he will only reason with you." He leaned forward, the chains on his wrists clinking softly. "My son might have inherited his mother's eyes, Aether...but he sure as damn inherited my heart."

"Don't you dare—" I started.

He continued as if I hadn't spoken. "He took *Alaric* out of his name—Damien Alaric Azarios, thinking cutting my name from his will make his heart less of mine." A hollow, knowing smile touched his lips. "But he hasn't yet found the hex he would give it up for. Until you."

"He loves me. Fiercely. But he would never, ever be like you." My own voice sounded uncertain to my ears.

He shook his head, a gesture of disappointment. "He spent decades carefully building his reasonable, rational life, and he would simply throw it all into a corner if someone so much as looked at you wrong. You are that single rose in his graveyard, child. And he would burn the whole garden to the ground to keep one petal from wilting. So, no, he is no better than me. And one day, he will understand why I had to sacrifice my Clan to take a chance."

I stared at him, completely lost. "To take a chance for what?"

"To get me more time with my Eternis."

The air left my lungs. "So she is...still?"

"She is the same. She never woke." The confession was ripped from him. "I—I hunted for solutions. I begged the Dominion. I traveled the whole Realm seeking a cure...and I failed. So, when the Empress of Nyxaria offered a potion that brought her back for weeks at a time, I took it. I took it because I could not bear to hear nothing but the memory of her breath. It made her open her eyes for a few nights...before she slipped back into the slumber. And I was addicted. Addicted to seeing her look at me, to hold her awake again. I would have done *anything* to see her look at me just once more, to feel her love, even if it was only for a few days, once a year."

"What kind of potion—why can't we make it?" I whispered.

"I don't know how it's made. The Empress never disclosed it to me. But I know it's something no one would approve of. Because once she mentioned she had to sacrifice something...or someone... every time she brewed it. And she couldn't make it more often without raising suspicion."

A wave of nausea washed over me as the truth crystallized. They were killing others to make this potion? How could that ever be right?

"I know what you're thinking, but those were not really innocent souls," he said quietly. "And I did not know for certain. I suspected, but even if I had known, I would not have said no." His gaze fell to his hands before lifting it again, steady on mine. "And all the Empress ever asked in return was my cooperation. To allow her niece, Ophira, to remain here—a voice in my court, a thread tying my decisions to the Empress's influence. It was not a difficult decision for me to make. And lately, to see my son Bonded to her lovesick daughter."

This man helped them erase me. The Abyss. All of it, a price for a fortnight of a dying woman's consciousness. "So you allowed them to sacrifice your own Clan?" My voice rose, trembling with revulsion. "To unleash the Untameables? To break the damn sigil?"

"I was not aware of any of those specifics!" he snapped, a flicker of his old fire returning. "Haldric and Ophira were behind that, scheming to seize Etheris. They acted without my full knowledge, but I had to cover for them. Because I was in too deep. And I couldn't lose my source. I couldn't lose her. I had to act reasonable, normal."

"You could have used that cursed crown's wish! To restore her health!"

His smile was bitter and sardonic. "I wish it were that simple. The wish never meddles with life or death. What do you think, child? If it were possible, the Nyxarian Empress would have wished you dead with it long before I ever got the chance to fail my son."

I pressed my palms flat to the bars until my knuckles whitened. My mind reeled, struggling to grasp the depth and tangle of the mess Atlassian had fallen into, all of it heaped upon Damien's shoulders and conscience, along with every brutal decision he was forced to make.

Alaric's shoulders sagged. "I announced you as Tamer so the Empress wouldn't kill you," he said, his voice devoid of all emotion. "It would have been easy for her to do. With Damien's devotion withdrawn in the days after the Abyss, you were exposed. I prevented your death."

"Why?" The word was a breath.

"I have never been his father, and I never pretended to be," he said, jaw tight. "Still, his blood is mine. If he were to remember—if he were to realize he'd lost you—he would consume this entire Clan in vengeance, with me in the center of the pyre. So I let it appear the council pressed me to make you our Tamer, to keep the Empress from reaching for you. She did not reckon Damien would fall for you again, not when I was to forge a Bonding with her daughter to appease her."

He paused and exhaled, then looked back into my eyes. "Even I had hoped he would not, that both of you might pass unnoticed through the mesh of politics. Seeing him choose you anyway angered me. It felt like watching him remake my worst mistakes. Yet I could not deny what he had become. He is, by whatever fate or fault, destined for you. And I had to accept that."

I pressed my forehead to the cold iron and let out a breath that was more a sob than air. NyxRathis nudged my calf, trying to calm me in her own way.

Alaric was insane. The sheer twisted scale of his warped love and his chillingly accurate read of his own son left me dumbfounded and dizzy. How could I tell all this to Damien without shattering him?

"My healers are still taking care of Zeryn." His voice broke on the name. "I want you to ask my son...to ensure it continues. Until...until she..." He stopped, unable to finish the sentence, the words dying in the space between his failure and his hope.

He looked down again at his manacled hands. "I deserve to die. But I never knew about the betrayal, or about the backstabbing. I wouldn't have let it happen. All of it spiraled out of my control after the Abyss. They held a lot of their secret meetings without me. I had no way to tell Damien without condemning myself and losing any chance to be with Zeryn." A humorless laugh escaped him. "Now, I've ended up here anyway. Wasn't such a bright thinker, I suppose. Age makes you desperate, not clever."

Curiosity broke through my heartbreak. "Where is she?"

"I have a chamber inside my own wing. My guard has the key, and my healers. She...won't be conscious." The sorrow in his eyes was gut-wrenching.

"You don't hate me?" I asked, the question feeling strange. "For killing the Nyxarian Empress? For taking away your only way to..."

"The Empress was done with me," he cut in, his voice flat. "She withheld the last potion. She knew the leverage was gone, that she had already squeezed out all I had to offer, and more." He looked away, into the shadows of his cell. "It was already over."

I didn't have it in me to address the horrifying *what-ifs* his story implied. I knew the answers, and I couldn't bear to hear him saying them out loud.

"I am not sure how to tell Damien any of this," I said, my voice trembling. "But I will. And we will take care of her." I met his gaze, forcing strength into my words. "But you had no right to keep her from him. He had the right to know his mother wasn't dead."

"I would have told him," he insisted, a flicker of defensiveness in his hollow eyes. "If the potion had not been the only fix, or if it hadn't been born from such...darkness. I couldn't risk revealing this to a just man and expect him to understand the choices of a desperate one."

I exhaled hard, ignoring the headache blooming behind my eyes. How had I ended up here, the bearer of this terrible, tangled tale?

I turned to leave. "Mirabelle."

His voice stopped me, softer now, stripped of its former pride. He sounded...nervous. I turned back. "What?"

He swallowed. His Adam's apple bobbed. "Ask him...ask Damien to grant me one last time with her. Just once. To feed her. To bath her. To tell her...to tell her not to be scared if she doesn't feel me near, that I have to go away for a while..." His voice broke completely, his eyes glazing with unshed tears. "I know you can convince him."

I looked at this broken man, begging for a final moment with the ghost of his love. I didn't trust myself to speak. I simply nodded and turned, walking away from the dungeon as quickly as my unsteady legs could carry me, wiping furiously at the tears that refused to stop.

CHAPTER 48
MIRABELLE

For a day and a night while I waited for Damien to come back from Ledgerdeep, I'd been spiraling. The weight of Alaric's confession felt like a leaden cloak on my shoulders. I had visited his mother's chamber, a silent, warm-lit room that felt more like a shrine. Zeryn. She was beautiful, even in her endless slumber, her dark hair fanned across the pillow, her face strangely unlined, untouched by the years of grief her existence had caused. I'd sat with her for a long time, the silence a heavy contrast to the storm in my head. I spent my evening there, helping healers to feed her, to gently massage her hands, just to watch her sleep.

Afterward, I found my sanctuary in Amara's kitchen, hiding among the spice jars. She took one look at me and immediately launched into the story of her recent encounter with the non-affair, the Thrall she'd known in Etheris before Abyss, completely forgotten, then literally tripped over in the market. "I was dying of embarrassment," she said, vigorously grinding peppercorns. "Turns out, I needn't have bothered. The oaf saw me, blinked, and then proceeded to passionately kiss a woman three feet away. He didn't even *recognize* me. Can you imagine, like, not recognizing *me*! So. There's that ego bruise." And we broke into fits of laughter.

Now I was walking back to our chambers. My fingers still smelled faintly of flour from the kitchen; my braid had come loose and tickled my neck.

I never heard the footsteps. One moment I was alone in the dim corridor, the next I was spun around and slammed against the cold stone wall, the breath knocked from my lungs. A hard, familiar body pinned me there, and his mouth crashed down on mine.

A startled giggle escaped me in surprise, but it was quickly swallowed by his ferocity, morphing into a muffled moan as Damien's tongue plunged into my mouth, tasting of wind and cold night air and a desperate hunger. His hands were everywhere, tangling in my hair, yanking my head back to deepen the kiss, sliding down to grip my hips, grinding his hardness against me through the layers of our clothes.

"*Bloody stars*, I missed you," he growled against my lips, the words a rough vibration against my mouth before he was kissing me again, biting my lower lip, sucking it into his mouth until I cried out.

He didn't wait for a reply. He scooped me up into his arms, his mouth still sealed to mine, swallowing my gasps as he carried me to our chamber. He shouldered open the door, kicked it shut with a slam that echoed through the corridor, and then I was falling, landing on the soft furs of our bed with him looming over me, his eyes blazing with a feral blue fire.

"Do you have any clue," he rasped, his voice dangerously low as he ripped his tunic over his head, "what you do to me? Being in that sterile, political pit, tallying numbers and negotiating terms..." His hands went to the laces of my dress, yanking them open with a sharp, efficient tug. "All I could think about was this. Was you. Under me. Screaming my name."

He stripped me, his movements rough and impatient, his gaze devouring every inch of skin he exposed. "Tell me you thought about me," he demanded, his mouth finding the pulse hammering at the base of my throat, his teeth scraping against the sensitive skin.

His mouth closed over my breast, his tongue circling the peak before he drew it deep, the pull echoing straight to my core. I cried out, my fingers fisting in his hair. His hand moved lower, trailing down my stomach. He hummed an approving sound when he found me wet. His thumb began a slow, torturous orbit around my swollen bud, the pressure just short of enough.

"I asked you a question, Bella." His thumb lightened to a feather-touch, a maddening hover, as he nipped and nibbled at the puckered peak of my breast.

"Maybe," I gasped, trying to grind against him, arching into the empty air for more. My thoughts, my fears, the terrible secret —it all burned away in the inferno of his touch.

"Hmm. Not good enough to earn this, then?" He stopped applying pressure entirely, his hand a taunting, still presence while he sucked and nibbled, sending sharp, sweet shocks through me.

"Stars, I dreamt of you like this... Now, please," I begged, and he rewarded me with a single, firm circle of his thumb. I gasped, my hands clutching at his shoulders. "It was all I could feel when I slept. Like I was hollow until..."

"Until what?" He leaned in, his teeth closing on my earlobe in a sweet warning.

"Until now," I moaned, one of my hands sliding down to try and pull his back to where I needed it. He caught my wrist easily, pinning it to the bed beside my head, and chuckled. "That's not how it works, wildcat."

I whimpered in a sound of pure frustration. "Until I felt you against me. Your skin, your weight, your...everything. I needed it."

He growled in savage satisfaction. One of his hands slid down to my hip, then lower, clamping possessively. "Show me how." His hand slid further between my legs, his fingers finding me soaking. He pushed one inside, then two, without letting me adjust to the first, his eyes locked on mine, watching me writhe.

"Yes... Yes, like this," I choked out, my hips bucking against his hand. "Needing you. Just like this."

A dark, satisfied sound rumbled in his chest. "Good."

The furs against my back were indifferent to the heat between us; all that mattered was his weight, his urgency, the way his hands read my body like a map he'd been studying for decades. I wriggled, trying to pull him closer, to feel more of him.

"You're all I've ever needed." His eyes shone with devotion, a stark contrast to the way his hand kneaded my bare breast with roughness.

He leaned in and bit the soft underside of my other breast, earning a yelp from me that melted into a helpless moan as he soothed the sting with his tongue. Then his mouth closed again around my hardened peak, all while keeping his finger moving in an out of me with a wild flow.

He withdrew his fingers, and in the same moment, he drove into me, a single, brutal thrust that filled me completely, stealing all the air from my lungs. I hadn't even registered when he'd freed himself. I choked, and cried out, my nails digging into the hard muscles of his back.

He didn't give me a moment to adjust. He set a violent rhythm from the start, each thrust a primal punctuation to the words he kept growling into my ear.

"You are so deliciously mine." *Thrust.* "Every sigh." *Thrust.* "Every moan." *Thrust.* "This perfect, tight heat." He drove deeper, making me sob. "All. Mine."

"Yes!" I gasped, my legs wrapping around his waist, pulling him closer, deeper, wanting to erase every inch of space between us.

"Say it. Bella."

"Yes, yours, Damien! Stars, all yours!"

He hummed in satisfaction and rewarded me with something harsher. He shifted, hooking my legs over his shoulders, changing the angle, hitting a spot inside me that made my vision whiten. I was seeing stars behind my eyelids.

"Eyes on me, Bella." His voice was a sharp command that brooked no argument.

"Bastard," I gasped, my gaze snapping to his, helpless to disobey. The curse turned into a choked half-laugh as he squeezed my other breast in retaliation, his hips never ceasing their relentless rhythm. The storming sensation made my eyes roll back, pleasure striking that deep place within me, making it a constant battle to keep my focus locked on his burning, owning gaze. He moved with the kind of pace that erased reasoning.

Fingers tangled in his hair. I tugged closer, forcing more of him against me, letting every sound that rose from me be a confession. And I let him murmur filthy, breathless things in my ear. There were kisses stolen like promises and bites that left angry marks.

"Come for me, love, let that sweet heat of yours squeeze me like a velvet fist." His voice was ragged with his own impending release.

Waves of pleasure shattered through me, waves of pure, blinding ecstasy that made me cry out his name as my body convulsed around his.

He followed me with a guttural curse, his own release pulsing into me as his body shuddered and collapsed over mine. His forehead, damp with sweat, pressed against my shoulder as he fought for air, his hard breaths warming my skin between the soft, almost reverent kisses he peppered across my shoulder.

We lay there for long moments, panting, slick with sweat, the air thick with the scent of us. He shifted, turning us so I lay sprawled atop him, my breath slowly steadying against his neck. The aggression had burned itself out, leaving behind a spent, trembling intimacy.

And as I lay there, I knew with a certainty that if I could, I would carry all his pain with me. I would bear every scar, every shadow, so his only concern, his only weight, would be the love he carried for me.

⋙⋘

I woke to muted light seeping through the thick velvet drapes, casting the chamber in a soft, gray haze.

Peace. It was a fragile, precious thing. But now I was relishing in it. The silence felt less like an absence and more like a presence, it was the stillness in my hand after the arrow has flown, the hum of the bowstring that had just released its purpose. But this was even more gratifying.

One of my legs was thrown over Damien's hips, the heavy quilt a tangled pool around our waists. Both of us were naked, skin still warm and smelling of each other. It had been so long since we'd had this, a quiet morning without the specter of battles or duty looming. The hours had dissolved into a rhythm of heat and respite.

That fevered cycle of need and fulfillment had kept us awake for most of the night. A hazy memory surfaced from the depths of the night—waking to the feel of his tongue pushing into me, coaxing me from sleep with insistent strokes until I was panting for more. He loved me slowly, easing into me before I'd even fully opened my eyes, moving with a rhythm that lulled me back into an abyss of pleasure and, finally, a sated, dreamless sleep.

Feeling every bit the improper lady he was making me, I casually lifted the edge of the quilt and peeked underneath.

Oh.

He was definitely...firm. *Very* firm.

I snapped the quilt down, a sly smile touching my lips at my own scandalous curiosity.

"Taking inventory, precious?" a sleep-roughened voice murmured above me.

I gasped and looked up to find Damien watching me, his head propped on his hand, a wicked smile playing on his lips. I blushed furiously, a helpless laugh bubbling out of me as I covered my face with my hands.

"I was...checking you were still...intact!" I mumbled into my palms, smiling.

He chuckled. "Intact, fully functional, and at your service." He gently pried my hands from my face, his fingers lacing with mine. "Though your reconnaissance skills need work. You're meant to be stealthier."

"I was stealthy!"

"You rustled the quilt like a startled bird. I've heard Dreadclaw move with more subtlety." He leaned in and kissed me, still smiling against my lips.

When he pulled back, I was breathless for a completely different reason. "How long have you been awake?" I asked.

"Long enough," he said, his thumb stroking the back of my hand. "Long enough to count those very tiny, perfect moles that form a little triangle on the inside of your right thigh." His blue eyes glinted with affection. "And to wonder what the story is behind the faint scar just below your left shoulder blade."

I fell back against the pillows with a soft smile, looking up at the carved stone ceiling. He trailed the back of his knuckles down the valley between my breasts, a feather-light touch that made my skin tingle.

"The scar is from falling out of a fruit tree when I was seven," I said.

He hummed and bent his head to press a soft kiss to the faint mark. For a few moments, he was silent, his lips resting against my skin. When he turned onto his side to look at me again, his expression had sobered, the playful glint replaced by an unsettling gravity.

"My mother is alive," he said, his voice quiet but clear in the hushed room.

"Wha— How do you know?" My voice must have sounded small. I had seen too many halting truths already this fortnight.

His brows furrowed. "You knew?"

The air crackled. "I just... I visited your father yesterday—" I began, my words tumbling out too fast. And stopped midway, seeing his expression began to darken, a storm of fury gathering in his eyes. I placed my hands on his chest, pressing down firmly.

"Hey. NyxRathis was with me. I was safe. I—breathe." I exhaled. "Damn it, Damien."

He took a controlled breath, the muscle in his jaw feathering. "I had to interrogate them all, one by one, to get the truth before their sentences are carried out. To wring every last secret out."

"Did you see her?" I asked softly.

"No," he said after a beat of heavy silence. He searched my face. "Did you?"

I held his gaze, my heart aching for him. "Yes." My hand tightened on his arm without meaning to. "She's...stable. Healers watch her all the time."

He was silent for a long moment.

"How do you feel?" I asked, taking in his passive expression.

He looked away for a fraction of a breath, then back, eyes steady but hollow. "Nothing." The word landed flat. Then, after a beat of heavy silence, he added, "Nothing, because I don't allow myself to think about it."

I took his jaw in my hand, forcing him to look at me. "Why haven't you visited her?"

He looked into my eyes, his own still terrifyingly devoid of emotion. "I am afraid." The admission ripped through me. "Afraid that if I go, I'll feel everything I've kept padded and stacked for three decades."

He was so vulnerable in this moment, and I knew how excruciatingly hard it was for this man, who was always strength and certainty, to admit it. I just moved into him, wrapping my arms around his neck and pulling him close. He buried his face in the crook of my neck, inhaling deeply.

"But you will...?" I asked quietly.

"I will, precious," he murmured against my skin.

"Whatever you feel, you won't feel it alone," I whispered against his ear, holding him tighter. "You will never feel anything alone again."

His arms locked around me in response, like I was the only

solid thing in a world unmoored. We lay in silence for a few moments, the weight of the unspoken future pressing down on us.

Then, with a sudden, decisive movement, he swept me into his arms and stood, as if physically carrying us both away from the precipice of that conversation.

"Where are you taking me?" I asked, breathless from the sudden lift.

"To wash the war off you and the world out of you," he stated, carrying me towards the bathing chamber.

I let out a watery laugh, clinging to his neck. "You're melodic but also incredibly melodramatic."

"Becoming a bit of a brat, aren't you?" he countered, and nipped my earlobe, sending a shiver down my spine.

Steam hit us as we entered the vast chamber—a warm, cedar-scented fog that softened the edges of the soaring onyx walls and grand, gilded fixtures. He set me down on a wooden stool and began the meticulous task of untangling the nest my hair had become after the night. His fingers were so gentle. I melted into his touch. The sound of water filling the bath echoed softly in the background.

It was in the middle of this quiet that he spoke in a tone as casual as if he were commenting on the quality of the bristles in the hairbrush. "Ah, I forgot to mention. Our formal Bonding ritual is in three days. Make sure you have everything you need."

I stiffened. "You forgot to mention what?!"

He finished with a knot and guided me into the sunken marble pool, with a stoic face. "Is there a problem?"

"Three days? Damien! That's no time at all!"

"I gave you three," he countered, sliding into the water opposite me. His tone still sounded infuriatingly reasonable. "And you have the entire royal treasury and every artisan in Atlassian at your disposal to make it perfect. I made sure of it."

I stared at him, flabbergasted by his logic. "And what if I say no? Let me guess, you'll drag me there screaming and kicking?"

A faint, almost imperceptible smile touched his lips. "I would prefer you conscious and willing, but I am adaptable."

With a growl of frustration that was half real, half a release of the morning's tension, I lunged forward through the water and bit his pectoral muscle, hard enough to leave a mark.

He grunted, more in surprise than pain, and his arms instantly came around me, pulling me flush against him in the warm, swirling water.

"She's feral," he murmured into my wet hair, "Aye, wildcat?"

CHAPTER 49
DAMIEN

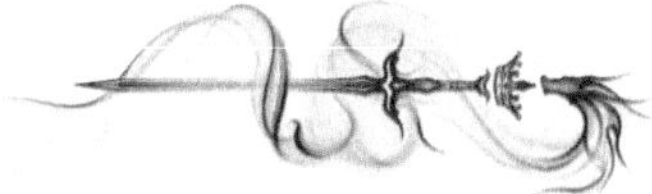

The door shut behind me with a finality that echoed in the hollow of my chest. I leaned against it, the solid oak a poor bulwark against the void within. A sharp exhalation left my lips, and I let the back of my skull meet the wood with a soft thud.

A curse was all I could muster.

It had been a miscalculation of the most profound order. I had thought, in some vestigial part of my spirit, that to look upon my mother's face would unleash a torrent. That some dam, long fortified, would break.

I had not intended the visit. Passing the open door to my father's chambers, some impulse—a ghost of a son's duty, perhaps—had drawn me within.

And then I saw her.

Zeryn. My mother. Her visage was preserved as if in amber, the dark hair I inherited fanned across the pillow, untainted by time. I beheld the woman whose absence had been the cornerstone of my existence, the spectral figure for whom a Clan was nearly sacrificed.

And I felt...nothing.

No grief.

No longing.

No filial piety.

A great, yawning emptiness where a son's heart should have resided. The silence in that chamber was not peaceful; it was accusatory. It confirmed my deepest suspicion: he had succeeded. My father, in his wretchedness, had not merely hardened me. He had carved out the core of me and left a monument of stone in its place. I was incapable of the very sentiments that defined a breathing, bleeding soul.

I pushed myself from the door and strode into the corridor, the polished marble a cold mirror to my soul. I had expected a flood. I found only a desert.

I needed proof that I was not merely a sculpture made of flesh and blood. That I was not wholly wrought of ice and duty. There was but one place to seek such absolution, one soul who held the mirror in which I might glimpse a reflection of something warmer.

My feet carried me through the palace, past archways and into the light-drenched Royal gardens.

ON MY WAY to the Royal gardens, my thoughts drifted to the new shape of the Realms, settled at Ledgerdeep. Two Clans risen and borders redrawn. A calculated risk taken: fifty Aether-wielders from defeated Kaldorix were invited into our heart. A viper's nest, perhaps. But with Bella, it was a risk that became a strategy for transformation. New dwellings on the outskirts were already built to accommodate the failed Clan, and the old districts renovated into order and dignity.

The air was thick with the cloying sweetness of jasmine and the murmur of courtiers. And there, amid a cluster of Royals, I found her. I leaned a shoulder against the cool stone of a marble pillar, one boot crossing over the other, and watched.

She was seated between Amara and Lyria. It was a tableau of attempted assimilation, and her very effort made her stand apart.

The others were at ease, their postures languid, their laughter flowing like water. Mirabelle sat with a spine of iron.

A young woman leaned forward, speaking of some inconsequential matter of ribbons and lace for the upcoming gala. All eyes turned to Mirabelle, expecting a contribution. I saw the delicate shell of her ear flush a brilliant crimson. Her fingers, resting on her knee, twisted together.

"Oh, indeed," she said, her voice a fraction too high. "Ribbons. They should be...very long. And thin. And...lengthy."

A beat of silence followed. Lyria coughed abruptly into her hand. Amara chimed in, "What she means is that their simplicity is often overlooked. A *very* good observation, Bella."

Mirabelle, sensing her misstep, pressed on with a desperate sort of courage. "And the...color. A most vigorous shade of...green. Like a...a determined Celestia. Oh and they should definitely look rich."

She was trying so hard to belong. I had even caught her attempting to befriend some of the Thralls by helping them cook, *of all things*. An effort I would need to gently dissuade her from soon. Her flustering attempts to please them were endearing and entirely unnecessary.

In time, she would learn that she only needed to stop trying so hard. And as for the few who proved too dim to see her brilliance, well—how fortunate that I've always been so devoted to improving the overall standard of our court.

I let my gaze wander.

To the soft curl of her wrist where it rested on her knee.

To the stray ribbon still tangled from where I had mangled her braid in my haste this morning.

To the hollow of her throat, where her pulse fluttered like a captive bird.

To the way her lashes cast shadows upon her cheeks, fine as cracks in porcelain.

She was the most stunning creature I had ever beheld, and the stars must have mind-veiled the day it bound her to me. I was just some brute holding a masterpiece, terrified I would smudge the paint.

The conversation shifted, and another Royal asked about the care of a rare, moon-pale blossom found in the wilds. Mirabelle's eyes lit with genuine knowledge. "It needs a specific moss, gathered from the north-facing stones near the cliffs."

"Truly?" the woman replied, intrigued. "Would you show me sometime?"

"Yes. Of course," Mirabelle said, before catching herself and downplaying it with a slight shrug. "I mean, I wouldn't mind."

Amara beamed with pride, seeing what I saw: Bella's slow emergence from her shell after years of coercion had convinced her that she'd never belong in some circles. I would have gladly gutted every last one of her tormentors, had I ever managed to get their names.

Amara threw her arms around Mirabelle for something she said and leaned in to brutally smother her cheek with kisses while laughing.

Alright, that was quite enough.

I pushed off from the pillar and walked toward them. Bella's eyes snapped to mine, instantly lighting in a way that never failed to unbind me. I smiled, a slow curve of my lips meant only for her and extended my hand.

"Mind taking a walk with me?"

She arched a brow, a delightful impertinence. "Are you commandeering me, my Liege? I was in the middle of a *very* important discussion."

Her friends giggled, and she looked inordinately proud of herself. And my smile widened despite myself, loving the way she was enjoying their company.

"I am," I replied, my hand still waiting for hers. "I find my schedule has a sudden, critical opening that only you can fill."

She looked back at Amara and the other women, a flicker of insecurity in her eyes. "I will...see you later?"

"Of course," someone said warmly, while Amara waved a dismissive, flour-dusted hand. "See you at night!"

Ah, no, she will not.

The reassurance seemed to settle her. She placed her hand in mine, her touch the irrefutable proof I needed—I was not made of stone.

I was made for her.

ETHERIS SPREAD OUT BEFORE US.

The very light had changed. The once-dominant, purple hues of the Celestia had softened into subtle, calming shades of gold for the nonce, casting the floating isles and bioluminescent forests in a vibrant, warm glow. Even the air tasted different—not just the familiar crisp and clean, but something sweeter and lighter.

It was as if the Realm itself was exhaling after a long-held breath, blending together with Veldorian Etheris.

Mirabelle gasped from beside me, her head tilted back, eyes wide, drinking in the shifted Celestia. "It's...so..." She turned in a slow circle, momentarily forgetting whatever word she'd meant to find. "It's ridiculous. It's like the Realm put on clean linen."

I smiled at the way her wonder eclipsed everything else. "The merge of Realms has expanded the space for Clans and Etheris," I explained, watching her rather than the view. "You have more Tameables to charm now."

I led her to the heart of the central isles of this part of Etheris, where the ley-lines converged in a nexus of pulsing energy. "This is the core of the joined Etheris. The control of its portals, its rhythms," I said. "Do as you please with new ones assigned for Atlassian. Name rules and make ordinances, Empress."

A mischievous glint entered her eyes. "I could declare that all official edicts must be sung in a high-pitched falsetto when entering Etheris."

"You wouldn't dare."

"Test me. I'm holding the nexus. I could make it a requirement for accessing the portals. Your move, Your Majesty."

"My move?" I asked, but she was already gone, a flash of laughter and flying hair as she darted away. I caught her in a few strides, my arm hooking around her waist and spinning her back against my chest. She let out a squeal, squirming in my hold. "And what exactly was your plan after the running part?" I murmured in her ear. My free hand found the laces at the back of her dress, my fingers loosening the top ties.

She breathed against my neck, her smile warm and reckless. My voice dropped to a husky murmur. "Because my plan involves something much, much more interesting than falsetto—"

A sudden, bone-deep chill cut through the warmth with a snarl. I instinctively tightened my arm around Mirabelle, pulling her fully behind me.

Mirabelle, however, just laughed, peeking around my shoulder. "You came!"

The very air groaned as Rak'Thalgar's colossal form materialized in front of us, his immense shadow falling over our embrace like a sudden eclipse. The Bone Tyrant's massive skull tilted, hollow sockets fixed on her. I heard nothing, but she nodded as if in response to a question and stepped forward.

The beast's skeletal form coiled around her, lifting her as if she was a ribbon caught on the wind. She laughed up to its maw, full of the ridiculous affection she reserved for things that should not be adored. Still, I watched, my arms crossed, a faint smile touching my lips. The sight of this nightmare treating my Eternis with the delicacy of a precious relic was one I doubted I would ever grow accustomed to.

The Tyrant exhaled through cavities like bellows.

"He says he felt a *disturbance of intent* and came to ensure his Lady was not being...unjustly detained," she translated, her voice laced with amusement, clearly embellishing the statement with her creativity.

"You can inform the overgrown ossuary," I retorted, my gaze

locked on the creature's hollow sockets, "that *my* Lady is perfectly, and quite willingly, detained. And that her Sovereign takes a rather dim view of interruptions."

She listened to the silent response, her smile widening. "He says my contentment is debatable and that my squeal sounded distressed."

"It was a sound of her unadulterated anticipation." I called her bluff, my tone flat. "A concept I am certain is lost on a pile of sentient bones."

Mirabelle patted my arm placatingly before addressing Rak'Thalgar again. "It's alright, really. I can easily handle an overbearing Sovereign."

Then they communed then in that low, silent hum of their Tether, and I stood there, not at all appreciating being so thoroughly excluded from a conversation happening a few feet away. The Tyrant let out a low, grinding sound that I felt in my teeth. It leaned its massive skull into her, and she pressed a kiss to its ancient, filthy brow.

"If you're quite finished bestowing affection on a creature that predates our civilization," I stated, making a conscious effort to unknit my brows.

It nuzzled her once more and gave a final nod. Its form began to dissolve into shimmering particles of light and shadow, leaving the golden glow of Vael'Thir where we stood and returning to the deeper heart of Etheris where he resided.

"We like it when you're grumpy," she informed me cheerfully.

"Noted." I said, my tone dry. "What were you talking about?" I asked, my gaze steady on her.

"We need to...test something," she replied, a flicker of secrecy in her eyes.

I narrowed my eyes but didn't push. She could do whatever she wanted with that creature—testing or otherwise. My focus shifted back to the present.

"As I was saying," I stated. "I have to get you somewhere before releasing you back to the *very important matters* you left behind."

She looked up at me, the sparkle returning to her eyes. "And if I've decided my important matters also involve testing how fast I can make you chase me again? This time, I'll put my real effort into it."

A slow, predatory smile touched my lips. "Then you will find my retrieval methods become significantly less gentlemanly. And the rewards I demand for your capture will be far more than you can possibly give in the middle of these open woods." I took her hand, lacing our fingers together in a firm grip. "Now, walk with me."

CHAPTER 50
MIRABELLE

I had tried everything—fussing over the new Aether-wielders, reorganizing the Hold's feeding schedules, even letting Amara drag me into a debate on the merits of different stitching techniques for ceremonial gowns. Anything to avoid the inevitable, ever since I heard my family had arrived a day prior to our formal Bonding and ceremonies. But I never expected that confrontation to be here, in this wild, beautiful corner of Etheris, in Nyxarian territory.

My breath hitched when I saw the sight of my father waiting for us, his back to us near their caves. I felt like a ghost drawn to a forgotten hearth.

I looked at Damien's face. His expression was a carefully schooled mask of neutrality, but his eyes held a Realm of silent support. His hand, resting on the small of my back, was a steady warmth.

"Tell me if you are not ready," he said, his voice low, meant for my ears only. "We will turn back. I know you have been anticipating this as much as you have been avoiding it. The choice is yours."

I swallowed, my throat tight. "No," I managed, my voice barely a whisper. "No, I think I'm ready."

He gave a single, curt nod, then led me forward. The moment we stepped into the clearing, my father jumped to his feet. His eyes shimmered with a hope so raw it was painful to behold.

Damien's voice was cool and formal. "You have until the shadow reaches the standing stone. I will be there," he said, his gaze sweeping the perimeter. Then he did the most Damien thing possible. He walked to a nearby outcropping of rock where a stack of ledgers rested and sat. He opened one, his posture that of a Sovereign reviewing tedious reports, a clear declaration that he would occupy himself, giving us the illusion of privacy.

My father gestured toward the chests. "It's all there. The compensation for everything Atlassian lost because of my dead Eternis and Lorenza."

Damien didn't look up. "It is a start," he said. "The families of the Majors who fell in the Abyss will receive their due. And every last nickel that remains belongs to Mirabelle."

"I don't—" I began, instinctively wanting to refuse, but the words died in my throat as I saw the look on his face. This was not a gift I was being offered; it was his decree and it was futile to argue over it.

And then we were alone.

I started fidgeting, my fingers twisting together. "I...I hope the accommodations are...acceptable?" I blurted out, then wanted to cringe. *Of all the things to say.*

He smiled, his expression softening. "You are beautiful like your mother, little one, all grown up."

"Thank you," I mumbled, my face heating. "I...I think I got her nose. And the hair. It's very...hairy. And red. Others used to ha— think it's quite different. I mean, it's just...there's a lot of it. Up here." *Stars, someone strike me down.* I wanted to evaporate.

He let out a warm, genuine laugh. "You are so like your mother. She always used to talk about the weather in excruciating detail when she was nervous."

Ah, such a comforting and charming trait to inherit.

He grew quiet, his smile fading. "I thought you would be enraged at me, for failing to protect you."

The shift was so sudden it threw me. "Why?" I asked, genuinely confused. "Did you want to get rid of me?"

"Stars! No!" The words burst from him, fervent and pained. "Stars, my pretty girl, how could you even think that? I would have torn the Celestia apart with my bare hands if I had known you were alive and in need."

My eyes blurred with tears from the unexpected rush of emotions. I wiped them away with the back of my hand and surprised myself by smiling.

"Ah, come here," he murmured, opening his arms.

I stepped into his embrace, burying my face in his tunic. The truth washed over me like the first, fragile warmth of spring after an endless storm: somewhere in the long, dark years of my life, there had been someone meant to stand as a shield against every cruelty. I was not an unwanted burden. I was a daughter, wanted, born to be cherished.

And I had missed all of it. I had lost a decade to a loneliness that this single embrace could have filled. Maybe I should have felt wrong for accepting it so fast—but perhaps I'd simply endured enough to finally stop questioning something that felt good.

The thought that followed was a cold tremor beneath the warmth: what if no one had ever found me? What if I had never learned this truth? The terror of that near-miss made me cling to him tighter; my tears were a mix of grief and an even more trembling gratitude.

He held me, his voice a soothing rumble. "I was such a dumbstruck fool when I first saw you during the ball. I was invited there to discuss alliances, and then I saw you. The resemblance shocked me so thoroughly I forgot my own name. Your overprotective shadow of an Etern practically burned a hole through my skull with his glare, and I still couldn't look away. I believe I had tried offered to buy you a new horse. It was the most insane thing I could have said. If I wasn't held back by Damien..."

I let out a wet laugh against his chest, the sound muffled by the fabric. The warmth of his hold, the overwhelming sense of being wanted, was a new feeling I haven't experience before. I had thought the way my adopted family treated me was what love felt like. It was somewhat kind.

But this...this spoke a different dialect of the heart. Like a final piece clicking into place within my soul. It was neither heat nor light, but an unshakable stability.

"You came that day to see me?" I asked.

"Yes," he said, his hand gently patting my back. "To talk about the alliance. Damien made it clear that day, it would be you, not Lorenza. I was invited to talk about you, to give him evidence of my lost daughter."

A genuine smile touched my lips, one that reached my eyes and held all the warmth blooming in my chest for my father.

"Nyxaria is always your home," he continued, his voice firm. "I will pass you the whole Clan, your brothers—who are desperate to meet you as their blood—and I promise, no more surprises like Lorenza." He paused, a twinkle in his eye. "Unless you count the fact that a brother of yours has a truly alarming number of semi-feral pet rocks. That might be a shock."

I laughed again, the sound clearer this time. "I think I can handle a few pet rocks."

We fell into the easy rhythm of sharing our lives, the stories flowing, making up for our lost time.

⊱❈⊰

IT WAS all coming together now. This was the third time I'd asked the Royal attendants to redo my hair, and it was sort of good the first time. But it was nice they were being so patient, or else I'd have gone with it anyway, too awkward to insist. They kept murmuring that this was the most perfect style to fit the crown.

I could not believe any of this was real. But the strangest part was that I was not nervous. At all. Perhaps it was because all the things I faced had carved out a hollow in me where fear used to reside. What is a ceremony before the eyes of a Realm compared to staring into the eyes of a man who had forgotten your soul?

A sharp rap sounded at the door. "Bella! It's me! I've brought you some...peeled grapes!" Amara's voice was muffled through the ornate wood.

"The Lady is not to be fed before the ritual, Lady Amara," a Thrall said, her tone long-suffering, as she expertly laced the final silk shoes onto my foot.

"It's a very calming grape!" Amara insisted. "For...her nerves!"

I chuckled at her increasing desperation. "They are almost done Am," I called out.

I heard her mutter something low and distinctly *un-ladylike*, followed by the sound of her stomping through the corridor.

This is the fifth time she'd tried to barge in with increasingly ridiculous excuses: an urgent question about the proper way to fold a napkin, a dire need to confirm the shade of my lips, and, most recently, a concern about whether the candles on the table were positioned symmetrically that I was fairly certain she'd invented on the spot. The Thralls had become a silk-clad barrier.

I smiled to myself, my thoughts drifting over the past day. I tried not to let my mind replay the court scenes, but failed: standing in that throne hall, summoning Irin and others to weave a tapestry of truth that proved Alaric's innocence in the broader conspiracy. The verdict was the stripping of his Aether and confinement to his chambers with his Etheris. It was a justice that fit. I did not want Damien to make a decision in cold fury that he would later come to regret. However wretched his father was, the man I had visited since was a ghost haunted by his own choices, and he had not been involved in the plots that truly harmed the Clan.

Suddenly, the attendants stepped back, their work done.

I rose and turned to the full-length mirror. The woman staring back was a version of myself I had never dared to imagine—woven from elegance and strength. The gown was a cascade of white that deepened to ivory, shimmering as though it had been spun from the heart of a fading star.

It shimmered with every breath, catching the light on intricate patterns of gold embroidery and stones that sprawled across the fabric like ancient constellations given form. At the shoulders, the gown flared into ornate pauldrons edged in gold and crowned with slender tassels, giving it a quiet command, almost like armor disguised as grace. A cape of the same impossible fabric trailed behind me, whispering against the floor.

At my waist gleamed a single multifaceted jewel—its gold veins holding centuries of silence. My hair had been shaped into a constellation of braids, each strand pinned and woven with care, as though designed to bear the weight of a dynasty.

I looked like...an Empress.

Amara, who must have finally slipped past the Thralls, gasped from the doorway. Then, without warning, she burst into loud, messy tears. "Oh, my—" she wailed, dabbing frantically at her eyes with her sleeve. "You're all...shiny and gorgeous and...and *important!*"

I almost laughed and almost cried at the same time. "Really?"

"Of course... Arghh, it's too much for my heart to handle!" She crossed the room in animated strides and then, with all the subtlety of a small thunderstorm, tried to smother me in an embrace without flattening the embroidery. Her fingers fumbled clumsily at the cape edges, and she planted a wet, emphatic kiss right at the hollow of my throat, careful not to disturb the brooch.

I giggled, feeling ticklish and loved, seeing her unguarded joy.

A soft throat-clearing came from the doorway. We both turned. My father stood there, his composure visibly fraying at the edges. His eyes, glistening, swept over me from head to toe, and a tremor passed through him.

"My gorgeous child," he whispered. "Look at you. A dream given form. How I wish your mother could stand where I am, to see the woman you've become." He swallowed hard, mastering his emotions with a visible effort. "She would have told you that no crown could ever outshine you. And she would have been right."

My throat tightened. "Thank you, Father." The words left me in a trembling whisper, surprising even myself.

He closed his eyes, his entire frame stilling as if savoring a long-awaited wish. A Thrall glided forward silently, offering a linen square to dab my eyes before melting back into the shadows.

He stepped forward, offering his elbow with a formality that was both regal and deeply personal. "Shall we? Two Clans await their leader."

I placed my hand gently in the crook of his arm. Together, we turned and walked out of the chamber, leaving the ghost of the girl I was behind and stepping toward the eternity that awaited.

CHAPTER 51
MIRABELLE

My world narrowed to the span of his hand in mine.

Damien looked at me as if the stars had been scattered for this moment alone, and I was the reason they burned. He was looking at me as though he couldn't decide whether to fall to his knees or pull me into his arms. He was looking at me as if I were the line between the dark and the dawn, the brief moment when the Realms forget which it belongs to.

It was devastatingly flustering. He had been drinking me in since the moment I entered with my father, his throat working in a deliberate swallow. His gaze pinned me where I stood, burning through every scrap of composure I had so carefully practiced among the Royals the night before—and stars help me, I blushed like a girl who'd never been looked at before, though I had grown used to his stares by now.

He was a vision of regal darkness. His attire seemed woven from the night, a velvet coat deep as shadow, its silver embroidery tracing the constellations of Telmoria. At his shoulders gleamed the sigil of the Azarios line, forged in polished metals. A long, dark cloak, lined in silver, cascaded from his frame like a river. Upon his head rested his silver crown set with dark gems that caught the light of the newly aligned Celestia, stark against the rich waves of his hair. He looked every inch the living embodiment of the throne.

We were in Etheris. The entire scene was enchantingly projected across the streets, cities, and distant outskirts of Atlassian. Feasts and celebrations would fill the coming days. Yet here, within the heart of it, the moment felt intensely private. Only those dearest to us—and the two allied Clans—stood witness.

And then there were the Tameables. They moved like living shadows and storms around the periphery of the gathering.

The head of Sage's council started, his voice echoing around us. "From two souls to one flow. From two wills to one destiny. Let the blood speak the truth."

Damien's gaze never left mine as he brought the obsidian blade to my offered wrist. A line of darkness welled up. I took the blade from him and did the same to his palm. But this time, as he pressed his wound to mine, our blood did not just mingle. It remembered the path it had flowed the first time we did this, ignited along our skin, a faint, glowing black trail that flared with the memory of a Bond the Realm had forgotten.

A ripple of murmurs and sharp intakes of breath went through the crowd. Now they all knew.

His voice, low and resonant, was for me alone, though it carried to the edges of the universe. "By blood and bone, by death and dawn, we are one."

"We are one," I repeated, the words a key turning in the lock of my soul.

As our blood mingled and dripped into the silver chalice held beneath our joined hands, it transformed. The plain silver bands within turned molten, then hardened into a dark, gleaming black. The chalice itself shimmered, its metal warming with the power it now contained. Damien lifted the darkened ring and slid it onto my finger. I took the other and did the same for him, my hands steady despite the tremor in my soul.

The voice of the Sage rang out then, clear as crystal and deep as the earth, sanctifying the space between heartbeats. "By the ancient rites, witnessed by land and Celestia and the very blood of destiny, the Bond is sealed, now and forever. Cherish the Bond until death parts you, and beyond."

And then Damien's hands were on my face, and he was kissing me. It was long, and slow, and deep, a seal upon the vows we had just spoken. My senses dissolved into the taste of him.

I smiled against Damien's lips. He broke the kiss, but only to press a soft, lingering peck to my forehead. Then he leaned in, his voice a husky whisper meant only for my ears. "At last the entire Realm knows who you belong to, Mirabelle Azarios."

My mouth curved of its own accord. "Do they?" I murmured, letting my breath brush his jaw. "Or do they finally know who *you* belong to, Azarios?"

A dark, approving smile curved his lips. Until a familiar, gruff voice shouted from the background, "For stars' sake, we get it! Some of us are starving!"

Izmer. His interruption landed like a dropped stone, and the frozen solemnity of the ceremony cracked into laughter. I could not help my own quiet laugh. Damien shot a look over my shoulder that was more amused than annoyed.

The Head Sage stepped forward once more. "Now, let the Crown affirm the rule."

A velvet cushion was brought forth, bearing the Crown of Atlassian. It was a masterpiece of artistry and power, wrought from gleaming gold that spiraled into intricate filigree, studded with deep, blood-red gemstones.

Damien took the crown in his hands. He did not immediately place it on my head. Instead, he turned to face the assembled multitude, his voice projecting, not just across the clearing.

"To the Clan of Atlassian," he called out. "You have bled for this Realm. You have endured. Today, we do not just crown an Empress. We crown a new era. An era of strength forged in unity, of power tempered by compassion. I give you your Empress— Mirabelle Azarios. My equal. My Eternis."

Then he turned back to me, his eyes blazing with contentment.

He placed the crown upon my brow. Its weight was significant, of history and hope.

He offered his hand and drew me forward to stand beside him, facing the crowd.

The Sage handed me an ancient scroll unfurled in his hands. I read it aloud, my voice steady, letting the words bind the air around us. "I, Mirabelle Azarios, do swear by stone and star, by blood and Bond, to hold this crown as a shield for the weak, a sword for the just, and a beacon for the lost. My life for the Clan, my breath for its civilians, from this day until my last."

Then I looked out at the sea of faces—Elders, Royals, Commoners, Legions, and Tameables. My heart swelled, and the words came from the very essence of who I was.

"I was not born in a palace," I began, my voice surprisingly clear. "I was raised in its shadow. I learned the value of a single nickel, the strength found in communities, and the dignity of hard work. I do not come to be a figure on a throne. I come to be a hand in the work. I promise you, I will *never* forget the lessons my life taught me. This crown is a symbol, but my vow to you is real. I will cherish this Clan, protect its inhabitants, and honor its spirit, from the highest spire to the most humble hearth. We have faced the wars and emerged. Together, we will build an *after* worthy of our sacrifices. We will mend the torn, welcome the lost, and remember those who cannot stand for themselves."

A cheer rose, at first small, then swelling until it filled the clearing and chased light into the far alleys of Etheris. Damien's fingers tightened around mine; his thumb rubbed my knuckle in a small, steadying cadence. And his eyes held mine, shining with a fierce, unspoken pride that held a future I had once only dared to dream.

And so, the story we had survived was over, and the one we would build together began.

EPILOGUE
DAMIEN

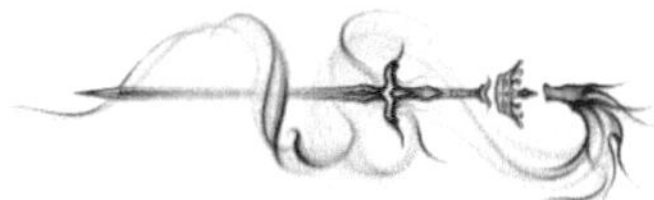

I nursed an awful cold ale while wishing it was something far better. I didn't like the thing one bit, but I was nursing it so Bella could have it. She leaned back against me, giggling at something inane her friend said from our opposite side, then tipped her head to ask for another sip.

My Tamer had opened a channel from the Hold to Etheris, allowing our Tameables to cross when they wished—though the tamed ones still preferred Atlassian. We'd come for yet another of Amara's *garden gatherings*, which was really just another flimsy excuse to see Bella. Most of them ended here, in Etheris.

Not that I minded being here with Bella. But her attention inevitably drifted to her friends, and I preferred being at the center of it—always. Fine, I was a selfish bastard. And I made no apology for it.

A shriek of laughter cut across the clearing. Little Adena waddled through the grass on her unsteady legs. "I told you not to run and fall," I called out, though my voice held no real sting. Our daughter had just turned two a few months ago and never rested. Especially here in Etheris, where that overgrown skeletal beast lived for the scraps of her attention.

Adena looked exactly like me—same hair, same eyes, even the

same fire in her blood. The Sages confirmed it. But her spirit...that was all Mirabelle. Stubborn in that adorable way. And I was fairly certain she'd inherited her mother's unsettling kinship with beasts. Bella told me Rak'Thalgar had confessed he could sense when Adena was sad or tired. Useful, if unnerving.

"Damien, let her be," Bella chided softly, as if I were the unreasonable one, and not the giant beast currently whirling our toddler in dizzying circles.

"Yes, let her breathe, brute," Izmer drawled, arriving with a platter of pastries. He handed one to Amara. "You worry like an old nursemaid."

"I will take your parenting advice when you have a pet rock that survives a week," I shot back.

Izmer scowled at my response. "What a slanderous lie. That tragic pebble was Amara's." Amara laughed, then squealed when Izmer hooked an arm around her waist and murmured something that made her elbow him.

I tucked a loose strand behind Bella's ear and gave her another sip of our tasteless ale. She sipped it and kissed my cheek, her lips a sweet burn against my skin.

Life after the Dissonance was...peace. As I'd always imagined, yet softer. Loving her wasn't a choice; it was a fundamental law of my existence. She was the fire in my veins and the quiet in my soul. My anchor and my storm.

"Amara! You've fed him enough of that sweet garbage. You know he gets lethargic after you visit. Every damn time!"

I followed her gaze to see Whip-tail licking cake crumbs from his maw, purring contently against Amara's legs before Bella could snatch the last bite away. Rak'Thalgar had taken Xal'Veyra to revive him since he'd lost his soul in our Realm. A place where her Aether wasn't bound by Dominion rules. I knew how much Bella adored that gentle creature. His death had hollowed her in some ways. And she'd lived in quiet hope, remembering how Xal'Veyra had revived Dreadclaw during the Abyss.

He saw Mirabelle coming and had the decency to look sheepish.

"You absolute glutton," Bella huffed, wiping his snout and cake crumbs with a linen. Her small hand moved in slow, soothing circles over his rough scales in a tenderness she reserved for very few. He nuzzled her palm in apology, which was entirely performative. We all knew he'd leap for the next cake offered.

Then he was off again, nudging Adena into another fit of giggles as he nuzzled her neck.

So much for not overstimulating her.

Mirabelle came back to me smelling of Ether-light, of beasts, and sugar. She settled against my chest, leaning her full weight into me, and took an unapologetically large bite of a glazed pastry. Then she lifted what remained and offered me a taste.

My hand slid to the front of her throat, tilting her head back just enough as I leaned down and took the rest from her lips, tasting the sugar and the warmth of her. She made a soft sound of surprise that melted into a quiet laugh against my mouth.

Then she leaned her head against my shoulder with a contented sigh, watching our chaotic, perfect world. "Happy?" she asked softly.

I looked down at her, at our daughter shrieking with joy, at the beasts who were our guardians and kin, resting in the eternal twilight. I thought of the cold halls of Atlassian, the weight of the crown, the silence that used to be my only companion.

I pressed a kiss to her temple. "How could I be anything else?" I murmured against her skin, inhaling her scent, and took a slow swallow of the terrible ale before offering her another sip.

I was still not speaking to my father. I couldn't bring myself to, after the secrets, the hiding, the plotting, and his unethical attempts to claw my mother back from the beyond. Still a quiet corner of me understood why he did it. I was no saint where my own morals met the love of my life. But I ignored that corner. It was easier that way.

Bella, however, was clearly on forgiving terms with him. She'd often bring Adena for visits, then return to tell me how our daughter had tamed *Alaric the Ironheart*, who now spent more time pretending to be a lion so Adena could *tame* him with a ribbon.

My mother hadn't woken. I visited her once in a while, just to sit. To see her. The second time, I took Mirabelle after she'd told me she'd give anything to see her own mother again. Her words left a hollow ache in my own chest. A shared, silent understanding of a permanent loss. We walked into the chamber and without asking, she picked up the bowl of broth and started feeding my mother. She did it like it was the most natural thing in the world, like she was just tucking in a child who'd fallen asleep mid-meal. When she was done, she held the spoon out to me.

And I did exactly what she'd done. As I did, a strange, fragile feeling unfolded in me. Not a feeling, but more like a memory of a feeling. A ghost of how my life was supposed to be as a child—my mother awake and scolding me for something trivial, my father smiling in a chamber that wasn't this one, me being a different kind of person altogether. *Someone softer.*

AND THROUGH IT ALL, my father sat in his chair by the window, watching his Eternis. He never left her side, even now that he was no longer confined to her chambers.

Now, Bella's skin had grown cool against me in the gentle Etheris breeze. I took my cloak and started wrapping it around her. Our little one finally waddled over, exhausted. She collapsed onto Bella's lap, ready for her midday nap. Bella dusted the grass from Adena's hair and clothes, cooing back at her while listening to her babble a stream of unintelligible plans for the afternoon, *"...an' then fly mii...bif star, an' we'll find the sugar-draf, an' I fly him..."*

Ah yes. Not going to happen.

Bella straightened her little dress. Then, Adena toddled over and settled onto my lap—apparently I had more space to offer as a bed. She lifted her arms in silent, sleepy command. I pulled her up, settling her against my chest and kissed her forehead. "Are you tired, little one?"

"*Nof 'tired. Waitin',*" she mumbled, her voice thick with sleep. She was already drifting, mumbling more plans into my tunic.

We all began to stand to part ways. Bella and Amara shared a long hug and a dozen promises to meet again in two days. Even while she was busy ruling Atlassian by my side, being a great Empress loved by the whole Clan—taking reports from the farthest outskirts, caring for commoners and Royals with same passion, arranging new trade routes for poor, and tending to the endless matters of the Hold, she still found time for whatever this was.

Rowane appeared then, accompanied by the healer from Vael'Thir—the serene heart of Etheris. He'd finally Bonded with the healer last week, after a campaign of subtlety so transparent it was a miracle she hadn't fled the Clan. He'd brought her along, ostensibly to show her more of Etheris and impress her. He was playing the gentleman, offering her his arm with a stiff formality.

Izmer nudged him with an elbow. "Careful, Rowane. You're being so noble you're starting to glow. Might scare the wildlife."

Rowane shot him a flat look. "Unlike some, I prefer to court my woman without involving a public spectacle."

"Public spectacles are memorable," Izmer countered, grinning. He was referring to the time he'd shouted his intentions for Amara across a training yard when she refused to kiss him. Her face was now beet-red.

I shook my head, adjusting the warm, sleepy weight of Adena against my shoulder. I pulled Bella close by her waist before we could waste another moment on this circus. "Come on, wildcat," I murmured, my lips brushing the shell of her ear. "You promised me undivided attention if I suffered through this torture party. Now it's your turn to pay up in more pleasurable ways."

She shushed me, her eyes darting to see if anyone had heard, but the look she gave me had already darkened with promise.

"You can start by walking faster," I added, my voice a low rumble meant for her alone.

We parted ways at the edge of the clearing. Bella's hand was warm in mine as we approached our portal, the hum of Etheris a gentle song around us. Adena sighed in her sleep, a small, contented sound against my neck.

In the quiet that followed, with the scent of crushed grass and distant blooms hanging in the air, I knew this was everything I needed. Her hand in mine, our daughter's steady breath, and the peaceful, unbroken horizon of a tomorrow we had built together.

I spent thirty years building something worth inheriting. And then she walked into it, and the only thing I wanted was for her to stay. Everything else—the crown, the wars, the legacy—it was all just the life I built before I understood what living was.

The portal shimmered before us, a doorway to home. Together, we stepped through.

Also by Fabins

Reigns of Telmoria

Aether and Ash

Of Ashes and After

About the Author

Fabins is a fantasy romance author with a weakness for slow burns and a fierce love of character-driven stories. A software engineer by day and a storyteller by obsession, she balances logic and longing with the careful precision of someone who has probably over-thought both.

When she isn't drafting, she is likely halfway across the world, gaming past midnight, arguing passionately about things that don't pay bills, or reading (either swooning over fictional characters or hurling the book at the nearest cushion after a terrible twist).

Join Fabins' newsletter
https://authorfabins.com/mailing-list

A small press bound by the belief that every voice matters.

Sign up for our newsletter to learn about new releases and more.

Buy directly from us to save on ebooks, book bundles, and special editions.

Follow us on social media:

facebook.com/oliverheberbooks

instagram.com/oliverheberbooks

tiktok.com/@oliverheberbooks

bsky.app/profile/oliverheberbooks.bsky.social

youtube.com/@OliverHeberBooksPublisher

oliverheberbooks.substack.com

amazon.com/oliverheberbooks

www.ingramcontent.com/pod-product-compliance
Lightning Source LLC
Chambersburg PA
CBHW031108160726
47991CB00004B/1288